DOUBTING CASTLE

DOUBTING CASTLE

Rebecca Kavaler

SCHOCKEN BOOKS · NEW YORK

First published by Schocken Books 1984
10 9 8 7 6 5 4 3 2   84 85 86 87
Copyright © 1984 by Rebecca Kavaler

Library of Congress Cataloging in Publication Data
Kavaler, Rebecca.
  Doubting castle.
  I. Title.
PS3561.A8685D6   1984   813'.54   83–40461

Designed by NANCY DALE MULDOON
Manufactured in the United States of America
ISBN 0–8052–3899–9

OUT of the way we went, and then we found
What 'twas to tread upon forbidden ground.
And let them that come after have a care
Lest they, for trespassing, his prisoners are,
Whose castle's Doubting, and whose name's Despair.

The Pilgrim's Progress

DOUBTING CASTLE

Chapter 1

I T was already late afternoon when the train pulled into the Jersey City depot, and dusk by the time she debarked from the ferry on the New York side. The growing darkness lay on the city like a coating of thick soot, and the view was as ugly as her thoughts. Nothing but gloomy warehouses, iron-shuttered against thieves, and stark telegraph poles hatched with a dozen or more crossbars, lining the street like the standards of a conquering Roman legion.

The dampness of the air, fresh off the river, intensified the January chill. Ada shivered, more from nervousness than cold, overcome by the din and confusion, the mad jumble of wheels, boxes, whips, horses. There was a logjam of hansom cabs, but the raucous cries of "Keb, sir? Keb, sir?" were directed over her head at more prosperous-looking prey than a lone young woman with only a gripbag in hand. She owed her rescue in the end to the gallantry of a fellow passenger—a stout paterfamilias in a derby hat, who commandeered a cab for her and assisted her in before waddling off to his own restless brood and glowering wife.

"To the Fifth Avenue Hotel, please." She hoped the false tone of assurance would convey a native's knowledge of the exact distance and the proper fare. The Fifth Avenue was, in fact, the only hotel in the city that came to mind. Twice Papa had taken her there, meetings that had a hurried, almost clandestine air. But this time she must pay the bill herself from a limp purse depleted by her long journey to a single twenty-dollar gold piece and a few silver coins. She had not counted on the expense of an overnight stay. Had her train arrived on time, she would have driven straight to the Grand Central depot, taken the suburban train and before day's end come to rest in dear Papa's arms.

In dear Papa's arms. Even in her present state of shock, she mocked herself. The longing had the discouragingly familiar ring of history repeating itself. A younger traveler, a longer journey, the same promise of Papa's arms at the other end. The sour memory of that earlier welcome—how quickly he had sent her packing!—was a warning not to set her hopes too high again. Nor was she arriving this time as the orphaned daughter he had sent for, with a rightful demand upon his sympathy. She tried to picture Papa's face registering surprise, delight at her unexpected apparition. Even imagination balked at that, dissolving his features in a wash of dismay, disillusion, shock. He would not believe her. He would not understand. More likely, he would accept the version of her disgrace the Dean would have posted by this time. But no such letter could have arrived as yet—not all the way from Michigan. Papa would first hear *her* story. What really happened. What didn't happen. Then let him judge her. That was the only purpose of her flight from Ann Arbor, which in itself would condemn her in all the prim, white-frame, tree-shaded houses on Ingalls Street, in all the dark corridors and musty labs of the medical school.

She closed her eyes in a fresh agony of shame and clung to the strap as if the jostling of the cab were too much for her. But for that moment, with the hot rush of blood to her head, she was oblivious to the evening crush of city traffic, the jangling bells of horse cars, the screeching of an elevated train taking a curve, the coarse cries of the teamsters maneuvering their heavy drays across the stream of elegant carriages and hustling hacks. She was hearing instead the soft tinkle of sleigh bells in clear midnight air, hoofbeats muffled in a new fall of snow. The spot on her neck where Francis had fixed his lips throbbed like a raw burn. A farewell kiss repulsive as the sucking of a leech. The remembering itself was nightmarish. There was no way to stop it once it began . . . .

A man! Harold, there, on the porch roof! Poor Mrs. Nichols's cry of horror.

Halt! Stop, I say! You rascal! Poor Reverend Nichols's ineffectual command.

Running. The crunch of feet breaking through the buried crust of last week's snow. Poor Reverend Nichols's ineffectual chase.

Ada! They remember her at last. *The poor girl was all alone! Oh, pray God—*

Yes, pray God. Inside the jouncing cab, Ada finished the prayer for them savagely. Pray God that Ada Traherne is lying in her bed with her throat slit, her body besmirched, but not her good name.

The driver tapped with his whip, his face peering down at her from the hole in the roof.

"Here you are, miss. Thank you, miss. Watch your step."

A little late for that, Ada thought bitterly. She caught up her skirt with her left hand, her gripbag with her right, and marched haughtily into the hotel.

Haughtiness was not hers by nature; it had been painfully acquired.

"A lady does not attract attention, I hope you will remember, Ada."

The occasion for that bit of advice from Mama was their first glimpse of the pretty Mrs. Deventer causing a veritable traffic jam along the Promenade des Anglais at Nice. (Pretty was the epithet then applied to Jack Deventer's bride. It was some years later, when fully authenticated as a femme fatale by the more lurid elements of the press, that she became the ravishing Mrs. Deventer, the enchanting Mrs. Deventer, the exquisite Mrs. Deventer, Mrs. Deventer the nonpareil.)

In Ada's memory, the pretty face had long ago dissolved into a vague radiance. All she clearly recalled was the sashaying walk; the billowing froth of flounces, ruffles, ribbon and lace; the twirling parasol of bespangled chiffon. A long golden curl snaking down a white neck. Mama's stiff-backed disapproval. The gossipy whispers above her head, recounting the scandalous conduct of Mad Jack Deventer, constrained after the latest casino incident to remain on his yacht at the polite request of the local authorities.

The child was more interested in that magnificent white-and-gold steam yacht than in those you-know-who and you-know-what comments about its owner. Night and day it was surrounded by a swarm of small bobbing boats, like pilot fish attendant upon a shark. At any moment Mad Jack himself might appear on deck and toss overboard a slop bucket full of gold coins. Better than a circus, Ada thought (as presumably did Mad Jack). Having once witnessed such a scene, she longed to see again the scrambling divers, the wild scrimmaging in water, the spluttering mayhem as men struggled with men and olive-skinned slippery boys eluded them all.

"Demimonde?" Mama's answer to her new English friend had been preambled with a scornful laugh. "My dear Mrs. Carlisle, for her that would be a step up. An actress of the cheapest sort, who did her best work off stage, if you catch my meaning." The voices momentarily lowered to an indistinguishable buzz. . . . "It's not as if the Deventers were new money, they're Knickerbocker to the core. No one will receive her in New York, which is why this honeymoon trip to Europe has been so protracted. Mad Jack? Oh no, my dear, the marriage merely confirms the name, I'm afraid he had fully earned it before."

6

All that was before Papa had come down from Vienna to join them on their Mediterranean vacation. Before the pretty Mrs. Deventer, suffering from some ill-defined complaint, had sought out the services of the young American doctor, preferring to place herself in a compatriot's hands. Or so she said. From the beginning, Mama had been suspicious of those urgent summons from the yacht, those professional visits occurring more and more often, lasting longer and longer. Papa's stay was no vacation at all, she complained. Had he abandoned a growing practice back home, on the pretext of needing further study abroad, simply to take on a single disreputable patient in Nice? In delicate health? In her distress, Mama rose almost to the level of wit. "If so, that is the only thing delicate about her."

Then one fine day the yacht sailed away, and Papa on it. Poor fatherless child, Mama cried. Abandoned orphan. Piteous words, but uttered ferociously, with a gaze fixed over Ada's head at the Eternal. Thereafter any mention of Papa brought about that unnerving cast in Mama's eye. As for the pretty lady on the promenade—Ada had most admired the way she used her parasol, like the balancing tool for a high-wire circus act— she turned out to be the Whore of Babylon, who rode astride a scarlet beast with seven heads and ten horns, much like another circus act. Soon that black beetle of a priest, Monsignor Fragetelli, scuttled across the threshold, and Mama sallowed into a religieuse, obsequious in her devotions but haughty as a duchess whenever they went abroad.

Ada now wondered if Mama's haughtiness too had not been acquired, if unhappiness was not a kind of Bessemer process of the soul, converting brittle pig-iron hearts into unbreakable steel. Yet she thought she had endured the minor miseries of the first two years at school rather well. Not once had she complained to Papa, knowing his answer in advance: Had he not told her a medical school was no place for a member of the gentler sex? Had he not warned her of the sordidness, the indecencies to which she would be exposed? Indecencies imprinted in medical texts! Patients uncovering themselves before a young lady's eyes! To which she had argued back there was nothing sordid or indecent about the human body, when scientific study was the aim. (True, the human body she had in mind was a smooth Greek marble, or a modern bronze of M. Rodin. Or maybe Mr. William Muldoon, billed as the "World's Champion Graeco-Roman Athlete," who rippled his oiled muscles on stage in "poses representative of classic statuary." Certainly not the sad broken bodies of derelicts and paupers that found their way to the dissecting room.)

Papa had proved right. Indecencies there had been, and sordidness too. Not as yet from patients—that awaited her diploma—but from her fellow students. Jeers, sneers, and most insulting of all, the groping, panting outbursts of ardor. Over Bunsen burners, over metal sinks, against glass-doored specimen cabinets, in dark corridors, in dusty library cubicles. A haughty girl, they finally called her. A stuck-up miss. "Who do you think you are—one of the High-and-Mighty Astors?"

So be it, she thought, and wrote brave letters to Papa about how nice her room was at the minister's house, how she had witnessed her first operation without fainting (although two of the male students did), how exciting she found the lectures on Semmelweiss and Koch, how she and Emily and Gertrude—three females in a class of eighty-five—had sworn to be "best friends" forever. As best friends, Emily and Gertrude counseled her frankly: "*We suffer no such persecution, Ada. This is because we know how to make ourselves respected.*" It was, Ada thought with chagrin, like poor Mama being brought to life again.

Her haughtiness grew, a hard calciferous accretion, the skeletal deposit of some tender form of life that had long since died. Only Francis had broken through that hardness. *He is from the Wyoming Territory, Papa,* she had first written, *and is the brightest student in our class.* Suddenly no more mention of her growing interest in pure science, or the need for further training in some laboratory abroad. Instead she was soon writing, *We plan to open a joint practice in Wyoming when we marry, and I have agreed he can have all the men for his patients if he will allow me the wives.*

Oh, what a fool! But she was like Mama at last, hard and impervious as steel, quite capable of countering the impertinence of the desk clerk ("My trunks have been sent on ahead since I am taking a train in the morning"), or quenching the insolence of the call boy ("That will be *all,* thank you."). She washed herself as thoroughly as possible in the basin (no suite reserved by Papa this time, no luxurious bathing room), brushed out and recoiled her hair, refreshed her traveling dress with a clean white collar.

On the train she had eaten little, had seen herself as pining away in a manner befitting the broken-hearted. In truth, neither the sight nor smell of greasy meat pies dredged up from wicker hampers, nor the stale sandwiches vended through the coaches at occasional stops had stimulated her appetite. But now that she was at least surface-clean of soot and grime, and had thought of the lavish bill of fare provided by the dining room upstairs, she acknowledged a ravenous hunger.

Hard as steel, she had to remind herself when she confronted the professional hauteur of the maître d'. She followed with eyes fixed on a certain spot between his shoulder blades, the better not to see the rustle of attention, the quivering of bonnets, the turning of fat necks in stiff white collars that marked her passage to a small table close to the swinging doors of the kitchen, reserved for just such questionable unescorted females.

The enormous carte du jour placed in her hand set her mouth to watering. Just in time she remembered her depleted purse and ordered oysters (quite cheap) and chicken patties (quite filling). As soon as the waiter left, she bit hungrily into a roll. Not daring to look about, she stared straight ahead, to find in her line of sight a table where two men sat in the final stages of their dinner. She began to count, first with envy, then with disbelief, the number of covered dishes the waiters removed. Eight courses, at least, and these two were now demolishing a snow-covered mountain of dessert. From a purely medical point of view, the man facing her was deplorable—enormous girth, beet-red face, bulging eyes. Apoplexy would be his end, without a doubt.

9

Quickly she looked down at her plate, the examination abruptly terminated. He had caught her staring at him. A flush of annoyance warmed her cheeks, but lest it be misinterpreted as a maidenly blush, she forced herself to stare back. With a fatuous smile, he did that ridiculous grooming bit with his moustache. He must have said something—she could guess what—to his companion, of whom she had seen nothing but a tall straight back and a head of blond hair. Slightly unruly, that hair, in spite of obvious efforts to make it lie flat. The head swiveled, bringing into view a young clean-shaven face. She stood her ground even against that arrogant appraisal, but was relieved when her own waiter finally arrived, and she had a legitimate excuse to shift attention to her modest repast.

"If you please, miss—"

She looked up, seeing first the note on the extended salver, then the well-trained remoteness of the waiter's expression.

"From the gentleman—a family acquaintance, I believe—at the table straight ahead."

Her first instinct was to refuse it, but she had a better thought. She scanned the note quickly, then extracted from her purse the ingenious Waterman fountain pen, initialed in gold, her last birthday present from Papa. The lengthy reply fully covered the reverse side of the notepaper. The waiter returned to her old "family acquaintance," who saluted her with a lifted wine glass. She acknowledged the salute with an ironic smile. Continued to smile even when his young companion turned around again, pale brows arched in surprise.

She snapped shut the cut-steel frame of her purse and allowed the waiter to pull back her chair. Like a cooked lobster now—that fat bon vivant. Red face growing redder, popped eyes protruding on stalks, wax-tipped moustache quivering like feelers, as he silently mouthed those words she had chosen with great care: *Pray accept my apology for staring. As a practicing physician* (she had indulged herself in that small lie) *I could not help but observe, even from this distance, all the signs of an impending apoplectic stroke: choleric color, gross overweight, overindulgence in food, drink, tobacco, and, as evidenced by your note, in even more health-taxing pursuits. I fear that a closer examination would reveal blood pressure too high, an enlarged heart, a diseased spleen, and a liver damaged beyond repair. My prescription would be an immediate blood-letting and a more spartan regimen, my good sir, but you are free, of course, to seek another medical opinion.*

On the way out, she passed close enough to hear the young man strangle on laughter as on a bone. "I told you, uncle, you were mistaken! Serves you right."

Then she was encaged in the elevator, descending slowly on the hydraulic lift, every muscle in her body still gripped in a tetany of pride. She turned the key in the lock and faced the loneliness of her cold, high-ceilinged room. Mama was right. Men were beasts. She hated them all. Papa dancing attendance all these years on that infamous beauty. Francis protesting his love even while he stabbed her in the heart. That fat fool in the dining room, daring to assume . . . the look in his young companion's eyes, when he turned around. . . .

Still leaning against the door, she began to shake, only now feeling the full impact of events, the sickening humiliation of the past few days. She reminded herself that she had left behind forever those nightmare faces: Francis's dark handsomeness disintegrating before her eyes as if passion were as soul-endangering a draught as Dr. Jekyll's potion in Mr. Stevenson's strange tale; the lantern-jawed dismay of the Reverend Nichols; Mrs. Nichols's lugubrious moue of Christian kindness; the clinical detachment of Dean Thwaite's regard, usually reserved for female patients in the charity ward.

But the words they had uttered had not been left behind. The words had traveled with her day and night, clicking telegraphically along the iron tracks, as if sending on ahead the news of her disgrace. She closed her eyes and immediately the room was invaded, occupied, taken over by those hateful voices. . . .

Francis's hot breath: "So beautiful, my darling . . . I cannot bear to think of you defiled by sickness and disease. . . ."

Reverend Nichols's plangent twang: ". . . we would never

11

have believed it, Ada, had we not seen it with our own eyes . . . ," orchestrated to his wife's thin wail, ". . . in our own house . . . in our own house. . . ."

Dr. Thwaite's bloodless eastern drawl: "You realize, Miss Traherne, I cannot possibly provide you with the required certification of character . . . you will not be issued a diploma this March. . . ."

"All is not lost, Ada," the Reverend's voice insisted, "the young man stands ready to marry you. . . ."

". . . in our own house . . . in our own house. . . ."

Ada opened her eyes, unable to bear Mrs. Nichols's Greek chorus. The chambermaid had pulled back the covers of the bed, closed the curtains. She walked listlessly to a window, held back a corner of the worn velvet, which from a distance had seemed so luxurious but under her fingertips showed a manginess of nap. Like life itself, all its rich heaviness turning into a dreary accumulation of dust.

She looked down on the pallid granite of General Worth's monument—a moon-bleached obelisk. Across the street lay Madison Square Park. As if conforming to her own low spirits, the park looked empty and bereft. A great gaping hole of blackness. Ada clutched at the curtain, loneliness attacking her like a sudden fit of nausea. More history repeating itself. She should have chosen any other hotel but this one where she and Papa had held their first reunion. Better to remember the joy, not the tail-end disappointment. The confusion in the customs shed, Papa's arms about her. Strange asthmatic noises over her head. The discovery of what a man sounds like when he is crying. And if his red beard was strange to her and his blue eyes seemed faded, the same could be said of the sky, the water, the buildings, all the milling people to eyes so long adjusted to a Mediterranean sun.

Fiercely returning Papa's embrace, she had remembered to be grateful to the Deventers. When Mama took the typhoid and those eyes were fixed forever, they had sent their lawyer, Mr. Kerne, to fetch her home again. He had appeared suddenly, out

of the blue, a gaunt old man she had never seen or heard of—
come, he said, to collect Dr. Traherne's daughter. On holiday in
Rome, he had explained—just happened to be free to undertake
this sad mission for her papa. The poor man had a rude reception. What was she to Papa or Papa to her that she should cross
the Atlantic now? She rather thought—a childish bluff, of
course—she would accept the kind offer of Mama's English
friend, Mrs. Carlisle, who had opened both heart and home to a
poor orphan doubly abandoned now by Mama's death.

Abandoned? Mr. Kerne was shocked at an accusation so patently false. "It was your mama's own choice to remain behind
in this playground of the rich. She preferred the climate, I am
told." As for the scandalous implications of such a charge, he
could only assume her poor mama had been a victim of her
nerves. Not too uncommon a state in ladies of a certain age, as
this papish lot knew full well and never scrupled to take advantage of. It was the only reference made to Mama's conver-
sion, though the reading of the will had drawn from him an
eloquent sniff, as if the singed odor of Satan had suddenly
filled the room. "Everything to the Roman Church," was his
translation of legal verbiage Ada hardly understood, "every tot
and tittle thrown on that popish dunghill." But then, he had
admitted with a shrug, even her mama was not so foolish but
she knew Ada would be cared for by her papa.

Ada was unmoved. The talk of female nerves did not impress
her. Nor lawyer's reasoning tagged with Latin ("Let me ask you
this, young lady. Do you think Mr. Deventer would countenance an irregular relationship under his very nose, within his
own house? *Res ipse loquitur!*"). Oh no, Mama had been abandoned, Mama had been wronged—she held to that belief with a
splendid stubbornness, too confident of her own guilt to doubt
Papa's. Had she not failed to love Mama as a daughter should?
Had she not preferred the reading of French novels to *Tracts
for the Times*? Had not Mama warned her that her fits of temper
would drive her loving parent to an early grave? She had even
thought at times that riding on a scarlet beast was preferable to

such a glum existence as she and Mama led. No, Mama had been wronged, and nothing Mr. Kerne could say would alter her loyalty to the dead.

And yet Mama was proved a liar after all, and by her own hand. Why these dismal quarters? Mr. Kerne had asked—from what her papa sent them, he had expected a luxurious villa by the sea. Ada was almost pleased with the dark apartment, the shabby furnishings. What better proof of abandonment than their forced retirement into genteel poverty? Mama had always said they must live on her own small settlement now that Papa had quite forgot them, Ada told Mr. Kerne, mimicking Mama better than she knew in her look of sour resignation. She stood firm even against the lawyer's shocked denial—he himself had sent the quarterly payments to the bank, and goodly sums they were! But when they went through the papers in Mama's desk, they found the statements from the bank, the quarterly entries—goodly sums indeed!—matched by those quarterly drafts, all payable to Monsignor Fragetelli.

"Salvation comes dear," Mr. Kerne had said drily.

Staring at the finely penned notation of monies in and monies out, Ada could see only an accounting of Mama's hate. She knew better than Mr. Kerne. All that money spent, not to save a soul, but to damn one. Papa's? Mrs. Deventer's? It didn't matter, nothing mattered but that Papa loved her. Had always loved her. He rose Lazarus-like from the underworld to which Mama had consigned him, to take his rightful place in her heart. She had sailed for home, loving the sound of that word—the wonderful mix of America and Papa! And he had been there on the docks, his arms open to her. And he had wept. And they were to live together happily ever after. . . .

An Elysian state that had not lasted out the afternoon. She could remember very well that young girl of fifteen, still swathed in the black bombazine of bereavement, standing at just such a window, looking out on the same park across the street—ah, she saw now what was missing, why it looked so empty! There, on that very spot, implanted on the grass, had stood a gigantic arm of a goddess, holding aloft the flame of Liberty. Truly a dumbfounding sight.

Even when Papa explained that the rest of the statue was still in France, that the arm was being displayed to encourage the donation of funds for a pedestal, the image of a goddess buried deep in the earth, one uplifted arm protruding from the grave, had remained fixed in her mind. And when Papa explained she was not to live with him at Kirkewode—"I do not wish to ever see you there, Ada"—she had known how the goddess felt, being buried alive.

"It is that woman—" somehow Mama's hard voice had found its way across the ocean to this New World too—"she's the one who doesn't want me there."

"Nothing would please Mrs. Deventer more," Papa said. "It is I who do not want you there. Come, Ada, I am thinking only of what is best for *you*. As your papa, I am the best judge of that."

Each conciliatory word of his was another clod of earth tamped down on her.

"I have enrolled you in Miss Porter's School in Connecticut. It's a very desirable seminary for young ladies, I assure you, and we are quite lucky that, in view of the sad circumstances, they are good enough to accept you in midterm."

She remained by the window, arms held stiffly at the side, standing in a grave filled shoulder-high.

"The Inwoods—your mama's cousins in Boston—have agreed to take you during your vacations. But as often as I can get away, I shall come up to visit you. We shall take little trips together, you and I, that will be fun now, won't it?"

There was no agreeable nod from the black-bonneted head. How could there be, when the dark loam now filled her nostrils, lay heavy on her eyes?

"Come, give Papa a kiss, he's missed you so much. Tell me your heart's desire, my darling, and you shall have it, no matter what it costs."

Only the flame of ambition was left to breathe in air, to burn all the brighter because the rest of her was underground.

15

"I want to be a doctor, Papa."

Papa laughed—a short explosive sound as if someone had jabbed him in the ribs. Across the street a pigeon perched on Liberty's upheld lamp.

"What's this? What do we have here? Another Miss Nightingale?"

Woman too will sound the abyss of science and the secrets of the mind! Almost Ada flung it at him—that passage from *The Princess*, which had become more comforting to her than any bedtime prayer. Even Papa could not disapprove of Lord Tennyson.

"Not a nurse, Papa. A doctor."

The laugh came easier the second time. "Well, let's leave such weighty matters to the future, shall we? Now let me have a good look at you. I swear, Ada, you show every sign of becoming an exceptionally pretty woman, did you know that? I'm willing to bet that in a year or two you won't have time for playing little Miss Sawbones, you'll be too busy fending off your beaux. In preparation for which, I shall take you out this afternoon for a stroll down Ladies Mile, and we shall look in all the shop windows and see the latest styles. Even for mourning, there must be something a little less—black."

Seven years later, looking down on the same spot, Ada told herself she had almost made it. Just three more months and she would have been Dr. Traherne. Dr. Ada Traherne. She had tried on that title as other young ladies rang married changes on their name. The Lady out there would have approved, she was sure.

The Lady was no longer visible, of course. Its arms were all of a piece with its magnificent towering form somewhere out in the bay, welcoming the daily arrival of Europe's "huddled masses, teeming poor." But her gaze remained fixed on the empty spot in the park just beyond the gaslights. A grimly playful thought: the Lady had not really been removed. She was still out there, but even the arm was buried now. Even the lamp. Even the flame.

Chapter 2

THE Hudson Division local was almost empty at that hour of the morning, the commuter rush being all the other way. As the train resurfaced amid the shanty towns of upper Manhattan and picked up speed, Ada's lips moved silently, testing the various ways of breaking her bad news. Stubbly fields ran by her window, the desolation of a ballpark in midwinter, the long swoop of a toboggan slide, a yellow-and-black advertisement in praise of Hood's Sarsaparilla. She caught a side view of romanesque arches as the train passed over Spuyten Dyvil, and surprisingly soon her stop of Riverdale was called.

Outside the long roofed platform of this depot, no fierce jungle cries of competing cabbies greeted her. Would that they did, was Ada's regret as she surveyed the muddy small-town street. No traffic at all after a heavy dray laden with feed sacks rumbled by. A buggy was drawn up to the curb in front of a small box-like building on stilts, which on closer approach turned out to be a post office. As good a place as any to ask directions to the nearest livery stable.

The postmaster, as potbellied as his stove, patted his bald head as if consoling it for the loss of hair. "Folks here don't rent their horses," he said and spat into a brass receptacle that bore evidence of his poor aim.

"Where you fixing to go?" asked an old man with the look of a farmer.

Ada displayed her most charming smile. The owner of the buggy outside, she deduced. He was about to offer her a ride. "To Kirkewode." Encountering nothing but a blank stare, she added, "The Deventer place." Still no sign of recognition. "I did get off at the right stop, didn't I?"

The right stop, the postmaster admitted, but beyond that seemed disinclined to be of further help. The farmer tightened his scarf as a sign that he was on his way. The offer she had hoped for would evidently not be made.

"Try the smithy down the street," the postmaster finally suggested. "Travers has got a buggy he lets out sometimes. When folks bring theirs in to be fixed."

"To Kirkewode," Ada announced for the second time, and held her breath. The blacksmith was an unexpectedly small man. No large and sinewy hands. And the muscles of his brawny arm, if brawny it was, were concealed by grey woolen underwear, to which he had stripped down to the waist even in the January cold. His hammer continued to beat down on the anvil, shaping the red-hot iron. By his side, on a table with a box-like top, were spread the implements of his trade, as neatly arrayed as a surgeon's tools in an operating room. He chose a little sharp-edged tool to bite off a jagged bit of excess metal, and plunged the hot iron into its bath. Only when the strangled hiss had died down, did he answer her.

"It's no business of mine, young lady, but you'll never get past the gate. If you was expected, they would have had you met. If you ain't expected, they'll never let you in."

With an effort she held back the retort that it *was* no business of his. "I *am* expected," she chose instead to lie. "There has simply been some confusion over the time of my arrival. I understand you have a buggy for hire. Will you take me there or not?"

"Can't even if I would, miss. Ain't had time to fix the broken axle from a little accident we had here last week. Women drivers—there ought to be a law."

"I'll take you, miss."

In the open doorway stood a tall young man, helmeted and brass-buttoned, truncheon at side. "You'll not be minding a ride in a patrol wagon, will you? I'm supposed to give the horses a run this morning and I might as well head toward the castle as any other way."

The blacksmith, already heating another piece of iron, laconically advised her to accept the offer. "Maybe he can get you through. He's full enough of the blarney, that's for sure."

"Thank you," Ada said, seeing no other choice. She leaned over to pick up her bag, but the young patrolman was there before her. Her elbow was firmly gripped as soon as they reached the curb and he solicitously guided her across the perils of the empty street. She waited in the small portico of the station house, a white frame, green-shuttered building that gave no external sign of harboring the police, while he vanished into the stables across the street. Emerging with the imposing wagon hitched to a fine-looking pair, he pulled up for her. With a shy confusion—rather sweet, she thought—he suggested it would be better for her to ride up front beside him to avoid giving the wrong impression.

"That I'm under arrest?" She could not help smiling. "But if I ride up there, won't they think something even worse?" Was that really a blush under the shadow of the helmet? Effortlessly he spanned her waist with his hands and lifted her up. As the horses trotted up the hill, she eyed sideways his impressive hulk, wondering when he had left the green shores of Ireland. Not very long ago, she guessed from the freshness of his brogue.

He was eyeing her too, she suddenly noticed, with a more open admiration. "Patrick Cullen is the name, miss. Patrolman Cullen. Soon to be Roundsman Cullen, I've the sergeant's word for that. Any day now my promotion will be coming through."

Fixing her eyes impersonally on the road ahead, she offered him her congratulations when it was obviously her name he had hoped for in return.

"Would you be a member of the family now?" he probed, after geeing the team onto a narrow dirt lane.

"Not exactly," was all she said. The closer her approach to Kirkewode, the more anxious she became. Even were she arriving in triumph rather than disgrace, she had reason to doubt her welcome. When Kirkewode had first been placed beyond the pale for her, her imagination had risen to the occasion: life with the Deventers must be a continual round of debauchery (with Papa as disinterested spectator, of course) to which no man would expose his daughter. An interesting prospect, long ago discarded. The reformation in Mad Jack's character had become as much a part of the Deventer legend as the restoration of his wasted fortune. A rare example of virtue being more than its own reward, it provided a favorite theme for sermons both in the pulpit and in print.

Then why, Ada continued to ask, and Papa continued to give no reason for their continued separation, beyond his autocratic decree. Little wonder that she began to think there might be more truth in Mama's dark suspicions than Mr. Kerne had been willing to allow. Perhaps Mama had lied only about the money, perhaps Papa was indeed held captive in a rich man's castle by an illicit passion.

What began as pure fantasy was given hard substance by a shocking piece of news. It was during her last year at Miss Porter's school that she read of Mr. Kerne's demise. Dead by his own hand! An old man like that, killing himself for love— and Mrs. Deventer the object of his desire! She remembered him in Nice—all stiff propriety. Even in that land of palms and olives, under an Italian sun (only the flag had changed to

French), he had kept to his black silk hat and formal lawyer's garb and spoke with disapproval of the looser forms of dress he saw about him. A stuffy hidebound fogey, she had thought. Who all the while was lusting for his client's wife! And then the following year, another death, this time a quite young lad, heartsick for the same unobtainable lady. Ada considered afresh the likelihood of Papa falling victim to such an enchantress. True, he had not killed himself for love—the very thought pinched her heart white—but Mama would have had an answer to that. For him, the lady had not been so unobtainable.

She was glad enough when Cullen interrupted such imaginings by a resumption of his inquisition. "Then you'll be visiting like?"

Taking her silence for consent, he chuckled with pleasure. "Now won't that give the biddies in me boardinghouse something to talk about! All them rooms in the castle, and never an overnight guest—'tis the first thing I heard about the Deventers when I was stationed here, and until this glorious day, it was the truth."

Ada was not sure if there was an amorous roll to that "glorious day" or if it was just the brogue. The fact that the sky was overcast and threatened either snow or rain gave more weight to the first supposition. Prone to quick judgments, she was already forced to revise the one she had made of this young patrolman. Not quite so naive, not quite so sweet. And much more good-looking. Beneath the helmet, tilted back, his hair curled damply in ringlets the glossy color of a prize bay. That openness of countenance, she now suspected, was the unclouded reflection of pure self-esteem. And what she had mistaken earlier for a blush was the almost constant rise and fall of the rich red blood in his veins, his easy response to the myriad delights of life: the soaring flight of a peregrine falcon overhead, his own fine handling of the reins as the horses took a sharp turn without breaking gait, the passing glimpse of a grand house topping a hill. Or just a pretty face.

Under the heavy serge skirt, her knees drew closer together

and she leaned a little farther to the side. "I have come to see Dr. Traherne," she said stiffly. "I have no acquaintance with the Deventers at all."

Oh, the doctor. Sure and he knew the doctor. Wasn't it wonderful now to be so rich you could have a doctor all your own.

Ada shrugged. Some wealthy people had their own chaplain—much the same just-in-case kind of thing, she assumed.

"Oh, they've a reverend too." It was his suspicion, which he cheerfully voiced, that the built-in chapel and resident parson were maintained for the sole purpose of keeping the servants close to home. The few Catholics in service had to be driven to the village for Sunday morning mass, but the coachman waited outside St. John's to take them right back.

If the Deventers hoped thus to starve local gossip, Ada could only conclude they were not very successful. Nor was her escort's store of information limited to Kirkewode; it encompassed all the baronial estates in the neighborhood. As other souls were stirred by poetry, so this young man seemed moved by wealth and the trappings thereof. She saw again that flush of pure pleasure as they reached the gateway to an obviously magnificent estate. Kirkewode? Her heart stopped. No, they were passing on beyond the elaborate wrought ironwork hung between stone pillars, on top of which perched two stone lions. She deciphered the initial "M" in the iron curlicues and caught the name Elmhurst carved on the stone. The Morosini villa, she was told.

"The Eye-talian gentleman," Patrolman Cullen prompted when she failed to respond. "The right-hand man of Mr. Jay Gould himself. Came over with Garibaldi, they say, and not a penny to his name—just his good looks and a strong pair of arms and maybe a little something in the way of brains. And now look at him! Living like a lord and twice as rich."

It struck Ada that "good looks and a strong pair of arms and maybe a little something in the way of brains" described her companion equally well. She suspected it had struck Mr. Cullen too, and that he foresaw for himself an equally bright future. There was certainly no doubt about the strong pair of arms.

With no visible effort, he was reining in the fresh horses, keeping them to a slow trot. The local scandals, recounted with great relish, required his full attention, and Ada resigned herself to listening with ambivalent emotions. Half of her wanted to cry out faster! Let's get it over with! The other half was more than content to crawl along, to postpone forever the unpleasantness that was likely to attend her arrival.

Mr. Cullen reached the pinnacle of rapture at the next imposing estate. A grand villa that, he crooned, belonging to a fine gentleman, a Mr. Jessup. Not that the rich didn't have their troubles, which Mr. Cullen seemingly could bemoan as if they were his own. Take the Jessups now: unlike the Deventers, they had been blessed with children—a wastrel son and a headstrong daughter. Ah, Miss Julia, *there* was a beauty! Many a time he had seen her tooling along in her tallyho, behind four matched bays, handling the reins as well as any of those young bloods in the Coaching Club. Not many women had the hands to control four high-steppers like that, but then Miss Julia was a bit of a high-stepper herself.

"Of course some say she'll break her neck yet," he said with a chuckle. "That was her coach that sideswiped the blacksmith's buggy—it happened right there at that turn we just took."

"Oh, the woman driver," Ada acknowledged absently, scanning the road ahead but seeing nothing yet that could be called a castle.

As if aware of her flagging interest, he passed on quickly to juicier gossip. Treated like a princess, Miss Julia was, no man good enough for her, or so her father thought. And then one fine day, she up and ran off with the coachman. Now what was a body to make of that?

The protracted pause grew in significance. Ada turned her head to meet a sharply querying look. Querying, she uncomfortably sensed, her own susceptibility to such story-paper romance.

"She must have broken her father's heart," she said primly. "Do you think the horses could be made to go a little faster?"

He flicked the reins with a grumpy giddyap. "If it's her father's heart you're worrying about, it's been mended by now. She's back at home, right enough, none the worse for wear."

"Oh. And her husband?"

"They do say he's been given a handsome sum not to show his face in these parts. Seeing as how life went so hard with them the poor man was driven to blacking her eyes now and then, he'll be thinking he's finally on easy street. Still—" he gave her a mooning look—"it's a romantic story, wouldn't you say?"

"Yes," she said. "It touches the heart."

Pat Cullen gave a disappointed sigh. There was the castle, he said.

Kirkewode! Throat suddenly dry, Ada grasped even more tightly the wagon seat. A heavy stone arch showed the way, the one visible break in a wall that stretched as far as the eye could see, seeming to diminish in perspective to infinity. The gate itself was locked. The design of its grillwork was simple. No curlicues or initials here. Just straight bars with triangular heads, like the shafts of so many spears thrust into the ground.

Cullen handed her the reins and leaped down to pull the bell chain. From her perch, Ada could see the stone gatehouse beyond the wall, a languid plume of smoke trailing from its chimney. The man who emerged was a heavy-set black-bearded fellow with all the civility of a prison guard.

"Oh, it's you, Cullen. What the devil brings you here? Nobody turned in an alarm."

No move was made to unlock the gate.

"Good day to you, Blackie. Sure and I've come all this way just to see your smiling face."

The heavy black brows remained drawn together. The man's only answer was to pick his nose.

"If you'd just look beyond that fine nose," Cullen continued unabashed, "you'd see I've brought you the young lady that's come to visit."

The man so aptly called Blackie looked her over, an inspection which only deepened his scowl. "Nobody told me nothing about a visitor—young lady or otherwise."

Ada leaned forward, almost dropping the reins. "It's Dr. Traherne I've come to see—you must let me in!"

Cullen cut short her plea with a little warning shake of his head and a wink that said, *leave it to me.* "Now, Blackie, there'll be trouble enough when they learn the young lady was not properly met, you'll not be wanting to cause more by keeping her out here in the cold."

"I've got my orders, you know. She'll just have to wait until I send the boy round to the house to check."

"Use your brains, me lad. What would they do if this *was* a case of unlawful entry or trespass? Why, summon the police to arrest the perpetrator. And ain't the police, in the presence of yours truly, right here, with the paddy wagon and all, ready to haul the culprit off said premises, if that be your master's wish?"

Not a quick-witted man, this Blackie, who picked at the hairy lining of his nostrils as other men scratched their heads. It took him a few moments to follow that impeccable logic, searching in vain for a flaw. Sullenly he unlocked the gate and drew it back, with the warning that it was all Cullen's responsibility now, that he had never admitted anyone before—not even Mr. Henry, the master's own brother—without specific instructions from the house.

Once the wagon was safely through, Ada said admiringly, "That was very well done."

Cullen grinned at her, with no undue modesty. "Sure and I'll have to talk me way through the Pearly Gates, I can use the practice."

The formidable barrier of bronze spears by no means marked their journey's end, Ada soon realized. The winding road continued with no further sign of habitation. An enormous buck, followed by two does, leaped across their path, and even Cullen had all he could do to keep the startled horses from bolting. In summer, one would be gliding down a green tunnel, but through the present bareness of the trees Ada could see the

25

surrounding landscape and appreciate how artfully a wilderness could be tamed.

With a sharp pull on the reins, Cullen brought the wagon to a sudden stop. "Look at that, will you?" he whispered hoarsely.

Her first thought was that he had spotted some exotic animal imported from the other side of the world. If the Deventers kept a fully stocked zoological garden, she would not be surprised. But there was nothing to be seen on the road ahead.

"There!" he said urgently, nodding toward the right. "On the wooden bridge. 'Tis the great man himself!"

Two men. One towering over the other. The shorter turned, and her heart leaped into her throat. Papa! But of course it was not Papa. Not like him at all. It was the beard that had confused her—the same old-fashioned "chin warmer," merely fringing the jawline, presenting the full bare face like a sunflower with its corolla. Beneath the plaid Inverness cape, worn carelessly open, this stranger was oddly dressed in knee breeches and low shoes. He smiled and made a move as if to approach, but whatever his giant companion whispered in his ear caused a sudden change of heart. He settled for a limp but friendly wave of the hand, and the pair strolled on, soon to be lost to sight.

Not until then did Cullen release his breath. As if it *had* been some exotic animal, Ada thought with amusement, which even his breathing might have frightened away.

"There now!" he exploded. "Ain't this me lucky day, though. The first time I've seen him with me own eyes."

"Then how can you be sure it's Mr. Deventer?"

"Oh, I've consorted with them as knows him well, and they have described him to a tee, beard and all," he said, and added with a grin, "I'm no heathen, miss, I go to Sunday morning mass at St. John's too."

Now if it was a romantic story she wanted—his tongue in motion as soon as the horses were again—surely the Deventers' was the greatest of them all. "Mad Jack, they used to call him, before he was married, and she was no better than she should be, if you believe the stories they tell. He was a loose screw, no doubt about it, flinging his money away like there was no bottom to the barrel, on the sure road to a pauper's grave. Truer words were never spoke than that God works in mysterious ways. His high-toned folks wouldn't have nothing to do with her, so they moved up here, shut themselves away. Sassiety, you can have it—that's what they said. And being just the two of them, a pair of love birds in their private nest, that was the making of him. No more high jinks, no more wild living. He don't even show his face, and bejesus, don't the money come rolling in! He's made back the family fortune and ten more besides! They say he's got so much money now he can't even count it."

"She still shows *her* face," Ada pointed out, more interested in this low gossip than she wanted to admit. "There are music hall songs about the effect of that."

"Oh, the poor lady," Cullen groaned, "beauty must be a terrible burden sometimes." With surprise, Ada realized that the sympathetic look directed at her implied that surely *she* could understand. "If a man be so foolish as to lose what little sense his Creator gave him, why should she be held to blame? Take that lawyer fellow who shot himself—I don't know much about the gent, it being before I was assigned up here to the 35th— but he was old enough to know better, that's for sure. It was when the young 'un did himself in that people began to talk. Poor lad, hardly out of leading strings—but that's when love strikes hard."

Had she heard about that bad business, he suddenly wondered? It had happened right here, two summers ago. "And yours truly answered the call. I seen him myself and bejesus, the sight was enough to make me—"

Yes, Ada interrupted the gory account, she had heard all about it. Who had not? Even out West, the papers had been filled with the lurid details. And then someone had written a song about her, soon to be heard in all the music halls. *Goodbye, goodbye forever, oh my Cloistered Rose.* It had been appalling, the strange hysteria sweeping the country. A spontaneous eruption of madness. A nationwide rash of suicides. Young men who had never met her leaving behind passionate notes of farewell, addressed to their Cloistered Rose. (In the pathology lab, where Ada had just been introduced to her first cadaver, Dr. Widener chewed his thick cigar and quipped, "A sure sign of spring.") The newest fashion color was a pale pink. Young ladies brushed back their fringes and wore their hair swept smoothly from the forehead à la Rose. A new phaeton model was christened the Dashing Rose. A new species of the flower for whom she was named in turn was named for her. But Dr. Widener was right, of course. As was the way with such phenomena, it had a seasonal transience. By summer, fringes were back. Pink was out. The suicide rate dropped sharply and young men who persisted unfashionably in killing themselves for love addressed their notes to unknown Ednas and Berthas and Mary Janes.

"'Tis all to her credit," Cullen pronounced. "The lady sticks to her marriage vows. If that foolish lad—or that even more foolish gent long past his prime (a family friend he called himself, would you believe it?)—well, miss, if you'll forgive me saying it, had they had their way, they would never have felt the unholy urge to do away with themselves, now would they? So where is she to blame?"

Ada did not attempt to answer that question, having glimpsed what could only be Kirkewode rising above the trees. A turn in the road and it came into full view. Indubitably a castle, though the Rhine and not the Hudson should be flowing past its door, was Ada's first impression. Decorative arches of stone were lifted like eyebrows over pairs of narrow windows. Stiletto towers with conical slate roofs. A meaningless crenellation everywhere, even on the chimney pots. She counted four stories up the walls of pale grey stone, and two more pitched under the sharply angled roof. Why in these modern times build walls so thick, windows so narrow, when the only assault to be feared was on one's privacy, the only slings and arrows those of misfortune?

As the patrol wagon pulled up in front of the imposing entrance, it struck her how ludicrous was her equipage. With

Cullen beside her, erect now and respectfully solemn in policeman's uniform, she felt like a convicted felon being delivered to her prison cell as they awaited the answering of the bell.

The butler who opened the door regarded them impassively. "Ah, Patrolman Cullen. What brings you here? Not more tickets to the Policemen's Ball, I trust?" The accent was unmistakably English and so was his presence. The pale eyes turned to Ada. She wished she had changed that morning into her one fresh dress, instead of merely brushing out her tailleur.

In the struggle to make any sound at all, her voice came out excessively loud. "Would you be good enough to tell Dr. Traherne that his daughter is here?"

If the butler was too well trained to exhibit surprise, Patrolman Cullen was not. "So you're the doctor's daughter, are you? Now why didn't you say so?" Her desirability may have diminished (not so wealthy as he had hoped) but her accessibility had increased. When the butler signaled that she should step inside, he boldly took her arm as if they were already united by an indissoluble vow. "I've me orders to stick by the young lady's side until Mr. Deventer or his lady says it's all right for me to go."

Those orders were not to be literally obeyed, the butler made clear. "Then you may wait here, Mr. Cullen," he said, and to Ada, "If you will step this way, miss. . . ." Ada followed, craning her neck to peer upward into the dim heights of the baronial hall. Along three sides, at second-story height, ran an open balcony with a marble balustrade, behind which a grim formation of armored knights stood ready to launch an attack. Another repelling force, Ada thought, like those gates, like the butler's eyes. There was even an advance guard stationed below at the foot of the grand stairway—two visored forms who held their lances at quite an intimidating slant.

The reception room in which she was deposited was by contrast almost cozy. Certainly much warmer. The fireplace had been freshly tended, and Ada chose to sit at a discreet distance on a spraddle-legged chair, all gilt and silk damask. One glance about the room revealed that Rose Deventer had yet to tire of her own color. The walls were dressed in pale rose brocade and underfoot an Aubusson repeated the rose in a deeper shade. On an easel reposed a landscape painting, which Ada would have liked to inspect more closely, but felt too much the uninvited guest. Instead she catalogued the objets d'art that crowded the pink marble mantel, her eye held longest by an alabaster copy of the Brownings' loving hands. Her own began to sweat in their kid gloves as she heard, even through the closed doors, the click of heels on the marble floor of the great hall.

"Quite right, Caxton. And you must thank that nice young policeman for escorting her here."

It was a low husky voice, not at all the clear soprano deemed most befitting the female form. Yet not for a moment was Ada in doubt as to whom it belonged. When the door opened, she would be face to face with Rose Deventer for the first time. She would see with her own eyes this woman whose beauty was by now a legend. A beauty that could drive a man to reform his dissolute ways, or leave a loving wife and child, or put a bullet through his head.

"My dear, dear Ada," Rose Deventer cried, sweeping into the room. "What a delightful surprise!"

Obeying the regal command of those outstretched arms, Ada rose.

Why, she's not *that* pretty, was her only clear thought.

Chapter 3

THE eyes were beautiful, Ada admitted when she was again seated, sharing the small sofa, her hand held captive. Grey eyes, cut long and narrow, as if squinting through mist or slitted by laughter. But there was a subtle coloring to lips, a little too red, and cheeks, faintly ablush, that made Ada suspect the woman used paint. Eddies of conflicting emotion swept over her: First an almost giddy recurrence of that childhood fascination, free of any moral judgment, recognizing only that here was someone out of the ordinary; then Mama's memory called shame that she should so easily forget the worm of evil embedded in this falsely blooming rose. The warm squeeze Mrs. Deventer gave her hand alarmed her—she needed time to put her heart in order.

The elegant head drew back, as if to better examine a work of art. "You, a doctor! A pretty thing like you! I simply cannot believe it."

Ada extricated her hand. "Could I see Papa please?"

"Yes, yes, of course. I have sent for him. But I

31

hope you don't mind my coming down to take a peak at this paragon I've heard so much about. How proud your father is of you, my dear! That is all we hear about these days—his brilliant daughter. Do you know what I expected to see? Some dreadful creature with a muddy complexion and weak eyes and the kind of skimpy hair that sheds hairpins all over the place— you know, a *strong-minded* face! Instead, to look at you, one would never guess you had a brain in your head!"

A paragon of modesty as well, Rose Deventer might have assumed from Ada's lowered glance. But the struggle under smarting lids was to hold back tears. Papa was proud of her, this woman had just said. Not once had Papa told her that. *How's my little Miss Sawbones?* he still greeted her, as if joining in some childish game.

"And why aren't you in school, dear?"

Ada did not trust her voice or dare look up, lest this woman see how close she was to crying.

"I see. Only your papa has the right to ask such questions. And here he is."

In rushed Papa, almost at a run, looking for once like a real medical man called away from a busy practice, too much in haste even to put a coat over shirt sleeves and vest. Under faded gingery brows, the glare of anxiety could have been no fiercer had it been fired by anger.

"Ada! What is wrong? Are you ill? To show up here like this—and not even a telegram—"

Oh Papa! trembled unvoiced on her lips, as if there were some failed connection with the loud cry of agony within. She had arrived at last, and there was Papa, but as she had feared, he was not exactly offering her the shelter of his arms. With the automatic concern of a gentleman for proper dress, he was rolling down his sleeves, fumbling with his cuffs, and eyeing her with unconcealed dismay. The sleeves were damp, she noticed, and his hands, when they were free to grasp hers at last, felt cool and freshly washed.

"Did I take you away from a patient, Papa? I'm sorry—there was no need for you to rush so—"

"No, no, child, a mild case of hysteria—easily handled—" Ada submitted to his searching look. Abloom with good health he could see, and he smiled with relief. "I do not know what they teach you in the schools today, my dear, but I have always found a good dousing with ice-cold water a most effective restorative to composure."

"You see, Ada, what a comfort it is to have your papa at hand." Ada turned to see Mrs. Deventer's gracious smile. "Even when Mr. Deventer and myself are in tolerable good health, there are the servants—a small township of them—and one or another always suffers from some complaint." Papa was the recipient of an admiring look from Mrs. Deventer that seemed somehow connected with her index finger's absent-minded stroking of Mr. Robert Browning's alabaster hand.

"What are we talking about?" Papa exploded. "Am I to know why my daughter has done this incomprehensible thing—left school with but three months to go for her degree? What in the good Lord's name has happened, Ada, to bring you *here?*"

The dreaded moment had come to put into words the unspeakable. Not since the tortures of adolescence, the first onset of womanhood, had Ada felt so intense an embarrassment.

There was a susurrus of silk petticoat, a sudden comforting hug of Ada's shoulders. The two of them needed to be alone, Rose Deventer suggested tactfully. And her dear kind doctor—the index finger drew a lingering, loving stroke down Papa's shirt sleeve—was not to bully this charming child. Could he not see how exhausted she was? Such a long tiring journey.

"I will see that a room is readied for you, Ada. As soon as you have 'fessed up to your papa, Caxton will have someone show you up. Pay no mind to the hour of day, my dear. What you need is a good long rest." Then the door closed behind her.

"Oh, Papa!" Ada hurled herself against his breast. At last the tears came, the sobs, and in between, not the composed recounting she had rehearsed on the train, but broken phrases.

Sitting on the sofa beside her, Papa looked stunned. "I don't understand, I don't understand," he repeated, dabbing helplessly at her wet face with his handkerchief. "I thought this young man loved you, wanted to marry you—"

Ada grabbed the handkerchief from him and briskly finished the job. "Oh yes, he loved me all right," she said bitterly. "He kept saying so all the time that he—that he—" She squeezed the crumpled linen into a ball, determined not to start crying again. "And he wanted to marry me. What he changed his mind about was marrying a doctor. Don't you see? He simply took this way to put an end to that."

The worst of the retelling was the reliving, the memory almost more painful than the event. Even that quiet time early in the evening had grown ominous with foreknowledge, the faint hum from the gas light like the spluttering wick of a bomb. Yet it had begun so peacefully . . . a cold Sunday night supper, the fire lit in her bedroom, the evening reserved for Dr. Gerster's newly published *Rules of Aseptic and Antiseptic Surgery*. Impossible to concentrate at the spindly desk Mrs. Nichols had provided her. She could never study properly sitting upright, fully dressed, weighted down by the heavy drapery of her skirts. And her bustle scratched. Though she had recently forsworn corsets as injurious to health, even a tight bodice was too confining at such times. She had stripped to her undergarments, stretched out before the fire on an old buffalo robe—so she had been wont to read in childhood, lying on the floor, kicking pantalooned legs in the air. A comfortable position, too comfortable by far. The fine print thickened, blurred . . . she dozed . . . struggled into consciousness from the torture of a dream to find a man's knee pressing into the small of her back, both arms held tightly behind her back . . . strangled back the scream when she twisted her head and saw the face of her assaulter. *Francis!* His name was all she had time to say. The gag was slipped in place, and she was roped, hand and foot, like a calf for branding—that was no doubt that Wyoming cowboy expertise he had so often boasted of. Yes, like a calf for branding, memory told her.

She was carried to the bed, and he lay down beside her, fully clothed, covering them both with the feather comforter. Just to keep warm while waiting, he assured her, turning her on her side, wrapping his arms around her. Nothing would happen, he would not touch her, did he not love her? His breath was hot on the nape of her neck as he told her all the ways in which he loved her. So they waited—waiting for *what?* her thoughts screamed—until they heard the tinkle of sleigh bells in the frosty night.

Papa sprang to his feet. "I'll kill him, I'll kill him! A devil like that has no right to live!"

"No, no, Papa—nothing *did* happen! I swear it—he didn't—hurt me. He didn't—touch me." She did not want ever to recall the particulars of that restraint, what at the time had seemed a death agony occurring behind her back—the groans, the galvanic twitching, and the long last shudder of a soul expiring. "Don't you see? All he wanted was to have it known that he was in my room that night. As soon as he heard the horses turn in, he untied and ungagged me, making sure that they saw him leave. . . ." They came running upstairs, expecting to see me dead—or worse—and in truth I could hardly move, Papa, there was no circulation left in my legs—"

"Then there were surely marks! Could they not see that you were held against your will? I shall write immediately to the Dean—no, by God, I'll go there myself! A horsewhipping is what that scoundrel needs—yes, first a horsewhipping and *then* I'll see the Dean!"

So even Papa did not believe that nothing had happened. He was convinced of her shame. What difference did it make then whether she had been taken by force or had succumbed to carnal desire? To prove herself unwilling victim was at best to exchange contempt for pity—a trade not worth the effort, to her way of thinking.

"He must marry you," Papa finally said. "I shall see to that, at least."

For a moment Ada almost hated him. She had already been offered *that* solace. *The young man is still willing to marry you.*

There was nothing but admiration for the young man's character in Reverend Nichols's voice. His wife, still suffering from the shock, smiled feebly and offered their own house for a quick quiet ceremony. *In my own house, in my own house* was still her refrain.

Ada answered Papa as she had answered them. "I wouldn't marry him even if—even if there were the need. Nothing could make me marry him now."

"But, Ada, you have no choice. These things get around, you know. There will always be a shadow on your name, whispered conjectures by those who do not know. . . ."

"I don't care about my name! I don't care if I never get married! Don't you understand, Papa? It's not just my name Francis has ruined—it's my life's work!"

Papa could think of nothing to say. He patted her helplessly. She saw now why he had ranted of horsewhips and parsons. These were textbook treatments, promising a cure for the lesser hurt; for the more damaging blow, there was nothing he could do. His silence was the agony of helplessness only a parent or a doctor could know—and he was both. Aware of his suffering, she forgot her own and insensibly her spirits lifted.

"Oh well, Papa, it's not the end of the world," she said briskly, as if he, not she, had made such a pronouncement. Straightening her bonnet, she became aware of a few loose hairpins, and firmly thrust them back in place. "At least I can stay here until we sort things out." Papa's silence was unbroken. "Can't I? Do you think Mr. Deventer will object? His wife seems agreeable."

Papa seemed to feel a sudden need to put some distance between them. He walked over to the fireplace and leaned against the mantel to stare into the dying embers. But he did not touch the coupled alabaster hands, Ada noticed, feeling oddly pleased. "*I* mind, Ada. I'd rather you were anyplace in the world but here. But now that you've come . . . under the circumstances . . . I suppose you'd best stay. Just until we sort things out."

Chapter 4

THE sun just clearing the trees had all the pallor of a recent rising. It took Ada a groggy moment or two to realize she had slept through not only the afternoon but the night. So late in the morning? Ada felt a momentary panic, then remembered there was no need to rush out barely combed and washed, fumbling under her coat for the unbuttoned placket of her dress. On so many cold winter mornings, when the sky still held its darkness like a bated breath and the ice in the washbasin had to be broken before she could douse herself awake, had she not longed for just this freedom to lie in bed, comforted with goose down, forever?

Forever. She let the heavy lined drapes fall again and the room returned to its sepulchral dimness. The bed assumed the form of an ornate sarcophagus. Around its ponderous carved frame, fat cupids danced in bas-relief, fingers to pursed lips, demanding silence for lovers. To her the silence was of the grave. She had her wish, she could lie here forever, life turned to fairy tale.

There were fairy tales enough of wishes granted just to prove the foolishness of the wisher.

Ada struggled against the onset of a deeper panic. From this room. From this house. She would settle for even a temporary escape. Her own clothes, even the worn gripbag, were missing but there was fresh fine linen in the drawers and in the mirrored clothespress she found an array of dresses approximately her size. The boots, thank heavens, were her own, although they had acquired overnight a miraculous shine. In a dress of striped wool and a cashmere shawl whose lightness belied its warmth, she ventured into the corridor and found her way to the open gallery that looked down on the great hall. The suits of armor, at stiff attention, made an honor guard for her passing. Below she saw a scurrying of black forms that recalled the scurrying of roaches when one walked unannounced into a kitchen pantry. No less a consternation did her appearance on the marble stairs create among the black-clad servants. After a moment's gawking, they resumed their attack with feather dusters and floor brushes and polishing cloths, bobbing an embarrassed curtsy to her polite good-mornings. She threaded her way among them to the heavy front door, pulled it open with an effort and walked outdoors, but not before catching a peripheral glimpse of the apron-swathed butler frozen on the threshhold of a side room. With the door closed behind her, she laughed out loud at his agonized look at being caught in dishabille.

Now that she was outside, she realized it was the stuffy air entrapped within a canopied bed that had made her feel she was being buried alive. Calmly she took the pulse of her own emotions: unaccustomed to such rich surroundings, she was suffering a mild case of mental indigestion, as a child might suffer from a surfeit of sweets.

And there was, in fact, a confectionary look to the rococo castle on this crisp clear morning, as she discovered when she took a backward look. The grey stones were awash in sugary pastels and the javelin-slim towers, the crenellated battlements, seemed neither ridiculous nor imposing but a charming jeu d'esprit. Sunlight on the castle was like putting gay flags out. She approved the effect and walked on, crossing a wide esplanade studded with marmoreal statuary, descending into a formal garden. What had begun as irrational flight was now a salutary constitutional.

At first she kept to the avenues paved in intricate patterns of brick and lined with pollarded trees. Poor trees, their cropped heads as pathetic as the bound feet of Chinese women. She had lost her taste for such formal vistas lifted from European courts. Three years in the West had re-attuned her to her native country. America at first had seemed raw to her, but she had come to see it differently. The very unkemptness of the landscape—even in this long-settled East—was proof that here men were not yoked to farms like oxen but had the liberty to move on. To move West.

West was Michigan. Cold blue lakes of glacial purity. Thick forests of evergreen, like lustrous fur on the back of this animal Earth. Roads leading north like streaks of rust cutting through hills of iron. And farther west—a name keened in an Indian tongue—Wyoming! Too late she saw the real direction of her thoughts. Francis! her heart keened and Francis's face appeared—nut-brown, high cheek-boned, straight black hair, the sardonic droop of his thin long mustache. How like an Indian memory made him look, as if taking its revenge. Francis hated Indians. That was their first argument.

"But the fighting is over, dearest."

"You don't know them, my girl. The fighting ain't over until the last one's dead."

When she pleaded for the vanquished, she looked mighty pretty, he told her fondly. When he cried "kill, kill," she secretly admired the firm set of his jaw. It hardly mattered, such third-person, past-tense events to lovers living very much in the first-person present. As for the future—their two futures to be joined as one in partnership—the vista was one of unending delight. Wyoming! She had yet to see it, but it was beautiful she

39

knew from its name, and though just a territory, more advanced than any state. Women could vote there and serve on juries and even hold office, she had heard.

"No hen doctors," Francis cautioned her, "at least not yet."

He chose to boast of other things: the vast ranges of the cattlemen—his father one—and the booming railroad and mining towns. Number of cows, miles of track, tons of ore. He spoke in figures, but his love of the land held more poetry than that, she was sure. He was just being manly, by speaking so. "You're fit for me, Ada, and I can handle you," was the blunt way he had asked her to be his wife. No poetry there. She had taken such plain speaking as proof he truly loved her.

She was to learn soon enough—even before that night of which she refused to think—what a paltry thing his love was. In his hands the telegram, yellow flag of defeat. Terrible blizzards sweeping the plains had frozen the cattle by the thousands. "Ruined." His voice was without timbre, as scratchy as if it were coming from a wax cylinder played on a Gramophone. "Pa has lost everything." Still keeping to figures.

"We can manage, Francis. A few months more and we will have our diplomas. With both of us in practice, we will feel no pinch at all."

The hand she offered was squeezed so hard she felt the bones rub against each other. "In a few months you will be my wife, Ada, and it will be up to me to manage for us both. Do you doubt I'm man enough?"

She said nothing. Now was not the time, she thought.

But later: "I am serious, Ada. You may take your diploma and frame it, but that will be the end to it."

Poor Indians, she had cried, unfair! Where was her eloquence now? Why could she not speak out like a Miss Woodhull or a Mrs. Stanton? She knew her worth. She had proved it. Francis was the under-demonstrator chosen by Professor Earle, a sign that he stood first in the class; but she had been told in confidence that had she been a man—And she was to hang her diploma on the parlor wall like an embroidered sampler touting home sweet home?

Again later: "There is nothing worse than a stubborn woman! You said you loved me and I accept that love as a sacred trust. What kind of a man would allow his wife to expose herself to dangerous diseases, to touch foul bodies, to enter strange houses, to consort with all kinds of low people?"

Just like Papa. Was this what love turned out to be—a cannibalistic feast in which one devoured the other? Was it love that formed this hard bolus in her throat so that she could not speak?

The ring was off her finger, sparkling in the palm of his hand. It said all she had to say.

He had then the same stricken look as when he held his father's telegram. "I love you, Ada." The same flat voice tightened beyond resonance, as when he had announced his father's ruin.

But it was she who was ruined—a thought bitter enough to abort any fresh crying spell. Walking rapidly, as if to outpace heartbreak, Ada crossed the whole length of the formal gardens and entered a more rustic lane, muddy enough from recent rain to require a careful lifting of her skirts. The sun, blocked by a passing cloud, made its absence felt with chilling effect. She pulled the shawl over her head, ready to turn back. It was then she smelled the smoke. She had to look hard to find its wispy track in the sky. Her first thought was that by some shortcut she had reached the gatehouse. Impossible, she quickly decided, remembering how long it had taken a team of horses to cover the approach to the castle. Curiosity urged her to round one more bend of the path.

There, nesting in a dale, was a sprawling one-story house of the same grey stone, roofed in the same red tile, as Kirkewode itself. Like a newly conceived organism whose cells have just begun to divide, she thought with amusement. In summer it would be shaggy in a full coat of ivy, but now the leafless hemp-like vines were exposed in all their coarseness, as if the house were held in a strangulating net. From a rear yard came a sporadic clucking, the breakfast conversation of chickens scratching for their feed, and from the house an appetizing whiff of fried ham.

Ada gave a self-disgusted snort—no wonder she had awoken in such a state of irrational anxiety. She was hungry. Starving. She had not only slept half a day and a night, she had fasted as well. As eager now to return to the castle as she had been to leave it, she turned back to find the path blocked by a large dog. Very slowly she advanced. An ominous growl brought her to a complete halt.

Never run. Do not show fear. A barking dog never bites. All the injunctions, prescriptions, bits and pieces of dog lore she had ever heard flooded into her mind. The barking dog adage was not reassuring, for this one was silent save for an unpleasant noise deep in his throat. "Good dog," she said, eyeing the hackles on his neck. She forced herself to hold her hand limply before her, though inwardly flinching. Was that not the proper introductory gesture? Perhaps protocol required her to remove her gloves. "Good dog," she repeated with no conviction and dangled bare fingers for him to sniff. But the ruff of hostility still framed his powerful head, and there was a coiled-spring tension in his haunches. Yet he did not move. It was almost as if he were awaiting orders.

Some primitive instinct, an atavistic awareness of another's presence, caused her to turn her head. A woman stood by the rear-yard gate, silently watching, the look on her face as savage as the dog's.

"Call him off!" Ada cried out furiously, certain that the dog belonged to this grim apparition in unrelieved black.

The face which a moment before had seemed so distinct suddenly collapsed into a sagging inconsequential blur. The intimacy claimed by those glaring eyes was withdrawn, a stranger stared dully at her now, with no interest in her presence. Or in her fate, Ada feared, for the woman quickly withdrew behind the house without a word said either to her or to the dog. Yet, after first paralyzing her with fright by bounding toward her, the beast passed her by with a disinterest that matched its owner's, leaped over the low gate and vanished too. The woman must have given some sign, Ada realized, feeling something less than gratitude. She hoped it was safe now to show fear, for she was sweating with it. And whether or not it was safe to run, she ran.

She regained her composure when she was back again on civilized brick, among the barbered trees, but was still somewhat short of breath when she ran into Papa on the esplanade. He was pacing with hands clasped behind him, head bowed as if intent only on the pattern of the paving. She ran up the shallow steps to greet him, eager to tell him about her unsettling experience.

He hardly seemed pleased to see her. His face was drawn with fatigue and he listened to her tale of near dismemberment by a ravening beast as to a complaining child interrupting a man confronted with serious adult problems. His only response was to ask what she was doing at the parsonage at that ungodly hour of the morning.

"I was just taking a morning walk, I didn't even know it was the parsonage." She saw no reason why she should have to defend her presence there, she told him angrily. It seemed to her that Kirkewode's resident clergyman was at fault in keeping such a ferocious animal. She would have thought his clerical duties required of him more hospitality. "That woman—whoever she is—looked as if nothing would give her more pleasure than to see that dog sink his teeth in me."

"Poor lady."

Such displaced sympathy did little to assuage Ada. Had curiosity been less strong, she would have stalked away. "I gather you know the woman."

Papa grudgingly allowed he did. The lady was Mrs. Haygood, the parson's wife. "Obviously she mistook you. Had you been wearing other clothes, I am sure you would have found nothing amiss in her behavior."

Ye gods, Ada silently addressed the statue of a Greek athlete with exceedingly prominent rectus abdominis muscles. At least Papa admitted that something was amiss besides his daughter. And what had clothes to do with it, she opened her mouth to ask, but the answer was already there: she mistook me, my back was to her, I turned my head, she saw my face. And hers crumbled like a mummy suddenly exposed to air. As if only hatred could preserve her.

"I see, she thought I was Mrs. Deventer. But why, in heaven's name, should she wish to see that lady torn apart? I tell you, Papa, I am sure that had that dog attacked, he would have only been obeying her command."

Ada had a sudden thought, of which she was immediately ashamed. Had Mrs. Haygood been driven to such extremes by jealousy? Was not even a man of the cloth safe from Rose Deventer's charms? Shameful the thought might be, but Ada could not dismiss it. Had not Mama been ravaged beyond repair by that emotion, though driven to more reputable extremes? She could still remember the corseted maternal breast to which she had been pressed, its hard ungiving feel. *My little girl is all I have now . . . my one consolation,* Mama had cried, then thought immediately of another. *Your poor Papa, my torment will be over when Jesus takes me in his arms, his torment will be everlasting . . . consumed by fire and brimstone . . . cast into the bottomless pit!* By contrast, Mrs. Haygood, siccing on her dog, seemed almost kindly.

"Mrs. Haygood has suffered much mental anguish, Ada, and it has obviously affected her mind."

So she had guessed right—another victim to be tallied to Rose Deventer's account. Papa need say no more.

What had she heard about the Deventers, Papa asked with a scowl that seemed to accuse her of knowing more than she ought. That both had an unsavory past, she replied matter-of-factly, but at present were devoted to good works and the piling up of millions. Of course, Ada could not resist adding, Mrs. Deventer had achieved a certain renown all her own. She was reputed to rival the monstrous Juggernaut of the heathen Hindoo. Disappointed suitors in droves committed suicide before her.

Papa visibly winced. "Not droves," he corrrected. "There have only been two—er—"

He was searching for a euphemism. She provided one. "Unfortunate occurrences?"

"Yes," he said. "The Haygoods' tragedy is that one of them was Jonathan, their son. Their only child, you see, so it is understandable that Mrs. Haygood never quite recovered from the blow."

"Oh, Papa!" Ada felt the deepest shame at having misjudged the situation so. "How terrible!" Never, never would she jump to conclusions again.

"Yes, terrible." Papa's voice fell to an apologetic mumble. "Sometimes a tragedy occurs and no one is to blame, Ada. Certainly not Mrs. Deventer—she held out no encouragement, I can vouch for that. Perhaps love unrequited, or otherwise forbidden, naturally leads to such excess, for then one is lured on by a false sense of security, believing that no real transgression will be committed, that nothing will come of it if the reins on the emotions are loosened. In the end, one loses all control."

Ada found the sadness in his voice unbearable. It was as close as he could come, she felt sure, to apologizing for himself. In this timid confidence, disguised though it had to be, he was opening his heart to her. Perhaps her fantasy of a true comradeship with Papa might yet be realized. First he would see that she, unlike Mama, understood the imperatives of love (the French novels she had read were full of that); then he would see that, unlike Mama, she had forgiven him long ago; and then—all clear thought failed her in favor of a cloudy vision of Papa and herself walking hand in hand discussing the profundities of the human heart.

"Oh, Papa, I do understand," she began, but caught herself in time. She had seen the flash of panic in his strained blue eyes, before his face had stiffened into a mask. She must not push, she must not grab. If he chose to disguise his meaning, she must disguise her reading of it. "The poor boy," she said quickly, to make clear whom she had in mind. And Papa was so

45

relieved that he had not betrayed himself, he grew almost loquacious on the safer subject of the Haygood boy.

Until the last summer, Jonathan Haygood had spent little time on the Deventer estate, being boarded away at school. The best schools—the Deventers' kindness had seen to that. He was a good son, devoted to his mother, obedient to his father, destined for the ministry. After a brief period of what Papa called the "usual doubts and self-questioning," he had entered the divinity school at Harvard, had just completed a first successful year. Quite naturally, his patrons expressed their approval by inviting him to dinner.

"We thought that first evening he was merely befuddled by the wine. He did not cover his glass as his father does—Harvard breeds a more modern type of clergyman, it seems—but if he imbibed too much, he never sobered up again. Wherever Mrs. Deventer went, he was at her heels. He stripped his mother's garden for bouquets, delivered them with tedious poems of such metaphysical yearning Mrs. Deventer had to ask me what they meant. He was engaged to visit a classmate at his summer cottage in Maine—he refused to leave, telegraphing that he had fallen ill. More truth than lie to that. When I look back, it seems an eternity he was mooning about, always underfoot. In fact, it was a mere few weeks. And we were amused." Papa paused, then grimly repeated. "Amused. Mrs. Deventer and I had many a good laugh at his expense. Until the night he climbed an old tree shading her apartment, made his way into her bedroom, and showed us all what true devotion really is."

The unforgiving hardness in his voice was meant only for himself, Ada was convinced. In an effort to console him, she asserted firmly that neither he nor Mrs. Deventer could be held to blame.

Papa shrugged. "On that point, and that point only, the mother's mind has given way. There is no reasoning with her. I always thought her a soft-spoken woman, but to hear her speak now of Mrs. Deventer—murderess is the mildest epithet—one wonders how she acquired a vocabulary like that."

46

The Bible was a sufficient source, Ada thought, remembering Mama. She remarked, with the condescension of a stronger mind, that the wife of a clergyman should have found comfort in her faith, the greatest bulwark against despair.

"You have yet to meet Dr. Haygood," Papa said gloomily. "There's not much comfort there."

Ada doubted that such gloom was all in Mrs. Haygood's behalf. He himself could use some comfort, but she did not know how to offer it. She had tried before and sent him scuttling like a hermit crab back into his shell. Just so had Francis, reeling under the blow of his father's ruin, rejected any offer of help. Her own thoughts took on a gloomy tinge, as she considered whether all men had such soft underbellies that they feared a woman's pity would do them in.

As if afraid she might yet employ some kind word against him, Papa pulled out his watch, found some unnamed duty called him, and dismissed her with a scolding that eradicated the last vestige of the sympathy he found so subversive. Young ladies did not roam abroad at such an hour, he told her. She looked a hoyden with her hair in disarray, mud on her skirts. He suggested that she repair immediately to her room and avoid being seen in such a state—it lowered one in the eyes of the servants.

Contrary to her expectations, that was easy enough to do. The early morning horde seemed to have melted into the woodwork. Or were they like the cobbler's elves in the fairy tale, coming out to do the household's work only when the master and the mistress were asleep? Some such magic seemed to operate, for she found her bed already made, the bathing room steamy from a freshly drawn hot bath, and a lacy peignoir draped in limp readiness to receive her. More magic, when after a long soak, she found awaiting her in the bedroom—though she had heard no sound—a tray of heavy Georgian silver, on which rested a pot of tea, fresh rolls swaddled in white linen like a newborn babe. Sampling the variety of jams in little Limoges pots, Ada felt a rapturous content. By the time she had eaten and poured the last of the tea, she was restored sufficiently to pass judgment on the world.

Mrs. Haygood showed a regrettable weakness of character, perhaps even a native infirmity of mind. But Rose Deventer could not be held entirely blameless, nor Papa either, from his own account. *We were amused.* No doubt they let the poor boy see that. If her own experience was any guide, laughter was what no man—much less a thin-skinned boy—could bear. And Mr. Deventer—had he laughed too? Papa had not mentioned how the husband took this young Jonathan's gallantries, this open courting of his wife. Papa had yet to mention Mr. Deventer at all.

With all due sympathy, Ada found even the victim at fault. Humiliated, an object of ridicule, the whole world reflecting his self-disgust—yes, she could see what moved him to take so foolish a revenge. *You'll be sorry when I'm dead,* a little girl in Nice had also phantasized, composing in her head the letter Papa would receive informing him of her death. But even as a child she had known that death had its facts as well as life. Not to savor the remorse firsthand. Not to hear the wild regrets, or witness the ungovernable tears. Oh no, there was nothing more foolish than being really dead.

She moved to the chaise and settled down in a froth of lace. For the first time in days, she felt well fed. And, not coincidentally perhaps, reassured as to her worth. There was a moral superiority just in being alive. Her body followed the dictates of the padded satin upholstery and fell into an unaccustomed pose of feminine allurement. Mirrored across the room was a sensuous odalisque. That warm ivory sweep of throat. The half-exposed breast, uplifted by the raised arm which served as headrest. The sideways look of hazel eyes, naive in color but interesting in their shape. A head haloed by a swath of sunlight, rendering brown hair opalescent with radiant colors. *That's me,* she realized and sat bolt upright, flushed with shame that recognition had sent pulsing through her an instinctive surge of pure delight.

Chapter 5

ADA was not surprised when Maxwell informed her, through a mouth full of pins, that her presence was desired in the smoking room. Quite proper that Mr. Deventer should wish to meet his self-invited guest before taking her in to dinner. Ada acknowledged the right with a slight nod at her reflection in the mirror, by no means averse to seeing a notorious tycoon in the flesh.

"There, miss, the best I can do without the proper undergarments."

Even with the pins removed, the mouth remained pursed in disapproval, but Ada could find no fault with the gown of Nile-green China crepe embellished with a double-ruffled tablier of ecru gauze. More gauze, its fullness shirred, swathed the shoulders, which seemed to rise out of a cloud. Recalling Mama's admonition against the pitfalls of vanity, Ada cut short her pleased self-appraisal and turned her critical attention to Maxwell's intruding image.

A quirky humor flashed in Ada's hazel eyes. If Mrs. Deventer was right in equating strong-mindedness in women with an unprepossessing face, then this lady's maid must be the brainiest woman around. A patently false fringe merely emphasized the sparseness of the greyer hair behind. Two pendicular moles sprouted from the sallow cheeks. As for the eyes, they were hardly visible through what seemed to be a permanently suspicious squint.

Maxwell re-positioned a frilled double bow of ribbon in Ada's hair and expressed herself as satisfied with the result, although the sour pucker of the mouth remained. Poor teeth, Ada suddenly wondered? Over which the mouth kept a concealing clutch, the look of disapproval as permanent as the squint? For disapproval had entered with her: "Maxwell's the name. I'm Mrs. Deventer's dresser. It seems I must do you too." Then that look, at which Ada now could laugh—the look of a surgeon called in too late, prognosis very doubtful.

Before sending her on her way, even Maxwell must have felt some compliment was called for. She paid it to her mistress. "Lucky for you my lady has not parted with her figure. She'll be pleased to hear how little alteration there was to do—just that little bit taken in at the waist. And the hem, of course, you not having so fine a stature."

Still Ada felt grateful for her ministrations as Caxton led her down a hall mirrored à la Versailles. However difficult this interview might prove, she felt far more confident, more self-assured than when, tired and grimy from her travels, she had awaited her first encounter with Rose Deventer. For the moment she agreed wholeheartedly with that lady of fashion quoted by Mr. Emerson: To be perfectly well-dressed gave one an inward tranquility which religion was powerless to bestow.

Caxton discreetly closed the door of the smoking room behind her, leaving her in a small anteroom enclosed within screens of Cairene lattice work. She walked through a hazy curtain of beads and glass prisms, setting off a wild tinkle, and drew her breath in. Before her was a scene lifted from the Arabian Nights. Low divans. Embroidered pillows. Moorish banners dripping from the ceiling. Inlaid Damascus tables. A two-foot-high nargileh with coiled snake-like appendages. A bronze elephant holding in its lifted trunk an enormous ashtray. Incense burners of repoussé brasswork. Enough oriental rugs to fill a bazaar, small ones tossed over large ones and over all a tiger skin or two. It was a room packed with so many exotic objects that for a moment Ada failed to see the most exotic of all.

This time her gasp was audible. "Mrs. Deventer!" That airy ribbon of smoke came from the loveliest of houris, afloat on a sea of pillows, not from the beard-bristling captain of industry she had expected to see. "I thought it was Mr. Deventer who—they said the smoking room—"

"You are shocked to see a woman smoke?" Rose Deventer performed a feat Ada thought impossible: she leaned even further back. "You disappoint me, Ada. I had thought your ideas were more advanced than that. If women can possess a man's virtues—as you lay claim to by your studies—why not his vices too?" Ada flushed at the mocking tone. The smile grew kinder. "Come, dear, sit here beside me. Mr. Deventer is not here, true, but I am his envoy, so to speak. He wishes me to welcome you—on his part as well as mine—and to apologize in advance for his absence at dinner tonight. A touch of malaria, I'm afraid. We do suffer from that complaint in this neighborhood—the War brought it north, your papa says, he calls it the rebels' revenge. Mr. Deventer's bouts are not so severe, but your papa thinks it best that he keep to his bed as long as he has the slightest discomfort." The long grey eyes narrowed with amusement. "Like most men, my dear husband has a highly developed sense of discomfort. You may not see him for some time, I'm afraid."

"I am so sorry," Ada said politely. Nowhere in the room was there a proper chair. She sat gingerly on the edge of the divan. "But then I have seen him already, I must confess."

"You have?" Rose Deventer reached out to the elephant as if to pat its trunk, but merely extinguished her cigarette. "Mr. Deventer did not mention that to me."

Ada flushed again. This soigné woman made her feel like

an awkward schoolgirl. A mere conversational gambit now sounded like an indiscretion. Quickly she explained that Mr. Deventer had been pointed out to her on the drive up to the house. Unless her guide had been mistaken in his identification: beard rather like Papa's, plaid cape, somewhat unusual knee breeches? That was all she could make out from such a distance, but Patrolman Cullen had been suitably impressed.

Rose laughed outright at that. "Oh dear yes, that sporty getup of his. So comfortable for country walks, he says. As long as he keeps it out of the drawing room, *I* say—and he does."

And as long as they were on the subject of clothes, Mrs. Deventer had a suggestion to make. Although Ada looked very fetching in that dress—a Worth creation, trust Maxwell to choose well—the first thing on the agenda was a shopping trip into the city to see what they could do.

"I am sure my trunk will arrive in a few days," Ada said stiffly. "And if my own things are returned to me, I will need nothing else."

Mrs. Deventer gave no indication that she had heard. "Madame Modeska can copy any Paris style and we shall set her to work immediately, but still you'll need some ready-mades to tide you over. Lord & Taylor's, I think. And, heavens, we must do something about boots. I cannot help you *there*." Smugly she extended a narrow little foot that made Ada's look like a clodhopper's. The glance she threw at Ada, back straight as a poker, feet primly together on the floor, left her struggling to contain her laughter. "My dear girl, that may be the proper way to sit on a chair, but not in a Moorish den. Come, curl one foot under you, like this. Then lean back against those pillows. There. Much more comfortable, isn't it?"

To Ada, not comfortable at all. Too sinfully languorous for that. Her sense of sybaritic decadence was enhanced by the passing of a little dish of bonbons, each wrapped in gold foil. Undeterred by Ada's abstinence, Mrs. Deventer unwrapped and popped a candy into her mouth with a sigh of ecstasy. "Huyler's of course—but these are made especially for me. My one weakness. Maxwell warns me I must take care of my figure, particularly at my age, but—" She took one more, vowing it was the last, that Maxwell was right. Alas, the transformation marriage made in so many women. Take Edith Kingdon—had Ada ever seen her on the stage? A lovely thing when the Gould boy married her (quite laughable the fuss his mama made about a misalliance—who were the Goulds anyway? Rose asked loftily) but now after one child, as fat as a house.

The form half-revealed by the loose-fitting robe of silky gauze showed no danger of such a fate. Nor did that way of sitting seem so indecent when the legs were encased in harem trousers gathered at the ankles, the feet shod in golden slippers with long curling toes.

Pleating the foil into what looked to Ada like a tiny doll's fan, Rose Deventer leaned forward with a strangely beseeching look. "Dear Ada, *I* never had a child, you know, and—"

A rush of air from the rudely opened door set the beaded curtain jangling. "Damnation, Rosie! Did you tell Caxton not to send up any more beer—" The bellow of outrage came to a spluttering halt as a burly man of towering height stepped through the curtain.

Mrs. Deventer turned. "What do you mean by coming into a room like that?" Her voice had an edge as sharp as any Moorish scimitar. "How dare you use that tone? You are dismissed. Pack your things and leave immediately."

Though a look of shame suffused the heavy bloated face, the man merely stood there, shifting his weight awkwardly from foot to foot, tugging at his disheveled livery. Ada surmised that, unless the Deventers had recruited an entire regiment of giants, this was the same man she had seen in company with his master.

"All muscle and no brain," Rose said, nodding with contempt at the giant. "Yet not so stupid but he knows Mr. Deventer will never part with him." She made a charming gesture with her hands— what am I to do? those upturned palms lightly pleaded of her young guest—and conceded that so long as Mr. Deventer must have a bodyguard, he was no doubt right to insist on keeping Slade. It was all the fault of those terrible anarchists, those bomb-throwing socialists. "The foreign element, you know," she said with a significant lift of the brow. Had Ada heard that Mr. Gould was once confronted in his office by a wild man with a gun?

As Ada recalled the well-reported incident, the poor demented soul had been an American businessman, not a foreigner at all. Hardly the first, certainly not the last, to be ruined by Mr. Gould's nefarious tricks. She made an effort to correct Mrs. Deventer's mistaken impression—"I do not think that foreigners should be blamed for *everything*," she added staunchly—but found that the lady had a proclivity for not hearing any contradictory response. In truth, Ada thought, those "huddled masses" welcomed by the Lady in the harbor were finding a cooler reception onshore.

Rose continued unabashed to shudder at the dangers Mr. Deventer faced from those imported undesirables. Taking Mr. Gould's narrow escape to heart, Mr. Deventer never went to his office in the city, she was glad to say. Still, these were times when all men of substance had reason to be afraid. One had only to think of that dreadful Haymarket affair—thank heavens those villains had finally been hanged though it had taken two years to do it—and today all these strikes, a veritable epidemic—the ludicrous demands of the Knights of Labor, what else could one do in a time of depression but cut wages and lay men off? Was Ada aware that just this New Year's Eve the gas works in the city had exploded, obviously the work of some malcontents? Slade's manners left much to be desired, but as an ex-pugilist ("he lasted four rounds with the great Sullivan himself, if you will believe him"), he was Mr. Deventer's best defense should some anarchist breach the castle's walls.

Ada saw no reason to doubt Slade's pugilistic past. His credentials were in his face, once handsome enough but now quite a mess with its flattened nose and grainy scars. And if a life in the ring explained the face, the beer explained the rest—that puffy overflowing of a still imposing frame.

A dumb but loyal brute, Ada summed him up, observing how his eyes turned from speaker to speaker. Faithful dog (though hangdog at the moment), to whom all language is incomprehensible, who must search for meaning in the tone of voice or expression of the face. But he had been voluble enough before he saw a stranger in the room. Rosie, he had called her.

"Very well, Slade," his mistress said with a sigh, "Mr. Deventer will deal with you himself. But something must be done about your appetite for liquid refreshment at all hours of the day."

Having received a dismissal he could accept, Slade nodded humbly and left the room. But Rose Deventer was no longer in a mood for idle chat. "Mr. Deventer will be too easy on him. Only yesterday he was so bosky, Mr. Deventer started out alone on his morning walk, was halfway to the gate before Slade caught up. Mr. Deventer laughs it off, but I shudder at what might happen if some rascal chooses such a time to do his mischief."

Hypothetical or no, such a rascal seemed to fully occupy her mind. Concern shadowed her eyes, tightened her mouth. It was true then, this fairy tale of loving man and wife? Poor Papa—a confusion of emotions moved Ada to such pity—what role did he play in this woman's life?

"What am I thinking of?" Rose exclaimed, uncoiling from the low seat. "Maxwell is waiting to do me now—and dinner is promptly as six. We collect in the blue drawing room, my dear. Caxton will show you there."

As soon as Ada entered the room, she knew she was in the presence of death.

"Ada, may I present Mr. Witten, a business associate of Mr. Deventer." Papa made the introduction brusquely.

"More than that," Rose objected. "Mr. Deventer's right-hand man. And our dear dear friend." No longer in harem attire,

55

she was sitting quite properly on the sofa, transformed into a lady of high fashion in dove-grey silk.

Ada placed her hand in Mr. Witten's—an act which required an effort of her will, for all her medical training. Deplore it as she would, she still felt an atavistic dread of death in such a form, shrinking from it as from an evil contagion of the spirit rather than a mere failing of the flesh. Three months at most, she gave him. The clothes of a once stout man hung in pathetic folds, testifying to a loss of weight so rapid there was neither time nor inclination for retailoring.

With the arrival of Dr. Haygood, their little dinner party would be complete, Rose announced. "I'm afraid we ladies are outnumbered. Mrs. Haygood is indisposed and cannot join us. The poor woman rarely goes out these days—I don't know if you're aware of the sad story, Ada—"

Ada quickly indicated that she was. Thus spared a recounting of the tragedy, Rose cheerfully hoped that Dr. Haygood would not be too late. "Our chaplain, I'm afraid, is kept as busy here at Kirkewode as our doctor." The teasing smile she sent Papa went unacknowledged.

"And why not?" Mr. Witten asked, with a death's-head grin. "One drums up business for the other. Little black bag or little black book, you takes your choice, but if you ask me, it's all soul-butter and hogwash."

Papa looked uncomfortable. "See here, Witten, if you don't have confidence in me, you're perfectly free to—"

"Oh, I got confidence," Mr. Witten said. "You say you can't save me, maybe the good Lord can—I got confidence in that. The reverend says sure, the good Lord can, but he gives me odds the good Lord won't. I got confidence in that." For a moment Ada thought the man had been seized by a convulsive fit, then realized it was soundless laughter. "Don't know but I prefer your hogwash to his soul-butter at that—at least you give me something for the pain."

Rose looked shocked, as at a naughty child speaking out of

turn. She beckoned him to sit beside her on the couch—"my dear friend, what nonsense you are capable of"—and reached out toward a dish of bonbons. Were they provided in every room, Ada wondered? How appropriate for a millionaire's taste—candies that looked like gold nuggets, piled high as a miser's hoard.

Still as if dealing with a child, a child on the verge of tears in need of instant distraction, Rose Deventer crooned: "Now close your eyes and open your mouth. . . ." Meekly Mr. Witten obeyed. The gaunt face on its stick-like neck, eyes tightly shut, mouth agape, reminded Ada of an unfeathered chick, pathetic in its scrawniness, opening its beak for regurgitated nourishment from the mama bird. "There now. Wasn't that a nice surprise?" But more than the candy, those thin lips seemed to savor the brief taste of the lady's fingertips.

Ada took Papa aside on the pretext of examining a deluxe edition of General Grant's memoirs. Papa nodded in answer to the question she mouthed: yes, the cancer was in its terminal stage. How the Deventers would manage without him, Papa found it hard to imagine. Witten was invaluable in executing the intricate financial maneuvers Mr. Deventer so cleverly devised—transmitting orders, delivering documents, buying, selling, bribing, spying, lying, threatening—the man had all the social graces of a real tycoon and had placed them totally at Deventer's service, content to remain little more than Mad Jack's runner. Inexplicable conduct, the shake of Papa's head conveyed, though Ada found in Mr. Witten's adoring gaze sufficient explanation. "He could have become a millionaire twice over had he struck out on his own."

Well, Ada thought, that was exactly what Mr. Witten was about to do—strike out on his own. And nothing Rose Deventer could do would hold him. But even at death's door, her vassal displayed a pathetic fealty to that beauty, eyes watering in gratitude at her kind attentions. With glazed inattention Ada tried to read the General's account of the battle of Shiloh, distracted all the while by the soft indistinct murmuring at the other side of the room. Even at its most serious, she noted, that contralto voice could not forbear a flirtatious rise and fall.

Her eyes wandered from the book to Rose Deventer's face. Honest puzzlement knit her brow. What was it there (aside from the eyes) that held men in such thrall? The nose was too long, too sharp; the mouth too thin, too wide. At that moment, Rose leaned over, the better to hear Mr. Witten's low reply, and the Song of Solomon sang itself in Ada's ear: *Thy neck is like the tower of David builded for an armoury, whereon there hang a thousand buckles, all the shields of the mighty men. . . .*

At the entrance of the last expected guest, Ada gladly abandoned the General. Mrs. Deventer gave Mr. Witten a conversation-ending pat and moved gracefully across the room to greet her chaplain. What a strange pair, was Ada's first thought when the new arrival shook hands with Mr. Witten—one lost in clothes too big, the other extruding from clothes too small. Yet a closer look revealed that the clerical garb was of decent fit, the fault lay in the odd construction of the wearer's frame. Although of average height, he had enormous bony hands that protruded gawkily from the tight black sleeves, an enormous bony head suitable for a man twice his size, and presumably enormous bony feet encased in those narrow outsized boots. With an inward smile, Ada fancied that before her stood a specimen intended to be displayed at the Museum of Natural History, but somehow misplaced in a lady's drawing room. A kind of new-found dinosaur, reassembled from fossil remains, but the job somehow botched—with certain pieces missing, or misaligned by an ignorant hand.

Under the craggy brow, small eyes of glacial blue found Ada of little interest, surveyed the room expectantly only to fall in disappointment into a study of the floor. "I had hoped," Dr. Haygood addressed the blue Chinese rug, "we would be honored tonight with Mr. Deventer's presence. In view of the unusual circumstances." The heavy head teetered in a nod at Ada, granting her a minimal value as a drawing card. "It is not often we have an addition to our intimate little circle."

"Often?" From Mr. Witten another paroxysm of laughter. "Never is more like it. This intimate little circle is what you might call closed—just Rosie and a small sprinkling of her admirers."

A remark dismissed by the lady with a tolerant smile, as at a court jester whose sally had misfired. "Poor Mr. Deventer," she sighed, addressing herself to her chaplain's complaint, "a touch of malaria again. But I too have grounds for disappointment. I had hoped Mrs. Haygood would feel fit enough to join us."

"Not one of your admirers there, Rosie," Mr. Witten cackled and received no smile at all that time.

A slight relapse, Dr. Haygood apologized to the floor, and just when time had begun to show its healing effect. Rose suggested airily that something in the line of vile vapors and miasmas might account for the poor lady's continued indisposition, as well as the recurrence of Mr. Deventer's ague. The conversation turned then to the weather and the possible untoward effects of so mild a winter—a safe topic, not yet exhausted, when Caxton appeared to announce the serving of dinner.

To Mr. Witten fell the honor of leading in their hostess. Then indeed Ada found herself within the circle of the lady's admirers, seeing how Rose placed her hand on the skeletal arm without the slightest hesitation, seeing her smile at that disease-ridden form as if it belonged to the handsomest gallant in town.

The dining room was awe-inspiring. Evidently the Deventers had taken to heart Mr. Oscar Wilde's injunction to be Early English ere it was too late. Paneled in dark oak and furnished in Tudor style, it was of baronial dimensions, with a fireplace large enough to roast a Tudor ox. And Ada suspected that the table, when fully let out, could seat comfortably a sizable portion of a Tudor court. As it was, reduced to the ultimate degree, it made the company seem sparse, ludicrously outnumbered by the footmen who moved silently but purposefully about under Caxton's all-seeing eye.

To Ada's surprise, a full setting had been laid at the head of the table, as if the master of the house were momentarily expected back from a journey but dinner could no longer be delayed. Seeing the direction of her curious glance, Dr. Haygood whispered that she must not get her hopes up. "His cover is never removed. It is the custom. But even when he is enjoying good health, Mr. Deventer rarely dines in company. I myself have been honored with his presence on but two or three occasions and even then he joined us in mid-course, as it were, and retired even before the ladies." All great men had their eccentricities, Ada was gravely instructed. Mr. Deventer's, it seemed, was a morbid shyness of strangers.

"How he must have changed," Ada remarked drily, recalling those scandalous escapades on the Côte d'Azur.

"Even as Saul on the road to Damascus," Dr. Haygood said with such reverence that Ada was struck dumb.

The vicissitudes of life had never been so evident as when Ada compared her last frugal dinner with this interminable banquet. After the oysters, a clear turtle soup. Then a poached fish coated with a fine French sauce. Then a gigot of lamb, followed by succulent green asparagus ("from our own glasshouse," Rose explained when Ada expressed surprise at the out-of-season treat). Fingerbowls were removed and a filet of beef presented *en croustade*. After all this, Ada found herself staring with something less than gustatory delight at a brace of canvasback ducks.

Surfeit brought in its wake a dyspeptic mood. "Do you not find it disturbing, Dr. Haygood, that in these hard times so many people are actually starving, while we sit down to a dinner such as this?"

"What you should find disturbing, Miss Traherne, is that there are so many sinners in this world."

An incredulous stare had little effect on a man who would not raise his eyes from his plate. There was more of the dinosaur here, Ada began to suspect, than a disproportioned frame. Such Calvinistic harshness belonged to an equally antediluvian time.

"But surely you cannot mean that the unemployed have only themselves to blame? That when businesses fail and factories close and farms are foreclosed, it is *their* fault? Believe me, sir, in my work, we see much of the destitute: men maimed by machines, destined never to work again; widows who have sought to take their own lives, unable to feed their children, unwilling to watch them starve; men still young, though they don't look it, who at death's door must be tied down to be kept in bed. They cannot *afford* to be ill, they will tell you, not even in a charity ward. A few, I grant you, are shiftless, have taken to drink, or fallen into other disreputable habits, but for the most part they are good decent folk, as pure in heart as any of us sitting here." Ada could not forbear a quick look at the vacant place at the head of the table. "Or purer."

At that Dr. Haygood did look at her. A glint of icy blue from out of the shadow of the bulging brow and the head bent down again. But his voice, hitherto a soft mumble, was transformed into a clear instrument of scorn. "What do you know, young lady, of the evil in men's hearts? Or God's justice? We are on this earth to serve God's needs, not He ours." He too darted a look at the empty place. "Sinners are we all, but do not doubt it, God knows his own."

It was not that stern ministerial counsel that silenced her. It was the echo of her own words. *In my work.* She no longer had any work. She had regressed into being a young lady, with no other occupation than the pursuit of a husband. No doubt Papa was even now marshaling in his mind a list of eligibles, hence his abstracted state. How else to dispose of her, he must be thinking. Not an easy task—she found a perverse satisfaction in that—once the scandalous account of her dismissal from school got around.

Francis. The stabbing pain surfaced again. There was a sudden burst of laughter at the distaff end of the table, toward which Ada turned in desperate hope of diversion. For some minutes she listened, but those risible anecdotes were being told in a foreign tongue. Puts and calls. Selling short. Bear raids and bull corners. Watered stock. Something secret called rebates. Something to be wary of called a trust. And such strange characters too, referred to by faintly contemptuous sobriquets—the Little Man, Livernose, Uncle Dan'l. Better known to Ada, the talk eventually made plain, as the execrable Mr. Gould and the formidable Mr. Morgan and the wily Mr. Drew. Still, their exploits were no easier to follow.

"Highway robbery, old Livernose called it!" Mrs. Deventer was reporting with unabashed delight. "As Mr. Deventer said, coming from *that* brigand, high praise indeed."

Observing Mr. Witten's spasm of laughter, Ada felt dimwitted not to get the point of such a joke. Shyly she asked why Mr. Morgan would pay all that money for what they had just described as a few miles of broken-down track.

Mrs. Deventer shrugged her lovely shoulders. "My dear, it's beyond me too. The games these men play! All Mr. Deventer said was that it had a certain nuisance value. I can't tell you how much money he's made simply by being a nuisance. We ladies could learn a lesson from that!"

Mr. Witten buried his face in his napkin. He was laughing now at her, Ada was sure. Not that she begrudged a dying man his amusement. Perhaps it was true that women had no head for business. In all these machinations, she could see only skullduggery and blackmail and a careless disregard for every Christian ethic. Ada doubted if Rose Deventer understood the subject either, although in parroting her husband she had been drilled to perfection. *As Mr. Deventer says . . . as Mr. Deventer says . . .* Ada was sick of hearing that model of American business enterprise quoted.

Sensing her boredom, Mrs. Deventer smiled and suggested they speak of more uplifting subjects. "Our young guest does not approve of Mr. Deventer's operations, I have the feeling."

"If so, you merely show your ignorance, young lady," Dr.

Haygood said coldly. "Do you realize what mankind owes to such men as Mr. Deventer? Those iron rails of his carry forward our great civilization. Without them, the wild grandeurs of this continent would never be tamed and put to the service of the Lord. I am reminded of the words of the Psalmist: O Lord how manifold are thy works! in wisdom hast Thou made them all; the earth is full of Thy riches."

The heavy head turned almost imperceptibly toward the undisturbed setting at the head of the table, leaving Ada in some doubt as to whom the chaplain had in mind as the Divine Creator.

"Not to mention the untold numbers of savage souls saved thereby," Papa said and Ada looked up just in time to catch his sardonic wink.

"True, true," Dr. Haygood murmured. "The banners of Christ march forward too."

It was with relief that Ada followed her hostess's lead and rose to leave the gentlemen to their cigars. Ladies' gossip and fashion talk would be easier to bear than such conversation as this, whether centering on Mr. Witten's Mammon or the Reverend Haygood's God, interchangeable as they were. But the two ladies had not crossed a quarter of the great hall before their way was blocked by a perspiring Slade, tugging at rumpled vest and holding out a folded note.

"Just came over the telegraph machine, ma'am. Thought it might be important. Did I do right?" The furrowed brow did not relax until Mrs. Deventer absolved him with an impatient "Yes, yes, quite right."

She held the note unopened between thumb and forefinger as if on a balance that was literally weighing its importance. "I gave strict instructions that Mr. Deventer was not to be disturbed, but Slade is right, it might be urgent. I know Mr. Deventer has been waiting for some information from Kansas City—"

Slade grinned, his confidence restored. "That's from Kansas City, you hit it right on the nose."

"Then I shall have to wake him, however much he needs the rest." To Slade she issued crisp instructions not to disturb the other gentlemen but to let Mr. Witten know his presence might be required upstairs. Of Ada she begged a little patience in waiting alone in the blue drawing room. "I shall not be long," she promised. "Just long enough to be sure that Mr. Deventer behaves himself."

Rose swiftly mounted the stairs and Slade was off to summon Mr. Witten. Ada stood in a momentary quandary as to the direction she herself should go. So many rooms, so many doors. She vowed never again to simply follow where she was led. Down those two shallow steps and turn the corner? No, that was the hall of mirrors—

"Psst!"

The sibilant demand for attention came from above. She looked up, saw only the shadowy array of armored knights. An enormous hall like this must have constant drafts, freakish eddies of air, she reasoned. A much more likely source of that hissing noise than a chivalric ghost from the fifteenth century.

"Psst! Girl! You—down there!"

At this undeniably human sound, she looked. From behind one stalwart knight appeared another figure, of much the same stocky dimensions but *sans* lance, *sans* armor, garbed instead in a long velvet robe. Leaning over the balustrade, he waved at her, coaxing her closer until she stood directly beneath him, looking up into a broad rubicund face. The head was covered with a velvet skullcap of Venetian design, beneath which no hair was visible, but there was no hiding the bright red fringe of beard.

"Mr. Deventer?"

She knew without a doubt that it was he. At this close range, she marveled that she could ever have mistaken him for Papa. So this was the great Deventer, maker of millions! Slinking about the hall like a naughty child who knows he should be in bed! The thought amused her. But there was nothing amusing in the gesture he suddenly made.

"Beautiful! Beautiful!"

There was no mistaking the object of that ardent gaze. Her hands flew up to the gauzy shirring of her bodice, crushed it against her chest. She stumbled backward, hoping to get out of range, and her heel caught in the hem Maxwell had hastily basted in. The sound she heard was definitely a rip in Mrs. Deventer's Paris gown.

"Now look what you've done!" she wailed, contorting herself to see the damage.

"That's nothing to what I'll do if you'll just stand there until I come down!" Hardly more than a hoarse whisper, yet the threat carried clearly in the cavernous hall. "Damn me, it's been a long time since I saw such a fine-looking piece—"

To her horror, Ada saw him lope toward the stairs and she gathered up her skirts, determined to seek sanctuary on the run behind the nearest set of doors.

"Jack! I've been looking everywhere for you, you bad boy!"

Ada froze in her tracks, but if she were to judge by Mr. Deventer's easy laugh, he was not a whit dismayed.

"Ah, Rosie, you always turn up at the wrong time."

"No, my love, at the right time."

Heart in mouth, Ada prayed that Mrs. Deventer would not take another step into the gallery. As yet, neither woman was visible to the other, and Ada took increasing comfort in the light banter passing between man and wife. There was yet hope that the shameful encounter might pass unobserved. It was not the first time she had received an amatory advance from a married man (though none of such crudeness), and as always the greatest agony was her own overwhelming sense of guilt, the excoriating thought that there was something wrong with *her* to provoke such an unseemly response.

"Come now, Jack, I have something here you will be more interested in than any of your sly games."

There was not the slightest edge to that sweet coaxing voice. No, she could not have overheard—Ada calmed herself with that assurance. A few shuffling steps of slippered feet, the closing of a door, and Ada was left weak-kneed with relief, feeling like a criminal who had once more escaped detection by the narrowest of margins.

She found her way back to the drawing room, thankful that she had a few minutes alone in which to recover her composure. A beautiful room—walls hung in blue silk brocade, ceiling tinted a more delicate blue, carved into garlands of flowers, fluttering ribbons, intricate scrolls—but she longed for the Spartan simplicity of her quarters on Ingalls Street. If only this were a bad dream. Perhaps it was. Any moment her eyes would open on the dying embers of a fire, and stretching her cramped limbs she would feel beneath her the mangy buffalo robe and know there was an examination tomorrow, with studying still to do . . . Oh, Francis, she would tell him afterwards, I had a terrible dream about you. . . .

The dream of a dream was shattered by the approach of Papa and Dr. Haygood, carrying with them in all its heat some argument brought to a boil over wine and cigars. Even before they entered, she could hear them at it in the hall. On no, she groaned, needing to hear no more to know that the source of their discord must be the Gladstone-Ingersoll debate in the North American Review.

Papa entered with a short bark of contemptuous laughter. Dr. Haygood came behind him with a tight-lipped smile of scorn.

"This man still holds to Ussher's chronology, Ada—in the face of all the evidence, my dear girl! Unlike us poor bumbling scientists, whose estimates admittedly may err by a million years or so, he knows the exact date of Creation—the year, the month, the very day. I tell you, sir, every time I open my Bible and see that foolish date, September 1, 4004 B.C., staring at me at the top of the page, I am tempted to read no further."

"You are misquoting me," Dr. Haygood said stiffly. "I do not hold to Bishop Ussher's chronology. My own researches lead me to conclude that he was off by some fifty years—"

Papa hooted. "Fifty years! Ye Gods, I am speaking of millions

66

of years! A hundred million—who knows? Those very railroads on which you bestowed your blessing speak out against you. Every fresh cut the Chinamen dig, every mile of track they lay, provides new proof of the earth's antiquity. And as for evolution, sir, our bone hunters are having a holiday out West. Are you aware of the collection of Eohippus fossils they now have at Yale? Old as man is, our noble friend the horse turns out to be still older—"

Dr. Haygood raised an enormous hand with the meek air of a man ready to compromise. "Please. Enough. We have had this argument before. Let me just put it this way, doctor. The Bible teaches that man is a little lower than the angels. Your science teaches that man is a little higher than the apes. Do you agree so far?"

Papa nodded. The meekness vanished from his opponent.

"Then each of us has chosen the truth that describes him best."

"Papa," Ada whispered, tugging at his coattails to remind him he was in a lady's drawing room.

"You're quite right, Ada," Papa said, "there is no point in arguing evolution with a fossil."

The ensuing silence was almost as painful to bear. Ada tried to think of some harmless subject.

"I am surprised they do not have the electric light here," she said brightly. "Could they not have their own generator installed the way Mr. Morgan did?"

"Ah, but gas light is more flattering to an aging face," Papa said, and then had the grace to look ashamed.

The glass-domed French clock on the mantel informed Dr. Haygood that after-dinner etiquette now permitted him to take his leave. His poor wife, he mumbled. Would they convey to Mrs. Deventer his best wishes for her husband's speedy recovery?

Ada took his early departure as a stroke of good fortune. Now was her chance, before Mrs. Deventer returned, to speak to Papa about the latest unpleasant turn of events. She had no intention of recounting that little adventure of the hall—no more horsewhippings, please!—but she would make it clear that she did not care for an extended stay at Kirkewode. Papa himself was no longer happy here—she had seen that on the esplanade this morning. Take me away, Papa, she would plead with a cunning helplessness that, if properly played, might rescue them both. Ada was not immune to the thrills of martyrdom. For one satisfying moment she saw it all as part of the Grand Design—her hopes dashed, her career aborted, her heart broken, her name besmirched—all that to bring her as savior to this castle where Papa was immured in a dungeon of despair.

Such a thought, however briefly entertained, left her feeling very close to him. And besides, their minds seemed to work alike. "It was all I could do not to laugh aloud when you called Dr. Haygood a fossil, for I had been thinking of him as a dinosaur all evening, and most so when he spoke of God."

To her amazement, Papa turned on her a look of outrage. "How dare you speak so flippantly of God?"

"Not of God, Papa, of Dr. Haygood—"

But no words of hers could assuage his wrath. Never should he have permitted her to enter medical school, he roared. Was it not bad enough that she had lost her good name, must she brazenly flaunt her loss of faith? He should have listened to those who warned him against such studies for a female, who predicted they would weaken her moral fiber. As apparently was the case. He could only hope she had been removed from that pestilential environment in time. Perhaps this was God's way of saving her before it was too late—

Ada laughed. A short harsh laugh. Their minds did work alike. She had been thinking it was God's way of saving *him*. "Coming from you, Papa, your concern about my loss of faith sounds strange. From all I heard tonight, you are fully in agreement with Mr. Ingersoll. The Great Infidel, isn't that what he's called?"

"Do you compare yourself with me?" Papa looked aghast. "Do you forget your sex? A daughter should pattern herself on her mother. God knows, your mother was all that a woman should be."

"Again, coming from you, Papa—" Irony dripped from those words, and a bitterness never before expressed.

"Yes, I was a fool. Fool! Fool!" Papa was tearing himself apart with a fury before which her own anger paled. "Fool not to value that pure woman more! It's true I found her piety her most tiresome fault, but I know better now." Suddenly his voice took on the measured tones of a reasonable man. "Listen to me, my girl. When Voltaire said if God did not exist, it would be necessary to invent him, it was Woman he had in mind. There is something so savage, so uncivilized, so primitive in the female heart that man must exercise the greatest care to teach the moral virtues, to constrain her by God's laws, or else it will break through and destroy us all."

"I see, Papa," was all Ada could say. She saw indeed what Papa meant. Women needed religion as wild beasts needed cages. Were the walls of Kirkewode to suddenly collapse, he like Seneca would thunder: *Where is the woman?* It hardly mattered that she could not speak. He would not have heard her anyway. He did not even hear her cry of pain when he seized her by the shoulders, crushing the gauze drapery, squeezing her so hard. She doubted if he even saw her, though he thrust his face so close she could smell his winey breath.

"Tell me, girl, do you believe in hell? In eternal damnation? In fire and brimstone?"

"You sound like Mama now." She did not bother to conceal her disgust. Suddenly she wondered if, like Mama, he had a particular candidate in mind. "You are hurting me. My shoulder. . . ."

Ada held her injured pose, awaiting his apology, but Rose Deventer swept into the room and all apologies were hers.

"You must forgive me for being so long. I do wish Mr. Deventer had never installed that telegraph machine upstairs! If your patient suffers a relapse, doctor, I'll have you know it's not my fault. It took me forever to get him back to bed—he's like that, you know, once he gets his mind fixed on business." Head cocked on side, she surveyed Ada and began to chuckle. "My dear girl, if this wasn't your papa, I would think you two had been cuddling. How have you managed to so disarrange that dress?"

With little clucking sounds, she puffed up the frothy folds around Ada's shoulders and stood back to admire the result. Oh yes, it would be a pleasure, she declared, to outfit such a figure. She was looking forward to their little jaunt into the city.

There was nothing disarranged in *her* appearance—hair and gown in perfect place—yet something about her held Ada's attention. The real, not painted, flush to her cheeks. The exhilarated sparkle in her eyes. The vibrato of excitement in her voice. With her, something sexually disturbing had entered the room, like a strong odor of musk (although the fragrance she wore was light and floral). Hastily Ada looked away, yet the thought of what wiles the lady may have used to bring her husband back to bed could not be erased.

"Poor Mr. Witten." The voice was neutral now, the face somber. "He's going fast, isn't he, my dear—doctor?"

Ada did not miss the quick addendum of a title to what was obviously a customary endearment. Her lips curled. Did these two take her for a fool? Apparently, for Rose Deventer continued with the charade.

"I can't bear to see it, doctor. Just that little bit of business upstairs, and he was too exhausted to come back down. I insisted that he retire. Ah well, Mr. Deventer has chosen his replacement, I'm glad for that. I am to stop by the office while I am in town and arrange for the young man to come up immediately, while there is still time for Mr. Witten to acquaint him with his duties."

"And how will that sit with Witten?" Something had happened to Papa. He seemed drained of all vitality. As if that outpouring of rage had served as the lancing of a carbuncle, drawing off the vile pus, but with it some elemental life force as well.

"He suggested it himself—brave man, he breaks my heart." In sadness Rose Deventer showed her age. As if she knew it, she gave a little shiver, shaking off dark thoughts of death. As easily as a dog shakes off water, Ada thought. Once again those

70

grey eyes were shimmering with gaiety. "A young gentlemen your own age, Ada—you will like that, won't you, dear? And quite personable, I am told."

"I am sure of that," Papa said with heavy emphasis.

"Your papa too is tired, Ada. We women merely add to his cares. He is glad, I know, that we will be out of his way for a little while. Since your arrival, he is brimful of new plans and has weighty matters to think about."

"Yes," Papa said and looked at Ada, really seeing her at last. Ada looked coldly back. He had discussed no new plans with *her*. She would make her own plans, but that would take time. Meanwhile, Mrs. Deventer was providing an escape from Kirkewode, who needed Papa? A temporary absence, it was true, but nonetheless welcome.

Good-nights said, she accompanied Rose up the stairs, leaving Papa behind. ("I think he wants a whiskey, dear," Rose whispered.) Somewhere to the left, in the Deventers' private wing, a door closed sharply. Ada hoped that Mr. Deventer, once in bed, had stayed there.

Rose acknowledged the sound with a smile. "Maxwell has been alerted that I'm coming up. I'm afraid you'll have to undo yourself tonight but never fear, we'll get you a maid of your own when we return. Heaven knows, there are plenty of these young girls about." Ada thought the smile dragged a bit at the corners, as if Rose Deventer too was tired. "You know your way?"

Ada nodded: through the archway on the right was the guest wing, her bedroom at the end. She allowed the soft powdered cheek to brush against her own, and walked briskly down the hall, alert for any lascivious "psst!" She did not fully relax until she reached her own room, there to luxuriate before a fire so warm she felt impelled to open a window for a breath of air.

Once she had wondered how Mr. Deventer felt about his wife's admirers; now she wondered how much Rose Deventer knew about her husband's roving eye. And there were yet other grounds for wonder occasioned by her closer view of Kirkewode's master. Admittedly the glimpse was brief and in poor

71

light, but she had seen no signs of either ague or fever in that ruddy face. Ada reviewed what she knew of malarial attacks: in this climate, the odds favored the intermittent tertian form, in which a full twenty-four hours elapsed between paroxysms. Still, even during such a respite, it would be extraordinary if the patient were restored to full libidinous vigor. Rather he would be gathering his strength for the next inevitable attack.

Turning restlessly in bed, Ada convinced herself that some other reason accounted for Mr. Deventer's seclusion. Perhaps, knowing there was a young female guest in the house, he was trying to avoid just such temptations as he had succumbed to this evening. *Even as Saul on the road to Damascus.* At the memory of that ecclesiastical encomium, testifying to the miraculous transformation of their host, she smothered in her pillow a most unladylike giggle. One thing was certain: Mad Jack Deventer had not changed *all* his ways.

Chapter 6

THE Deventer party moved through Grand Central Station with the pomp of a royal progression. An advance guard of two bowler-hatted footmen cleared a path through the jostling crowd of commuters while Maxwell secured the rear. Rose Deventer, swathed in chinchilla, was very much the queen, complete with crown jewels (or so Ada imagined the contents of the slim silver-tooled case in Maxwell's firm grasp). In the modest tailleur freshly cleaned and now restored to her, Ada made a rather shabby lady-in-waiting. It was a role she did not relish, nor did she share the preening satisfaction of her companion in the stares of gawking strangers. But sinking into the padded comfort of the carriage that awaited them, Ada granted there was something to be said for this mode of travel.

The old-fashioned brougham maneuvered through the traffic jam of hansom cabs and the gloomy sky was darkened further by an elevated structure overhead. But surely Fifth Avenue was the other way, a disoriented Ada asked. Rose's eyes squinted with amusement. Their destination was, alas, a less famed thoroughfare, she said, those vulgar palaces of the nouveaux riches were not for the Deventers. In her husband's family, the word "new" was anathema, whether applied to wealth or houses or—Rose chuckled reminiscently—even clothes. "Would you believe my dear departed mother-in-law kept all her new Paris gowns in a trunk for a full year, curing them like hams or whiskey, before she felt it proper to wear them?" The present building craze on Fifth Avenue was a phenomenon the Deventers had watched, unmoved, from their house on Second Avenue. "Not so fashionable an address, I'm afraid, but it will do for *us*."

Ada marveled at the inverse snobbery of that modest statement, that perfect mimicry of a patrician drawl. Recalling the woman's low origins, her disreputable past, Ada decided that Mama had been quite wrong to question the acting credentials of Mad Jack's bride. In speech, in dress, in bearing, in manners, Rose Deventer played the fine lady to Knickerbocker perfection. It took more than a pretty face to effect such changes, Ada conceded with an inward sigh, aware of how little she had done to remedy her own imperfections. The woman had character. And charm, Ada was forced to also allow, feeling its irresistible pull. Like a mindless cellular excretion, it seemed to envelope all in its vicinity regardless of sex.

To distance herself, Ada pulled back the velvet curtains and turned her attention to the passing view. Fashion had undeniably passed Second Avenue by. The side streets were sour and treeless, given over to grim brick tenements. Once they had crossed the impressive width of Twenty-third Street, gas works dominated the eastern sky and the cold gusts of wind brought up from the south a slaughterhouse stench. On the avenue itself, once fine houses now advertised for roomers, and even the little square they were approaching had a derelict look only partially the fault of winter. Yet Ada was pleased when the carriage pulled up to the curb. Any open space was welcome in a city with such a monomania for building.

Of red brick, adorned only with a Greek Revival marble porch, the Deventer town house seemed simplicity itself after the turrets and towers of Kirkewode. Once inside, Ada was sure that in this modest residence she would feel more at home. Here was a staircase one could mount without passing a display of military might. Here were rooms sized for humans, not for giants.

In the flurry of their welcome by the resident staff, the need for those two footmen imported from the castle became evident. However simple the exterior, this was still a roomy mansion, requiring more than a cook, a coachman and one maid to function smoothly when the owner was in town. With a brisk competence that Ada observed in silent awe, Mrs. Deventer took charge. The cook was reassured (five courses would do for that evening since the ladies would be dining alone); the maid scolded (her work downstairs should have been finished at this hour); the imported footmen sent about their business (they must see immediately to the central heating, since the females wouldn't touch the blasted furnace and the coachman held it was not in his jurisdiction). There were instructions for Ada too—she was not to linger over her toilette, they would be off again within the hour.

The flustered maid, arms filled with billowing muslin covers, fled down the rear passageway behind the stairs. Ada sent her a commiserating glance, which hardened into a stare. There was no mistaking that wall-mounted contraption encased in oak. A telephone. She ascended slowly in Mrs. Deventer's wake, certain half-formed plans taking clearer shape.

Having brought only the clothes on her back, Ada found little cause to linger at her toilette in the room assigned her. With the telephone in mind, she quietly retraced her steps down the hall. Outside Mrs. Deventer's door, she could hear Maxwell's disapproving voice, advising against the heliotrope faille, suggesting instead the Suède-colored ladies'-cloth. No doubt the woman kept an entire second wardrobe here. But then, was that not her life—the putting on and taking off of clothes? With a pitying shake of her head, Ada knocked on the door.

The husky voice responded pleasantly to Ada's soft call, granted her permission to enter. Standing akimbo, Rose was enduring the torture of having her corset laces tightened.

"Oh dear, I'm keeping you waiting," Rose apologized. She looked charmingly abashed at her unreadiness and blamed it all on Maxwell, who was fussy to a fault.

Ada was quick to protest that they should not hurry on her account. "I just wondered—perhaps you could tell me how long we'll be in town?" To explain her concern in terms such a fashion plate would understand, she added, "I brought no change of clothes, you see—"

"But that's what we're here for, isn't it?" Rose's laugh was reassuring. They would return this afternoon with so many packages, Ada's problem would be to make a choice. Of course, for the important gowns, they must call on Madame Modeska tomorrow. Then there was the bootmaker. And the milliner. "Not to mention a few trifling errands of my own. We'll be utterly exhausted, my dear, but two days will have to do us— Mr. Deventer swears he can spare me no longer. I suppose that in our seclusion we have grown too dependent on each other, but then—" she eyed the narrow span of her waist approvingly in the mirror—"that's what they mean by a happy marriage, isn't it?"

A rhetorical question, Ada assumed, and managed to look as if all her troubles were over, now that the question of her wardrobe was settled. And perhaps they were, she thought, since she had the promise of one more day in town. Here in New York—she was a fool not to have remembered earlier!— lived the one woman qualified to advise her, even to extend a helping hand. If only that name had occurred to her when Papa was raving and ranting about over-educated females with their poor scrambled brains. What better answer to that calumny than the shining example of Dr. Mary Putnam Jacobi? There was a woman with not one but three degrees, whose eminence even Papa must recognize—yet a wife and mother too. What about Dr. Jacobi? she should have demanded. Did *she* lose her femininity, Papa? Has all her learning weakened *her* moral fiber?

The best thing on endometritus published yet, her pathology professor at Michigan had admitted, recommending Dr. Jacobi's paper to all his third-year students. Ada had been quite puffed up with pride. So much for that old medical text Francis loved to taunt her with, defining a woman's head size as "almost too small for intellect, just big enough for love." Of course, he was just teasing her. A lover's playfulness. A playfulness that turned deadly with the reversal in his fortune. Her independence, it seemed, was something he could no longer afford.

The shock must be wearing off at last, for she was thinking of Francis without a shudder. She could even sigh "poor Francis," half in sympathy, half in scorn for one who measured everything in terms of money, even his manhood. A peculiarly American disease, according to visitors from abroad. The conversation last night at dinner—all that low gossip of high finance—was a case in point. Each time she asked who was so-and-so, the answer came with dollar marks, expressed not as what the man *possessed* but what the man was *worth*. Francis would have fitted right in at the Deventer dining table. Such was the man she had agreed to marry, trusting in his love, relying on his support. Consigning him to oblivion, Ada firmly cranked the side lever of the telephone.

"Dr. Mary Putnam Jacobi, please." She gave the name to Central as if it bore the magic authority of Ali Baba's open sesame. Central rudely brought her back to earth: New York City was not the boondocks, she must give a number.

"Please consult your list of subscribers."

With no list at hand, Ada threw herself on Information's mercy and was finally connected with Dr. Jacobi's office. The voice that answered was deeply guttural, faintly Germanic, definitely male. It was hard to hear through the spluttering, fizzing, scratchy noises traveling along the wire; in addition, the hall radiator was hammering and hissing now that heat was coming up. Convinced that she and this new invention were engaged in a life-and-death struggle, she all but shouted into the perforated disc: "I'm sorry, sir, you are the wrong Dr. Jacobi!"

"Surely, madam, that depends upon the point of view."

The voice crackling over the wire made light of her flustered apology. Dr. Abraham Jacobi could only tell her that his wife—the *right* Dr. Jacobi, he mischievously added—was not at the moment available. Her mornings were spent at the Women's Infirmary, her afternoons in lectures at the Women's Medical College. Office hours for patients were necessarily limited. However, if madam wished to make an appointment, he would be glad to give her the correct telephone number—

"But I am not a patient," Ada interrupted, hearing a stir upstairs that made her anxious to complete her call. "I am a medical student at the University of Michigan and wish to consult her on a purely professional matter." This was not the time to quibble about the truth of her position. She emphasized the brevity of her stay in town, hence the urgency of her request. His response was sympathetic, and she rang off with the assurance that her call would be returned that very evening.

Mrs. Deventer found her waiting in the front hall, bright-eyed, slightly flushed—just the right glow of anticipation that a young lady should show at the prospect of a shopping spree, she complimented Ada.

"Such a plain hat, my dear," she said, as if noticing its plainness for the first time. Her own plush bonnet was decorated with ribbons, plumes and a stuffed bird posed in flight. "If you really prefer that Quakerish mode, we might look in on Redfern's. He has just opened a New York branch, and though he doesn't suit *my* style, I must admit there's no one like the English for your kind of tailored things. In any case we can order your riding garb from him." But she must plead patience of her young friend; first certain important papers had to be delivered to Mr. Deventer's office downtown.

"The Street, ma'am?" The coachman let out his breath in a noisy labial flutter that rivaled the restless whinny of his horses. But it was the route not the destination he wished to argue, a point on which his mistress proved adamant.

"The usual way, Duncan. And I do not wish to hear again how much longer it takes."

If Mrs. Deventer preferred a circuitous route, Ada reasoned, it would no doubt be justified by scenic wonders. And indeed they soon turned south on Fifth Avenue, here in its lower reaches somewhat sedate in tone, with a prevalence of somber brownstone. As they wheeled past a fine row of Federal houses into Washington Square, Rose murmured something about great plans afoot to celebrate the upcoming centennial of Washington's inauguration. "I think Mr. Stanford White is to design something Napoleonic here."

"I should think they would be satisfied with that outrageous obelisk in the Capital," Ada replied sharply. "I find it ironic— all this hullabaloo for the man our history books tell us hated public adulation."

All conversation ceased as soon as they crossed the little park. Never had Ada seen so abrupt a change from the genteel to the disreputable. This southern end of the square was flanked by decrepit wooden buildings, housing nothing but stables and saloons. Down narrow streets the horses slowly picked their way through rotting straw and manure heaps rendered soupy by the recent rain, gutters ankle-deep in sodden garbage. Mrs. Deventer held back her curtain, the better to take in the view. The faint trace of a smile lay like some forgotten pleasure on her lips. She sees some pretty scene from her past, Ada thought, that makes her blind to the ugliness outside.

"Coontown," Mrs. Deventer announced, as if needing to account for black faces on the street. "One of Mayor Hewitt's campaign promises was to clean up the city's streets. You see what politicians' promises are worth."

Another block and the faces lightened, but not the depressing aspect of these rookeries for the poor. *Boulangerie . . . Char-*

cuterie . . . peeling letters on old store fronts in the act of being displaced by another tongue. *Farmacia . . . Pesce. . . .*

Ada was surprised to see still standing so many ramshackle wooden houses, reminders of the city's past, jerry-built even when new and now more like piles of kindling than human habitats. In the muddy yards stood desolate washtubs collecting rain; from the sagging porches, wet ropes drooped like storm-damaged telephone wires. In summer it was all much gayer, Mrs. Deventer assured her—the ropes were aflutter with rag-pickers' gleanings, children danced to the organ-grinder's music, and all that verminous throng now huddled in the dank indoors made merry under the open sky. So that is why the lady chooses to come this way, she finds it colorful, quaint! Ada thought with disgust.

So handsome a carriage drew curious stares on these poor streets. Ada shrank back in the curtained depths. She could not bear the sight of shivering children huddled over a street grating, warming themselves by the ejected steam. There was such resignation in the worn faces of the women, such bleary hostility in the faces of the jobless men, lounging against the corner lampposts. But Mrs. Deventer did not spare herself the sight of these poor souls, nor them the view of her in all her splendor. With that straight back, the one gloved hand upraised to hold back her curtain, and the unwavering half-smile on her lips, she might have served as a model of the English queen on her recent jubilee.

They passed too close to a peddler's cart, were assaulted with the rotting smell of overblown cabbages.

"Oh, stop! Stop!" Ada cried, looking back. "That poor horse has collapsed—the awful man is beating it!"

For the first time, Rose Deventer showed a crack in her composure. The smile turned ugly. "You have a bleeding heart, I see, for our brute friends. One old drayhorse drops dead in the street, and what an uproar we hear from all you kindhearted folks who call yourselves humane. Shall I tell you what I think of animal lovers who have the cat's-meat man come round each day to tempt their pets with goodies, while children—like those out there—are left to root in garbage on the streets?"

The surprise attack left Ada speechless. Even when she found her voice, she was capable only of a weak sarcastic thrust. "It seems I have misjudged you. I did not know you cared about the poor."

"Care? Why should I care about such spineless creatures? I agree with Dr. Haygood—these are the *deserving* poor. Just think of their numbers, girl! Had they the brains, or the will, they could take it all, without a by-your-leave, instead of sniveling about their hard lot!"

Truly astonished, Ada gave a nervous giggle. "I don't think that's what Dr. Haygood had in mind—"

"I know what Dr. Haygood has in mind," Rose snapped. "If it's original sin you're looking for, you'll find it here. Poverty is the indelible stain on these damned souls. And Dr. Haygood and I agree on yet another point." A rasping sound of harsh amusement, not at all like her usual soft chuckle, emerged from her white throat. "It's not in good works that they will find salvation."

What did this surprising woman really mean? There was an almost revolutionary import to her words, and yet such unfeeling judgment in her voice.

"If I follow you," Ada suggested, almost timidly, "they may yet be saved. Are they not beginning to recognize their power? The Knights of Labor—"

"Knights!" No chuckle this time, an outright laugh. "What has chivalry to do with labor? Do you think that Mr. Deventer made his money by fancying himself a knight? Or Mr. Morgan? Or those noble slumlords, the Astors? Or this Mr. Rockefeller, who, I swear, will one day swallow us all? Let them strike—who can hold out longer, the starving man or the man with a full belly? Not that they stick together even on that. Mr. Gould put it best—why should we be afraid of the working class, we can always hire one half to kill the other. I do admire that little man—he doesn't bother to dress up an ugly truth."

81

So repellent a statement deserved no reply. Ada stared stonily ahead. There fell a silence in which the rhythmic clop of hooves on wet cobblestone exerted a calming effect. Mrs. Deventer withdrew into her private thoughts, and Ada's belligerency receded, to be replaced by sheer puzzlement over the real nature of this woman who could speak so forcefully when she chose.

"You must forgive me," Mrs. Deventer said abruptly, giving Ada's hand a conciliatory squeeze. "I lost my temper back there—taking you to task for pitying a poor horse. It called to mind a very unpleasant story I once heard—about a little street arab, a girl not more than ten. She was found wandering in the streets faint from hunger, with bruises on her body easy enough to see since the rags she wore barely covered her. The lady who found her—a tenderhearted soul—did not know what to do with such a deplorable bit of humanity. In a quandary, she asked advice at the nearest charitable institution, which happened to be a watering station of the S.P.C.A. While the men were arguing among themselves as to the nearest asylum for homeless waifs, the child stupidly confessed to having a home—if you could call it that. No mother, but most definitely a father, the bruises being his handiwork. Whereupon the men threw up their hands: there was nothing to be done. Now if she were an orphan, it would be different, they said—a thought the child herself must have entertained, don't you think?—but in those days there was no Society for the Prevention of Cruelty to *Children*, you see. No one dared interfere in the sacred relationship of parent and child."

"Stories like that are nothing new to me," Ada said grimly. "Half the bones that are set on any children's ward are broken by some drunken brute of a father, and the doctors just patch the poor things up and send them back to be abused again, I'm afraid."

"Ah, but *this* child was not sent back. The Good Samaritan who rescued her was a very determined old lady, not about to have her good deed go for naught. Granted that the child was the property of its parents, she argued, were not the horses they protected equally the property of their owners? If they saw a horse maltreated, they could take him from its master, such a scoundrel could even be arrested. Surely they could do as much for one of God's children, who had not only a body but a soul to be saved? It was the law—that was all the men knew to say—it was the law. Read me your law, she demanded. So they read her the law. They got to the part that forbade the abuse of any horse, mule, cow, sheep or other animal—at which point she let them go no further. 'Animal!' she cried. 'It says animal, does it?' She hooked her umbrella around the girl's neck and pulled her forward. 'Look at this creature, gentlemen!' she demanded. 'The louse-infested hair, the mangy skin, the filthy paws, the wildness in its eyes! It snarls, it whines, you cannot say it talks. What is this if not an animal?'"

"The poor child!" There were tears in Ada's eyes. Mrs. Deventer looked impatient with such weak sentimentality. The point was, she instructed Ada, that the old lady got her way. The men examined the squirming specimen pinned before them and agreed it was an animal—and as an animal protected by their law. As a result, one of the gentleman volunteers, a substantial citizen with a fine brownstone house and a delicate, childless wife, took the little girl into his own home.

Ada thanked the Lord there was a happy ending to such a heartrending tale.

"I'm not sure that was the ending," Mrs. Deventer said vaguely, looking out the window. "If I remember correctly, there was some kind of trouble later on. It could have been no easy job domesticating so wild an animal, but the wife made a noble effort. For four years, she tutored the girl at home, not only in the three R's but in the necessary social graces. With remarkable results, I understand. Unfortunately, she discovered that her husband had devised an educational curriculum of his own." At Ada's naively inquiring look, she added delicately, "Of an unsavory nature, I'm afraid. Quite naturally, she blamed the girl, diagnosed her as congenitally evil and kicked her out. By then the girl's father had drunk himself into his grave—that's as much of a happy ending as I can report—and her brother (did I mention she had a brother? well, she did) took her in hand." As if suddenly losing interest in her own story, Mrs. Deventer abruptly brought it to an end. "What became of her after that, who knows."

Ada knew. As soon as she was released from the spell of that accomplished storyteller's voice, recognition came in an intuitive flash. *A story I once heard.* Oh no, Ada silently refuted her companion, her eyes drawn to the strong white neck, imagining it caught in the crook of an old lady's umbrella—*you* were the little animal cleaned up, fed, taught a few tricks, and then kicked out again. No mystery now why Rose Deventer chose this route. These were the streets she had known as a child, a reminder of how far she had come, how high she had risen. Yet, staring at the lovely head swaying with the motion of the carriage—yes, like a queen, acknowledging the plaudits of her subjects—Ada could hardly believe her own surmise. Here was a metamorphosis more astounding than any to be found in Ovid. How to explain it, save in Dr. Haygood's terms: that Rose Deventer was one of God's elect.

For all her new understanding, Ada was relieved when they finally reached the commercial liveliness of lower Broadway. She had had enough of slums, enough of peeping through a velvet curtain at the misery of the poor. But the detour had acted on Mrs. Deventer like an invigorating tonic. Her prattle about the latest fashions reached an almost feverish pitch. Redingotes and polonaises . . . Venetian pearls and Chantilly lace . . . figured velvet and watered silk . . . Ada listened meekly to it all. She saw no virtue now in her own disregard for appearances—she who had never been other than suitably dressed. Compared to the brutalizing poverty of Rose Deventer's childhood, what Mama had bemoaned as their "reduced circumstances" was better called the lap of luxury. *Little animal!* Ada could not erase the picture of a child answering to that description, with not enough rags to even hide her bruises. Condemn as vanity, this preoccupation with peacock finery? As well accuse a starving man of gluttony because he could not take his mind off bread.

They crawled at a snail's pace through the bedlam of traffic that required great skill of the coachmen and even greater courage of the pedestrians. Ada shuddered at the thought of having to make a crossing through such a pack of carriage wheels and horses's hooves. And never had she seen so many tall buildings bunched so closely together, although Trinity's spire still rose above them all. If it proved true that as man's buildings ascended, so would man's ideas, how blessed would the twentieth century be.

The building before which they pulled up was somewhat of a disappointment—a dingy grey granite front dwarfed by its ten-story neighbors. Not even a brass plaque outside with the Deventer name. With assurances of her immediate return, Mrs. Deventer vanished inside with a fat leather portfolio. Left to her own thoughts, Ada drew the fur carriage robe over her lap and allowed herself the additional luxury of a brief daydream, anticipating Dr. Jacobi's call that evening.

Of course Dr. Jacobi would grant her an interview. On hearing her story—not so hard to recount woman to woman—Dr. Jabobi's eyes flash with indignation. The eminent physician takes up arms in her behalf. Ada will be admitted to the Women's Medical College—hang the rules! As for the dastardly behavior of her ex-fiancé, Dr. Jacobi thunders, *he* is the one who should be drummed out of the profession. Here Ada raises a restraining hand to urge upon her militant champion a more forgiving attitude (with faint overtones of Mama). Let him be, she pleads, I do not wish him more unhappiness than that which even now must be tearing him apart. Dr. Jacobi, impressed with Ada's noble character as well as with her academic accomplishments, advances from behind her desk to clasp Ada's hand—

And the door of the carriage opened. The toe of one bronze kid boot remained poised on the threshhold as Mrs. Deventer took her leave of the gentleman assisting her up the step.

"You shouldn't have come down, Mr. Vance. There was no need. And you in that thin office coat—you must be freezing. Back you go before it starts to drizzle again."

"Oh, I am warm enough!" Ada's view from the curtained recess of the carriage was annoyingly restricted. She could not see the man at all, but she was sure from his tone that an ogling look accompanied that remark. "Would you assure Mr. Deventer that I shall repay his trust with a devotion to my new duties equal to Mr. Witten's?"

"More than that, I shall compliment him on his choice." When Rose's voice was in its lowest register, Ada noted, anything she said took on a caressing note. "It is not too short notice then?"

"A bachelor's life is not too difficult to rearrange. I shall be ready to accompany you on your return to Kirkewode."

There was something in the man's light-timbred voice that Ada found provokingly familiar. She would have liked a peek at him, but not for anything would she allow Mrs. Deventer to discover her leaning across the seat, craning her neck. Still, there was the slim fawn-colored umbrella the lady had left behind—more a fashionable accessory than a protection from the weather. Ada's fingers closed on the carved amber handle. Retaining her aloof expression—as if there were no connection between her and the movement of the umbrella—she held back the opposite curtain with the stiletto tip. All she could see, however, were their hands—Rose's gloved fingers resting lightly on his bare palm.

A few last gallantries and Mrs. Deventer entered with head bowed low to keep unruffled the feathery plume, the outstretched wings of the bird.

"A nice-looking young man, don't you think?" After a great rustling, she was finally settled and laid a now flat portfolio between them. Ada must forgive her for not presenting him, but she had not wanted to keep him out in the damp air. Nestled deep in her corner, Ada displayed a total lack of interest. She had not seen the gentleman, she said.

Now that Rose had delivered a few papers for her husband— an onerous task, she made it seem—she became almost giddy, like a schoolgirl on holiday. Shopping, she laughingly proclaimed, was the real business of their sex. If so, Ada was to think at the end of an exhausting afternoon, Mrs. Deventer deserved the title of tycoon as much as did her husband. Their first stop was at Lord & Taylor, where they were greeted at the door by an overlord in formal attire, who passed them on to an equally imposing dowager of lesser suzerainty. The regiment of young salesgirls under her command advanced with garments for their consideration, retreated with those rejected, returned to the attack with fresh supplies.

"How much?" Ada asked, fingering a lampas skirt with a garniture of wine-colored velvet, only to be shushed by Mrs. Deventer. Ada was not to concern herself with such matters—it was her papa's wish. Ada submitted with an outer complaisance that masked an inner chagrin. Even as she asked the question, she realized how meaningless the answer would have been. How was she to know what was too dear for Papa's purse? Her dressmaker's bills were always sent direct to him and half the time she did not even know the cost. His complaint was never that she spent too much but rather that he feared she spent too little. *I have a horror, Ada,* he once wrote, *of your becoming one of those frumpy creatures who advertise their learning by a certain negligence in dress. Whatever high degrees you may acquire, see to it that you always look the lady, for that is the title that does you most honor.*

Until now, Ada had thought herself obedient in this regard. At the beginning of each term, she would choose one new gown in the latest color, refurbish her old dresses with new ribbons or fresh lace, mend, clean, brush, replace the dust ruffles on her skirts—and then forget about such matters until another term began. But to look the lady by Mrs. Deventer's standards was harder work than that. By midafternoon, Ada's head ached, her feet throbbed, she wanted nothing more than to go to bed. She could only marvel that Rose showed no sign of wilting (but then it was not *she* who had to dress and undress, stand to be pinned, look at herself in three-way mirrors, be pulled and pinched and patted and disheveled). In spite of Ada's pleading, not one item was deleted from the shopping list and when the end was reached, Rose added yet another.

"It won't take but a moment, dear, to pass by Huyler's and pick up a fresh order of my candy."

At that shop, however, Ada was allowed to remain in the carriage, staring glumly at the white-coated girls pulling taffy in the window before the enraptured gaze of a sidewalk audience. Their hygienic attire reminded her of the lab coats at medical school and a sudden rage, such as she had not felt since childhood, swept over her. She felt like kicking in the whole pile of boxes they were bringing back, rending the pretty ribbons into shreds, stamping the mountain of cardboard to pancake flatness with both feet—in effect, she felt like throwing one of those wild tantrums that had caused Mama such distress.

"There, we've done for the day," Rose said, adding another ribboned box to the pile. "If only the weather weren't so bad. It's just the right hour to drive in Central Park, but not even the sporting set will be out today. What a bore, I do so want to exhibit my lovely visitor from the West—but never mind, the sun may come out tomorrow, and then we will take the phaeton, the better to show off our fine feathers—" Growing aware of the black hole of silence into which her words were falling, Rose looked searchingly at Ada. The tenseness in the young figure struck her. "You're tired, I expect. We shall go right home and enjoy our tea by the fire."

But the moment they entered the house and saw the calling card on the hall table, Rose's geniality was extinguished. "Damn the man!" she swore, shocking Ada, who wondered what there was in the short message penned on the card to make Rose so forget herself.

Maxwell must have heard the carriage, for she was waiting for her mistress at the head of the stairs. "It was that silly maid who let him in," she called down. "You know Mr. Henry and his ways—he must have chucked her under the chin and called her a pretty little chicken and she told him all she knew. One thing's for sure, you can expect a caller this evening, she told him you'd be in."

"What I should like to know," Rose said grimly, "is who told him I was in town at all. Does he have a spy at Kirkewode, or does he keep a watch at this end?" Suddenly she remembered Ada, and her ill humor fell away with one careless shrug. Her brother-in-law, she explained the card, flicking it back on the salver. "Mr. Deventer won't see him, so he tries to get at me."

Thinking only of the call she herself was expecting, Ada cared nothing about the internecine struggles of the Deventers. While Rose retired to change (yet once again!), Ada moved restlessly about her room, moments of euphoria (yes, Dr. Jacobi would admit her to the school!) alternating with moments of gloom (no, Dr. Jacobi would not even hear her out). A knock at her door sent her heart racing—she was wanted on the telephone! But it was only Maxwell, who looked with disapproval at the unpacked boxes, avowed it was not her job to put those things away. She had come to see if there was something in that pile of ready-mades (a word she uttered with great disdain) fit to be worn at table.

"Ah, wait until your papa sees you in that," Mrs. Deventer said at dinner, applauding the pink faille with its cascade of blonde lace. Ada was equally certain of Papa's approval—she looked the lady, no doubt about it. There was even a momentary pleasure in behaving like one, so seductive was the elegance of her attire. Following Rose into the drawing room, she caught her own body imitating that sashaying walk. A memory flashed into her mind with the stabbing luminescence of a migraine: Mad Jack's new bride twirling her parasol on the promenade at Nice, and from Mrs. Carlisle, Mama's friend, that very English titter. . . . *So very American, my dear, if you will forgive my saying so. Just as Mr. Trollope described it, the walk of a fourth-rate French woman in a second-rate French town! . . .* And then Mama's answering laugh. . . .

"Come join me," Rose said, patting the sofa. "If we go through these pattern books tonight, we can give Madame Modeska a clearer idea tomorrow of what we want."

All Ada could think of was that Dr. Jacobi had not returned her call. She sat on the appointed cushion with a dispirited droop that only caused Rose to smile approvingly at such languid grace. Suddenly the smile gave way to a soft tsk of pity. "Your poor hands—I hesitated to speak before but it pains me to see even one flaw in what would otherwise be perfection. They're worse than a washerwoman's, Ada. What have you been doing to make them red and raw like that?"

Touched on a sensitive spot, Ada reacted automatically, snatching her hand away from the book they jointly held. "It's just the carbolic acid we use when we assist in surgery."

"That awful stuff? But why? Don't you see it ruins your skin?"

"Would you rather have the patients die?" Ada snapped. "That's what happens in any operating room that doesn't follow Lister's procedure." Remembering she was done with all that, she forced her hand to come out of hiding, take hold of the book again. "Don't worry, Mrs. Deventer, they'll soon be as white as yours." And as helpless, she sneered at herself.

"In the meantime," Rose said doubtfully, "you must wear pomade gloves at night. And for the day, I shall give you a pot of my burnt-almond cream. It works wonders and hardly leaves a trace."

The door opened and the footman entered. Foolish hope! Ada rebuked herself as the card was presented to Mrs. Deventer. With a sigh of resignation, Rose picked it up. Apparently another urgent message on the back.

"Henry, of course. I suppose I must see him. Show him into

the library, Thomas. It's bound to be an unpleasant interview, Ada—I'll spare you that."

Hardly had Mrs. Deventer left the room when the footman reappeared.

"For me?" Ada jumped up with an alacrity the footman found alarming.

"Yes, miss. A Dr. Jacobi on the telephone."

Resisting the impulse to shove him out of the way and run, Ada followed Thomas into the hall. Through the closed door of the library came a stentorian rumble, the muffled sound of a very angry man. The footman listed slightly in the direction of the interesting noise and slowed his pace. As a substitute butler, he lacked Caxton's English polish, Ada observed.

"Thank you, Thomas, I can find the telephone." She brushed past him, terrified that Dr. Jacobi would grow impatient and ring off. But when she picked up the receiver, she was answered with a crisp, business-like voice.

"I understand, Miss Traherne, that you are presently attending the University of Michigan Medical School? Are you interested in transferring or do you look forward to continuing your studies on a postgraduate level?"

"In a manner of speaking, yes. I mean, both," Ada temporized. There were special circumstances, she pleaded, difficult to discuss over the telephone, if only Dr. Jacobi could spare her a few minutes tomorrow—and all the while her hand stroked the golden oak housing Mr. Bell's invention as if it were Aladdin's lamp from which a genie had been summoned.

"Let's see, tomorrow I have a tight schedule, but you return to Michigan the day after, my husband tells me. Very well, can you be at my office in the Infirmary at nine o'clock sharp? I should be through with the morning rounds by then."

"Oh thank you, doctor, thank you," Ada breathed into the magic instrument. She rang off without correcting the impression that, in leaving the city, she was returning to school. A small misunderstanding. She would explain it all tomorrow.

Mrs. Deventer returned to the drawing room to find a very

different young woman awaiting her. Gone was the listlessness, the drooping fatigue. Ada was waltzing around the room in such high spirits that Rose stood in the doorway and smiled.

"Ah, youth," she apostrophized. The violent slam of the front door forcibly recalled her recent visitor to mind. "Poor Henry," she said, though little sympathy came through that conventional sigh. "Family connections can be trying—and Mr. Deventer's more than most, I do believe."

But Ada was not to think that Mr. Deventer was by nature lacking in proper family feeling. Rose held herself to blame for the estrangement of the brothers. Mr. Deventer had never forgiven his relatives for their hostility to his marriage. In fact, before Mr. Deventer had recouped his fortune, they had been content to ostracize the loving couple, demanding nothing more than to be left alone. "Extend to your brother the same Christian charity he now displays to us, I beg Mr. Deventer. To no avail."

The faintly ironic tone seemed to Ada fully justified. She too had had experience with Christian charity, as exemplified by the Reverend Nichols and his wife.

"They must be a greedy bunch," Ada said bluntly. "I can't imagine a Deventer in need of cash."

"True—by your standards and mine," Rose said, drawing yet tighter the bond of understanding between them. But there was the small matter of primogeniture—a Deventer tradition—which no doubt added to the dissension between the brothers. Both Henry and the youngest son, Alsop, had received a respectable sum in cash, but Jack, as oldest, had been left in sole control of the bulk of the family's financial holdings. Alsop, a man of high moral standards and scholarly pursuits, gave no trouble, although he refused to speak to his oldest brother until the day of his death—"Or thereafter, so far as I know," Rose said, with a quiver of a smile. "And his son, from what I hear, continues in his father's footsteps. At least he makes no move to restore the family connection. It is Henry who has been the gadfly. He has been as profligate as my husband ever was, though his taste runs more to horses than to women, I am told. Trotters are his passion, and a ruinous one. Were it not for the monthly allowance Mr. Deventer grants him, he would be in bankruptcy court. But still he is not satisfied, he believes it is I who bar him from his brother, that if he could only see Mr. Deventer, he would get more. And yet I assure you, Ada, were it not for me, he would receive nothing at all."

The woman has a truly generous heart, Ada thought, feeling an equal generosity percolate through herself. She felt kindly toward everyone now that her future was rich with promise again. There was such good feeling between them that evening, Ada was loath to say goodnight. Rose kissed her on the cheek and warned they must get an early start. "First thing in the morning—" she began, but Ada interrupted.

"Oh dear, I forgot to tell you, I have an appointment at nine o'clock. But I should be free by ten—will that be early enough?"

Only by the upward tilt of her head, did Rose betray surprise. "With whom, may I ask?"

Ada raised her own chin a notch. Why should she be accountable for her time, she demanded coldly.

"I do not mean to pry, Ada, but your papa has entrusted you to my care while we are here."

"With a Dr. Jacobi, if you must know."

"A medical doctor?" Rose asked, her voice rising in alarm.

"Yes. At the Women's Infirmary."

Rose's sharp intake of breath, like a suppressed cry of pain, brought Ada quickly to her side. "Are you not feeling well, Mrs. Deventer? Shall I loosen your corset—"

"Oh you poor thing!" Ada found herself pressed to Rose's perfumed bosom. "In your condition, you think of me? You sweet child! But perhaps you are mistaken—surely it is too early to tell. I know you have read all those medical books, but as a married woman I may know a thing or two that—"

Ada freed herself, her face a fiery red. "Dr. Jacobi is a professor at the Women's Medical College. I plan to seek admission there. I am consulting her for that purpose—no other." Ignoring Rose's profuse apologies, Ada rushed upstairs. It was Papa she was most furious with—Papa who had betrayed her confidence. And it was clear that he had never believed her story. For him, she was ruined in fact as well as in report. He had as narrow, ugly, bigoted a mind as any she had thought to leave behind in Michigan. And why had she hoped otherwise—was he not a man? Her trust lay now entirely in her own sex—that she must remember. On cooler thought, she absolved Rose Deventer of any blame. Believing only what she had been told, Rose had uttered not one word of censure, had only offered help. Ada fell asleep with the consoling thought that on the morrow Dr. Mary Putnam Jacobi would do the same.

Chapter 7

THE gods were smiling on her, Ada felt, as she walked out into morning sunshine. With the sun had come a precipitous drop in temperature. Suddenly atop the horsecars there were white flags with red balls in the center, signifying (as she gleaned from two truant youngsters, skates over shoulders) that at last the ice in Central Park was frozen hard. And this the middle of January! Ada smiled condescendingly at the passersby huddled in their coats, muffled in their scarves, noses and cheeks nipped red as the skating flag. As Francis would say, even the winters were effete back east.

It seemed equally auspicious that in this neighborhood, once an enclave of the landed rich, so many hospitals now were clustered. It was but a brisk short walk to the Women's Infirmary, an old red-brick building that seemed to belong to the days of crinoline and army blue. As soon as Ada entered its halls, properly reeking with a carbolic odor, she felt a wave of homesickness. A young woman in a nurse's cap and apron was speaking earnestly to an older woman, bare-headed, neatly dressed in some dark stuff. "Thank you, doctor," the nurse said and sped away with her tray of stoppered bottles. A simple encounter yet Ada's heart leaped with joy. Women, all women—the nurses, the patients *and* the doctors.

Even the clerk in the small glass-enclosed office was female, working with incredible speed at a typewriting machine. Following her directions, Ada mounted the stairs and found a small room on the second floor with its door open, its desk unoccupied. Books climbed one wall, unopened cartons were piled high against the other; there was hardly room to turn about. Ada sat nervously in the high-backed wooden chair facing the desk, wondering if she had mistaken a storage room for Dr. Jacobi's office.

"Miss Traherne?" Ada had no doubt that this compact mass of energy invading the room was Dr. Jacobi. "Forgive this disarray but by next year we shall be in new and more commodious quarters." A brisk shake of the hand and the square-faced woman took her seat behind the desk. Meeting the direct gaze of those brown eyes, Ada was glad she had chosen to wear her simple tailleur rather than any of her new finery. It was not the first time she had the feeling that her looks worked against her, that she would have to prove she was serious.

"Now tell me why you wish to transfer from one of the best medical schools in the country to our modest institution," Dr. Jacobi challenged her. "Do you find the work too difficult there? Do you think a purely female institution will have slacker standards?"

Ada stared at the hands resting on the desk—square, spatulate fingers interlocked. Such competent-looking hands. She squared her shoulders and replied, "Quite the contrary. I think you will find my standing—"

"So sorry to interrupt, Dr. Jacobi." The young woman from the office downstairs had left her typewriter to deliver the message she held extended. "From Dr. Blackwell. I am to bring her back an answer."

As Ada watched, the sallow cheeks took on a carmine tinge, the dark eyes that lifted from the page were aglow. As soon as Dr. Jacobi spoke, Ada recognized the strong emotion as rage, however tightly controlled.

"You may tell Dr. Blackwell yes, I shall meet with her this afternoon to discuss the questions I submitted for the examination. Just a moment, Edith—" she called back the young woman and turned on Ada her fierce gaze. Like an eagle's, Ada thought, all atremble, seeing herself pinpointed as the prey.

"How would *you* answer this question, Miss Traherne? When is atropine contraindicated in ophthalmic practice and why, with particular reference to the drug's effect on the vagus nerves."

Why, that was easy! Ada took a deep breath and began, "In cases of incipient glaucoma, where any increase in intraocular tension is to be avoided . . ."

Dr. Jacobi looked pleased, glanced quickly at the note. Oh test me, test me again, Ada dared her silently. "Now this one, Miss Traherne: describe the Koch plate test for airborne microorganisms. How can this technique be modified to give a quantitative as well as qualitative result?"

Ada's face lit up. In bacteriology she excelled. Succinctly she described the exposure of plates covered with nutrient jelly to the air, then the incubation under cover of the trapped microorganisms. "If you want to obtain a count per liter of air, you should use Hesse's method: coat a tube with the nutrient jelly and draw a given quantity of air through at a given rate. . . ."

A brilliant smile transfigured Mary Jacobi's face, immeasurably lightening its stolidity. "I see such questions do not tax your female brains." To the young woman still waiting in the doorway, she gave an additional message. "You may also tell Dr. Blackwell that we shall soon have at least one student who does not find my questions impossible to answer."

Alone with Ada, Dr. Jacobi could not resist venting her exasperation. "All these excuses made for young women who simply will not buckle down to hard work, who still have more of an eye for a man than a book! I am told I cannot expect from them the same caliber of work expected of men, we must go slowly, take it by degrees, allow for past generations of neglect. Frankly, such cautionary urging to go slowly smacks to me of the same advice given would-be educators of the freed slaves." She gave a final snort of disgust—"Midwives, not doctors, they want me to turn out—" and shook herself like a hen settling her ruffled feathers. "Forgive the outburst, Miss Traherne. I am accused, perhaps rightly, of having a temper on short fuse. But this is a matter on which I feel strongly. If we must have women's medical schools—and the time requires it, there are few schools as liberal as Michigan in admitting women—they must maintain the same standards as the men's. They tell me I am the exception, not the rule. But you prove my point. Women have the intelligence, what they lack is the application, a sense of calling which our society instills in the male when he is still in skirts. The way we rear our girls, on the other hand, particularly if they are pretty—" the ardent speech came to an abrupt halt. Dr. Jacobi looked directly at her. "Pretty," she repeated as if she had suddenly forgotten her train of thought. A frown drew together her dark brows. "Tell me, Miss Traherne, why *do* you wish to come to this school?"

Even as she began haltingly to tell her story, Ada knew she could not have found Dr. Jacobi in a less receptive mood. Nor was she telling it very well, feeling as she did like a common criminal in the dock. And aligned against her was a packed jury (Papa, Reverend Nichols, the dean, Mrs. Deventer), whose verdict of guilty had already been given. Truth, it seemed, was not a constant but a variable, determined more by what people believed than by what actually transpired. She could hear her voice trailing off . . . how unconvincing, that plea of innocence . . . she herself did not believe it. . . .

"I see," Dr. Jabobi said coldly. "I am afraid I was premature in sending that laudatory message to Dr. Blackwell."

I see, Ada silently mimicked that icy opening, I was to have been used as a shining example; this woman feels it is she who has been betrayed, not I.

"I think you were mistaken to come to us, young lady. We are a woman's school, true, but you will find no Woodhulls here, no confusion of women's rights with women's license." That brown competent hand gripping the desk revealed the tight hold she was keeping on her temper. "I do not take it upon myself to censure your dalliance with young men. But that you could not control your natural instincts, that you should allow them *precedence* over what promised to be a fine career, *that* I find insupportable."

There was a momentary pause which Ada took as a token display of judicial fairness, a willingness to hear what else the condemned might have to say. Ada let the silence grow. There was nothing left her but her pride. She would not beg.

"I would say you have sold your birthright for a mess of pottage, Miss Traherne." Dr. Jacobi rose from the desk and held herself in a rigid pose of dismissal.

In a daze of misery, Ada made her way down the stairs and out of the building, not even seeing the nod of farewell and admiring smile the woman in the office sent her through the glass partition. She was not at all surprised to find that the sky had reverted to its former January grey. She had already discovered the gods' true intent.

No need to ask how the interview with that woman doctor had gone—one look at Ada's face told Mrs. Deventer all she needed to know. Just as well, she had reason to conclude as the afternoon wore on and their final whirlwind of shopping was accomplished with no fidgeting, no impatient protests from her young protégée. Even Madame Modeska had been impressed with Ada's unmoved composure, her somnambulistic grace. "Every inch zee lady," she complimented Mrs. Deventer on her young friend, not forgetting in her enthusiasm to belabor her French accent, "and *such* inches, ooh-la-la! Zee measurements are *parfait*—as you say in English, perr-fect," she condescended to translate. She draped her cloth tape around her neck and led Mrs. Deventer aside, nullifying the discretion with a whisper that penetrated to the farthest corner of the room. "I am indeed grateful, madame, for zee little custom you give me. *Bien entendu*, I am no Worth, I can provide no Paris label—but if you will place zis young lady exclusively in my hands, I promise you she will outshine them all!" Struck by a terrible thought, she clutched the tape dangling over her compact bosom like a dowager in fear for her pearls. "She *does* go into society, yes? She will not hide my creations up there in the *faubourgs,* as you do?"

Mrs. Deventer tossed an amused glance at Ada, who gave no indication that she had heard. She seemed to be engrossed in a view of rooftops afforded by the unbroken row of tall arched windows that gave the atelier its fine light.

"One hardly knows with young ladies nowadays," Rose said, "but I shall speak to her papa—"

"That will not be necessary."

Rose looked at Ada with a quickened interest. Such a clipped definitive remark, yet the girl still seemed miles away in thought. "That could be either a yes or a no, Ada. Which do you mean?"

"That's what young ladies do, isn't it? Come out. Go into society. Whatever it is called. Why should I be different?"

Why indeed, she asked herself. She turned away from that westward view of a river front, pierced by the sharp bowsprits of the freighters, the sky aswarm with gulls. So many birds. What was it Papa had once written her, knowing her love for the Lady with the Lamp? Birds, yes birds—thousands of them attracted by the torchlight the Lady held aloft in the harbor, dashing blindly against the iron structure, leaving at the Lady's feet a mountain of corpses. . . .

But she was beautiful, it seemed. Madame Modeska had just said so—and she made her livelihood by knowing things like that. And Rose Deventer—rather famous in that line herself—agreed. If hitherto she had refused to consider herself in such terms, that was Mama's doing. *Beauty is a snare. Handsome is as handsome does. Beauty's but skin deep. Love built on beauty, soon as beauty, dies.* According to Mama, beauty and wisdom were rarely found together, beauty and virtue even more rarely conjoined. True, she had come to understand, even as a child, that those barbed adages were being flung in quite another direction, but it was into her young mind they had stuck. Hence the film that glazed her eyes whenever she looked into a mirror, screening out all but the essential decencies that must be checked: face clean? hair tidy? dress properly buttoned? Now she walked over to the full-length mirror and looked at herself boldly, examining every detail of her features. When she turned back to Rose, there was a new light in her eyes. She was satisfied that one career, at least, was still open to her.

"I should particularly like this gown, Madame Modeska. How long would it take to make?" She pointed at a fashion plate of Modeska's own design.

"My masterpiece," Madame Modeska admitted modestly when she saw the elegant ball gown Ada had chosen. She asked the ladies to observe the pointed corsage trimmed with lace and tulle, the loops of fine pearls and crystal pendants that garlanded the bust, continued on a diagonal all around the skirt. "I see it in a ciel-blue damask—but perhaps zee décolleté is too extreme? I must confess, when zis inspiration struck me, I did not have a *jeune fille* in mind—"

"I should like it made up in palest pink, not blue," Ada said firmly. "And you are not to alter the design in any way."

Madame Modeska looked questioningly at Mrs. Deventer, who was struggling to contain her laughter. In vain. It broke out—a loud joyous peal that reverberated in the high-ceilinged room. "Ada," she cried, holding out her hands, "you're a girl after my own heart! You had better watch out, I'll have you for my daughter yet!"

Unsmiling, Ada allowed her hands to be seized, suffered the enthusiastic embrace before returning to the mirror to adjust her new bonnet. She tied the pea-green ribbon under her chin with a vicious tweak. "There is only the bootmaker left to be seen, I think? Shall we be on our way?"

The enthusiasm for Ada's new social prospects remained all Rose's. At dinner, after dinner, even following Ada into her bedroom when she retired, Mrs. Deventer was full of plans. Ada noted without surprise that no further mention was made of consulting Papa—that had been mere window dressing, it was Mrs. Deventer who called the tune.

Was Ada concerned lest Mrs. Deventer's standing in society be not of the best? Showing no delicacy on a subject Ada would have never broached herself, Rose bid Ada not to worry. Her brother-in-law Henry but followed the crowd in wishing to press Mr. Deventer to his bosom once again.

"Even I would be graciously received, they have contrived to let us know, should we care to end our self-imposed exile. Self-imposed! That's the way they put it, dear—a nice way of denying that they once felt otherwise. The fact that we have rejected all their overtures has whetted their appetite—I swear, if I ever gave a ball they'd come in droves—out of curiosity if nothing else. Well, we shall satisfy them at last. For myself, I do not care but oh! to see the havoc you will wreak among these New York beaux, to put the noses of the Astor girls out of joint, to have your triumphs touted in *Town Topics,* to bring those bride-shopping English lords and Italian counts to their knees! What a triumph I see before us, Ada!" But sobered by some other thought, Rose fell silent. With a sigh, she confessed that Mr. Deventer posed a problem—he had grown too fond of privacy to ever give it up. Still, he might allow her to spend more time alone in town. "Your papa will know how to handle him, I'm sure. He listens to your papa more than to me sometimes."

As if the problem of Mr. Deventer were thereby solved, Rose grew euphoric again. What a season they would make it! First they must procure an invitation to the Monday evening Patriarchs' balls. An afternoon tea just for the ladies. A small evening reception. A theater party or two. For all of that the Deventer house would do. But of course Ada must be formally presented at a really grand affair, and for that they would rent Delmonico's. . . .

She's off again, Ada thought wearily, brushing her hair with conscientious strokes. Perhaps it's just the talk I find so dull, she thought, unable to repress a yawn; perhaps when I actually find all those men at my feet, it will be more interesting.

"There I go," Rose said contritely, "forgetting how tired you are. If I get carried away, you must forgive me, Ada. In bringing out a daughter, most mothers merely relive their triumphs—I shall be having mine for the first time." And playing the role of mother to the hilt, she insisted on Ada getting into bed immediately, tucked the covers in and placed a maternal kiss on Ada's brow. "Have a good night's sleep, dear. We leave for Kirkewode early in the morning." She turned down the gas jet and gave a soft rich chuckle in the dark. "I was just thinking of your papa—he will have to admit now that, where you are concerned, I am right and he is wrong. So much for his silly plans!"

She was gone. The heavy double-lined curtains were drawn against the cold, the air was dense, the blackness thick, and yet there seemed a denser, thicker, still palpable presence in the room, as if the darkness retained Rose Deventer's form. It was just her perfume lingering on, Ada realized at last, and curled up for sleep.

Chapter 8

My thoughts on awful subjects roll
Damnation and the dead.
What horrors seize the guilty soul
Upon the dying bed.

THE lusty singing came from the servants in the rear of the chapel; even in the Lord's house, masters had the best seats, Ada noticed. Her own thoughts rolled on less awful subjects—the baroque tracery, the fan vaults, the gilded pulpit carved into a writhing mass of figures that looked more pagan than Christian from where she sat. This proprietary chapel was but another extravagant worldly room in a many-roomed house, a bravura display of the architect's eclectic skill. In so richly dressed a place of worship, Dr. Haygood's stern Calvinistic sermon had resounded strangely. He had taken for his text a passage from Job: *But where shall wisdom be found? And where is the place of understanding?* *Not* among the diggers of old bones (aha, Papa, so much for your dinosaurs, Ada thought, and smiled). *Not* in the sterile halls of science (oh, dear, he's looking straight at me, Ada realized and squirmed). Behold, the fear of the Lord, that is wisdom; and to depart from evil is understanding. Raising her eyes from the hymnal she shared with Mrs. Deventer, Ada caught Nicholas Vance in the act again. Always staring at her! Flushed with annoyance, she looked back down but refused to lend her voice to such repulsive words. Mrs. Deventer, however, showed no such qualms, although her soft contralto, so musical in speech, was painfully off-key in song. She could not carry even so simple a tune as

Where endless crowds of sinners lie
And darkness makes their chains
Tortured with keen despair they cry
Yet wait for fiercer pains!

Ada hoped the service would be ended with that grim admonition, but there was still a final homily to be endured. She resisted the urge to look in Mr. Vance's direction to see if he was still looking at her. She looked instead at Papa, whose attention was focused so intently on the pulpit. But she knew Papa: when he seemed that engrossed, he was not listening at all.

On Mrs. Deventer's right, an empty place marked her husband's absence, just as at table. And Mr. Witten was wise to be absent too, for there was little comfort for the dying here. Finding her eyes sliding again toward the new recruit to Rose's circle, Ada fixed a stern gaze on the pulpit. Dr. Haygood's large head, that awesome cranial bulge, suddenly reminded her of a baby. A newborn had just such monstrous proportions. Ada no longer wondered that so learned a theologian, as his doctorate implied, had accepted this private sinecure. What congregation, other than this captive one, would have overlooked his strange appearance, exposed itself to such uncomfortable and outdated dogma?

"Did not our great teacher, Martin Luther himself, instruct us in sacred nature of all work—even the most menial?" Dr.

Haygood might mumble pleasantries in the drawing room, but in the pulpit his voice took on a precise cutting edge. Ada was sure it carried well to the back of the chapel, where it was aimed. "Did he not teach us that the servant girl sweeping out a room is engaged in as holy an office as I myself in this pulpit? That the servant who cooks well for her master and mistress is, in truth, cooking for her dear God?"

Ada stole a quick look at Nicholas Vance, whose face was held in an impassive fixity. But something about the serious mien set her off—she could feel the giggles moving up her throat, her eyes watering. She looked away to avoid exploding into laughter. Papa's face swam into view—a sobering sight. He was leaning forward, eyes shaded by his hand. For a moment, she thought he was ill, but at her touch he raised his head and glared as if some importunate demand of hers had disturbed him in prayer.

She clung to his arm as they left the chapel, feeling a Sunday need to be his "good little girl," as he used to call her. It did not escape her that Mr. Vance stayed behind with Rose Deventer, who was conveying to Dr. Haygood her warm appreciation of his concluding oratory. Down the long corridor and into the great hall, Papa remained unresponsive to her beseeching closeness.

"Papa," she pleaded, "are you angry with me? Have I done something to displease you?"

Papa released himself, snapped his cuffs, tugged at his vest, smoothed the sleeve of his coat. He was shaking off her touch like a wet dog shaking off the rain.

"So. I understand you have a new profession. Belle of the ball. Of course I know only what your new confidante cares to tell me. Perhaps I have it wrong?"

So much for the new image of herself—the meek and mild loving Christian daughter. With his first words, he had made her very angry.

"I but follow your lead, Papa. She was first of all your confidante. She knows everything I told you in strictest confidence."

She was glad to see that he looked uncomfortable, thrown off stride. "Now, Ada, she caught me when I was still reeling from the blow—"

"And your plans—you do have plans, she tells me." Ada pressed home her advantage. "You see fit to discuss them with her, but not with me."

There was a dangerous jutting forward of Papa's beard. "You forget yourself, my girl," he said coldly. "It is a child's duty to confide in its parents, not the parents' to confide in the child. Such plans as I have take time to mature. And although you are now in the market for a husband, until such time as you acquire one, I shall tell you what I think right, when I think right, and as your father I expect to be obeyed."

"Of course, Papa," she said with great dignity, and walked up the stairs, beneath the tilted lances of the visored knights, down the corridor to her bedroom, slammed the door and muttered under her breath, "You may *expect* it, ha!" After which she felt considerably relieved.

She now had her own dresser—a dour young girl named Marie, still with the raw red cheeks, fiery as a rash, that her Breton countryside seemed to produce. "An inexperienced chit," Rose had apologized, "but at least she's French—of a sort. The French are very clever about clothes, you know—she'll learn quickly, with Maxwell's help."

Contrary to Rose's preconception, Marie was proving not very clever about clothes—hardly knowing, in fact, which was front and which was back, and all thumbs, to boot. This morning she had done up the back row of tiny buttons three times before coming out even. Ada was rather relieved that she had been bundled off with the Catholic contingent to St. John's in the village, where even now that handsome policeman, Patrick Cullen, was probably giving her the eye, wondering what he could ferret out from this new addition to the Deventer household.

Not much, Ada concluded, smiling at the thought. Unlike Maxwell, who clucked and complained and issued edicts and dealt out reprimands, Marie performed her duties in silence. Thinking of that tight face, closed on its thoughts like a miserly

107

fist clenched on coin of the realm, Ada wished Patrick Cullen luck.

A yawn convinced Ada that, even emerging from a coma, she would know a Sunday, there was such a Sabbath vacuum in the air. She pushed out the narrow mullioned windows to test the rawness of the weather, hoping it was not too unpleasant for a walk. The view that stretched in front of her was enticing in any kind of weather: the long sweep of rolling land with magnificent trees so ingenuously arranged, as if by Nature, ended in the sudden drop of a ha-ha, beyond which a true wilderness lay. An indraft of balmy air assured Ada that a walk was just the thing.

She was heading for the esplanade when some movement caught her eye and she turned her head. Close to the grey stone face of the castle, under a towering tree, stood Rose Deventer and Nicholas Vance. An animated chat, at least on the lady's part, with much pretty play of hands in and out of a fur muff, and charming Gallic shrugs, the last of which dislodged the fur-lined wrap, sleeves dangling, draped over her shoulders like a cape. Mr. Vance picked it up and replaced it—rather dawdling at the job, Ada saw. Another shrug and he almost had to do it again. But the wrap was clutched just in time and Rose made a laughing exit from the scene, vanishing indoors.

Now, sir, Ada silently addressed the gentleman, what will you do with the rest of your Sunday? She was completely unprepared for the little bow he gave the stone wall before moving off. A Mussulman making obeisance to the east? she questioned scornfully. Then saw the figure in the window just above. That was the Deventer wing of course. *Her* bedroom window. And that *the* tree—a shiver-provoking thought. In its leafless state, it had the gnarled and crabby look of old age, but in summer it must have seemed a green inviting bridge to the poor Haygood boy. The suicide tree, she would always think of it now, as if it were a separate species.

She turned away, the better to put that tragedy out of mind. At least the little scene she had witnessed removed any suspicion that Mr. Vance was interested in her. If his eyes seemed always on her, it must be from puzzlement, not with any amatory intent. The moment he stepped into the carriage, she had recognized him—this young man they were carrying back to Kirkewode as Mr. Witten's replacement—last seen in the dining room of the Fifth Avenue Hotel. No doubt he was always on the lookout for unescorted women, with the same sordid design that had moved his fat uncle to approach her.

At first she was sure he too remembered their earlier encounter, but at Mrs. Deventer's introduction, he expressed nothing but the usual polite delight. She may have looked familiar, but who or where or when, he must be struggling to recall. You have the advantage of me, was the way to describe such a state. Ada let her mouth out in a tight ungenerous smile: she certainly had the advantage of Mr. Nicholas Vance.

But if boredom had impelled her to seek distraction out-of-doors, boredom was reason enough not to rebuff him when he encountered her on her walk.

"Ah, Miss Traherne. Are your steps as aimless as mine? May we then join forces?"

Ada indicated that his company was acceptable, but continued at the brisk pace she had set herself. To maintain his sauntering air, he had to lengthen his stride, but had plenty of breath left for leisurely conversation. Evidently in awe of his new surroundings, he marveled at every turn. Had she ever seen the likes of this fountain, that Chinese pagoda, such a beautiful topiary garden. They paused to peer through a Claude Lorrain glass, admiring how the scenery had been designed for just such viewing, the glass tinted to give the proper hues.

"This is really my first opportunity to enjoy these pleasing prospects," he said, eyeing Ada's profile. "Mr. Witten has been giving me such a cram course in the Deventer holdings that I have had little time to venture beyond the office upstairs."

"Yes, you have been truly cloistered there," Ada said, and smiled. The tearful refrain of "My Cloistered Rose" was playing in her head.

As if his ear could pick up inaudible vibrations, his next words were: "Mrs. Deventer has been most gracious. Attentive to my every need. And deeply attached to her husband, I am sure. Only a great love could keep so active and charming a woman imprisoned for so much of the day within the narrow confines of their apartment. Mr. Deventer rarely stirs outside, yet demands she dance attendance on him day and night. I must confess my curiosity is aroused. What is he like, this paragon who arouses such uxorious devotion?"

"You mean you have not seen him? But you spend all your time up there—surely he gives you orders, papers to be delivered, things like that. You have already made two trips into the city—" she broke off, embarrassed to have revealed how close a watch she kept on him.

With obvious chagrin, Mr. Vance admitted he had yet to set eyes upon the great man. He was relegated to the antechamber, which contained the files and safe, the ticker and telegraph machine. Beyond that lay the sanctum sanctorum, which Slade guarded with a Praetorian vigilance. Only Mr. Witten and Mrs. Deventer had the proper credentials to pass through that sacred portal. Excepting the butler and the lady's dresser, even the servants were denied access.

"The rooms are turned out by no less a personage than Caxton himself. I wonder that he should so lower himself," Nicholas said with a seriousness that Ada found amusing. Poor fellow, she thought, he is disturbed at finding himself ranked among the lowest. "Of course, your father is particularly favored."

"What do you mean by that?" she asked haughtily. Was he implying some irregularity?

"Well, I could not fail to notice that his coming and going is erratic—sometimes one without the other—and I questioned Slade. There is no secret about it. Mr. Deventer has constructed a private stairway connecting his room with the doctor's quarters directly overhead. Sick people seem to always fear being taken in the middle of the night. There are certain disadvantages to a house this size, I suppose. Just think of how long it would take, using the main stairs, to respond to a medical emergency."

Ada laughed at his awestruck tone. "No doubt in time you too will become one of the favored ones."

No doubt, he sighed. Meanwhile he had much to learn. Would learn much more, he was sure, when Mr. Deventer worked with him directly. As it was, his orders had to be transmitted either by note or word of mouth through Mr. Witten and Mrs. Deventer.

"I confess, Miss Traherne, to wild imaginings at times—that my employer fears me as a source of some dread contagion, or wilder yet, that behind that door exists no mere mortal, but a sphinx, a sybil, an idol carved of stone." He ended with an apologetic laugh that denied the seriousness of his complaint.

"Oh, he exists," Ada reassured him. "And I can vouch that he is flesh and blood," she added. The shameful memory of her brief encounter with Mad Jack translated into a visible blush.

Astonishment brought Mr. Vance to a standstill. "You have actually seen him? In the flesh?"

Ada found his incredulous response rather overdone. "I see no reason why you should doubt my word, Mr. Vance. Perhaps you think I am one of those toadies who claim an intimacy—"

"No, no," he quickly interrupted, "it is just that—" Just what she was left to wonder, for a new idea struck him. "Look here, perhaps it was your father you saw, they do have the same kind of beard, the same coloring—to judge from the portrait of Mr. Deventer in his office downtown."

"Are you suggesting that I do not know my own father when I see him, Mr. Vance?"

"No, no, Miss Traherne—I merely suggest that from a distance—"

111

"Ah, but I saw Mr. Deventer quite close up. And quite close up, Mr. Vance, there is no resemblance at all."

They resumed their stroll at a slower pace, and in silence. Both were too absorbed in thought to spare further attention to the beauties of the landscape. Ada stole a glance at her companion. She had not believed the smooth clean-shaven face capable of that momentary animation. Now it was once again impassive. Such rigid control of facial muscles, she decided, was as concealing as the conventional hairy covering. Still, the single vertical line between his brows was more noticeable than usual.

"No, not this way," she countermanded his choice of direction. Just in time she had recognized the path that led to the Haygood house. With no wish to encounter again either the intimidating dog or its equally ferocious mistress, she suggested that it was time to begin the journey back.

Mr. Vance reversed direction and offered her his arm with a gentlemanly concern Ada took in poor grace. Did he really think her legs failed her? To disabuse him of any such idea, she insisted that they digress onto an upward-winding path so faintly marked she had missed it before, so narrow two could not pass abreast.

"It promises a fine view," she answered his cautious objection and took the lead, her step unflagging even when the ascent grew steeper.

"I think we shall be able to see the river," she called back. She was filled with a sudden exploratory ardor, forgetting even the man behind her, intent only on scaling the heights. They emerged into a semicircular clearing held in the embrasure of dark evergreens, its open end providing the fine view Ada had foreseen—broad river in the near distance, towering cliffs on the farther shore. But the vantage point was already occupied. One look at the formless black-shrouded heap sent Ada edging backward, her heels grinding down on Mr. Vance's toes. Hushing him indignantly for his sharp ejaculation of pain, she resorted desperately to sign language: Be quiet. Let us go.

Too late. The misshapen monument of grief rose, unveiling a small stone marker.

"Mrs. Haygood. I hope we did not frighten you." Putting the best face on it, Ada came forward with a strained smile. She had no need to read the lettering on the stone to know whose grave this was. "We were just exploring—we had no idea that—I mean, no wish to intrude."

The pale face seemed like a fading image on an old tintype that, exposed a little longer to the air, might vanish entirely, leaving behind only a blurred acid stain.

"You have the right, this is still Deventer land," Mrs. Haygood said. "For *him,* there is no leaving it." She turned her back to them, looking out over the rolling descent to the river, whose surface had a steely glint under the winter sun.

At Mr. Vance's questioning look, Ada whispered, "Her son." He had only to read the simple epitaph to see how recent was the loss. Obviously he knew nothing of the circumstances. She had a sudden premonition that some awkwardness was in store.

Doubting that her previous encounter with the lady constituted a formal introduction, Ada identified herself, then presented Mr. Vance as the gentleman who would soon be taking over Mr. Witten's duties. A brief three-quarter profile view and a bob of the black bonnet was all the acknowledgment Mrs. Haygood made, leaving Ada to search for some graceful exit line.

"My deepest sympathy, ma'am," Mr. Vance said smoothly. "I know myself how hard it is to lose a parent—how much harder it must be to lose a child. One has not even the consolation that it is in the natural order of things." Ada breathed a sigh of relief—so far there was nothing amiss in what he said. But the foolish man must go on. "I take it this was a favorite spot of his? I am sure he must be at peace here. Never have I seen so lovely a resting place."

Ada flinched. She had feared just such a solecism—there was only one reason why the boy's grave lay in so secluded a spot. She fully expected the bereaved mother to inundate them with a gusher of tears. For the first time, Mrs. Haygood looked at them fullface. Her composure was more unsettling than any tears.

"He has no peace." Mrs. Haygood's eyes had as steely a glint as the river. "Nor will he know rest until that she-devil gets her just rewards. But the truth will out—just the other night my poor baby told me so!"

Ada and Mr. Vance exchanged a meaning look, found they shared the same thought. The lady should be escorted safely to her home. "We found the path here rather arduous, may we offer you our company on the way down?" Ada asked gently.

"Allow me, ma'am." Mr. Vance offered his arm with a gallantry that would not be denied.

The startled look she gave them, the frantic eyeing to either side, made Ada think they had come upon a lunatic escaped from Bloomingdale. With the resignation of a prisoner who sees no way out, Mrs. Haygood allowed herself to be led away.

Does she know we think her mad, Ada wondered? If so, the lady made a valiant effort to deny it by such inane comments as must surely prove her sane. The weather, the beauties of nature, and the myriad virtues of the bark of the sassafras, which abounded on the path, were the only subjects of her discourse until they sighted the grey stone parsonage.

From the rear of the building, the huge dog came bounding, torn between greeting his mistress and rending the strangers in shreds. Ada was annoyed to see how quickly, with no help from Mrs. Haygood, Mr. Vance brought the dog to heel. Such fawning filled her with disgust. Bravely she reached out her hand to pet it too, but all she received was an ominous curl of the lip, an unmistakable sneer.

"Now that's unusual," Mrs. Haygood said to Mr. Vance, "he does not usually take to strangers. Argos is Jonathan's dog, and since—" her voice broke, but with an effort she contained herself—"since his dear master passed to the Other Side, he has not been himself. Sometimes I find him sitting here, right in the middle of the walk, as if Jonathan had just ordered him to stay. And such a patient look in those big brown eyes, fixed in the direction from which the boy used to come. We all know that dogs hear sounds that our ears do not pick up—I think they see as well things our eyes cannot discern. When he sits like that, his hackles up, and will not budge, though usually so obedient to my command, I know that Jonathan is somewhere near! I mentioned this to Mrs. Jenckens at our last sitting, she says it is a sign that Argos sees his astral body and that I, too, when my heart is strong enough, will one day see his dear form. . . . May I confess a wicked thought? Though I love the dog, I am at times almost impatient for his old age. When *he* passes over, I may be able to sleep a little better, knowing that Jonathan has his loved companion by his side, is not so terribly lonely wandering out there. How cold the antechamber to eternity, he tells me!"

She shuddered and fell silent, yet made no move to take her leave. Mr. Vance seemed to hold some fascination for her. Ada, restless to be off, remarked how chilly it had grown, how inconsiderate they were to keep Mrs. Haygood from her warm fire.

"Tell me—Mr. Vance, is it?" Mrs. Haygood had eyes only for him. The black-gloved hand plucked at his sleeve as if he were the one now in danger of escaping. "My husband says dogs have no souls, that heaven has no room for them. What do you believe?"

Mr. Vance made no effort to disengage himself. He placed his hand consolingly over the black-gloved fingers and spoke with more feeling than Ada had yet heard in that bland well-modulated voice.

"My dear lady, I believe that heaven has illimitable room and welcomes any being that is capable of selfless love."

A pretty speech, Ada thought, but Mrs. Haygood was affected more than was called for. Her clutch tightened on Mr. Vance's arm until he looked alarmed. She seemed about to swoon.

"Mrs. Haygood, are you ill?" Ada reached out, only to be thrust aside by quite a vigorous arm.

115

"*Veritas!*" With her free hand, Mrs. Haygood placed a fingertip on Mr. Vance's ring—an awed touch.

"A school ring, ma'am. Of no consequence." Mr. Vance released himself with difficulty, the faintest trace of embarrassment in his eyes.

"*Veritas!*" Mrs. Haygood crowed. "Truth! It is just as Jonathan said! A stranger will come under the banner of truth to uncloak her wickedness, disrobe the temptress, show her naked in all her evil designs! That was the very message we received from him. Oh sir, little did I expect that you would come so soon!"

"My dear lady!" Mr. Vance looked appalled. "This is merely a school ring—the Harvard insignia—"

"I know, I know." There was something almost coquettish in Mrs. Haygood's adoring gaze. As astounding to Ada as the poor lady's delusions was the miraculous transformation in her looks. Twenty years seemed to have dropped from her, as if like one of Homer's goddesses, she had been wearing the cloak of age merely as a disguise. Gone was the sad drag on her cheeks, the tired droop of her shoulders. Color bloomed in her face.

"How clever of you," she simpered, "to choose my dear boy's own school. . . ."

"Margaret!"

The lady's rejuvenescence proved short-lived, extinguished by the lowering presence of her husband in the doorway of the parsonage.

"So there you are. I thought I heard that dratted dog—" His reading glasses pushed up on his forehead, Dr. Haygood bent his head forward to distinguish the faces of his wife's companions. He had removed his black coat and wore instead a shaggy shawl over his shoulders. A buffalo, Ada thought, then revised the image. A buffalo about to charge.

"Not a word to *him*, I beg you," Mrs. Haygood whispered, "he does not countenance traffic with the spirits—"

"Ah, Miss Traherne. Mr. Vance. An unexpected pleasure,"

Dr. Haygood said, but the mumbling monotone conveyed no pleasure. "I think, my dear, you had better come inside." He opened the door invitingly wide.

She trotted obediently in and the door was closed on her. Dr. Haygood remained outside, hovered for a moment indecisively, and then approached them in a halfhearted effort to relieve the general awkwardness.

"I regret not asking you in, but I have a good idea where Mrs. Haygood has been—she has a morbid predilection for a certain spot—and she will pay for it with nervous spasms the rest of the day."

The grim satisfaction in his voice made Ada scowl. A moral Scrooge, she judged him, intent on balancing the books, never mind the pain. No wonder Papa had scoffed at her suggestion that the woman find solace in this man of God.

"It is we who should apologize, sir," Mr. Vance said with an unruffled politeness. "We were taking an aimless walk, encountered your wife, our steps fell in with hers, and here we are—we had no intention of disturbing your Sabbath rest— well earned, if I may say so, by your Sabbath labors."

Ada gave a faintly audible snort. Mr. Vance seemed to have an unending store of polite sentiments, soothing phrases.

"Does she have trouble sleeping?" she asked sharply. "Perhaps she should have a bromide—"

"Miss Traherne, spare me your professional opinion. As I spare you mine. *Dr.* Traherne—" a slight emphasis to remind her that Papa was the only Traherne with the right to such a title—"did leave some drops with her, I believe. I disposed of them."

"You did—*what?*"

"Dr. Traherne agrees there is nothing wrong with her—it is all in her mind. And in that province, young lady, I am better physician than he. I have instructed her to repeat the Lord's Prayer as many times as it takes to weary Satan, who will then send her to sleep to rid himself of it."

There was a dangerous look in Ada's eye. Mr. Vance quickly

117

interposed, "Perhaps if you say it with her, sir, Satan will tire in half the time. Come, Miss Traherne, we should not keep Dr. Haygood from attendance on his wife."

Her elbow firmly grasped, Ada was pulled away. Mr. Vance did not release her until they were out of sight of the parsonage.

"That man—how could you speak to him without—I should like to throttle him—did you *hear!*" Balked in her present inclination toward mayhem, she diverted her anger to him. "You certainly put your foot in it, up there at the grave! Going on like that about 'such a lovely resting place.' I'm surprised you didn't send the poor woman into hysterics. Don't you know the Haygood boy took his life by his own hand? Another case of unrequited love chalked up to Mrs. Deventer's account. That's why he's buried there all alone—they don't admit suicides into consecrated ground!"

Ada was satisfied with the effect. Mr. Vance smote his forehead and swore, "Ye gods! Why didn't you stop me? Of course I didn't know."

"I don't see why not—I thought our Cloistered Rose was a household name by now," Ada said, conveniently forgetting that when she arrived at Kirkewode her own knowledge of its mistress had been rich in rumor, sparse in fact. "Certainly it is common knowledge that she has a lethal effect on her suitors." She darted a quick look at him, wondering if already he considered himself among that lot.

"Of course I've heard something of the sort, although frankly, until I met the lady, I thought such talk the usual hyperbole of the press." He worried at his ignorance, as if to explain it would mitigate the blame. Mr. Kerne's death had made quite a stir, he remembered that very well. And he had heard of a young man following suit, but not by name. It had happened then in '86, if he had correctly read the stone?

"The summer of that year." Briefly Ada repeated the story Papa had told her, not neglecting to point out that the tree the boy had climbed to enter Mrs. Deventer's apartment was the one he had been standing under that very morning, chatting

118

with the lady in question. He need not think they could canoodle like that without being seen.

He shook his head pityingly. "At that age, the devil gets into a boy—" he winced—"that sounded like Dr. Haygood, didn't it? All I mean is that it is a time of great enthusiasms, uncontrollable emotions. I speak of young men, of course. Young ladies, as we know, never lose control." He managed to dispense a little bow in her direction without breaking stride.

Ada's instinctive reaction was to argue that point—if only it were clearer what argument to wage. Was it calumny or compliment to exclude young ladies from "great enthusiasms and uncontrollable emotions"? The resultant image of her sex, undoubtedly superior, was somehow too pallid for her taste. Moreover, she had sensed a tinge of irony in his courteous exoneration. What she could see of his profile was unrevealing; with no cue as to what thought lay behind it, she ridiculed its cut. Overly precise. Like one of those fashionable silhouettes snipped out by skillful scissors in a trice. The thought that next occurred to her made her want to giggle.

"I fear you do less than justice to your sex, Mr. Vance," she said demurely. "I am sure that not *all* young men are subject to such strong emotions." She was picturing this cool specimen in the throes of an ungovernable passion. It was hard not to laugh out loud at so ludicrous a picture.

But Mr. Vance's thoughts were still on the somber story she had recounted. "Poor lad. The summer of '86, was it? I was abroad that year, that accounts for it."

Ada looked at him curiously. "It seems to me that you have been accustomed to a higher station in life than your present employment. Or do most Wall Street clerks go to Harvard and take the Grand Tour?"

She had not thought his bland face had the limberness to be pulled into such a long moue. "Ah, Miss Traherne, you've found me out. But I hesitate to burden you with my life story—"

"Please do, Mr. Vance."

"Are you sure it will not bore you? Every day one hears of

119

just such unfortunate occurrences, a prominent family brought to ruin, a fortune dissipated overnight, father felled by a stroke, dear grey-haired mother loses her mind, daughter sells herself on the marriage block, and the wastrel son, never trained to any useful pursuit, is cast utterly adrift—"

Ada had grown impatient. "Come, Mr. Vance, one does not hear of that every day, one reads it—in some cheap story paper."

Mr. Vance looked injured. "I am surprised, Miss Traherne, that you should be familiar with such low literature." Evoking no smile, he assumed a heroic stance—the condemned man before a firing squad. Obviously he was ready to bare his soul.

"Very well, if you must know, I have never been to Harvard, I found the ring on a washbasin in a hotel room. I did inquire about the previous occupant, but the chap left no forwarding address—understandably since he had decamped without paying his bill. I have often wondered how *he* acquired the ring— could it be that even Harvard turns out a scoundrel now and then? I confess I simply took it, it seemed fated to be mine, fitting my finger to a tee.

"As for my stay abroad, that was no Grand Tour, believe me. I was a courier at the beck and call of a skinflint industrialist, who inconsiderately expired in Nantes and left me stranded. Perhaps it was his revenge for my having misrepresented my facility in French, although I picked up the lingo fast enough. In any event, I worked my way back home on a merchant ship and consider myself quite fortunate now to be in Mr. Deventer's employ, particularly with such opportunities opening before me. What else can I say, except that I am of poor but decent folk, am a great reader of story papers and even books (though unlike yourself I have never been to an institution of higher learning) and otherwise have led a dull and uneventful life."

It was Ada's turn to be embarrassed. All that her suspicious questioning had exposed was a harmless pretension or two. She hoped his pride was not hurt—men were so vulnerable on that score. Not that he looked particularly abashed. "Believe me, Mr. Vance, I have no wish to pry into your personal life. Nor the right. Let us talk of something else."

He took her cue willingly and changed the subject. Mrs. Haygood was still much on his mind. "She mentioned a Mrs. Jenckens. The name rings a bell, but I cannot place it. A spirit rapper, I gather—"

Ada too found the name tantalizingly familiar. They puzzled over it, moved on to casual chatter, until Ada suddenly cried out, as if stung: "The Fox sisters!"

He was immediately enlightened. Of course, that famous pair—or infamous, as some would have it—the original Rochester rappers who had started the whole thing. The younger one, Katie, had gone to England and materialized a very substantial husband there—Mr. Jenckens, he presumed. What the devil was she doing back in New York? Up to her old tricks again?

Ada recalled vaguely that Katie Fox had been widowed a couple of years before, at which time she had chosen to return to her native land. Left with two young children on her hands, Ada contended, she had little choice but to return to her old profession, if only to make ends meet.

"I'm afraid I have little sympathy for those who batten on the grief of others." Mr. Vance looked at her askance. "That was tactless of me. Perhaps you are a Spiritualist yourself."

Why should he think so, Ada demanded indignantly. Nor was she mollified by his reply that she seemed an independent-minded woman. Women's righters and female mediums and free-love advocates—it was too common an assumption that they were all one big crackpot group.

"If I did believe in such things, I would find myself in company with many prominent members of *your* sex," she retorted, and found herself making a heated defense of spiritual phenomena in which she believed as little as he. She struck what she hoped was a purely scientific stance—no prejudgment, impartial consideration of the evidence, a willingness to keep an open mind—to which Mr. Vance responded with such infuriating tact that she soon abandoned the argument and fell into a childish sulk.

Even in retrospect, she was not sure just how the conversation turned to her, or why she had bored him with that tedious recounting of her life. Perhaps it began with some mention of Nice—alas, he reminded her, his tour of Europe had been less than grand, terminating before he reached that fabled playground of the rich—and he had seemed most interested in her childhood memories of the place. When it came to explaining Papa's departure to take up residence at Kirkewode, she kept to Mr. Kerne's comforting account of a purely professional engagement separating man and wife. To her relief, Mr. Vance saw nothing peculiar in such a domestic arrangement. He knew of many such cases, he avowed, though usually the traffic went the other way: the wife departed with the children for Europe's more cultured shores, leaving Papa behind to continue turning out the wherewithal.

Having so good a listener must have gone to her head. Before she knew it, she had passed beyond a humorous recital of the daily grind at medical school and was confessing to ambitions that she had thought extinguished when she chose to marry Francis and practice by his side. To cure the sick was a noble calling, but how much nobler it would be to eradicate disease forever! Mr. Vance looked skeptical? Then he did not understand the full import of the discoveries being made, almost daily, by such geniuses as Koch and Pasteur. From what had already come to pass, one could with confidence extrapolate the future. Hers was a radiant vision: for every disease, a germ; for every germ, a vaccine; for every vaccine, one less plague inhabiting the earth. Smallpox, anthrax, cholera, diphtheria, consumption, and just this past year the dread rabies— Ada thrilled to the list of victories already won, the germs already known, the vaccines either here or shortly on the way. All in so small a space of time—more progress made in these last two decades than in all the centuries since Galen. What was happening in science, she would have him know, was no evolution on a Darwinian scale, but a cataclysmic event, a volcanic eruption of knowledge! In the field of knowledge, at least, Agassiz was right: mountains were toppled in a day, new mountains raised up overnight. Oh what an age to live in, she cried, with an open gesture that seemed to embrace a whole world filled with invisible animalcules.

"Do you know where I would like to be right now?" she asked fiercely. "In Paris!"

"Ah, Paris," he murmured.

"Ah, Paris," she mimicked that special bleat reserved for the land of romance, the font of high fashion. "Don't be silly. They're opening the Pasteur Institute this year—just imagine what it would be like to work there—under *his* direction!"

Mr. Vance dutifully imagined. "If you feel like that, I wonder that you did not stay for your degree. I understand from Mrs. Deventer that you have left school and have no plans to return."

Like an arrow, those words pierced her soaring thoughts, brought them back to earth. A rough landing. What else had Rose Deventer told him, she wondered angrily. Then reason told her the anger was unjust, that Mr. Vance would not have brought the subject up at all had he been more informed.

"I get carried away, I'm afraid," she said curtly. "Those were rather childish dreams. I now have other plans for my future."

"And they are—?"

She was suddenly reminded of the career she had chosen in Madame Modeska's atelier. Here was a man to practice on. Ada tilted her head to view him from the corner of her eye, and tried to emulate Rose Deventer's seductive smile. He blinked. Quite a triumph, she felt, to confuse a cool fish like that.

Though they were shivering now in Kirkewode's great hall, colder far than the outdoors, he seemed reluctant to take his leave, remarked that she looked as fresh as when they first set out, admired such a picture of perfect health. Since Ada saw herself as romantically languishing just then, it was not a description that pleased. Was Miss Traherne by any chance an advocate of physical culture? Miss Traherne, gritting her teeth, gave him a testy smile which he interpreted as yes. Then she might be interested in the exercise room the Deventers had equipped downstairs. All the latest body-building devices— dumbbells, trapeze, rowing machine, fencing equipment, even a punching bag. She did not know it? He must show it to her. He owed his own discovery of the room to Slade, who had been eager to demonstrate his boxing technique. She need not fear she would be poaching on a masculine preserve—Mr. Deventer never used it, he was told, only the lady of the house. Surprising, that. Not that he saw any reason why ladies should not develop muscles too, he assured her hastily.

Back in her room, Ada could not believe the clock, that time could pass so quickly on a Sunday. Reviewing her own performance on their long walk, she wished she had talked less, listened more. It was a fault of long standing with her, which could not be blamed on lack of education or sage advice from friends. Miss Porter's school might be weak on mathematics, but it was strong on ladyhood. Perhaps then she had been too young to understand why a lady's conversational art should be limited to drawing out the man, but she was older now, could see what women were about. Knowledge was power. Loosen a man's tongue and you soon knew him inside out; hold your own, and you were toasted as the eternal mystery, the great unknown, the dark continent which no man dare explore lest he be swallowed up.

She had thought to have acquired a modicum of the skill, but what a backsliding just now. *Her* childhood, *her* school life, *her* dreams of the future—not one word from Mr. Vance of his. It seemed to point to some incorrectability of character worse than nail-biting—she had conquered *that.* And adding to her discomfort was the obscure feeling that Mr. Vance had wanted it just so, that there was a trick to it, an ungentlemanly table-turning device by which he had gained the very advantage she had earlier boasted of, knowing more about her than she about him.

124

Chapter 9

ADA soon noticed that she was not alone in succumbing to Mr. Vance's conversational charms. She had once read arrogance in the assured arrangement of his face, but she had reason now to doubt that first impression. Certainly he was democratically inclined when it came to lending an attentive ear.

Marie, who favored her mistress with only curt monosyllabic replies, must have found her tongue with him. The little Ada came to know of her own maid, she had to learn from Mr. Vance: the girl's village of origin (Auray), the family's occupation ("in the oysters"), how many brothers (three) and sisters (four), and why her eyes so often matched her cheeks in redness (she cried herself to sleep, poor homesick Breton). Ada shook her head in admiring disbelief—all this information obtained from a few brief meetings in the hall. And one afternoon she herself witnessed Caxton relinquish his reserve—that double carapace of Englishness and butlerdom—to bemoan how flat, stale and unprofitable was Kirkewode to a man of his tal-

125

ents—no weekend guests, no house parties, no balls—he should never have left His Grace, whose hunting box saw more festivity than this dubious American castle.

She was not at all surprised, therefore, at Slade's growing chumminess with Mr. Deventer's new aide, particularly since both spent so much of the day in the same quarters, serving the same master. It was the bodyguard's argumentative bellow that stopped her at the head of the stairs as she was on her way to dress for dinner. The softer answer—unmistakably Mr. Vance's voice turning away wrath—drew her into the terra incognita of the Deventer wing. Instinctively her footsteps fell more lightly as she came to the massive double doors behind which Rose Deventer vanished each night. Here the armor-furnished gallery met its formal end, but beyond the private suite was a narrow passageway reserved for servants' use. Not only narrow, but poorly lit and thinly carpeted. She ventured on, observing that even the most splendid of mansions turned miserly and mean where only servants trod. From the back stairs at the end came another roar, so enraged in tone and volume that she felt alarmed for Mr. Vance's safety. But when she looked down the dark well, there was the object of her concern seated peaceably on the landing below, puffing on a cigarette, and the giant towering over him held only a disarming pitcher of beer.

"That rotten rag!" Slade growled. The foamy edging around his mouth lent him a rabid look. "Who gives a hoot what Fox says in his *Police Gazette*? It'll take more than that scum's backing to make Jake Kilrain the world's champeen. There's only one and you know it—the great John L. He don't waste time with all this sparring and fancy footwork, he's right in there with his dukes flying, and here's the jaw he broke to prove it. And tell me this, if he ain't champeen, what's the Prince of Wales doing inviting him over for lunch? The champeen of champeens—that's what his royal nibs wanted to see in action, and that's what he got an eyeful of."

Mr. Vance nodded yes; he had read about the exhibition in

the *Herald.* And quite a flap it caused, too. The good Queen did not approve.

From above, Ada saw Slade's shoulders heave a behemoth's shrug. It was not a ladies' sport, he said. "Though let me tell you, I seen ladies at his fights, eyeing him with their tongues hanging out. Not the sporting kind either, the genuine article. If I was to tell you some of their names—"

It was obvious that Mr. Vance was in no danger of bodily harm. There was no excuse for lingering further. And yet his interest in the pugilistic art was so unexpected, Ada could not resist hearing what next he would say.

"So you think he'll beat Charlie Mitchell—if they do meet this spring in France?"

"Birmingham Charley?" Slade spit his opinion on the bare servants' stairs. "John L.'s had him on the ropes before, would've killed the limey if the coppers hadn't stopped him. Wanna place a little bet? Two to one, that's how sure I am."

Mr. Vance took a last leisurely draw, apparently considering the odds. "I don't know, Sullivan's what—thirty, now? And he hasn't fought bare-knuckle under London Rules for at least six years. Not to mention that he does his training with one foot on the rail." He ground out his cigarette and got to his feet. "I think I'll take that bet."

Ada drew back quickly, seeing they were about to mount. To her confusion, Papa chose that moment to emerge from the Deventer suite into the gallery which she had yet to recross. Worse, the door remained open as he turned for a final word. Ada froze against the wall, trapped by her guilty conscience. She had behaved just like a servant, listening in on Mr. Vance; she could not bear now to be caught skulking in the servants' hall.

"Do you think it will bring on the ague this time?" asked Rose Deventer from inside.

"I don't know, it's too early to tell. And I've warned you that even so, the issue is in doubt. After a bout of fever, there has always been some improvement in the past, but I offer you no guarantee."

A fatal hesitation, Ada realized, to have stopped at all. Those homiletic stories she had learned her letters by were proving true: One wrong step (eavesdropping on Mr. Vance—mere harmless curiosity, it had seemed) led inexorably downward on Satan's path (here she was, eavesdropping on her own Papa!).

"See here, Rose—" the harsh impatience in Papa's voice astounded Ada. It was hardly to be recommended as a bedside manner. "I've discontinued the daily quinine, that's all I can with safety do. Without it, the fever will recur, sooner or later. Unfortunately it may be later. If you have more faith in noxious vapors, then go ahead, open the windows at night. In this weather you'll have him dead of pneumonia in a week. That's not exactly what you want, is it?"

"Hardly." The dry denial rang more convincingly in Ada's ear than would have a tearful protestation. "Well, send Slade back up, if you see him. He's probably taken the opportunity while you were here to guzzle down a bucketful of beer."

Papa grunted and was off, the door closed, and Ada seized the moment to speed across the gallery into the obscurity of her own wing. She felt appalled at her behavior—every movement that of a sneak thief—but that did not diminish her relief at escaping unobserved. Better private guilt than public disclosure. She looked around for Marie to help her change for dinner—the apartment was empty. That too was a relief; Marie's silences were more intrusive than the idlest chatter, forcing her to think constantly of something pleasant to say. Nor were those raw-knuckled, stubby-fingered hands more skillful than her own in handling the intricacies of dress. Of course, in the way of hands, she herself had nothing much to brag about. Hers had wrung even from Marie a spontaneous cry of sympathy: *la, la, ces pauvres mains!* Reminded of Rose Deventer's thoughtful gift, Ada sat down at the dressing table and began to apply the burnt-almond cream. The slow languorous rubbing encouraged a meditative blankness of mind.

128

I have discontinued the quinine. Until that moment she had refused to consider Papa's parting words, to admit that she had heard what was not meant for her to hear. Now she almost wondered if she had heard aright. Granted that Mr. Deventer was indeed subject to malarial attacks—hence the daily dose of quinine—he was certainly not suffering from one at the present time.

Had she not suspected as much from her one glimpse of the gentleman? A certain complacence indented the corners of her mouth, a fleeting dimple of self-esteem. But the next thought shattered all pleasure in being right. Why then would Papa discontinue the prophylactic dose? She went over every word, every inflection in his voice, to reach the same puzzling conclusion. Papa *wanted* his patient to succumb again, was actively encouraging the onset of a debilitating fever. Would Papa so forget his Hippocratic oath as to—? Never. Then Papa must believe a paroxysm or two would do Mr. Deventer good! What then was the matter with Kirkewode's master? How strange an illness to demand so strange a cure.

The puzzlement was still with her when she went down to dinner, though she tried to put it out of mind as a confidential matter between the physician and his patient. The surprise awaiting her, however, accomplished this in the twinkling of an eye. There on the pouffed satin sofa, the cynosure of the pre-dinner gathering, was an unexpected presence, its blackness like a storm cloud in that room of azure blue. Dr. Haygood had brought his wife.

Catching her breath, Ada took in Rose's high spirits, Dr. Haygood's unconcealed triumph, Papa's incredulous look, Mr. Witten's sly amusement. Only Mr. Vance seemed not to realize how extraordinary was the occasion.

"I understand from Mr. Vance you two have met," Rose said gaily. "Now you see our little circle quite complete."

"Not quite, dear lady," Dr. Haygood corrected her, "we had hoped to see Mr. Deventer restored to us as well." There was an accusatory ring to his mumbled inquiry as to Mr. Deventer's progress, as if in failing to produce *her* spouse, Rose had left him short-changed.

"You know the nature of the disease—it comes and goes, comes and goes," Rose said with resignation. Poor Mr. Deventer, she sighed, extorting sympathy from them all; such a pity that the vagaries of the ague still kept her husband from enjoying this good company.

In a discreet aside to Papa, Ada expressed a professional interest in the course of Mr. Deventer's illness. Surely a stiffer dose of quinine would bring him about? Though Papa merely grunted, she counted it nonetheless a lie. Poor Papa, he looked greatly relieved when Mr. Vance joined them to inquire of Ada if malaria was one of those diseases she had spoken to him about, ready to fall victim to the inexorable advance of science?

If he meant had they yet discovered a malaria germ, Ada admitted the issue was still in doubt. There were those now claiming to have found a parasite in the blood, but she herself still held to the bacillus theory. Although Mr. Vance seemed eager to hear from her lips the latest dicta from the scientific world, Papa's disapproving look reminded her that this was not a conversation in which a young lady showed herself in a becoming light.

Across the room, Rose Deventer's gaiety was acquiring a desperate edge as none of her gracious overtures to Mrs. Haygood met with any response. To Papa went out a silent cry for help which drew him to the uncomfortable grouping about the sofa. With his departure, there was an ominous change in Ada's demeanor. She listed slightly toward Mr. Vance, affording him a closer view of her décolleté, a sharper awareness of her perfume.

"Do you realize that you are living in a very perilous time, Mr. Vance?" she asked with such significance that he knew germs could no longer be the subject. Though he confessed himself nonplussed, something in those blue eyes told Ada that this man knew peril when he saw it. "Have you not consulted the calendar recently?" she prompted. "Is there not something special about 1888—something that occurs only once in every four years?"

"Ah, yes," he said, the lift of his brows conveying his enlightenment, "you mean the presidential election." She had not known a man could summon such demureness. "Do not tell me, Miss Traherne, that your interests extend to politics as well."

"I was referring to leap year, Mr. Vance." As she suspected, he had known all along. "When custom has it that a lady may be the wooer, need not wait to be the wooed. Have you taken steps to protect yourself against the droves of importunate females who will no doubt seize this opportunity?"

He begged her to give him a few pointers from her greater experience. Ada found it convenient that flirting required so small a portion of the mind, for even as she tossed her head and answered Mr. Vance with a soft trill of laughter, she was mostly occupied with the curious behavior of Dr. Haygood's wife. Why had the woman consented to come if she meant to sit there like an automaton, a piece of clockwork whose mechanism had run down?

"I have been so wanting to share with you some choice items from our glasshouses, Mrs. Haygood," Rose was saying. "The asparagus we have now is simply superb—may I send you some? That is, if your health will now permit you to enjoy it," she added delicately.

Eyes fixed blankly on empty space, an idiotic smile pasted on her lips, Mrs. Haygood made no reply. It was left to Dr. Haygood to fill the silence. "You are too good, Mrs. Deventer," he mumbled.

Papa took his turn, pronounced himself delighted with Mrs. Haygood's improved looks. The compliment went unacknowledged. Forcing a heavier joviality, he struggled on. "I recall, dear madam, you were the first among us to appreciate this fellow Wagner. All the rage now, they tell me, though I myself do not see what is so musical in all that screeching. Still, my daughter will be going to the German opera next week—

her first exposure, you understand—and it is my opinion she should be forewarned. Perhaps after dinner you would favor us with that Siegfried song on the piano—how well you used to play that—it almost made a convert of *me*."

Standing behind the sofa, one large hand encasing his wife's shoulder, Dr. Haygood was well positioned for his ventriloquist's role. "We are out of practice, I'm afraid. Perhaps some other time."

Not so much a social visit then, as a vengeful haunting, Ada decided. Banquo's ghost come to spoil their dinner. *Thy bones are marrowless, thy blood is cold; thou hast no speculation in those eyes which thou dost glare with!* Mr. Vance exchanged with her a look of dismay—the lady's presence had a dampening effect even on their casual flirting. Yes, the evening promised to be a disaster.

Until, that is, Papa returned in disgust to their corner of the room to suggest sourly that Mr. Vance should try his hand. Dutifully Mr. Vance took the empty seat beside Mrs. Haygood.

"And how is my good friend Argos?"

Mirabile dictu, Papa whispered to Ada. The automaton had come to life, an alert intelligence in its eyes, the rictus of feigned sociability transformed into a genuine smile. Dr. Haygood was left agape, the words from his opened mouth seized by the lady herself.

"How kind of you to ask. He misses his new friend, I know. We hope you will soon find the time to visit us again, Mr. Vance."

There was such relief at the miraculous cure of Mrs. Haygood's dumbness, everyone began to talk at once. Not much meaning survived the crossfire, but the animated noise was in itself gratifying. Alas for Mr. Vance, his bravura performance condemned him to be tied to the chaplain's wife for the duration of the evening. As they went out to dinner, a whispered conference between Caxton and his mistress resulted in a change of seating, with Mr. Vance placed at Mrs. Haygood's right, from which direction the lady never turned her head.

"Cry your heart out, missy. Your young man is spoken for."

Ada shrank from Mr. Witten's close breathing in her ear. "You are mistaken, sir," she said coldly.

"It ain't unheard of, you know, for old hens to like young roosters. I'd say she means to stick closer than one of your papa's leeches—just look at her over there."

"I mean, he's *not* my young man." Ada was furious to find herself blushing, certain that he had deliberately misunderstood her. She wondered if he had always battened on other people's discomfort, or if this repulsive trait was a function of his illness.

And yet, as the terrapin gave way to the salmon and the salmon gave way to the saddle of lamb, Ada came to see that what rendered Mr. Witten's remarks so venomous was the grain of truth they always contained. Mrs. Haygood's absorption in her young dinner partner was downright scandalous, however preferable to her previous agonizing silence. By consensus, the general talk ignored the unlikely couple, stranding them on a conversational island of their own. The occasional glance Dr. Haygood sent his wife reflected only satisfaction. If, as Ada assumed, the poor woman had been dragooned into coming to this dinner, a man of his conceit would find in her unwonted vivacity merely proof of his good judgment.

Across the table, Mr. Vance inclined his head closer to the lady to catch some softly spoken comment, one hand twirling the stem of his wine glass. Against the delicate crystal, the hand had an undeniable strength. A naked strength. The Harvard ring was gone. Locking the stable door after the horses were stolen, Ada thought, with a slightly contemptuous sniff. Its removal would hardly unconvince Mrs. Haygood that he was the truth-bearer whose advent had been promised by the spirit world. Quite the contrary, Ada could have told him. If the ring was not his customary adornment, all the more reason to assume it had been worn as a special sign.

A new thought came to Ada—unwelcome at first since it made of Dr. Haygood something less than a villain. Yet observing how Mrs. Haygood bloomed in Mr. Vance's presence—like some fragile heliotropic plant that tracks the sun, whose petals open only in its light—Ada could not deny that, far from being an unwilling guest, Mrs. Haygood might well have sought this invitation. Beneath that surface frailty was a steely will, she was beginning to suspect. And neurasthenes, she recalled from a neurology lecture, were skilled maneuverers. When the husband has a taste for tyranny, the clever wife arranges it so that he *commands* her to have her way.

The dinner followed the usual interminable course, but its aftermath was thankfully brief. Concern for his wife's still delicate health impelled Dr. Haygood to take an early leave. An awkward moment of good-byes, with Rose pressing a hand gone suddenly limp and lifeless, her gracious murmurings answered only by a resumed idiot's smile, and they were gone.

"Thank the Lord!" Rose heaved a tremendous sigh. "I have never known such an exhausting evening. I do not think I could have survived another minute. I suppose we have Dr. Haygood to thank for this reconciliation, but I think I prefer to have his good wife avoid me like the plague—it is more comfortable all around."

"I'd say she did just that, Rosie, in this very room," Mr. Witten jeered. He did not seem to share Mrs. Deventer's exhaustion. Ada had never seen him so lively at this hour. The social tension of the evening had proved a better painkiller than any medicine Papa prescribed.

"Yes, she did, didn't she?" Rose picked up a bonbon, began to peel away the gold foil in her careful way. Suddenly she cried out in an unrecognizable voice, so hoarsened with rage it might have emerged from a man. Her beautiful neck showed all its tendon cords. "Why in God's name did she come then? Does she think I have forgotten, that I need to sit here staring at her black dress all evening to be reminded of her son?" The fit passed as quickly as it had come. "Ah, what a mess I have made," she said, opening her clenched hand to reveal the crushed chocolate half-melted in her palm.

"There, there, Rosie, never you mind," Mr. Witten said,

though whether he was referring to the oozing chocolate or the Haygood tragedy was not clear. He was using his own handkerchief, a repulsive crumpled object, to wipe her fingers clean, but Mrs. Deventer's attention was elsewhere. It was from Papa she wanted reassurance, some small comfort—so the beseeching look in her grey eyes declared. Ada thought it heartless of him to turn away without a word.

Rose reached out to Mr. Witten, placed both hands on those sunken cheeks. Misty eyes examined the head thus cupped, like Hamlet seeking to recall the features that once belonged to Yorick's skull. "Oh, Sam, I could always count on *you!*" A silent "Oh" of dismay acknowledged the unfortunate past tense, and with a muffled cry she rushed from the room.

Ada glared at Papa's back, and followed on her heels. At least one Traherne was capable of human sympathy. "Mrs. Deventer!" The cavernous hall echoed that name. Ada wished she had not called so loudly—it sounded like a new arrival being announced in the waiting room of the gods. Rose turned to await her at the foot of the stairs, eyes quite dry again, head held at a disdainful angle. Ada's heart cried out to her—what battles this brave woman must have fought to rise above her past, what blows endured along the way, and always expecting yet another blow to fall.

"I just want to say—" But what to say? From somewhere came words Ada hardly knew as her own. "You can count on *me,* Mrs. Deventer."

For that declaration of loyalty, Ada was rewarded with a glowing look, a husky "thank you, my child," before Rose fled from her as well. Ada hesitated, then decided to follow her example and retire early rather than rejoin the men. She felt out of sorts, both with Papa and herself. Already she regretted the impulsive gesture which had drawn her out into the hall, blaming Papa for it. Had he not so cruelly denied his support, she would not have felt the need to offer hers. To Ada, the ebb and flow in her regard for this woman was almost frightening. At times the attraction seemed like a natural force, as uncontrollable and powerful as the moon's pull on the tides. But there were neap tides too, just as inexplicable, when all her liking for this modern Delilah was sucked away, leaving exposed a subterranean labyrinth of doubts. She was, in fact, the last person in the world Rose Deventer should count on.

"Psst!"

Ada's hand automatically pressed the top of her bodice.

"Miss Traherne!"

She let her breath out. It was only Mr. Vance calling her softly from below. He bounded silently up the stairs, puzzling her with his secretive air.

"Forgive me, but may I speak to you for a moment—confidentially?"

She guessed the writer of the note he gave her even before she had unfolded it. "I rather thought Mrs. Haygood came tonight for some such purpose." The message was penned in a spidery hand, showing the faint tremor of nervous debility. "She passed this to you on the sly?"

He nodded. "She doesn't want that husband of hers to know. You see why the sitting must be tomorrow night—she explains that Dr. Haygood will not be at home then. I should not really mind seeing the famous Katie Fox at work, but I feel I would be attending under false pretensions—that dratted ring, you know. I should like your advice. Should I humor the poor lady and attend the seance? Or would that merely encourage her pathetic delusions?"

Ada modestly disclaimed any right to advise him, then proceeded to do so, more preoccupied with correcting his impression that she was interested in spiritualism than with the problem he had posed. *She* would never lend herself to such a foolish parlor game, she announced, however harmless it might be. A properly designed scientific inquiry—that would be another story.

To her confusion, he seemed to feel that she had bidden him to go. He pronounced himself much relieved that she agreed it was harmless, thanked her profusely for putting his mind to rest. His ability to twist her words was remarkable—what was there in her caveat that Mrs. Haygood seemed dangerously unstable to make him assume that she was offering to accompany him?

"You're quite right, Miss Traherne," was his enthusiastic response, "there should be someone with professional training in attendance, just in case the poor woman becomes overwrought." The look of admiration added to her confusion. "Now why didn't I think of that? Of course you must come too!" And before she could make her protest heard, he was plotting how they might get away after dinner without betraying Mrs. Haygood's trust, using the full moon and the recent snowfall to propose a sleigh ride as the perfect excuse. To Ada it sounded strangely like a lovers' rendezvous—might that be really what he had in mind? As if to answer that unspoken question, he acknowledged that certain false suspicions might be aroused. All the better, he assured her soberly, they would serve as a red herring drawn across the track of truth.

Just how red was that herring, Ada wondered, aware that she had little experience with this flirting game. She recalled how Francis had announced without preamble that she was the girl for him, stamped her with a kiss, then returned to their discussion of Lord Kelvin's law. There was only one way to find out— she suddenly acquiesced, leaving the gentleman on the stairs somewhat off-balance, having just begun to exert his persuasive powers.

Marie awaited her in the bedroom to submit an apology for her earlier absence with her usual economy of phrase. *Crise de foie,* the girl explained. She was subject to these attacks. They soon passed. Ada smiled sympathetically, knowing that the liver was blamed for any pain between the collarbone and the thigh. Or perhaps it was the monthlies—a complaint the girl would deem unmentionable. "I really don't need you, Marie. My advice is to go straight to bed and curl up with a hot-water bottle."

But Marie shook her head stubbornly. She knew her duty and was quite capable of performing it, was the message conveyed by those clamped lips. Ada obediently turned her back and bowed her head.

"Ah, but you are cold, ma'mselle."

"My girl, you are hot," Ada said sharply. "Just where is the pain?"

Ma'mselle was not to worry, she was quite all right, Marie insisted.

"Come, I want an answer. I am a doctor."

Marie tittered, looked at Ada uneasily. Was this some English joke she did not fully comprehend? Lie down on the bed to be examined? The girl rolled her eyes heavenward at this assault on modesty, then dissolved into a fit of giggles. Ada was forced to resort to a higher authority. "As your mistress, I will not tolerate being disobeyed." It was infuriating to see how quickly then the girl moved to the bed.

But once the patient lay before her, there was only a cool professionalism in her questions. The fever, judging by her palm, was not dangerously high. Not her monthlies, then? Blushing, Marie shook her head. "But the pain is down there, isn't it? And it must have been worse this afternoon, for you not to get out of bed?" English failing her, Marie resorted to gesticulation. Ada nodded—chills and nausea, yes. Under the skirt which Marie refused to raise, her fingers probed, evoking from the foolish girl a wincing apology for leaving off her corset.

Abdominal pain in right iliac fossa. It was impossible to tell through so many layers of cloth if there was a dullness on percussion, but she flexed and adducted the thigh to test for sensitiveness, and received a satisfactory yipe of pain. She had had such attacks before? How many? How often? Marie squeezed her face together in the act of remembering, as in a constipated effort to pass a stool.

Ada felt her hand gripped as Marie was seized by a sudden spasm of intense pain. "It will pass, it will pass," Marie whimpered, half in promise to Ada, half in reassurance to herself.

"Yes," Ada murmured consolingly, "just lie still, there's a good girl."

Ada leaned against the headboard, her forehead against two fat cupids in flight bearing between them an unfurled scroll. *Amor vincit omnium.* Even after she shifted her head, she felt she wore the imprint like a phylactery of the Jews. Here she was, playing nurse when she should be preparing for the final examinations that would make her truly a doctor. It will pass, it will pass, she told herself, using Marie's words to address her own pain. These waves of unhappiness, moments of despair, came less frequently now.

"Stay here, Marie, I shall fetch Dr. Traherne," Ada said softly, thereby producing a remarkable cure. Marie sprang to her feet, proclaimed the pain had passed, there was no need of a doctor. Ada sighed in defeat, all efforts at persuasion failing. She found it hard to understand why so many poor and ignorant souls dreaded doctors more than death itself.

Chapter 10

THE next morning when Marie appeared with the breakfast tray, Ada took note of the dark hollows under her eyes and the mincing walk that betrayed her belly's tenderness. No more of such Breton stubbornness, Ada decided. She took a quick sip of the hot chocolate, slipped into a morning robe and turned into the bully that the occasion required.

"Downstairs we go. March!"

Dr. Traherne was in his office, Caxton informed her reluctantly. With Marie kept in lock step by a nerve-pinching grip on the upper arm, Ada passed the music room and conservatory and mounted the two wide shallow steps that marked the entrance to another wing. This rosy marble corridor studded at regular intervals with pilasters of a darker hue was new to her. Papa had discouraged her interest in his practice in Kirkewode. A dull sort of business, no exotic diseases, no dramatic surgery, nothing to interest an up-to-date little sawbones like her—such had been his response, teasing on the surface but underneath edgily defensive. Somehow he had never found the time even to show her his office.

Following Caxton's instructions, she went to the corridor's end and knocked on the last door. Taking the impatient "Yes?" for an invitation, she entered with her foot-dragging charge. Papa, busy scribbling at his desk, looked up, gingery brows knotted with annoyance. Had not Caxton told her he was not to be disturbed at this hour of the morning? Caxton, at least, had the sense to recognize a medical emergency, she countered sharply.

Marie was shivering now, though whether from fever or from fear, Ada was by no means sure. One look at the girl and Papa closed his notebook, locked it in a drawer. At Papa's approach, Marie began to snivel. Terror drove all English from her. To his questions, she responded first in her peculiar French, then began to utter the strange Welsh-like sounds that Ada gathered was her native tongue. Papa kept her struggling hand in his, murmuring an exasperated "there, there" while his fingers took her pulse and his eyes took stock of the rest of her. Into one ear poured the girl's Breton cries, into the other Ada's reasoned summary of her findings, until he shouted, "Drat it, shut up, both of you females!" whereupon Marie subsided into sniffles and Ada into sulks.

Asked to stand aside and leave the patient in Papa's hands, Ada turned a critical eye on the thick carpet, the imposing desk, the tapestried chairs, the glass-doored cabinets with rows of dark-tinted bottles, shelves of impressive books. It did not escape her that most of the medical texts were outdated, although there was a recent edition of Loomis's *Practice*. She turned her attention next to his desk, on which lay a surgical instrument box. Her hand stroked the beautifully polished wood, but she was almost afraid to open it, knowing in advance it would have a red plush lining. It was common practice, she had heard, for doctors to clean their instruments scrupulously and without a second thought place them in that deadly nest of infection. Yes—red plush. But, thank heavens, Papa kept his knives and saws rolled up in pristine Canton flannel.

"Stop fiddling over there, Ada," Papa ordered, "and give me a hand with getting this girl on the examining table. Perhaps you can assure her I have no evil designs upon her body, that she will be decently covered with this cloth—"

Half by force, half by persuasion, they managed to subdue Marie. Once on the table, she lay supine in the quiet paralysis of a stunned sacrificial animal. While Papa bared the abdomen, Ada held the cloth up in such a way that Marie was spared the sight of her own nakedness—all that modesty required, apparently.

"Perityphlitis, beyond a doubt," Papa said. Marie called out to the good God to save her! "No need for that, my good girl, what you have is an inflammation of the bowels. That doesn't sound so dreadul, does it? When did you last move them? I thought so. An enema for you, my girl, and a holiday in bed. Don't mind the needle, this nice stuff will relieve the pain."

Ada could no longer hold back her protest. Her "Papa!" was an expletive of such suppressed force, the needle gave a jerk and Marie howled, Papa scowled, and Ada's courage failed her. How could she tell her own papa that he was behind the times, that perityphlitis was as dead as last year's hats, and that the course he was prescribing might leave his patient deader than that.

"Be quiet! Lie still!" Papa looked so angry that Marie at once subsided, but Ada knew the anger was for her. He beckoned her aside. "Is it the morphine you object to?" he demanded. "Is there some new teaching I am not familiar with that says the patient should not be deprived of his pain?"

"Of course not, Papa. It's the enema I wish you would reconsider. The latest thought is against such measures. The bowels should be kept absolutely quiet in a case like this—no cathartics, laxatives, purgatives of any kind." Papa was standing with arms crossed behind an iron shield of silence, that pose of hearing one out which meant not hearing at all. She could feel her own anger mount, but this was exactly what Professor Scolby had warned her class about as their graduation grew

142

near: as young doctors fresh out of school, they must expect to rub up against old fogeys who had never been well schooled; eminent greybeards who would wash their hands, then pick their noses, and believe they were observing the latest rules of antisepsis; busy practitioners with no time for reading journals or attending meetings, who would defend their ignorance of the new advances with the claim that medicine was not a science but an art. Tact was the response that had been advised. Tact was what Ada, grinding her teeth, now employed.

"Perhaps you missed Dr. Fitz's article, Papa, which came out in '86. Everybody agrees that he has completely redefined this problem. For one thing, the source of the infection is definitely the vermiform appendix, not the bowel proper, so perityphlitis is something of a misnomer, you see. Appendicitis is the more accurate term. Dr. Fitz specifically warns that any agitation of the bowel increases the risk of perforation, and once the abscess spills out into the peritoneal cavity, even surgery has little chance of success. It is truly an important paper, Papa, I'm sure I have a copy of the journal in my trunk, if you would care to look it over?"

Papa's momentary speechlessness encouraged her to believe that he was digesting the new information she had provided. His explosion—a blast of anger that sent her edging backward—took her completely by surprise.

"Why should I read this Dr. Fitz, whoever he is—"

"A pathologist at Harvard, Papa."

"—when I have my own daughter to instruct me in the latest thought? Do you think that in my twenty-odd years of practice, this is the first case of perityphlitis I have seen, that I am in need of a consultation with a young female who has not even completed her third year of medical school? My advice to you, miss, is to acquire your diploma before you set out your shingle!"

Ada felt the sting of tears at such an underhanded blow. Pride demanded that she turn on her heels and leave the room without another word; only concern for Marie stayed her.

"Papa," she said urgently, "the only effective treatment for this is the knife—"

Marie's English did not fail her then. The injection was just beginning to take effect, but she scrambled off the table as if afraid of being disemboweled on the spot. No doubt she intended a scream. What emerged was a strangely detached-sounding drawl. "Not the knife, *monsieur le docteur,* not the knife, do not listen to that she-devil, save me, oh blessed Virgin, save me. . . ."

"Do not be afraid, my girl, no one will cut you up—" Papa tried to soothe her.

"Marie, don't be so stupid! It's for your own good that I suggest—" Ada scolded.

"She-devil. She-devil." Marie lethargically crossed herself.

"Ada, shut up!" Papa's raised hand, open as for a slap, knotted itself into a fist, boxed the air helplessly. "As for you, my child, the only thing my daughter has said that I agree with is that you are stupid. Can you make it up to your room? Then off with you, and to bed."

Marie kissed the hand of her savior, avoided any look at Ada and made her exit gratefully. Ada washed her hands of the foolish girl. She had more understanding now of Mrs. Deventer's contempt for the poor, who could but would not save themselves. She felt the same for such ignorant patients who preferred the superstitious practices of the Dark Ages to the bold measures of the new science.

Papa shook his head at her. "Sometimes I think this fellow Morton should have kept his laughing gas for pulling teeth. Without anesthesia, we wouldn't have this modern passion for the knife. I thank my stars I learned my medicine when surgery was a last resort—"

Ada steeled herself to make one last effort. "I am sure that in your day, Papa, you were right—sepsis followed as a matter of course, but nowadays, with proper listerization, miracles are performed. Particularly in this inflammation of the appendix, Papa. There is reason to believe that delay in operating—"

"I have no intention of discussing this case further with you," he said icily, and taking her by the elbow, escorted her to the door. His beard wiggled alarmingly. He could no longer contain himself. "In my day? In my day? My day is not quite over, young lady. Let me remind you that yours as a doctor is. I admit I did not much care to see you taken under Mrs. Deventer's wing, but I think now the sooner she introduces you to society, the better for us all. Except society, of course. Frankly, when I think of what is in store for it, I pity it."

"Very well, Papa," Ada said evenly, proud of keeping her voice at a ladylike level, "you will never hear from me again on this subject." To the door that closed behind her, she was blunter. When she thought of what was in store for his patients, she informed it, she pitied *them.*

Still the first thing that she did when she returned to her apartment was to search through her baggage which had arrived at last from Michigan. Caxton had suggested it be removed to the trunk room (for fumigation, one would have thought from his disdainful expression), but she had insisted it be brought up to her apartment, where it rested now, as yet unopened, an encumbrance in the dressing room. The clothes did not matter, but her books, her papers—she wanted them beside her just a little longer.

Her books were crated separately; what she sought now was packed with her clothes. When she threw back the hooped lid of the trunk, the odor of past dreams, failed hopes assailed her, stronger than camphor. The crushed dark stuff of workaday dresses ballooned up, spilling on the floor the odds and ends she had thrown on top: her brass slide rule, which Papa had acquired in France for himself and given to her when she entered medical school; her desk blotter, still bearing the imprint of study notes like a secret code; the 1888 wall calender which she had never had a chance to hang up but whose little sheet for March already had a circled date—graduation, it would have been. The effort to fight off weak and womanish tears gave her face an almost ugly set.

Ruthlessly she tossed out the neatly folded dresses, underskirts, chemises, flannel drawers—ah yes, there were the white lab coats, two freshly laundered, one soiled and with a new acid hole—and at the very bottom, like a protective lining, her lecture notes, loose papers, prized journals.

That afternoon she chose the hour she knew Papa would be in attendance on Mr. Deventer to slip into his office and leave the journal on his desk, opened at page 321: *Perforated Inflammation of the Vermiform Appendix. Reginald H. Fitz.* True, she had vowed he would never hear from her again on this subject, but was it "hearing"—she gave her rationalization an appreciative grin—when she was not making a sound? She felt a twinge of regret at letting the journal out of her hands—it was Francis's copy, borrowed and not returned—then mocked herself for making it a sentimental object, like a love letter or a photograph. *Francis.* She did not want to think of him. She closed the door of Papa's office firmly, as if shutting Francis inside.

Quite aimlessly, she next wandered into the billiards room. Caxton, passing by the open door, volunteered, "If you are looking for Mr. Vance, Miss Traherne, you will find him in the exercise room downstairs."

It was annoying that he should so misread her presence there. It was true that when Papa was closeted upstairs with Mr. Deventer, it was customary for Mr. Vance to be excused from his duties, encouraged to stretch his legs or otherwise relax. True also that at such times she had observed him often in this room, sending the ivory balls caroming in such an intricate pattern of angles that her interest in the game had been aroused. But his absence now was all to the good, she told herself. She could try out her own hand without a witness to her beginner's ineptitude. And yet her interest quickly waned. The stick wobbled between her fingers, the balls took their own strangely erratic course, and twice she left a chalk track on the felt. The better part of valor, she decided, was to return the stick to its rack and await instruction.

She recalled Mr. Vance's offer to show her the exercise room and felt slightly injured that he had not done so yet. The winter was closing in, she could put to good use those contraptions he had touted. It seemed as good a time as any to discover them for herself.

Glad that Caxton had vanished from the hall, she ventured down the first stairway she came to. On this lower level, the heavy masonry of the castle's construction was oppressively exposed. The low, barrel-vaulted corridors seemed more likely to lead to a dungeon than to so modern a convenience as an exercise room. She took a turn to the right and was momentarily alarmed by certain curious scuffling sounds, but was quickly relieved to hear a familiar bellow (Slade, beyond a doubt). The pair of brass-studded leather doors swung open at her touch. At first she was aware only of so much empty space—an enormous barracks-like expanse. Then, at the far end, she saw Mr. Vance and Slade. Naked! She had walked in where only men were allowed!

Only half-naked, she quickly realized. Panic subsided to mere embarrassment when she saw that jersey tights accounted for the clear outline of their lower limbs. And there were the dumbbells, the trapeze bars and rings dangling from above, the rowing machine beached on dry floor, the ballet practice bar running the length of a ten-foot mirror. This was indeed the gymnasium Rose Deventer used.

Ada had never thought to be a witness to a sparring match, but, seeing that both men were too occupied to be aware of her presence, began to enjoy the new experience. The mayhem always implicit in Slade's raised voice was actually taking place. There was a rivulet of bright red blood running from his nose. He brushed a hairy forearm across the flow as if he were wiping away a rheumy cold. And Mr. Vance—what had happened to the discipline of his smooth straight hair? It was hard to recognize his flushed face beneath that mess of sweaty curls. Ada was afraid he had the disadvantage, being so much the smaller. She gasped in alarm as Slade swung a huge fist at his head. Miraculously, the curly head was no longer there, the padded leather glove swiped empty air. Mr. Vance popped back up and somehow managed to connect his own fist with the side of Slade's head. Shaking it as if to clear his thoughts, Slade grunted.

"That's a powerful right-hander you got there, m'boy, but when a runt is up against a regular-sized fella, best stick to the straight body blow—" The giant grunted again as Mr. Vance's fist landed on his flabby midsection but suddenly—too quickly for Ada to be sure just how it happened—Mr. Vance was sitting on the floor and Slade was concluding his lecture—"but don't forget, you gotta guard against a counter to the jaw."

From the way he sprang to his feet, Mr. Vance could not be much hurt. The two men faced each other again, fists curled up, held out stiffly. Was that what was called "squaring off?" Seen in profile, the figures might have been taken from a frieze of some piece of ancient Greek pottery. It was surprising what a well-developed form had been concealed under the clerk's proper clothes.

Aware that such pugilistic bouts were not intended for ladies' viewing, Ada turned to make a discreet exit. Only then did she notice there was an audience of more than one. From an inner doorway across the room, Rose Deventer had made an entrance equally unobserved. Ada blinked at the imperial splendor of the oriental robe that enveloped her. The long grey eyes were fixed on the boxers, and there was something in the contemplative smile that made Ada uncomfortable.

Her move to leave caught Rose's attention. A smile, a shake of the head, an out-turned palm signaled her to stay. Rose moved soundlessly to her side, hugging the wall. Bare feet, just visible beneath the kimono, explained so quiet a step.

"He strips to advantage, doesn't he?" Rose whispered, adjusting her clutch on the slippery satin held together at her waist. Golden dragons breathed a crimson fire. Ada moved back as if feeling the heat.

Was she just reconnoitering, or had she come down for a workout, Mrs. Deventer asked. If the latter, she would need

148

proper clothes, something loose-fitting. There was sure to be a suitable garment in the changing room—she would be glad to take Ada back there now. "No need to feel shy, dear. The gentlemen will leave as soon as we take the floor."

Ada did not know where to look. Their presence had been discovered. With only a towel around his neck, Mr. Vance was approaching. She did not think she could converse sociably with a half-naked man—a healthy one on his feet, not a sick one in his bed. On the other hand, she dared not look at Rose Deventer, whose momentarily gaping robe had revealed lower limbs encased in boxer's tights as clinging as the men's and who wore above the waist—if that startling glimpse was to be believed—nothing at all.

With her eyes fixed on the tips of her boots, Ada pleaded some undefined duty. "I really *must*—" Unable to think of what it was she *must,* she simply fled from the room.

To be a femme fatale was not as easy as it looked, Ada decided. At dinner that evening, it became clear how much she had to learn about her newly chosen profession. She should consider herself fortunate, she told herself, to have before her so fine a practitioner to serve as an example. A slight change of seating had lowered Papa, raised Mr. Vance a notch. The clerk now sat immediately on the right of Kirkewode's mistress, whose charm had been turned up to an even greater incandescence. The lady made it seem as simple, as mechanical, as turning up the gas. But it was for Mr. Vance that Ada reserved her severest strictures. How stupid, the way he basked in the silly little attentions Mrs. Deventer paid him. Several of his jokes Ada judged as pitiful, but Mrs. Deventer never failed to reward him with her rich chuckle, that thick viscous sound like the bubbling up of some underground hot springs. And when he turned serious, Rose gazed at him with such ardent attention, one would think an oracle was speaking. Who cared why the *Thistle* had failed to win the America's Cup?

Ada turned to Mr. Witten, expecting some caustic comment on the flirtatious pair, but for once he failed her. Drinking heavily of the wine, he gazed woozily at his lady love, nothing but approval on his wizened face. Perhaps adulation of his employer's wife was just another duty he expected Mr. Vance to take over. In which case, he must be gratified by the performance of his new understudy.

Papa, on the other hand, seemed too engrossed in molding bread pills on the lace cloth to notice anything, or to be of much use as a conversational partner. Ada, feeling much neglected, was forced to listen in on *those two*—so she was beginning to think of them. Still on the subject of yachts, Ada noted, finding it an inappropriate subject for a man of such modest means.

"With so fine a yacht as Mr. Deventer must have," Mr. Vance was saying, "I suppose you made the transatlantic run last summer, along with the rest of New York."

Ada visualized a flotilla of—over a million and a half, wasn't that the latest census? But, of course, for those two, only yacht owners counted, the others didn't exist.

"I'm afraid Mr. Deventer is not impressed by royal pomp and ceremony—hardly a good American democrat," Mrs. Deventer said. "I would have been quite willing to join the exodus—after all, how often do you have a Pope and a Queen holding their jubilees the same year? But Mr. Deventer was convinced that was the worst possible time to go—he does hate crowds. Even when I can coax him aboard—and last summer we did take a short cruise—we shun the fashionable watering places and ports of call."

Ada foresaw no relief from her boredom even when Caxton brought in the brandy and cigars. At such purely family dinners, Mrs. Deventer preferred to remain with the gentlemen, bypassing the hard spirits but treating herself to one of her long Turkish cigarettes. Ada was therefore taken by surprise when Mrs. Deventer rose and gave her the signal to withdraw.

It became clear as soon as they entered the drawing room that Rose had seized an opportunity to speak to Ada alone.

"I understand that Mr. Vance has suggested a sleigh ride after dinner. Take care, my dear, there's a full moon tonight." Finding that her smile met with no response, Rose spoke more soberly. "I do think, Ada, a word of advice would not be amiss. Don't let mere propinquity entrap you into feeling more than you ought. An unexceptional young man, but I'm sure your father has something better than a mere clerk in mind for you."

Ada felt no need to ask why this sudden concern lest she become too intimate with Mr. Vance. She had only to recall him stripped to the waist, and the look in Rose Deventer's eyes—the studying look, the bemused smile. Ada tried out a look of sweet innocence, thinking: she is my teacher now, this is the way the game is played. And averred sweetly that nothing was farther from her mind, there was no cause for alarm, even as she fluttered her lashes and looked modestly down, thereby causing—as fully intended—a great deal of alarm. It was fun to pretend to be equally smitten with Mr. Vance's charms, knowing all the while that she was immunized forever from such silly mooning about. Yes, that had been Francis's role in her life—to serve as a vaccine, causing a transient rise in temperature, a short period of discomfort—small price to pay to be safe forever from a deadlier, more disfiguring disease.

When the gentlemen rejoined them, it was Mrs. Deventer's turn to be amused. Mr. Vance was reeled in to her side like some poor helpless fish (though hardly struggling, Ada noted sourly). And there he stuck, having eyes for no one else—or ears either, all his attention given to the high-society gossip Rose was delighting in (having just read the latest issue of *Town Topics*). Ada was ready to believe he had forgotten all about their plans for the evening, but apparently Caxton had been primed in advance, for he appeared promptly on the stroke of nine to announce the sleigh had been brought around.

"Already?" Mr. Vance looked surprised that time could fly so fast. Obviously he would like nothing better than to stay right where he was. Eating out of Mrs. Deventer's hand. Literally eating out of the lady's hand.

"Close your eyes and open your mouth," Rose crooned. She was not about to let her young gallant go before firmly staking out her claim. With a smile, she popped a bonbon into Mr. Vance's mouth. Ada did not much care for that smile. The two sharp peaks of the thin upper lip and the turning upward on either side formed a sinuous snake-like line, like the Egyptian hieroglyph for water. *I would not trust her.* The thought sprang from nowhere into Ada's mind.

Once outside, she felt ashamed of such an ill-founded judgment, based on nothing but a smile. It was clearly Mr. Vance who should not be trusted. He seemed to forget all about his new lady love with his first deep breath of cold air. All his attention directed now to his present companion, he made sure that Ada was warmly wrapped in the fur lap robe before taking up the reins. As he leaned over her with such solicitude, she felt a strange sensation in her body completely at odds with the cold disclaimer of her thoughts. The leaping of her pulse was an involuntary response to an embarrassing visualization of his half-naked body, so well muscled, so pleasing to the eye.

Her blush deepened with her next thought: was that not what men did, undress women with their eyes? Was so different from that odious pop-eyed man in the Fifth Avenue Hotel, whose stare had been so insultingly bold—uncle to this cool proper young man by her side? The possibility that in the deepest recesses of her mind she might have something in common with that repulsive specimen caused her to shudder. Shifting to a safe distance, she maintained a pose as frigid as the night air until she remembered that women were made of finer stuff. The gross advances of a man were transmuted by the female into a harmless flirtatious art. Why else had she accepted this invitation but to perfect that art? She began to respond to Mr. Vance's light sallies, and returned them in kind. Swaying with each curve in the road, she allowed herself, by imperceptible degrees, to come close enough for their shoulders to brush whenever he gave a little snap to the reins. She was so impressed with the skill of her maneuvering that she was rather sorry when the lights of the parsonage came into view.

Aroused by the tinkle of the horses' bells, Argos announced their arrival in time for Mrs. Haygood to await them at the door. Either her husband's absence, or Mr. Vance's presence, had restored her again to the comeliness of near-youth, with real blood flowing in her veins. With the flushed excitement of a hostess at a ball, she took their wraps and made them welcome. True, in that welcome, Ada was somewhat scanted, her presence acknowledged with cool surprise while Mr. Vance received a glowing smile full broadside.

They were ushered into the parlor, a low-ceilinged room so cluttered with furniture that Ada moved with great care for her bustled skirt lest she knock something over. Having seated her guests by the fire and insisted that they partake of some mulled wine, Mrs. Haygood made a faltering effort at polite chitchat. A painful effort, Ada thought, like the victim of a stroke struggling to relearn how to talk. The minutes passed and Ada shifted restlessly. Was Mrs. Haygood under the impression they were paying a merely social call? Mr. Vance smoothly helped her along, pulling the words that failed her out of her very mouth with his "As you were no doubt about to say, ma'am," and "May I expound on that, ma'am," and "If I understand you correctly, ma'am," until even he lost patience and brought the matter to a head.

"This Mrs. Jenckens, ma'am, I take it she has failed you?"

Mrs. Haygood gasped "Oh, no" and half-rose, as if afraid he was about to take his departure. "She's lying down, resting a bit. She needs to gather her strength, you know, before—" She looked askance at Ada. "I am to call her when we're ready, but—" Another look at Ada put her into an indecisive dither, from which she was rescued only by Mr. Vance's firm tone.

"I assure you, ma'am, that Miss Traherne's presence will be a help, not a hindrance. The more people there are, the stronger the magnetic field, and the surer we are to make contact, you know."

"So kind of you to think of that." Mrs. Haygood gave him a grateful smile and departed to produce the star turn of the evening. Overheated, Ada drew her chair back from the fire. Everywhere she looked there was evidence of some accomplished female hand, presumably Mrs. Haygood's before her breakdown: picture frames of sea shells, an autumn landscape above the mantel worked entirely in feathers, a great deal of berlin work made up into fat wool cushions that padded every chair, several arrangements of wax flowers unconvincing only in their perfection. There was a piano too, closed and bare of sheet music, its top covered with a fringed Indian shawl and weighted down with a cluster of small ornaments in the manner of an instrument not much used.

Ada ventured to approach it, curious about the arrangement of objects before which two small candles flickered. The centerpiece was a photograph of a young man, hand-tinted to better convey his blond handsomeness. A wash of yellow on the hair, a wash of blue in the eyes, a wash of pink on the cheeks, a finer brush stroke carmining the lips—a process Ada detested. Like the beautifying efforts made on a corpse, she thought, and drew back, shocked. This *was* a corpse, she realized. Jonathan Haygood, dead at nineteen, by his own hand. At the time the photograph was taken, he must have just been graduated from his preparatory school. He had that sternly serious look that boys adopted on that occasion, whereas girls found it easier to smile, either more amenable to the cajoling of the photographer or merely in relief that, for the most part, their education was over.

The pathos of his death was brought home to her in earnest—not even the painted prettiness of that face could hide the unfulfilled promise of its youth. She was less moved by the oval miniature atilt on a rosewood stand—a conventional little angel with blond ringlets. One golden curl lay preserved in a cloisonné box.

A bronzed infant's boot completed the pathetic collection, from which Ada turned with a sense of discomfort.

Mr. Vance, who was examining the feather-work, confessed himself in awe of the time it must have taken first to find the right colors, then to apply the feathers in that painstaking way. "The premise, I suppose, is that the Devil finds work for idle hands."

Ada's hands had never known such skills, a disability which had caused her some trepidation when she first attempted dissection. Much to her surprise, she discovered that she could wield a scalpel with the best, and that fingers confounded by the simplest embroidery stitch could still sew up a gut quite tidily, with a quickness that surpassed all but Francis's in her class.

"There is such a thing as idle work too," she said loftily and hoped she had not been overheard by Mrs. Haygood, who entered at that moment with a disheveled elderly woman in tow.

So this was Katie Fox! Ada felt a keen stab of disappointment at the sight of so commonplace a figure. It was evident she had been "resting" in the clothes she wore, for her bustle was sadly crushed and somewhat askew—as ludicrous a sight as if a camel had displaced his hump to the side. Her full waist, straining against the tight pointed basque, had popped a button which had not been replaced, showing she had a careless disregard for her attire. Not so for her face, for she had made a hurried effort to repair the ravages of sleep by furious powdering, which left a clear line of demarcation between the flour-whitened chin and the much darker neck. Many a magazine article had been written about the Fox sisters, illustrated by pen-and-ink portraits of two handsome dark-eyed women. Confronting the present reality, Ada decided the artists had either worked from old photographs or had exercised a journalistic license. This was the kind of down-and-out face uncovered daily in city morgues, unclaimed, unmourned. Puffy, jowly, the face spread itself in the puddles of an aimless smile, fixing finally on Ada. Katie Fox advanced with hands outstretched, and sent crashing to the floor an alabaster vase.

"No harm done," Mrs. Haygood gasped assurance, kneeling to pick up the pieces. She did hope that her maid, sent purposely to bed, had not been awakened.

Moving swiftly in Katie's wake, Mr. Vance rescued a glass-shaded lamp and led her safely to a chair. By then it was evident that the sleep from which she had been awakened was not an entirely natural one.

"My, *there's* a pretty girl," she said, leaning toward Ada in an attitude of delighted surprise. Ada caught a glimpse of pink scalp beneath the thinning black hair (surely dyed?), and the reek of brandy on her breath. "I bet you have more beaux than you know what to do with, you little fox. And do you have a favorite? There now, I know just how it is, you're in a quandary, you can't decide between the two or four or however many bees are buzzing around your pot of honey. Who knows, perhaps tonight your dear papa will send you some much-needed advice. He is still looking after you, my dear, though from his new quarters up above."

"Katie, Katie," Mrs. Haygood pleaded, trying to stop that foolish flow.

"If I need advice from my papa, Mrs. Jenckens, I have only to ask him. He is closer at hand than you seem to think." Ada spoke more sharply than she had intended, but she could not help but feel betrayed. This was the spiritualist whom she had defended against Mr. Vance's aspersions, and look at her—as bosky as Mr. Witten at his worst, and twice as foolish. Ada took more to heart the reflection on her judgment than on Katie Fox's character. Unforgivable, she found such behavior.

Katie pulled a disreputable handkerchief from her sleeve and stuffed it against her mouth to suppress a sudden fit of hiccups. "Strange, I see about you—hup!—the aura of an orphan—hup!"

Mrs. Haygood looked resentfully at Ada, as if she were to blame for this painful display. "I did mention she was orphaned, Katie, but I was referring to her mama. It doesn't matter. Miss Traherne is of no importance. It is Mr. Vance on whom you should concentrate your powers. Since Jonathan has sent him to us with a sign, I am sure that with him here with us, my boy will at last speak to me, I shall feel his presence beside me, in this very room!"

Mr. Vance, standing beside her chair, found his hand squeezed in a convulsive grasp. "I thought, ma'am, that he had already spoken to you—"

"Not himself," Mrs. Haygood confessed. So far, Jonathan had been able to communicate with her only through intermediaries, she explained. Messages had been delivered by Alexander the Great, Cornelius Vanderbilt, President Lincoln, her own grandfather (who had died in a madhouse but had completely recovered his senses in Heaven, she was relieved to learn) and lately by Dr. Beecher, who was still a little confused in his new quarters, having so recently passed on. All very interesting personages, she agreed, but what a mother's heart really wanted to hear was her son. Besides, a great deal of time was wasted by the emissaries, however well meaning they might be. The Commodore thought she wanted pointers on buying stocks; her grandfather, truth to tell, had never made much sense even when sane; and poor Dr. Beecher acted as if he were still on trial and kept refuting those calumnies about his womanizing (which she, for one, had *never* believed) so that it was hard at times for Jonathan to get a word in.

Getting a word in was just a manner of speaking, Ada quickly learned as a round table was cleared of its lamp and all encumbrances and four chairs drawn up. The spirits always began by rapping out their messages, Mrs. Haygood warned, although sometimes, if their thoughts came fast and furious, they called for paper. "You'll see Katie's fingers fly then—though you can't make heads or tails of it until you hold it up to a mirror." As for the rapping, Mrs. Haygood boasted that she was by now so well versed in the alphabet she could keep up with the most rapid fusillade.

No voices? No ethereal materializations? No unearthly hands suddenly taking one's own in an icy grasp? Ada expressed a deep disappointment.

"There are always charlatans to cast doubt upon the true guides to the Unseen World," Mrs. Haygood quelled Ada with an impatient glance. "You'll find no fake machinery here or gutta-percha limbs. Katie has no need for them, have you, Katie? You are not the first disbeliever she will have convinced before the night is over—"

"Now, now, Louisa, you know I promise nothing. All depends upon the spirits." If there were skeptics present, Katie Fox did not seem to care. Comfort was her paramount concern. She rejected the chair Mrs. Haygood had provided, directed Mr. Vance to pull up another one and tried out various cushions to obtain the best support for her back. Having kicked her slippers off, she was finally at ease and gave the order for turning down the lamps. A circle of joined hands was formed, with Mrs. Haywood on Ada's left, Mr. Vance on her right. In the first moments of silence in the semidarkness, Ada felt the flow of magnetism was unevenly conducted. She could not fault Mr. Vance for exerting any undue pressure and yet there was a definite sensation in her right hand that she found increasingly hard to ignore.

Nothing happened. The silence extended. The growing dampness of Mrs. Haygood's hand attested her anxiety. Katie suddenly broke the circle—"for a wee dram of restorative," she said, clearing her throat. The quick swig from a tiny silver flask must have given her the psychic strength she needed, for no sooner had they rejoined hands than a series of sharp popping sounds was heard. Ada jumped—like a string of firecrackers going off, she thought, wondering if some device had been set in that far corner of the room from which the noise seemed to come. But such dark suspicions evaporated as the cracks continued, changing position, hovering now almost at her ear. Mrs. Haygood's grasp tightened as she addressed the empty air.

"Jonathan? Is it you, Jonathan, at last?"

Two sharp raps, so close to Ada's head, she flinched.

"No?" Mrs. Haygood translated. "Who are you then?"

"MAMA."

"Mama!" It was the disconcerted cry of one opening the door to a completely unexpected, not too welcome guest. "I was going to ask about you, Mama, but—"

"ADA. ADA. MY CHILD."

"Oh." Mrs. Haygood gave a very deflated sigh, and frowned at Ada. "It's for you."

Presented for the first time with such a "telegram," Ada did not know what to do.

"Do hurry up and ask her what you want to know," Mrs. Haygood said impatiently, "I'll read the raps for you."

Ada cleared her throat. "Mama—er—how are you, Mama?"

"SUBLIME. SUBLIMELY SUBLIME."

Ada struggled to think of something else to ask. "I am glad you are happy, Mama," she temporized.

"I THOUGHT I WAS HAPPY ON EARTH, BUT WHAT IS EARTHLY HAPPINESS COMPARED TO THE HAPPINESS I KNOW NOW?"

"That's nice, Mama," Ada said feebly. That earthly happiness had been well concealed.

"I WATCH OVER YOU, MY CHILD. I WEEP WITH JOY TO SEE HOW PRETTY YOU HAVE GROWN. WAS AT BANQUET LAST NIGHT WITH EMERSON WHO SAID HE HAD HEARD FROM OTHERS I HAD BEAUTIFUL DAUGHTER. MADE ME PROUD."

Ada was stunned. Miraculous changes were wrought in spirits freed of the baser matter of this world. The Mama she had known paid no such compliments. *Praise to the face is open disgrace* was the closest she had come. To Ada's dismay, tears sprang into her eyes. If only it were true, if only Mama had looked on her with such loving eyes, spoken in so tender a tone. "Oh, Mama!" She could not help the broken cry.

Mrs. Haygood's patience was wearing thin. "That's all very well," she said, "but if you have no message from *my* child, would you please remove yourself and allow someone else to get through!"

Such rudeness had its effect. The raps grew fainter, erupting in ever sparser bursts.

"TELL PAPA—DEAR AS EVER TO ME—WAITING FOR HIM TO JOIN

ME—ROSE-COVERED COTTAGE—EVERYTHING HERE JUST AS HE LIKES—"

The raps ceased. "How strange—" Ada began, but was hushed by Mrs. Haygood.

"Concentrate. Think only of Jonathan. I count on you, Mr. Vance!"

Silence. Minutes passed. There was only the sound of Mrs. Haygood's rapid shallow breathing, and heavier breathing from Katie's direction. A stentorian sound. Almost—oh dear! Ada thought, fighting back a wave of giggles, she *is!* Katie was unmistakably snoring.

"Katie!" Mrs. Haygood cried out. "Not tonight! You mustn't—"

It was no use. The sitting was over. The other-worldly spirits were no match for the harder spirits Katie had imbibed. She was not fully awakened even by the turning up of lights and Mrs. Haygood's insistent shaking. In her befuddled state, she required the assistance of Mr. Vance on one side and Mrs. Haygood on the other to make it to a bedroom upstairs.

"I hope you will not be discouraged by this one failure. It happens now and then," Mrs. Haygood apologized to Mr. Vance as he assisted Ada with her wrap. "These sittings take so much out of her, I'm afraid she resorts at times to artificial stimulants. Just to keep her strength up, you understand. You *will* give it another chance, won't you? I beg you, Mr. Vance, do not abandon my poor boy now!"

Mr. Vance assured her he was still at her service, would await her call. Ada received no such invitation. Mrs. Haygood could hardly manage a polite goodbye. Ada could see the besotted woman held her responsible for the wasted evening—all that time taken up by a gab-bag of a mama! Once again, poor Jonathan couldn't get a word in edgewise.

For some distance, only the tinkling of bells disturbed the night, as if the evening's experience required a heavy digestive quiet. Ada's explosive laugh shattered the silence and the tall hemlock they were passing under shook in responsive glee, powdering them with snow.

"It's the thought of that banquet! I was wondering what they sit on, or if they sit at all!" The thought sent her off again. "Besides, I doubt if even in heaven Mama would dine with Mr. Emerson—he was far too much of a freethinker for her taste."

Mr. Vance's amusement was more restrained. "Still you must admit she was very clever in producing those sounds—I have yet to figure out the means. Her hands were being held and I kept an almost indecent watch for any movement of her limbs—there was none I could detect. I was wondering if your scientific observation uncovered something I missed?"

Was he making fun of her? Ada would have preferred to forget that she had ever called for an open mind on the subject of spiritualism. "Admittedly Mr. Vance, you were right and I was wrong," she said stiffly. "The woman is a fraud and that's all there is to it."

And yet for one moment . . . ADA, ADA, MY CHILD . . . she had felt a prickling of the skin, her heart had jumped, almost she had believed, she had *wanted* to believe. . . . "She is nothing but a drunken slut," Ada said, grinding her teeth. Had she but known it, her face had the same hard unforgiving look she had so hated to see on Mama's.

Mr. Vance was taken aback by her vehemence. He suggested, in an offensively calming way, that some people might find Katie Fox deserving more of pity than of censure.

"We seem to have reversed positions," she said and pointed out that when she changed her mind, it was in accordance with her training in a scientific discipline. A *priori* reasoning must always give way before the experimental evidence.

"That is very modern. As is befitting a Modern Woman." He bobbed his head in the suggestion of a complimentary bow. "You will find me downright medieval, I'm afraid, but I believe our opinions are more a function of our humours than any scientific evaluation of the facts. I myself am of the dyspeptic type—no doubt you'd find my bile running more black than yellow. Mr. Carlyle is my man, at least when I consider mankind en masse. A swarmery, a universal rottenness, a quagmire of mendacities—what else has he called it? I'm with him there and go him one better. At least he has his heroes, his Cromwells, those whom he considers as competent chargé d'affaires for mankind's business—Dr. Haygood would recognize them as the elect—whereas I think as little of them as of the rest. In my book, they cost far more than they are worth. Which, one could say, makes me a good democrat. You can see that with such predilections, I am pleasantly surprised by everyone I meet— none has yet lived up to my expectations."

Ada was surprised, both by what he said and his manner. His playfulness was suddenly anemic, the bones of earnestness stuck out. She was surprised as well by his choice of humour. Phlegmatic, she would have chosen to describe him.

"I suppose what you are saying is that I am too sanguine?"

"Humourously speaking, yes. I see you soaring high above us all, like an aeronaut whose balloon has carried him out of the earth's atmosphere into a purer ether. So far away, how lovely the earth must look, spinning like a top painted blue and green. But then to descend, expecting to find only the most beautiful vistas, to land instead in a desert or swamp or blighted forest or stinking jungle or, heaven forbid, in Hell's Kitchen or the Bowery! What a comedown!"

"Humph." Ada did not care for that aery picture. Besides, when he spoke of her, the playfulness grew thick, she was no longer sure what lay beneath. "You are harder on the woman than I am. *I* did not call her a swamp, a stinking jungle, anything like that."

"No, no," he laughed. "I was but trying to see her through your eyes. What I saw is that she means no harm. I very strongly felt that. I spoke to Mrs. Haygood when we were putting her to bed as to the fee she charges. Do you know she has asked only the expenses of the trip—which is all that Mrs. Haygood can contrive without her husband's knowledge. That speaks well of her, don't you think? As for the drinking, yes, there's that, but to be exploited from childhood, to be exhibited in public like one of Mr. Barnum's freaks, is hardly conducive

162

to the formation of a gentle retiring female character. And obviously she has had recent reverses—"

"Oh really, Mr. Vance, that is no excuse. Everyone has reverses. Not everyone takes to drink." It was a statement delivered with a superior tilt of the chin. "And to be frank, I am losing patience with Mrs. Haygood as well. Whatever blows life may send me, I hope I bear them with greater fortitude, less foolishness." Ada's declaration was one of conviction, not hope.

"I am sure you will, Miss Traherne," Mr. Vance murmured. "But then you are an extraordinary young woman."

Now what did that mean? She was not even sure it was a compliment. Immediately she determined to extract one less ambiguous. She snuggled deeper into her wrap and held up the dark cylinder of fur as if to protect her face against the cold. The eyes thus left revealed took on an enticing Moorish look, she was convinced. Mr. Vance, however, did not seem affected by her wiles. He kept up an easy flow of talk—all harmless compliments and mild jokes and casual observations on the fine effect of moonlight on the snow—as if they were circling each other in a ballroom under the eyes of the most watchful gossips. Perhaps he wished he were back at Kirkewode, nibbling chocolates from Rose Deventer's hand. If so, it was some consolation to know he was headed for a fall. Ada could not forget that afterglow of passion, the overwhelming aura of satisfied lust with which the lady had returned after putting her errant husband to bed. By comparison with *that,* this present interest in Mr. Vance's manly form was but the merest passing fancy.

The evening had been a waste. Katie Fox had proved to be a tosspot, Mr. Vance a block of ice. The horses were pulled up before the entrance to the conservatory and Mr. Vance stood waiting to help her out. Ada gave him credit for a certain thoughtfulness, hearing that he had prevailed on Caxton to not wait up. "You'll find this door open," he said. "I'll lock up when I return from the stables."

She made one last attempt to thaw the block of ice, tottering just enough in her descent to find herself within his arms. A flustered apology, a tremulous smile, and she would be gone, leaving behind the searing imprint of her body to torment him the rest of the night. To her amazement, one hand grasped her back hair and pulled her head up. It seemed to last forever, that kiss, but she had no clear idea of time, nor of any thought in her head. When he released her, she could think of nothing more original to say than, "How dare you!"

"What do you think I am?" he asked in a voice she hardly recognized. "One of Miss Alcott's boys?"

"A gentleman, I thought."

"A comedy of errors," he said, all blandness again.

She hated him for finding his composure so quickly, while she stood there, her mind still awhirl, watching him drive off with a salute of the whip as if they had parted in all propriety.

Furious with herself for having shown so little presence of mind (how dare you! was what women said in those cheap story papers), she mounted the stairs with unladylike haste to gain the privacy of her apartment and opened the door on a startled Marie, caught napping in a chair. It was a relief to transfer her rage to such a deserving object. "What the devil are you doing here? Why aren't you in bed?"

"I was waiting for you, ma'mselle, for the undressing. I am all better now, *voyez-vous*. Poof, the pain is gone, as the good doctor promise."

Ada glared at her. It seemed the vilest treachery, such a quick recovery, as if Marie had taken Papa's side against her and was determined to prove her wrong.

"Oh, go to bed, Marie," she said in exasperation. "I can undress myself."

She had to push the protesting girl out. Immediately she went to the mirror to see if there were visible bruises on her lips. Never had she been kissed like that! Francis had never dared pry her lips apart and—only the French did that, she had thought. And probably only to their mistresses, not their wives. There seemed to be no indelible mark. But even as she stared at her face, a dull red swept up her throat into her cheeks. A comedy of errors, he had said. Her head clearer now, she could fill in what he had left unsaid. If she had thought he was a gentleman, he had *thought* she was a lady. Had Mrs. Deventer told him about her expulsion from school and he now thought her *loose?*

The torment she had wished on Nicholas Vance was fated to be hers. Marie had warmed the sheets and the enormous room was almost cozy from a fire only now beginning to die. But in its flickering light, the bedstead's amorous design thrust itself on her sleepless eyes. The fat cupids made no attempt to conceal their lascivious leer. Pudgy fingers pointed straight at her, and she knew why.

Chapter 11

ALMOST she could like this city. The noise, the traffic, the hunched, nervous, shouldering herds of people, like cattle about to stampede, had an exhilarating effect after the close confinement of Kirkewode. On Rose Deventer too, for when they entered the house on Second Avenue, she sniffed approvingly the air—a mix of fresh polish and hothouse flowers testifying to servants on their toes—and swore she felt like an old workhorse kicking over the traces whenever she came into town.

"You don't look the part," Ada said, smiling at the thought of this elegant woman pulling any kind of load. In her high-plumed hat and frogged and tasseled coat she most closely resembled a gorgeous hussar of the Russian court. Still Ada was equally infected with a holiday spirit; there was pleasure enough just in thinking of what she had escaped from, she hardly needed to anticipate joys to come.

She had dreaded facing Nicholas Vance in broad daylight, but to her relief they had left so early only the servants were up and about. An embarrassment, if not avoided, at least postponed. With Papa she had not been so lucky. When she came downstairs, her new dressing case in hand, Caxton handed her Papa's note summoning her to his office.

"You seem to be getting along rather well with Mrs. Deventer." He was staring out of a long narrow window, his hands locked behind him. A quick glance at his desk showed Ada that the journal with Fitz's paper had disappeared, but apparently he did not intend to discuss it.

"She has been most generous, Papa." Ada addressed his back uncertainly. "I hope you are pleased?"

He turned around at that, but Ada found his face just as hard to read. "Are you being so amiable in order to please me? Or is there something in you that responds to her on its own— a case of like attracting like. You are a female, after all."

"I can't deny that, Papa," Ada said. The interview promised to be unpleasant. Definitely an accustory tone, but of what was he accusing her? Of having, like Rose Deventer, too frivolous a cast of mind? Once he had complained on opposite grounds— that she occupied herself too little with what were properly feminine concerns. *Why can't you be like other women?*—that was what he used to ask. Now it was, *Just like other women.* The same contempt.

"Sometimes I have looked at you, Ada, and seen your mama. She had that same overweening confidence in her judgment. But recently when I look at you, I am more apt to see Mrs. Deventer. I don't think I like the change."

Ada endured the reproving shake of his head in silence. It would be useless to ask why he did not look at her and see just Ada. For him, Woman was a separate genus, subdivided into several species, into one of which she must fit before he felt at ease.

It was not necessary for her to talk at all. Papa preferred that kind of vocal exercise so popular in elocution classes, where the other party to the conversation was invisible and unheard, whose comments were assumed from the progress of the monologue. "I am not blind, you know," he said now, as resentfully as if she had just questioned the acuity of his vision. "I see what goes on between her and Mr. Vance. That does not concern me, in fact I welcome it, a new interest will make it easier for her to accept the changes I have in mind. But when I see you display the same interest—no, no, don't deny it, Ada, I tell you I am not blind—in a man who has nothing to recommend him but his youth and passable good looks and a more than passable ability to mimic his betters, I wonder if I do right to leave you in her hands even for so short a time, if you are not beginning to fashion your tastes on hers."

Ada was too furious to attempt a denial. "Have you finished, Papa? The carriage has been brought around, I don't want to keep Mrs. Deventer waiting."

"All I wish to say, Ada, is that you must not count too much on this new life Mrs. Deventer plans for you. When you return, you may find that I have different plans. I trust you will approve of them."

"Life is much simpler without men, isn't it, my dear?" Rose said now, closely paralleling Ada's own thoughts. They were due at Madame Modeska's for a final fitting and Mrs. Deventer was behaving almost girlishly, hooking arms and forcing Ada, like a partner in a dance, to match her jaunty step. Once inside the carriage, however, she qualified that cavalier dismissal of the other sex. "Heavens, I almost forgot—admittedly men do have their uses." She leaned forward and changed her instructions to Duncan. They would first stop at the Fifth Avenue Bank. "Speaking of money," she began and, making an appropriate descent into seriousness, passed on some matronly advice. As soon as she was married, Ada must coax her husband to open a bank account for her—in her own name, Mrs. Deventer was very specific about that. Every woman should know how to handle her own pin money, Mr. Deventer always said.

Ada turned restless at yet another quote from that great man, but Rose mistook the quiver of boredom for girlish trepidation. "Really, Ada, it's not so difficult as it sounds, although I too had palpitations at first. But the gentlemen at the bank are most helpful in explaining the figures, and I must say very understanding about an occasional small overdraft or two. The fact is I am almost always in balance now. I take some pride in that, although I know there are some who believe it's not quite ladylike to be able to add a column of figures."

It amused Ada, who had mastered the calculus on her own during a summer's holiday, that Mrs. Deventer should look so complacent at having acquired that rudimentary ability. And when they entered the bank and passed into a special parlor set aside for the feminine trade, her amusement grew. Only a discreetly placed row of tellers' cages betrayed the fact that this was a bank. Otherwise, the rich carpeting, the plush-covered, heavily fringed chairs, the little tables so domestically arranged made it easy for any lady to believe she had not left her home. A cheerful fire burned in a small hearth faced with marble columns and topped by a classic pediment adorned with sculptured figures, all wearing togas and straining athletically at various mercantile pursuits. There was steaming coffee in a silver urn, in case a lady needed to steady her nerves. For direr emergencies, there was an escritoire—a charming piece of Sheraton design—from which she might dash off urgent pleas for help, stationery and pen and ink all provided. How ubiquitous, those little writing desks—they were to be found in every public room set aside for ladies. In hotel lobbies, in railroad depots, in theater powder rooms—now in a bank. Were all women presumed to have the epistolary stamina of Richardson's Pamela, eternally scribbling away en route, entr'acte, or just in passing?

Leaving Ada to sip coffee on a couch, Mrs. Deventer transacted her business with a whiskered gentleman behind the gilded bars and returned, triumphantly jiggling a much heavier purse. Though the coffee had been her suggestion, she now looked impatiently at the cup in Ada's hands. "We must be up and at 'em, Ada!" she urged, chuckling at the military turn of phrase.

All morning, as they briskly made their rounds, she retained the air of an ardent general, eager to engage the enemy, urging on her troops. But not so brave, those troops. Ada confessed to a growing cowardice at the thought of her approaching debut, which not even the good fit of her new gowns could check. It was one thing to imagine cozy scenes, always comfortably tête-à-tête, in which love-crazed suitors threw themselves at her feet; it was quite another to enter a ballroom and run the gamut of four hundred pairs of eyes. She listened to Mrs. Deventer discuss with the modiste what she should wear to the opera the following night, the two of them jabbering over her head as if she were not there, making her feel like a child again, having to stand still while Mama gossiped with her friends.

"You say she appears before the public for the first time? Then perhaps the white lace, with the little Damascene jacket— a *jeune fille*, you understand. . . ."

Mrs. Deventer did not agree. At her formal presentation, the girl would wear white, of course, but there was no need to proclaim her purity ad nauseam. What was wanted for this occasion was something striking—a gown that would draw every eye, turn every head toward the Deventer box. "It is our opening salvo, madame, and I intend to make it felt!"

Between them, it was decided that Ada would wear the original Modeska creation, even more magnificent in execution than in illustration. Madame even granted that pink was a better color than blue. *Mais certainement,* it could be ready in time—all hands would be put to work and it would be delivered early the next afternoon.

The vision of Ada in the pink gown, basted and pinned though it was, fired Mrs. Deventer with an impatient desire to hear the new Wagner opera. "I can hardly wait," she chortled and consulted the diamond-studded watch pinned to her waist as if literally counting the hours.

"We are running later than I planned. Perhaps I should not have asked Mr. Vance to come down in advance, tomorrow

170

would have done as well. You will have to entertain him, my dear, I must have my beauty rest."

Ada squealed—a pin had stuck her as she turned suddenly around. "Mr. Vance? Why is he coming into town?"

"My dear girl, did you think we would attend the opera without an escort? I have commandeered Henry's box, but not Henry, I assure you. Not even for you, my pet, will I endure my dear brother-in-law's company for an entire evening. Besides," Rose's deep chuckle erupted, "Mr. Deventer warned me not to be seen with him in public lest his credit go up. Henry could double his debt, you know, on the strength of that alone."

Mr. Vance had yet to arrive when they returned, and Mrs. Deventer immediately disappeared upstairs. That beauty rest, Ada assumed, tired enough to seek some herself. But there was not much rest in rehearsing over and over her impending meeting with Mr. Vance. Shrivel him with a cold cutting look? Act as if nothing had happened? Tossing on her bed, she played it out both ways, unable to decide.

Dressing for dinner, she was glad she had left Marie back at Kirkewode. In her present mood, she could not have borne with clumsy hands or inept fiddling with her hair. She, who never had headaches, felt as if in removing her hat she had left the hat pins sticking in her scalp. She dipped her handkerchief in eau de cologne and applied it to throbbing temples. But when Mama's remedy proved ineffectual, she knocked timidly on Mrs. Deventer's door and asked Maxwell if there was any camphor about. The door, opened only a crack, was closed again, leaving her outside while Maxwell went off to look. She could hear Rose's indistinct mumble. Something seemed to be smothering that stage-trained voice which usually carried so well. It took some time for Maxwell to return with the vial, looking as if she disapproved of headaches too.

"We will not be down to dinner tonight," the dresser regally announced. "I'm to give you this note, so you will understand we are not to be disturbed again."

The note was so impregnated with Rose's perfume as to need no other signature. *Maxwell will have it that I must prepare for our evening at the opera as if it were my own opening night. Poor woman, she feels nostalgia for long-ago times. With me it's not so much nostalgia as pure stagefright. I leave Mr. Vance to you.*

On her way down, Ada passed the footman bringing up a tray. "But that's raw!" she exclaimed at the sight of an uncovered platter lined with thin slices of the palest veal.

"Oh, not to eat, miss." Thomas had a tolerant smirk for the foolish fads of ladies. "This here's to be poulticed on her face. Cook tells me Maxwell has the recipe straight from Miss Lily Langtry's dresser. Still I wouldn't be surprised if soon enough madam don't tear into it with her teeth, considering what's waiting downstairs for her dinner. One slice of toast, a piece of fish not large enough to make one good swallow—starvation rations, I call it, and it's a standing order until further notice."

Her curiosity satisfied—Mrs. Deventer was submitting to the austerities of the Banting diet—Ada braved herself to face Mr. Vance. She found him in the drawing room, pouring himself a glass of sherry, and quickly decided on the cold cutting look. Like the cad he was, he refused to shrivel. As for her second choice—pretending nothing had happened—he was preempting that.

"I understand Mrs. Deventer is indisposed and we dine alone," he said pleasantly.

"Yes," she said, refusing a glass of sherry.

"Just a headache, according to Maxwell. I am sure she will be recovered tomorrow night. I know that you are looking forward to the opera."

"Yes." Magically, her own very real headache was gone.

"Perhaps you prefer Madeira. There's a very good bottle here. Are you sure you wouldn't like a glass?"

"Yes. I mean, no. Yes, I'm sure."

"See here, Miss Traherne." There was an abrupt directness in that cool address. "I will *not* apologize for last night. I am well aware of the great plans afoot for your coming-out, and that you

172

are not likely to waste your favors on one so humbly positioned in life as I. Like a cat about to venture out on serious hunting, you have been sharpening your claws on me. Don't do that again, please. In return, I shall keep my humble place."

Ada felt an unsettling mixture of emotions—part shame, knowing he was right, and part resentment at being called to task like a schoolgirl. "You don't do the humble bit very well." That was resentment speaking. But in the end she could not deny the shame. "You are right, of course, the apology should be mine. From now on, shall we be just friends?" she held out her hand.

"By all means."

He gave her hand a quick formal pump and they went in to dinner, with Ada vaguely dissatisfied with this resolution of their differences.

Mr. Vance had an amazing knack for pretending that nothing had happened. Here we are, Ada remarked to herself after dinner, lazing about in a most comradely way. To her surprise, she was very entertained by his stories of the Street, all garnered in his brief employ at the Deventer office—and he as financially naive as she when he first took the job as clerk, he swore. Ada wondered how she could have found the subject such a bore in Mr. Witten's mouth. Not that she fully understood the market operations which so aroused the risibilities of Mr. Witten and, she saw now, even the reluctant admiration of Mr. Vance. The basic principles, he assured her, were quite easy to understand. Rob Roy's code nicely summed them up: *The good old rule sufficeth then, the simple plan, that they should take who have the power, and they should keep who can.*

"Why do they call him Mad Jack still?" Ada suddenly asked. "He earned that in his youth, but by now he should have lived it down."

"The name has not been altered, but the meaning has. The Mad Jackal of Wall Street, that's what it stands for now. Not a

173

bad description, I'd say, from what I've learned so far. Mr. Deventer has a way of letting others make the kill, then stripping the carcass clean."

And had she really seen Mr. Deventer in the flesh, he asked again, still incredulous of her good fortune. *And did you once see Deventer plain, and did he stop to speak to you,* he might have been saying. Such awed curiosity was all right when applied to a Shelley, but not to a man whose only claim to fame was a scavenger's talent for making money.

Browning's lines suggested poetry as a welcome change of subject. They might read aloud to each other—did not Mr. Vance find that a pleasant way of passing time? Agreeable as ever, Mr. Vance accompanied her to the library, but refused to name a poet, insisted that she make the choice. With a glad cry of recognition, she pulled out a copy of *The Princess.*

"Do you know Lord Tennyson?" she asked, passing him the volume.

He thumbed through it thoughtfully. "I do recall a *Princess Ida*—could it be the same?" And without looking at her, he began to sing, almost under his breath:

> *Pouting lips that seem to say*
> *Kiss me, kiss me, kiss me*
> *Though I die of shame*
> *That's the kind of maid*
> *That sets my heart aflame. . . .*

Ada furiously snatched the book from him. "That travesty!" It was high time he was introduced to the original version of this great battle cry for women's rights. Nothing would further his education more.

How it had moved her at first reading—this tale of a princess who rejected her princely suitor to found a women's college away from all men and there to breed a new race of women, not mere fierce Amazons but philosopher-queens. Once she had thought the Princess Ida too fiercely set against man's love, but Francis had since taught her otherwise.

To share the book, they sat together on the sofa, closer than Ada liked, but that could not be helped. There were more longueurs than she remembered; impatiently she decided they should skip the greater part of the prologue. "We'll start here with the question: are there heroic women living now?" She took it upon herself to give the answer:

> *. . . there are thousands now*
> *such women, but convention beats them down:*
> *It is but bringing up; no more than that:*
> *You men have done it: how I hate you all!*

Her voice rang out with such fervor that Mr. Vance drew back in alarm, calling it unfair unless he had equally strong lines to read as a mere man. Ada assured him that he would: Cyril was surely gross enough and the King was all that was traditionally male.

Ada thought he played the King too well, intoning with great relish that man was the hunter, woman was his game. But she had not recalled that final love scene. What playacting this man was capable of. She actually felt a thrill, hearing those last lines: "*Indeed I love thee; come, yield thyself up: my hopes and thine are one: accomplish thou my manhood and thyself . . .*"

"It is later than I thought," she said quickly, "I must get my beauty sleep," and berated herself even as she broke away for the vapidity of that flustered remark. No Princess Ida she, but the soft and milky rabble of womankind.

Eyes fixed on the stunning figure descending the stairs, Ada wondered how she could ever have thought Rose Deventer almost plain. The color of her gown—an unrelieved black— had given Ada a momentary shock (obviously intended), but no one could deny it was a perfect foil for such fair beauty. Around that white tower of a throat, a magnificent strand of pearls was wrapped three times, the motif repeated in triple rows of seed pearls on her skirt. The only other decorative touch was a white aigrette that curled over the blond head like an exotic bird's crest.

Beside that stark beauty, Ada felt Madame Modeska's pink creation pale into insignficance. How could she have been so misled by the image in her mirror, by Maxwell's grunt of approval, by the receptive widening of Mr. Vance's eyes when, a few minutes earlier, she had descended those stairs? She was as nothing compared to this glorious Venus—look how Mr. Vance rushed forward to assist her with her wrap—and there was surprisingly little comfort in those old adages of Mama's about the superiority of moral over physical beauty.

The modest reappraisal of her own looks had the perverse effect of making it easier, not harder, to bear the limelight which her shyness had so dreaded. As they took their seats in Henry Deventer's box and Rose nudged her with delighted whispers—"See, every head is turned to you, my dear"—Ada remained tolerably at ease, knowing those stares must be directed at her companion, not herself. All through the prologue, while more fashionable patrons trickled in, the ogling continued. Ada wished that the enormous gas chandelier could be completely extinguished; perhaps in total darkness even this restless audience would quiet down. On stage, day was breaking, Siegfried entered in full armor, then Brünnhilde leading her white steed. Never had Ada heard music of such grandeur, such an intricate interweaving of themes. Hands clasping the rail, she leaned forward, lost to everything about her as the wild joy of the Valkyries subsided to a more human register, befitting a hero who was yet a man, a woman who was yet a hero. . . .

"Mrs. Astor's box is still empty—oh, I forgot, Monday is her night," Rose said. Finding Ada unresponsive, she turned to chat with Mr. Vance, who had taken a modest seat behind them. "What's happening now—is it time for intermission?" Informed softly that it was but an interlude between the prologue and the first act, she raked the first parterre of boxes with her glasses. "That must be Alva Vanderbilt, there couldn't be two iron jaws like that. . . . I think there, right across from us, must be the Whitneys, he *is* handsome, isn't he? . . . And that should be the Huntingtons, one of our Barefoot Millionaires, Ada; so that's the widow woman he married. . . ." Whenever the volume of sound recalled her to the action on stage, she demanded a quick summary of events from Mr. Vance. She could not understand a word of what was being sung, she complained.

"Oh, Mrs. Deventer, it's all in the program notes," Ada said, trying to control her temper.

Mr. Vance leaned forward to graciously explain. "Siegfried is promising to deliever Brünnhilde to Gunther in exchange for Gunther's sister."

"But isn't this Siegfried married to Brünnhilde? I'm sure that's what you said."

"He's been given a love potion, ma'am, that has made him forget his previous vows."

"Humph! Just the sort of an excuse a man *would* give."

To her obvious relief, Act One finally came to an end with a last crashing chord. For a moment Ada felt shattered, like a piece of crystal that had responded too perfectly to a note of a certain pitch. "Oh, isn't Lilli Lehmann wonderful, Mrs. Deventer!"

Mrs. Deventer's attention was elsewhere. Beyond recommending the Banting diet to every member of the company, she had no time to waste on the downfall of the gods. There were weightier matters on her mind. This was the time for receiving visits—look how crowded were those other boxes. Of course, since she had not made her presence in town formally known, they need fear no such invasion. Still it was for this moment she had endured all that caterwauling—

"Now, Ada, don't draw back, you are here to be *seen!*

Though of course you must appear completely oblivious to it all. Like this—mark me—you lay one arm along the rail, give a half-turn, lift the neck so (notice how that makes a lovely line from chin to fingertips) and look distantly into space. I'd say, about the level of that chandelier." Having induced Ada to smile, she chuckled herself, but without moving, keeping undisturbed the design of elegance she had created with a sweep of throat, a twist of white shoulder. "There is no better training for a woman than the stage, my dear, no matter what her station is to be in life. If we are to be honest with each other, it's all acting, isn't it? Only, if we're lucky, we get to choose our parts."

Mr. Vance professed a need to stretch his legs. Would Miss Traherne care to accompany him into the corridor for an ice? Ada would have gladly, but Rose said no, it was poor strategy to join the crush outside; that would allow a few too close a view, others none at all. Besides, who knows, someone might drop in after all. "You see?" she crowed, as the door to their box opened. But with the entrance of their visitor, all her graciousness curdled in an instant. "Henry! I thought it was understood you were *not* to—"

"Ah, my dear sister! How could I resist? Not only Rose in full bloom, but this sweet young bud—"

Smiling down at her—red-faced, pop-eyed, mustached and big-bellied—was the stupid coxcomb, the insulting fool she had encountered in the dining room of the Fifth Avenue Hotel! A stunned Ada could hardly take in the curt introduction Rose was performing.

". . . my husband's brother, Henry Deventer—Miss Traherne. . . ." And oh yes, Rose had almost overlooked him, so modestly withdrawn in the corner there—Mr. Nicholas Vance.

They shook hands. Uncle and nephew shook hands as if they had never met before! Ada's opera glasses slipped out of her lap, she leaned over, glad of any opportunity to hide the shock, the confusion that must be evident in her face.

"Allow me, Miss Traherne." Henry Deventer's face was redder

than ever from the exertion of bending over. Ada could see the strain of recollection in his eyes. "Have we not met before? Perhaps at Newport? Saratoga? But impossible—would I forget?" Ada averted her own gaze, thankful that he had forgotten.

Rose's playful supposition was being realized under her nose—Henry Deventer was making clear to all below that family harmony had been restored and with it, it was to be hoped, his credit.

"I tell you, sister, the world's agog tonight—you have no idea how many gentlemen have approached me for an introduction to your young friend, they were begging me to bring them to my box, but you see I obey your slightest whim, I came alone—"

"As I recall my slightest whim, it was to see neither hide nor hair of you tonight."

The full lips pursed in sad reproof, but the stiff spiked ends of his mustache still projected jauntily in the air. "Very well, Rose, I'll be off."

Rose gave a not so delicate snort. "Yes, now that you've accomplished your purpose. Before the night is over, you'll be borrowing money from some fool who believes you're back in Jack's good graces—"

Henry smiled. In full view of all the curious eyes fixed on this box, he had managed to kiss her fingertips before she could withdraw her captured hand. "My dear sister, your mere presence in my box established *that*. But should there be any doubting Thomases, your smile, Rose—do smile, Rose—will confirm it. Now that you plan to come out of hiding and join the world, better all round to bury the past, don't you agree?"

Rose considered him thoughtfully. Then smiled. "You *are* a blackguard, Henry. No wonder Jack will have nothing to do with you."

He looked fatuously pleased at so fine a compliment. "I always thought you and I could deal famously together, Rose. Ah, there's the bell, so ta-ta for now." He made Ada a creaky bow. "Miss Traherne, I am the envy of every man in this house." Something in the boldness of his admiring glance sent

179

a shiver of remembrance up her spine: it was Mr. Deventer again staring down at her from the balcony. Instinctively her hand crept up to cover her décolletage. She quickly called herself a fool—these two were brothers, a fraternal resemblance was to be expected, the eyes—not the look—were the same. And yet different too. A worrying distinction, it hovered on the edge of consciousness, important to make.

But then Henry Deventer was gone, with the most distant of nods to a Mr. Vance who sprang politely to his feet. From the orchestra arose an ominous, malevolent dedication to eternal hate. Though seemingly intent on the moonlit stage, Ada gave no thought to the greed of the Nibelungs or Siegfried's fate. Nicholas Vance was all she had attention for—or whatever was his name. Mr. Vance by any other name would be just as sly, deceitful, treacherous, underhanded. . . . Pretending to be a poor, upward struggling, decent, hard-working young man, he had certainly taken her in.

Wagner's great work had become nothing more than a musical accompaniment to her own thoughts. The Ring motif was sounded, Brünnhilde saw the flash of Rhinegold on Siegfried's finger and knew herself betrayed. Ada saw the Harvard ring instead. *His* ring, of course. A bad mistake to leave it on, but how smoothly the man had lied his way out. The dark cry for vengeance from the orchestra pit merely echoed what was going on in Ada's heart. Like Siegfried with the Tarnhelm removed, Mr. Vance stood revealed for what he was—a Deventer by name as well as by blood. By now, Ada had it figured out: Mad Jack childless, Henry unmarried, but the youngest brother, Alsop, had a son. There was no other nephew Henry Deventer could lay claim to. Ada remembered the tribute Rose had paid to Alsop Deventer: a man of high moral standing, she had said. Proof indeed that acquired traits were not inherited. Ada caught her lower lip in a sharp vicious bite, thinking of how tender she had been for Mr. Vance's sensibilities, how careful of his pride, how convinced that he felt inferior because of his low estate. A Deventer.

"Look, Ada," Rose whispered, "half the boxes are emptying, there is no need to hear this thing out."

To look without seeing, to listen without hearing, Ada found it equally pointless to stay on. "You are quite right, Mrs. Deventer, we have accomplished all that can be hoped for here, we might as well go."

Mr. Vance looked at her with concern but Rose was too gratified to question such unexpected obedience, other than to ask sympathetically if Ada's headache had returned. No wonder if it had, she clucked, taking Ada's silence for a tacit yes. German music was enough to give anyone a headache, the Italians at least wrote melodies that could be sung.

In the carriage, with Mr. Vance seated opposite the two ladies, Ada found it difficult to avoid his eye. That presumption of a headache must excuse her withdrawn silence. She leaned her head back, closed her eyes and saw not one but a multiple array of Nicholas Vances. The arrogant Mr. Vance, as first seen in the hotel dining room, looking over his uncle's choice of an evening's light entertainment. The ingratiating Mr. Vance, snuggling up to Rose Deventer under the suicide tree. The free and easy Mr. Vance, as seen down a servant's stairwell, making bets with a beer-drinking Slade. The attentive Mr. Vance, drawing her out with skillful questions on a quiet Sunday promenade. The disheveled Mr. Vance, naked to the waist, trading blows with the ex-sparring partner of the great John L. The impulsive Mr. Vance, all rough passion, kissing her full on the mouth—that too all pretense, like his other playacting. . . .

"Oh my dear, it's bad, is it?" Rose said pityingly. "I do wish I had some camphor with me, this jouncing about can't be much help."

Ada said she could bear it. Certainly she could bear it. It was nothing to her what strange parts Henry Deventer's nephew chose to play. Mad Jack's nephew too—the thought startled her into opening her eyes. She met straight on Mr. Vance's concerned gaze and quickly shut them again. How could he expect to pose as a stranger to his own uncle? Except that, considering

181

how long the brothers had been estranged, it was likely he had not been seen since a child.

But why, why, why? The question pounded in her head, almost convincing her she did have a headache. A man of such protean aspects, what could he be but a spy. A spy for Henry Deventer, hoping to foster that uncle's interest in some unknown way. Mrs. Deventer had voiced more than once a suspicion that her household contained such a creature—was not Henry Deventer too well posted on her whereabouts?—but naturally she had thought a servant was the culprit. Instead it was this fair ornament to her table, this new member of her husband's inner council, handpicked by him but, if there was truth to Papa's bitter aspersions, according to her own specifications. There was some slight consolation in the fact that Rose Deventer had been made a fool of as much as she. Would that lady not be surprised? She must be told, loyalty required it. First thing in the morning, Ada decided. She rather relished knowing more than that knowing lady, if only for one night.

As soon as the front door closed behind them, an anxious Maxwell made a rush for the stairs, calling down, "You're back early, what happened, ducky, was there some unpleasantness?"

"Just like old times, Maxie," Rose reassured her. An endearment from the past, Ada supposed—it was the first time she had heard it. "I wish you could have been there, watching from the wings."

The dresser's ugliness was leavened for a moment by reflected glory, and then she faded back into the shadows. Rose was obviously torn by conflicting desires: to stay below with her young friends prolonging her recent triumph, or to rush upstairs to share the details with her loyal dresser. Ada thought it to her credit that she would not keep the impatient Maxwell waiting, but urged Ada and Mr. Vance to toast the still young evening with the champagne she had ordered to be ready in the drawing room.

"Oh, we were a smashing success, weren't we, Ada? Not a

speaking part as yet, but how they stared!" She gave Ada a happy squeeze and for a moment seemed about to treat Mr. Vance to the same. Was it Lily Langtry's recipe or the approval of the crowd that deserved the credit for a radiance that increased rather than diminished with the passing hours? Running up the stairs, it was she who seemed the giddiest of debutantes, while Ada and Mr. Vance, left behind so sober with each other, seemed to belong to an older generation.

Ada found herself being firmly led into the drawing room even as she protested that she was far too tired for any further celebration. "Just one glass," Mr. Vance urged, "you see, Thomas has it chilled already." Ada accepted her glass silently, still unable to meet his eye.

"Miss Traherne—" he spoke in an explosive rush, as if the popping of the cork had unstoppered words held back all evening—"I am sure that something happened during intermission to upset you—I know that ladies are inflicted with these sudden onsets of malaise—headaches—whatever you wish to call it . . . but I don't believe that explains this change in you. See, you refuse to even look at me, and were we not the best of friends last night? My conscience is clear—"

Ada did look at him then, with so ironic a lift of brow he had to take another running start. "My conscience *is* clear, Miss Traherne—or at least I am no more guilty than you. For there is only one thing I can think of to account for your altered behavior. Confess, you remembered from the start having seen me before—"

"I see you remembered too. I don't recall your mentioning it."

"But surely you understand a gentleman takes his cue from the lady. Since you gave no hint that you recalled our encounter, and particularly in view of its rather unpleasant nature, it would have been the height of rudeness to remind you—"

Ada had only contempt for such maneuvering. "The problem, Mr. Vance, is not where I saw you but with whom."

"Ah, you mean Mr. Henry Deventer," he said, with the air of one suddenly enlightened. "I can explain that—if I may?"

Ada knew another lie was brewing. Not that his well-disciplined face betrayed the slightest shiftiness—on the contrary, a franker, more open countenance would be hard to find. And yet by now she knew that face so well, she sensed what was coming by the slightest rearrangement of its features. Beware him when his face takes on that earnest set. The truth he always treats lightly.

"Please do," she said, with a smile of treacly sweetness. It had just occurred to her that she held an advantage yet. Poor fellow, he had no way of knowing that she had overheard him call his dinner companion "uncle." Was he about to admit the connection? She thought not.

How awesome his proficiency in deceit. Ada heard him out, fully appreciating the fine embellishments (including a dash here and there of truth) he gave so beautifully simple a lie. He had known—it was current gossip in the Deventer office downtown—that a replacement would soon be needed for Mr. Witten. He had wanted that promotion badly, and had blessed his luck when, by sheerest chance, he met Henry Deventer at the "trotters." Naturally he had invited the gentleman to dine with him, hoping a closer acquaintance would place him on the inside track. *That* might be considered duplicitous, he conceded, but a working man could not always afford the nicest motives, and a bit of pull never hurt in getting ahead.

"Besides, Miss Traherne, if I sinned, I paid for it fast enough. It didn't take me long to learn that Henry Deventer was on the outs with his brother. Far from being able to put in a good word for me, he needed someone to put in a good word for him. There I was, stuck with a check that cost me a week's wages, and nothing to show for it—surely that's punishment enough."

"But still you got the job."

"Yes, there's a moral in that somewhere, I suppose," he said, more earnestly than ever.

"Please, let's not look for *morals,* Mr. Vance."

"May I ask one small favor of you, Miss Traherne? Not to mention this to anyone at Kirkewode? I've been there long enough to know how strongly Mr. Deventer feels about his blood relations—if he heard I had been seen with his brother, he would boot me out without even giving me a chance to explain."

Serve him right to be booted out, sent packing. Away from Kirkewode forever.

"I can't promise that, I'm afraid." Ada had every intention of telling him right out he was a liar. A Deventer and a liar. Why then was she temporizing? "It has been a very wearing evening—all these revelations, Mr. Vance. Let me sleep on it. I promise this—I shan't do anything without first telling you." *That* was a pleasure she would not deny herself.

A small favor indeed, but he appeared grateful. With one rash gulp, Ada drained her glass and excused herself. There was no sign of the fatigue she had pleaded as she mounted the stairs with a light-hearted step. It was a cat-and-mouse game she was playing. A repulsive kind of game, she had always thought, pitying the mouse. She had never realized how much fun it was if you were the cat.

Chapter 12

ADA was as glad to return to Kirkewode as she had been to leave it. Papa could be exasperating, yes, but now in need of his advice, she headed straight for his office, knocked, received no answer. The door was locked. Caxton, consulted, astonished her with the news that Dr. Traherne had left Kirkewode early that very morning.

"Oh yes, he mentioned certain plans—" Ada said vaguely, not wishing to seem so ill-informed about her own papa's whereabouts. She managed not to grab the note Caxton delivered, strolled leisurely into the Rose Room, there to read it unobserved. Exasperating was the word for Papa, beyond a doubt. What did he tell her that she did not already know? She refolded the noncommunicative note as Mrs. Deventer, still aflush with last night's excitement, threw open the door.

"I know your papa hates to be disturbed at this hour, but I'm sure he will forgive us just this once. I want to tell him how beautiful his daughter was last night—" The eagerness was real, Ada saw. Rose had not even stopped to change out of her traveling attire. The tasseled rope beside the mantel was pulled before Ada could share her disappointing news. "I shall have Caxton tell him there is a medical emergency," Rose said with a wink, "that will bring him running."

"I am afraid—" Ada began timidly but with Caxton's entrance lost Mrs. Deventer's ear. To be the bearer of ill tidings was not an honor Ada cared to fight for.

"Gone? To the city?" The usually low contralto reached the register of a screech. A deep breath, and Rose spoke more calmly. "And no address where he may be reached?"

Caxton had the good sense to disappear as rapidly as he had appeared. One look at Rose's face—puffy and red as if she were breaking out from some ill-advised dish she had eaten—and Ada wished she could do the same. The silence—a mere matter of seconds—seemed to last forever. To Ada it was more terrifying than the ensuing storm. The alabaster model of the Brownings' hands, so lovingly intertwined, went flying across the room to smash into the easel. The gentle landscape of Roman hills bathed in a golden light clattered to the floor.

"How dare he! Without a word, without so much as a by-your-leave! Skulking off behind my back, afraid to face me—and quite right! Just wait until he gets back—"

"Mrs. Deventer!" Ada's cry was one of professional alarm. The woman was shaking as if stricken with the ague. Ada's instinctive urge to rush to Papa's defense gave way to an uneasy concern as she sensed, beneath that screaming fit, an almost animal fear. Aware that the pink marble mantel supported enough projectiles for a full-scale barrage, she took a firm grasp on Mrs. Deventer's shoulders. "Compose yourself, ma'am. I am sure that Papa did not leave without first consulting Mr. Deventer—"

The grey eyes were once more clear and rational. Ada was relieved to have forestalled a full-blown hysteria that might have required Papa's water cure.

"You're right, Ada. I should not have rushed down like this, before I even said good morning to my dear husband. You must forgive me, it is for him I am so concerned—his state of health is so unpredictable, I don't feel safe without a doctor in the house—"

Judging Mrs. Deventer fully recovered, Ada grew indignant on Papa's behalf. Papa, she said sternly, would never leave a patient still in need of his services. In his note—Mrs. Deventer looked eagerly at the letter as if she expected to share it—he had said that Mr. Deventer's condition was sufficiently stabilized for him to take a few days leave. "He says he will be back within a week, and in the meantime—" here Ada ventured to express her own idea, not Papa's—"should there be any emergency, please remember that I am here." True, she did not have her diploma but that was a mere formality at her stage of training.

Rose's smile made it questionable whether she took Ada's assurances seriously, but she declared all her anxiety at an end. "I shall tell Caxton to notify you if any of the servants get ill," she said, leaving Ada with the clear impression that she had been entrusted with the care of only those inhabitants of the castle who were of little worth and could be easily replaced.

Alone in her room, Ada scolded Papa a bit herself when she reread his note. A whole week he might be gone. What was she to do then about Nicholas Vance? In truth, she had no taste for the role of informer. Yet to remain silent, to become an accessory after the fact, to so repay the Deventers for their kindness? Impossible. The answer, after a sleepless night, had come to her: Was not a dutiful daughter expected to submit matters of importance to her father's judgment?

The more she thought of it, the more convinced she was that she should do nothing until Papa's return. Mr. Vance would therefore have a short reprieve. And she too. The worst part of that sleepless night had been a prevision of life at Kirkewode *sans* Mr. Vance—boring, boring! It was a thought she preferred not to linger on. Instead she began immediately to plan how to use this extra time to best advantage. Close observation of that slippery gentleman should provide her with more information to report than his mere name. Hamilton Nicholas Schuyler

Deventer. That much she had learned from a quick foray into the Deventer library before they left the city.

Unfortunately the next two days provided little opportunity to closely observe Nicholas Vance—as she continued to call him even in her private thoughts, the better to avoid a slip of the tongue when in his company. Not that she was much in his company these days. With Papa away and Mr. Witten "indisposed" (so Caxton had answered her expression of concern at his absence), the Deventers laid claim to the greater part of Mr. Vance's time. The dining table had become a vast Sahara of unused space, with the three of them—Rose and Mr. Vance and she—clustered at a small oasis at one end. And since Rose had most of Mr. Vance's attention even then, Ada found herself carrying on an imaginary conversation with the empty chair and untouched setting that still awaited the master's appearance. *How interesting, Mr. Deventer . . . you sold them short? . . . and then the bubble burst? . . . Yes, of course, I understand, ha ha, how very amusing . . . but I'd hardly call you a bear myself, more of a bull from what I've seen. . . .*

Another grey day and I might have gone into a decline—so Ada saluted the sun, visible at last after so many days in hiding. One of those boxes brought back from the city had contained a riding habit from Redfern's. A necessity, come spring, for the display of her form in Central Park, according to Mrs. Deventer. But the sun, though February pale, was warm enough to make the morning mist seem like the steamy breath of trees coming to life. Ada saw no reason to wait for spring.

The elegantly draped skirt and tight basque fitted to perfection. She did not need Marie's admiring "*la!*" to tell her she looked absolutely smashing. Giving a final adjustment to the tall beaver hat, she sent Marie to answer the knock on the door.

"Caxton! What's happened?" Surely a catastrophe. His jowls were aquiver with emotion.

"It's Mr. Witten, miss—or should I call you doctor? Mrs. Deventer said that in an emergency—"

"But of course," Ada said briskly, "take me to him."

From Caxton's report as they rushed up the stairs, it seemed that the terminal coma had come sooner than Papa anticipated. "When I brought up his breakfast tray, he was acting a bit peculiar. Wanted me to dress him so he could go out to some stable—MacReady's, I believe. I know of none by that name in the neighborhood. My suggestion that he was not quite up to riding threw him into one of his laughing fits and then he just collapsed on the pillow. I can't wake him, miss, I'm afraid he's expiring."

Viewing the frail figure lost in the huge bed, Ada's first thought was Caxton was right, this was the end. But there was a pulse, surprisingly rapid. A profuse sweat had plastered the nightgown to his skeletal form. As she leaned over, prying open one crepuscular eyelid, she smelled his breath.

"He's drunk, that's all. Very drunk." She almost laughed with relief. This was one time she could not feel censorious about such overindulgence. Given the inexorable progress of his disease, Mr. Witten was far easier in his mind being out of it. "Come, let's make him more comfortable—look at the lumps in this bed."

Caxton no doubt shared her relief, but could not conceal his chagrin at having made a misjudgment. "He had just his usual nightcap, miss, and I brought him nothing this morning but tea and gruel. How he managed to get in this state, I'm sure I don't know."

"Here's your answer." One of the lumps had proved to be an empty bottle. She was staring down at the steel engraving on the label: a distinguished-looking gentleman in double-breasted cutaway and beaver hat but without the usual patriarchal beard of such healers. *Perry Davis's Vegetable Painkiller.*

"But that's just some herbal mixture, miss. Mr. Witten has a lot of those—he keeps them hidden in his dressing room." Hidden, Caxton understood, only because Dr. Traherne had expressed a certain scorn for patent medicines and Mr. Witten was reluctant to expose himself to ridicule.

"This is almost pure alcohol," Ada said with complete assurance. It had been the humor of her chemistry professor to assign that patent medicine—along with *Hostetter's Celebrated Stomach Bitters* and *Dr. Pierce's Golden Medical Discovery*—for analysis. All I hope, Francis had joked, is that they don't sell it to the Indians. "I think you had better remove his cache, obviously he's on the verge of delirium tremens."

While Caxton searched the dressing room, Ada removed a second bottle from the bed, tried to smooth the sheets, found yet another. And something else—an oilskin packet with dangling ties. "Oh, bother!" was her exasperated response when she saw that the contents were scattered throughout the crumpled linen. Theater programs, ticket stubs, a few letters—the mementos of lifetime. Poor Mr. Witten had been reliving his youth. Carefully she went through the folds of the sheets, picking them out like lint, knowing he would not wish to lose one.

All the plays he attended seemed to have starred a Rosie McMahon. Ah, his Rosie, even back then. She had need to skim only one of the program notes to understand what kind of a play it was. No wonder Mama had been so scornful of the new Mrs. Deventer's talents, that kind of dramatic production was designed solely to display the unclad female form. And the envelopes were addressed in a hand she knew well by now, postmarked Nice. So even on her honeymoon, the dashing Mrs. Deventer had kept in touch with her former lover.

With distaste, Ada restuffed the pouch, tied it firmly, only to discover she had failed to include one item almost hidden under the unconscious form. She pulled it out—a faded yellow sheet, crumbling at the edges. Apparently so old it threatened to come apart in her hands as she unfolded it. A handbill of the crudest printing. The address given was MacReady's Stables, off Washington Square, and the patrons were promised, as mere curtain raisers, a dog fight, a cock fight, and rat baiting. But the main attraction in the capital letters that had first caught Ada's eye was to be A SPARRING EXHIBITION BY THE TWO MOST PULCHRITUDINOUS FEMALE PUGILISTS IN THE WORLD. The illustration,

191

though roughly drawn, made quite clear what the pulchritudinous pugilists would wear—the usual male attire of close-fitting tights, nothing else. Horrified—yet unable to stop reading—Ada tried to decipher the pencilled note at the bottom:

> Want to see some pretty bouncing tits, Jack? You can have the other, but Rosie's mine—or will be, soon as I can strike a deal with Slade, her fancy man. Her *brother* too, worse luck, so he's holding out for a fancy price. Friday night? But lay off R. or I'll tell her you still got the pox.

In the corner, was the reply Jack had passed back: *I'm your man, Friday night it is.*

Ada felt as stunned as if she had been in a boxing ring, had just received a knockdown blow. Between the "little animal," whose pathetic story Rose herself had told, and the grand Mrs. Deventer of this vast estate, there had existed—like yet another incarnation of a transmigrating soul—this Rosie in a boxing ring. The first emotion to emerge was a kind of pity for Mr. Witten. Mad Jack had not laid off, had paid a pretty fancy price. But an even greater pity suffused her as she recalled Rose Deventer in her dragon robe, still keeping up her form.

Such a life as that. And such a brother. Slade. How obvious the relationship now seemed. The resemblance was still there in the battered face, if one knew to look for it. The liberties he took, the failings she overlooked, were easy now to understand. Ada had a new appreciation of Rose Deventer's worth. Left to himself, a man like that would sink into the lowest cesspools of society. But Rose could not forget that he was her brother, had taken him in, provided him with a job of sorts. Ada knew herself made of meaner stuff. She would have let him rot in the gutter.

As Caxton reappeared, she quickly returned the handbill to the pouch, placed the treasured bundle under the sleeping man's pillow. "See that he has nothing alcoholic to drink—

including that stuff," she said, indicating the bottles cradled in Caxton's arms. "When his pain returns, he is to be given only the powders Dr. Traherne prescribed, is that clear?"

As she was about to leave, it occurred to Ada that the less said about Mr. Witten's condition, the better. Until he completely sobered up, he should remain "indisposed," she suggested to Caxton. "Better give me the key to Dr. Traherne's office so that, if necessary, I can get him a sedative."

She left with Papa's key in her pocket, feeling she had served him well. Rose had been angry enough at his departure—no reason to let her know one of his patients had really needed him.

It was early afternoon before she set out again for the stables. Oh, the excesses of the excessively rich, she thought as she viewed the cluster of stone buildings, a mere two stories high but with tiled roofs and a decorative design even in the setting of the masonry. For themselves the Deventers required a castle; for their horses a mere manor house. And from the number of stable hands lounging about, she estimated that a full cavalry regiment could be formed on the premises in the unlikely event that another war was ever declared.

The sheer wastefulness of such an establishment was underscored by the excitement her appearance caused. She felt like the English queen paying a state visit to some distant outpost of the empire, where the royal presence had never before been displayed. Fine hunters were kept, but Mr. Deventer did not hunt; nor did Mrs. Deventer ride, although Ada could choose from six gentle mounts, trained expressly to carry ladies. Even the call for a carriage came rarely enough, except for Mr. Witten's—now Mr. Vance's—need for the runabout to get to the station.

On a white-stockinged mare, who proved livelier than promised, Ada covered miles of deer park trails without encountering a soul. Very peaceful, she told herself. Very lonely, herself replied. She should have accepted the groom assigned to ride with her—he looked downcast, poor fellow, on being told he was not needed. Why had she not allowed him to feel useful for a change?—so she read his dejection by her own. For she was suffering a reaction from that morning's exhilaration, when for the first time in many a week she had been called upon to do what she was trained to do. It was a painful thought that it had taken Caxton to remind her of her loss. All this luxury had a seductive charm. *Should I call you doctor, miss?* Caxton would never know how much that hurt.

A deer's white tail flashed through the brush—the third she had seen so far, and in broad daylight. Such lack of shyness must follow from the lack of hunting. Ahead the trail took a hairpin turn, doubling back on itself. It took her a moment to realize that she had reached a boundary fence, so cleverly was it concealed by a tall thicket of yew. She was reminded again that on this seeming wilderness some hand had imposed all the usual civilized restraints. But surely the deer must be convinced they lived in perfect freedom—until they tried to go beyond the bounds. Fortunate animals, to have so kindly a gamekeeper. Or were they so fortunate after all? If prison looked more like a prison, would they not try harder to escape?

On a wild impulse, she turned the mare round and put her into a gallop. The thicket loomed before her, higher than she had thought, but there was only a fraction of a second to wonder if the horse would take the jump or pull up short and send her sailing over it on her own. Her heart was in her mouth and then she felt the push of powerful haunches and she was flying, flying . . . back to earth with a jar, her leg still hooked over the saddle, and free, free!

The horse seemed to relish its freedom too, and there was a contest of wills before Ada could rein it in. She was now on rolling meadowland, spotted with an occasional old oak or clump of copper beech. There was something to be said for such open vistas allowing an unobstructed view of the great river. Turned into a mirror by the sun, it reflected a world upside down. At some distance a large villa could be seen, half-obscured by a ring of hemlock. The sight of its shingled mansard roof made Ada aware that she was trespassing on a neighboring estate. Doubting that she could recapture the fine levitating spirit which had carried her over so high a fence, she took her bearing by the river and headed in the opposite direction. There should lie the public road which would take her to Kirkewode's main gate.

It was not long before she came to a narrow lane down which she proceeded at a decorous gait, trusting that, in spite of its many turns, it retained the same general direction. Meanwhile she amused herself with a picture of the sullen face she would encounter at Kirkewode—how furiously Blackie would pick his nose, trying to figure out how she could have left unobserved.

Suddenly she heard an ominous rumble behind her and looked back to see a coach drawn by four bay horses careening wildly around a turn, bearing down on her at a terrifying speed. She was pulling off the narrow road to let it pass when a loud blast from a horn struck her horse with a panic that matched her own. It reared and bucked until it had relieved itself of the encumbrance of a rider, then ran madly off through the trees. Sitting unharmed in the shallow drainage ditch, Ada felt the ground reverberate as, with a thunder of hoofs and a creaking of springs, the four-in-hand whizzed by. A lackey, hanging on for dear life to his perch in the rear, turned back a startled face, as did the helmeted passenger in the driver's box. Before vanishing around the next curve, the coach threatened for one precarious moment to overturn but, much to Ada's disappointment, righted itself in time.

She rose, brushed herself off and cursed the driver, of whom she had seen only a tall beaver hat and a multicaped coat. And what the devil was a policeman doing up there, aiding and abetting such a public menace? For there was no mistaking the uniform of the passenger, who was running toward her at this moment, with the little groom hard on his heels. And not just any policeman, but Patrolman Patrick Cullen. Or was it Roundsman by now?

"Miss Traherne! Praise be, you're not hurt? Take it aisy there, you might have a broken limb!"

Ada continued to march toward him with a determined stride. "If I had a broken limb, I'd know it by now. I'll say this, it's no thanks to that blasted fool at the reins that I'm all in one piece. I don't know what you were doing in that box, Cullen, but your life was in as much danger as mine—are you aware the coach had only two wheels on the ground when it was making that last turn?"

"Don't I know it, miss!" Cullen lifted his helmet as if to give a little air to his sweat-dampened curls. "It's not a young lady you can talk reason to—"

"A young lady! You mean to tell me a woman was driving at that reckless speed?"

The driver himself—herself, as Ada now saw—appeared at the turn of the road, although the coach was still out of view. At the sight of Ada on her feet, the woman changed her hurried pace to a careless saunter, which did nothing to assuage Ada's anger.

"Are you in the habit of driving with so little respect for the safety of others? If you wish to break your own neck, that's your business, but you have no right to break mine in the process, Miss—whatever your name is!"

"Julia. Julia Jessup."

The approaching figure was much slighter than it had appeared in the driver's box. It was the hat that gave her height, the capes that made her shoulders seem so broad. Dark eyes stared at Ada boldly, without the slightest apologetic shift. From underneath the hat, the face was framed with short dark curls, coiled tightly as springs. With that high coloring, she was pretty enough, Ada granted.

"I know who *you* are—Paddy just told me. You're Ada Traherne, and your papa is the Deventers' doctor, and you're staying at Kirkewode, where none of us has ever been invited, and

I'm dying to hear all about the Cloistered Rose and her husband, that old moneybags—what do they do with themselves in that great big castle? I mean, it's all very exciting, I'm sure, when her lovers are shooting themselves all over the place, but it must be pretty boring in betweentimes, I should think. But, of course, you've got a lively young'un now to replace the old stick who's on his last legs, I hear—he's *very* handsome, I saw him the other day on his way to the station—you sly puss, I bet you weren't going to even mention *him*—"

To her amazement, Ada found herself walking down the lane, arm in arm with this perfect stranger, whose excited chatter implied they were the dearest of friends. Ada managed to disengage herself, attempted again to establish herself as an injured party. "Really, Miss Jessup, all I want is to find my horse and be on my way—on some other road than that on which you are traveling!" Since Julia merely giggled at that tart rebuff, Ada decided to dispense some much-needed advice. "I am willing to assume you were not deliberately going at such a dangerous speed, no doubt those horses were running away, but in the future—"

Dark eyes flashed fire. "Now you listen to *me*, Ada Traherne, no horse runs away when *I* have the reins! I can handle a four-in-hand with the best, as Paddy here can tell you—tell her, Paddy. And how the devil was I to know you would be riding on what is, after all, our private property? Not that I give a damn about that, but your Deventers sure do. Even so, I could have passed you, I'm sure—I've managed tighter scrapes than that, but that damn fool lackey had to blow his horn and scare the daylights out of your damn fool horse." As suddenly as it broke, the storm passed, Julia was all smiles again. "If I know horses, and I do, yours is back in the stable by now. I'll have to drive you back myself."

The young boy in puce and green livery gave his mistress a hand up. "Come on," Julia urged, taking up the reins, "you don't want to ride inside, the three of us can squeeze in up here."

While Ada still hesitated to so risk her life, Patrick Cullen begged to be excused. With a formality strikingly at odds with Julia's easy speech, he pleaded the call of duty. "I'd best be on my way, Miss Jessup, and see if I can catch them poachers you reported. No, no, miss, don't you bother about me, a policeman's used to pounding his beat, I can get back to my horse on foot. Best way to cover the ground, in fact. Even if I don't nab them thieving rascals, I'm likelier to come across one of their traps."

Bidding both ladies good-bye, he made off with such dispatch that Julia laughed. "I do believe he's afraid to ride with me. Are you?" she challenged Ada.

"Of course not," Ada lied, and climbed up into the driver's box.

With a sideways look, Julia took in the rigidity of Ada's spine, her tight grip on the side rail. "Don't worry about being late, I'll get you back in time," she promised demurely and cracked the long whip.

Ada never quite recovered from that jolting start which seemed to leave some part of her vital organs behind. At each turn, centripetal force threatened to have its way with her, only her desperate grip on the side rail kept her from being hurled into space. The long whip uncurled itself again and again over the horses' bobbing heads, with a snap at its tip like a reptile's tongue capturing its dinner out of the air. Apparently Miss Jessup was not satisfied with this vertiginous speed.

Once through the gate, however, and on the public road, Julia demonstrated the iron hand within that soft leather glove. Seemingly without effort, she slowed the team down. Ada soon understood why they were traveling at such a reasonable pace. Not out of respect for traffic (of which there was none) but to make possible a gossipy conversation. What was Mr. Deventer really like—it was common knowledge that he had been a lively dog in his youth, too bad he had to reform. Ada had nothing to add to common knowledge. Julia readily moved on to Mrs. Deventer—what did she look like in the morning with her hair undone and in her wrapper?

"When I was a girl, she was my beau ideal," Julia said. "I spent all of one year trying to be just like her, but I'm just not that type, you know—"

"How old are you now, if I may ask?"

"Eighteen," Julia said, unabashed. "I've been married, you know." Marriage, Ada gathered, added years.

"The truth is," Julia confessed, making a peculiar sound, "I like my men live and kicking, not dead at my feet." The pink tip of a tongue was suddenly visible, feeling out the open space between two front teeth. An amatory nature such a space was supposed to mean. Not that Ada believed in physiognomy as an index of character. Nor in phrenology either, although listening to Julia expound on the subject of men, Ada could not resist drawing an imaginary map of a cranium in which one enormous bump of Amativeness swelled from temple to temple, leaving room for nothing else.

"What do you think of my policeman?" Julia suddenly asked. "Ain't he a charmer?" Ada now identified that peculiar sound as a sigh in reverse, a gustatory sucking in of breath through the front gap.

"Ye-es," Ada said, wondering how to mention tactfully *that* one's excessively large bump of Ambition. "But I do think he keeps an eye out for his advancement—"

"You mean an eye on my money?" Julia laughed. "Oh, he's cute enough, but then so am I, my dear. Men are all right, you know, as long as you keep them in their place." The dark eyes suddenly widened, like the hood rolling back from a ship's turret gun to expose the glint of hard metal. This young girl, whose language at best smacked of the stables, was about to say something shocking. "Take them to bed, you'll come to no harm, take them to church, sound the alarm—how do you like that? I made it up. It's the first wise saying in Poor Julia's Almanac."

This was to be a ride that broadened Ada's sympathies. She found that she could feel sorry even for Patrick Cullen, whose affections were clearly being toyed with. This young woman would have her way with him, then toss him aside like a—like a—Ada sought a simile for abandonment, finding it hard to conceive of Patrolman Cullen as a used glove. A far more topsy-turvy world, this one Julia showed her, than the mirrored image in the river.

In those few months between her marriage to the coachman and its subsequent annulment, Julia had acquired a sentimental education which she was as eager to display as Ada was her medical one, flooding her new friend with the most intimate confidences. Where was the reticence, the modesty, the delicacy of thought, the refinement of soul which belonged by birth to the gentler sex? Most women would never have recovered from such a sordid experience, but Ada looked in vain for the disfiguring scars on this young girl—for so she still seemed in face and figure and irrepressible high spirits. As Cullen had once put it, the girl showed none the worse for wear.

"I'll tell you one thing, Ada, you'll never find me taking on another husband. Too much like turning over the reins to some booby who ain't half the whip *I* am. No, not for love or money," she swore, pulling up at Kirkewode's gate. "Money I've no need of, and as for love, one thing I've learned, you don't have to get married for *that*." She laughed aloud at Ada's blush and ordered the lackey to pull the bell.

Ada began to make her good-byes, but Julia would have none of that. Did Ada think she would be dumped out here on the public road? Oh, no, she would be driven right to her door.

For Ada, more confusion. How hateful, this phobia of the Deventers against strangers. Still she had to warn Miss Jessup that the gatekeeper would not let her through.

There was that widening of the eyes again. But "call me Julia," was all the girl said. When Blackie appeared—yes, at the sight of Ada, he began to pick his nose—Julia motioned to the lackey to resume his rear perch and called out impatiently to the gatekeeper to unlock the gate and give Miss Traherne a hand down.

Ada felt a twinge of disappointment. She had expected more of a fight from a girl so headstrong.

"All right," Blackie grumbled, "but I'm hanged if I know how she got out."

The gate swung open, pinning him for a moment behind its bronze bars. "Hold on," Julia said through gritted teeth and with a crack of her whip sent the coach barreling through. "Whoo-eee!" she cried, drowning out whatever cry emerged from the open mouth of Blackie, now far in the rear. Once again the trees were racing past and with her free hand, Ada made a grab for her hat. She was beginning to enjoy the sensation of such speed, cutting through a tangible wall of air, feeling the rhythm of the beautifully matched horses, now fully let out. "Whoo-eee!" Ada cried in unison with Julia as the grey stone walls of the castle came into view, and felt only regret that the drive had been so short.

"You'll do," Julia said with a congratulatory pat on Ada's knee.

"You know, Julia, I'm not allowed to ask you in," Ada said beseechingly, "I must thank you here."

But Julia's curiosity was fully rampant, not to be satisfied with just a view of the castle's outside. "Fiddle-faddle," she said firmly, "I've practically saved your life, I'm sure the Deventers will want to thank me themselves."

Ada did not quite understand how Julia, who had occasioned her fall, could present herself now as her rescuer. But her curiosity was as strong as Julia's. What would happen if this girl did walk in? She promptly whipped up a resentment she preferred to think had long been smouldering: why should the Deventers conduct their household as if Kirkewode were a real castle, and one under siege? And what right had they to keep her as cloistered as the legendary Rose?

"Yes," she said, matching Julia in firmness, "I'm sure that Mrs. Deventer will be delighted to meet you."

She had hoped to avoid Caxton, but the sound of the coach had brought him to the door.

"Oh, Caxton," she said, trying for a casual air, "I've brought a friend back for tea."

But Caxton was not a man to be barreled through. "I'm afraid that will be impossible, miss," he said, blocking the way. "Madam is indisposed."

"Then we shall have tea alone, in the Rose Room please." Ada stepped to one side, but still encountered that stiff white front. Impasse.

"Is that Ada I hear?" From the shadowy depths of the hall, Mrs. Deventer called out.

"Yes, madam. With a young lady."

A momentary silence while the opposing forces held firm. As if she knew her time was short, Julia was craning in every direction for all she could see of the great hall over Caxton's broad shoulders.

"And who have we here?" Rose appeared, looking particularly fine in sapphire velvet, with a Niagara of lace falling all the way to the floor. Julia would understand that no one put on a gown like that to be indisposed in. Ada was mortified.

"This is Miss Jessup, who lives next door—she—"

"I know *of* the Jessups," Rose said, cutting Ada off, "but I do not think we have exchanged visiting cards. I do wish we could ask your young friend in, Ada, but something untoward has happened." Only then did she speak directly to Julia. "I am sure you will forgive us, Miss Jessup."

"Yes, of course," Julia murmured. Ada could not bear to see her so cowed. The girl was actually apologizing! So sorry to have caused any inconvenience. Forgive her intrusion. Forgive her attire. Forgive her existence!

Some other time, Rose suggested with no attempt to be convincing. Some other time, Julia echoed, with no attempt to sound convinced. Ada refused to let her go like that, followed her out to the coach, showered her with thanks to make amends for that crushing rejection. But far from being hurt, Julia was starry-eyed.

"Isn't she wonderful! My beau ideal! If only I could be like that—" Ada's apologies were brushed aside. "It's not *her* fault—it's that husband of hers. Everyone knows he's the one who won't have people in the house. What did I tell you? The mistake is in getting married. No, truly, I don't mind, I'm just glad I got a look at her close up. Do you know, Ada, for a teensy-weensy moment I was disappointed, and then I realized it's not that she's so pretty—heavens, girl, you're ten times prettier—but she has—oh, I don't know—she has an *air!*"

Ada, even without an air, was welcome at the Jessups' any time, Julia said and drove off at a sedate pace as if afraid that her beau ideal still had an eye on her. But Rose was in the hall, waiting for Ada. Seeing the thin cursive line of those lips—that Egyptian smile—Ada was enraged. Never had she witnessed such rudeness, Ada stormed—and this to a young woman who had practically saved her life! Would Mrs. Deventer please explain why she was not allowed to ask even a neighbor to tea?

"Because she *is* a neighbor," Rose said, still smiling. "Mr. Deventer does not wish to encourage that kind of dropping-in. Do calm down, Ada, when we're in town you may have as many girl friends as you like—if they are of good family, of course, and properly brought up. I do not think your papa would approve of your acquaintance with that young person—her reputation is not of the best. Now come with me." Rose extended her hand with such a pleased look—surely she can't be pleased with me, Ada realized—that all thought of Julia vanished as her anger gave way to a cautious expectancy. "Something has really happened, my dear. At least I think you'll be surprised. Pity that you are dressed like that, I would suggest you change—you look as hoydenish as your friend—but we don't want to keep your young man waiting, do we?"

What was all this fuss about Mr. Vance? Had his identity been discovered? The thought was quickly dismissed. Mrs. Deventer would hardly smile like that. Deeply puzzled, Ada followed Mrs. Deventer into the Rose Room.

"Ada!" The teacup clattered in his hand as he jumped to his feet.

To a stunned Ada, time seemed to freeze, leaving them all congealed in a stiff unmoving pose—herself with mouth agape,

Rose with her hieroglyphic smile, Mr. Vance putting down his cup with steadier hand—and Francis.

The spell was broken by Rose. "There now, what did I tell you!" Hers was a theatrical delight in a particularly effective mise-en-scène. "Never have I seen a girl so surprised!"

Francis came toward her, taut with the eagerness of a panther about to leap on its prey. Ada moved back. "I promised I'd follow you to the ends of the earth, Ada—well, here I am!"

Behind her Mr. Vance emitted a scornful "humph!" and muttered a hope that the fellow knew more medicine than he did geography.

"I admit I'm surprised, Francis. I hardly expected you to leave school at a time like this. You—" once it would have been *we,* she thought—"you don't graduate until the end of March, shouldn't you be studying for your exams?"

"What does that matter?" Francis seized her hand. "What matters is that I am here with you."

The sallow, high-cheekboned face tilted in its familiar grin, and Ada's heart gave a familiar response. Was it possible he had abandoned his degree, even as he had caused her to abandon hers? Was he atoning at such great cost?

"The first thing I asked him myself," Rose said approving Ada's dry practical tack, "but there's no need to scold him, Ada. He got special permission to take his exams in advance, and he's a full-fledged doctor. Oh, we have a very clever young man here."

Ada found it easy to free her hand while Francis gave Mrs. Deventer a grateful look, the tips of his ears rosy from her praise.

"I don't even have to go back for the official ceremony, Ada, they'll mail me my diploma at the end of the term."

"There," Rose said proudly and Ada saw now the whole ear was red. "What do you say to that, Ada?"

"I think I'll have a cup of tea," Ada said.

Chapter 13

"**I** WOULDN'T marry you if you were the last man on earth!"

Story-paper words, Ada realized, were very useful at times. Like bobbing buoys they marked a safe conversational channel. Without them, what terrible things might she not say.

Francis was not disturbed by so conventional a sentiment. "I thought you would have simmered down by now, Ada," he reproved her. "You shouldn't have skedaddled like that, you know. It put me to a lot of trouble, having to clear things away so I could follow you."

Ada felt a strong desire to throw something *à la* Rose Deventer—preferably a breakable object right at his head. Unfortunately they had chosen the conservatory for this private interview after dinner, and the only object at hand was a stone Buddha weighing half a ton, whose ineffable smile was directed at a jet of water issuing from its navel.

"Sorry to have inconvenienced you. You really shouldn't have bothered."

"Aw, come on, Ada, don't be like that." Flowery

speeches were not his line, he unnecessarily declared; she must judge him by his deeds, not his words. Surely his presence here proved he loved her. And when that laconic speech failed to melt her, he pressed her rigid form against his chest as if to let her hear his thumping heart. An unexpected curiosity kept Ada in his arms, allowing him to stamp his lips on hers, a hot dry seal of ownership. Why, she thought contemptuously, he doesn't even know how to kiss. He looked pleased with himself when he let her go. Making love to a fencepost, it seemed, was all he required.

"You're fortunate that Papa is not here," she said, fastidiously plumping out the velvet bow on the shoulder of her dinner gown. "He would like nothing better than to use a horsewhip on you. And frankly I don't think I'd try to stop him."

From his easy laugh, it was apparent that not even the threat of Papa could shake his confidence. "If it's horsewhipping he wants, he'll have the chance. Mrs. Deventer has invited me to stay until he returns, and I don't reckon I'll pull your trick and run away. When he hears that all I want—that all I *ever* wanted—is to marry you, he'll change his tune, I bet. Mrs. Deventer—now that's a nice lady—she understands how a fellow feels about his girl. You talk to her, Ada, she'll put you straight."

One surprise after another. She could conjecture why Rose was letting him stay the night—for just such a tête-à-tête with the girl he had come so far to see. But a stranger within the gates, an intruder within the charmed circle, for a whole week? He must have won Rose over, convinced her Ada should accept his suit.

Ada's chin took on a stubborn set. He could stay until kingdom come for all she cared, she would never change her mind.

"Francis, what can I say to convince you that I do not *want* to marry you?"

It was no longer a question of want, but of must, he gently pointed out. Not that he would have placed her in such a position had he not known she really loved him. What he had done, he had done to insure their future happiness—he was sure her pa would see that.

His look wavered, so did Ada's. Neither wished to recall in specific detail the events of that night.

"All I see, Francis, is that you have made a great mistake to come here," she said, and left the fraudulent serenity of the green glade to rejoin Rose and Nicholas in the drawing room.

How great a mistake, she herself was just beginning to realize. For all her savaged pride, she had kept a lover's image of him in her heart—an image as falsely painted over as that photograph of the Haygood boy. But tonight, when she thought of how her heart had mourned his loss, she could only ask why all the fuss? He was good-looking enough, though she no longer saw the noble savage in his sallow, high-cheekboned face. And he might be as smart as she (and he) thought he was. But what she had admired as strength, she saw now was nothing more than arrogance and conceit. Back then (already her attachment had receded to the distant past), she had found his rough and ready ways a welcome change from the usual spooniness of men. Not so now; they offended her, betraying rather a ham-handed spirit, an uncouthness not so much of manners as of a certain cast of mind. Let him wait for Papa's return, Ada decided with a shrug. It would give him time to learn he could no longer handle her.

Having resigned herself to a week of unwelcome importunities, Ada was surprised that Francis seemed content to let the matter rest. Perhaps he believed he had said all that needed to be said until he met with Papa, when he would contract in a proper business-like way to take her (goods slightly soiled in transit, but not really damaged) as his wife. Or was it—Ada was ashamed to feel a twinge of pique—that he too could not resist the suction pump of Rose Deventer's charm, which in no time at all had him plastered to her side.

"Now there's a real lady, Ada," he said at the breakfast they were sharing alone. She had risen early just to avoid this and wondered if he had had the same aim in view. "She's content to let her husband make the money, so long as he lets her spend it. And she sure knows how to spend it so as to make it all worthwhile." He gave an appreciative glance at the sideboard with its row of silver chafing dishes. He approved, it seemed, of breakfast in the English style.

With some asperity Ada suggested that the Deventers were only practicing what the socialists preached: from him according to his ability, to her according to her needs.

"The trouble with you, Ada, is that you've got a man's brains in a female body, and you've let it go to your head. Let me warn you, my girl, that most peculiar hybrids—take the mule, for example—fail to reproduce themselves."

"Thank you for the warning. But I claim only a woman's brains, and find them more than satisfactory. Still, who knows what peculiar hybrid might result if I mated with a jackass!"

"Oh dear, she has you there, Dr. Stevens!"

In the doorway, Mrs. Deventer applauded Ada. An unexpected vision. Rose *never* appeared at breakfast.

"I never said that women don't have a tongue," Francis said cheerfully and jumped to his feet to pull back her chair. Ada had occasion to admire again the lovely line of that white throat as Rose, once seated, looked up to acknowledge Francis's courtesy.

"You and Mr. Vance should not have retired so early last night, Ada," Rose said, nibbling with a rodent's small fierce bites on a piece of cold toast. This morning, it seemed, Rose was back on her Banting diet. "Dr. Stevens and I had *such* an interesting conversation. But then, you might well have been bored. I'm afraid I was running on again about Mr. Deventer's exploits in the market. Your young man—"

"Not my young man."

"Oh, dear. I may yet plead his cause, but *not* at breakfast. Dr. Stevens, then, is not so narrowly concerned with science as you, my dear, but takes a broader view of life. I like that in a man— that he can be as interested in a successful operation on the Street as—shall we say?—on the abdomen of a poor girl with a stomachache."

"I see that Papa discussed Marie's case with you," Ada said bitterly. "*We* were taught that professional ethics require a strict confidentiality where patients are concerned."

Rose replied mildly that she and Mr. Deventer stood in loco parentis for their servants—especially those who had left all family behind in the old country. "Besides, your papa took your interference much to heart, Ada. I don't know when I've seen him so upset."

"Francis!" Ada turned to him eagerly, remembering for the moment only their past community of interest. "This was just the kind of case Professor Fitz had in mind—you would have advocated surgery too, I am sure, instead of waiting for pus to invade the whole system—"

"Really, Ada, this ain't the kind of thing to talk about at table. It's enough to take away any lady's appetite."

It was true that Rose had pushed away her plate, but Ada suspected it was the cold toast she found unappetizing. Her contempt for Francis grew as she listened to him assure his hostess that nothing would please him more than to meet the subject of their discourse last night—purely as an admirer of financial genius, he hastened to add, not in his capacity as a doctor, for he would not presume to intrude upon Dr. Traherne's practice. How he flaunts his degree! Ada thought, his new title like a bad taste in her mouth.

The effect on Rose, however, was all he could desire, although the soulful look, in Ada's sour view, was directed more at the thick slab of ham on his plate than at his face. "Who knows? Perhaps I can arrange just that." Smiling she shook a finger at Ada. Coyness did not suit her, Ada thought. "Since you are being so cruel to this young man, Ada dear, I am taking it upon myself to entertain him. First I shall take him on a tour of the castle and if the weather permits this afternoon, Mr. Deventer might join us in a survey of the grounds."

That these two had met at breakfast by prearrangement was already evident to Ada. But Rose had had enough of watching others eat, announced she would wait for Dr. Stevens in the morning room. "No, no, do finish your breakfast," she urged Francis, who had jumped to his feet with a large bite still squirreled in his cheek. "There's a week's supply of newspapers I have yet to read. And I shall have to see if Caxton has the key to Dr. Traherne's office."

As soon as she was out of the room, Ada demanded, "Why does she want Papa's key?" It lay, in fact, in her pocket, where she had convinced Caxton it should remain.

"I think she wants to show me what modern facilities Mr. Deventer provides his medical man. If it's like the rest of the place, they're probably medieval, but I mean to be polite. And after that she wants me to take a look at this Mr. Witten, who's been ailing, I understand."

"The man's dying of cancer, if you call that ailing."

"Yeah, she told me that. But he's not been out of his room the last few days. That butler fellow in the boiled shirts says it's just something he ate, but she feels your pa shouldn't have left him unattended. And I must say, Ada, I think it's pretty unprofessional for him to light out like that without getting another doctor to take his place. Especially with Mr. Deventer too not being in the best of health."

Ada refused to defend Papa to such a man. "I think you had better hear the truth about Mr. Witten's latest indisposition," she began, and quickly summarized the condition she had found him in.

She should have expected his disapproving reply: Just the kind of patient no woman should confront—a man in that condition was apt to show little respect for her sex. "As for this doctoring on the sly, Ada, one of these days you're going to walk into real trouble and I won't be there to get you out." He found it easier to understand her wish to spare Mrs. Deventer the truth. He would examine Mr. Witten in private before allowing the lady in, and if he found the fellow had sobered up, as Ada seemed to think, he would let Caxton's comforting diagnosis of dyspepsia stand. In his eagerness to join that lady, he was wolfing down his food, Ada noticed. She said nothing more until he had excused himself and was at the door.

"Francis."

"Yes?"

Her hands fingered the key in her pocket. She could not explain her reluctance to let it go.

"What is it, Ada?" He fidgeted, anxious to be off.

"You will need this, I believe—the key to Papa's office."

Her toss was a little wide of the mark, but there was nothing wrong with Francis's reflexes. He caught it with an almost lazy swipe of his long arm. To Ada it was as if some essential part of Papa was now gone.

At luncheon, a new Francis was on view. The rough tweed he had worn since his arrival had been replaced by black serge. His go-to-meeting suit, Ada had heard him call it. The drooping ends of his long thin mustache—it gave him the look of a western desperado, Rose had laughingly remarked at breakfast—had been whacked off, a neat trimming job that subtly altered his whole face. More dapper surely, and yet beneath the suave brush of hair the mouth had an oddly childish set. It was as if an unformed youth were trying on a grown-up look. It pleased Ada to think that, like Samson succumbing to the wiles of Delilah, he had shorn himself of all his strength.

"I have been given the afternoon off—an unexpected holiday," Mr. Vance announced. "Perhaps you would care to join me in a game of billiards, Miss Traherne."

"I took it for granted that you're to go with us, Ada," Francis spoke up quickly.

"In this world, one cannot take anything for granted," was Ada's sententious reply. She preened a bit to see them vie for her company, even though she realized that it was no special honor to be a bone of contention between two who had so disliked each other at first sight.

It was only at that moment she decided to take Julia Jessup at her word. She would be riding over to the Jessups', she said, but if Mr. Vance cared to join her, he was welcome. To herself she reasoned that a young woman willing to receive one guest without prior notice could just as easily accommodate two.

As they left the dining room, Francis drew her aside to issue some avuncular advice. He did not like to see her on such intimate terms with that fellow, he said, glowering after Mr. Vance's retreating back. Not even a professional man, just a clerk, he pointed out. If she wanted to set her cap at someone, she could do far better. He didn't want her to think he was pressing his own suit, he was only concerned that she remember who she was.

"Who am I, Francis?" she challenged him.

"You're a doctor's daughter." His soberness was suddenly fractured by a tilted smile. "And—when you come to your senses, Ada—a doctor's wife."

She looked at him curiously. "It seems I am nothing without the possessive." Then her lips curled in what could be taken as an answering smile. "What if I promise to set my cap at no one lower than a Deventer?"

Francis was delighted to be so teased—that was his old girl again. "Aw, come on, Ada," he protested and made a grab for her, "where does that leave me?"

She evaded him with an agility that left him not so pleased. "Surely that's for you to decide." Gathering up her skirt, she made a hoydenish run for the stairs. A surge of exhilaration made her want not just to run but to leap. I belong to no one, to no one—the thought raced in her pulse, gave her wings.

As they rode through Kirkewode's gates, with a friendly nod to Blackie, Ada was looking forward to a pleasant ride, perhaps a momentary embarrassment of the Jessups' staff when they arrived uninvited, but then a whirlwind greeting of delight from Julia to put all to rights. A girl with such an unconventional view of marriage would hardly be a stickler for the lesser rules of social intercourse. And a glance at Nicholas Vance beside her, astride a magnificent hunter that showed itself by much head tossing to be impatient with their easy pace, reassured her further. Not even Julia's mama would object to so handsome a young man dropping in for tea.

But the afternoon did not turn out as Ada planned. The weather failed her first. They had just reached the Jessups' gate when the sky took on a peculiar cast. Dark thunderclouds rolled in from the west, while to the east was the same fine sky they had set out under. It was like looking into another world to see in the distance placid cows basking in a golden light while overhead the blackness deepened. Thunder rolled and lightning flashed, and yet there was a costive stillness to the air, with only a drop or two of water squeezed out.

"This is the strangest weather," Ada said, "I've seen this kind of storm only in summer, never at this time of year."

A bolt of lightning split the blackness of the sky. For a fraction of a second it seemed to hover over the Jessup estate, so that Ada actually saw its jagged track. She felt a tingling in her palms, smelled something acrid in the air. Along with the clap of thunder could be heard a different crashing sound.

"Too close for comfort," Nicholas said, "that must have struck a tree nearby."

They put their horses to a canter, hoping to reach the Jessup house before those fat drops became a downpour. Another few moments and it was clear that all this rumbling and flashing was pure rhodomontade, there was to be no rain. As quickly as it had come, the storm was over.

Nicholas pulled up abruptly, turned in the saddle. "Someone is calling you, Miss Traherne—sounds like a woman in trouble."

A dark-clad figure emerged from the small copse of evergreens that crowned the hill on their right. Waving both arms in a semaphore of distress, the young woman began to run toward them, making awkward progress with much ankle-turning over the rough ground.

"It's Miss Jessup!" Ada cried, and following Nicholas's lead, turned off the road and cantered up to meet her.

No great harm had come to the girl, Ada decided quickly enough. Though gasping for breath, Julia could still cast a curious glance at a handsome male even while assuring Ada that she was a lifesaver, a real lifesaver! Her riding dress—shockingly short, revealing tall boots rather than trousers—was sadly mussed. Her hat was gone and her thick curly hair, undone in back, fanned out like a barbaric headdress. Ada found a certain justice in what had unmistakably occurred—it was Julia's turn to be thrown from a horse—and she was ready to rub salt in the wound with a commiserating speech. But "You ride astride?" she exclaimed instead, only then perceiving that the short skirt was divided.

"And why not? You should try it, Ada. Then you'll know what it feels like to be in real control."

"And yet I gather you took a fall," Ada said, resisting the temptation to smile.

Julia reacted as haughtily as when Ada had questioned her ability to handle a four-in-hand. "The horse took a fall—not I. You'll see what I mean, just follow me." With a peremptory gesture—somewhat like a captain ordering his men to follow him into battle—Julia scrambled back up the hill. Ada smiled to see Mr. Vance look so bemused, as if he had just encountered a hitherto unknown species.

They were led over the hill and down a shallow incline to a clearing, in the center of which was an odd brick structure, octagonal in design and windowless, its sole entrance marked by a door swinging tipsily, half-off its hinges. When the far side of the building came into view, they saw not one but two horses, both asprawl on the ground under an enormous elm almost split in two. One lay athwart the other, nuzzling its companion in death.

Mr. Vance dismounted and went over to examine the bodies. "So this is where the lightning struck—too bad they were both tethered under the same tree." Ada was almost as sorry for the elm, which an unusually balmy February had brought to the verge of flowering but which now would never know the spring. "Well, you were lucky not to be in the saddle. I take it your friend has gone for help?"

"No," Julia said, challenging him with her boldest look, "my friend is still here."

As if on cue, Patrolman Cullen, stooping to clear the low lintel, came out of the brick building. The red tinge to his cheekbones betrayed an embarrassment Ada would have preferred to see in Julia's face.

"Sure and our guardian angels have not let us down," Cullen began in his thickest brogue. " 'Tis a pleasure to see you again, Miss Traherne, and to make your acquaintance, sir—Patrolman Cullen here." Only when he flipped his hand up in a casual salute, did he become aware that he was helmetless, although he had still to discover he had misbuttoned his tunic. Finding no reciprocal pleasure in Mr. Vance's cold eye, Cullen addressed himself to the more sympathetic ear. "It's like this, miss—do ye mind them poachers I was after? Miss Jessup here advised me of this old smokehouse which the present owner— her pa, that is—don't use these days. Faith, I seys to meself, but that's a proper place to find sich perpetrators hanging out, and divvle a soul the wiser. So I seys to the lady, would ye be kind enough to show the way—"

"Oh really, Paddy, cut that twaddle," Julia said in disgust, having kept her eye on Mr. Vance. With a tilt of her chin at that gentleman, she allowed that she for one did not feel called upon to explain to just any passerby what was none of his business in the first place. Miss Traherne, however, was her *friend* and that was an entirely different matter. "Ada, could I speak to you for a moment in private, please?"

Ada somewhat unwillingly responded to the chummy pressure of an arm around her waist and was drawn inside the smokehouse. The only light was that afforded by the open doorway, and to her pain Ada discovered that iron hooks still dangled from an overhead beam. Recovering, she then stubbed her foot on a hard round object that clattered off to the side. *That,* according to Julia's little shriek, was Paddy's helmet. Ada was warmly thanked for the reminder. And while Julia groped for the helmet, she explained to Ada the exigencies of the present situation.

"We've got to get Paddy's horse away from here—" Julia's whisper was freighted with a significance Ada could not comprehend.

"But of course," Ada said, still rubbing her head. "I didn't think you intended to let it rot out there. We'll ride over to your stables and get a boy with a cart—"

"Don't be so stupid, Ada. If it was a matter of getting help from our stables, I could have walked. Why do you think I was so glad to see you—it's your horse, girl, your horse! That means we can drag it off our property with no one knowing I had Cullen here, don't you see?"

Ada did not see at all. Why all the secrecy, she asked sharply. It certainly looked as if there were going to be a dreadful storm, she could vouch for that. "No one will blame you and Patrolman Cullen for taking shelter." That "stupid" rankled, lending a waspishness to her tone. "I am sure you have talked yourself out of worse scrapes than this."

Julia seemed to realize that more diplomacy was required. Her voice dropped to a soft confiding level; in the semidarkness Ada could hear the purr, like that of an arch-backed kitten. Julia swore she had known Ada would understand—had she not recognized from the first moment of their meeting that they were soul mates?—but unfortunately her pa was not a reasonable man. And even more unfortunately, the smokehouse was the worst site those horses could have chosen to drop in their tracks.

Ada thought to object on behalf of the horses—they had hardly chosen to be struck by lightning—but was distracted by Julia's movements. It was hard to make out in the poor light what she had just picked up and was folding like a careful laundress. A horse blanket, it looked like. Ada decided not to question the smooth ironing motions of those hands, but soul mates she was sure they were not.

"You see, the smokehouse is where Jake and I—he's the one I made the mistake of marrying—would always meet. In fact, if Pa hadn't found us out and had a conniption fit, I doubt if we would have run away, so in a way it was all his fault." With an effort Julia forbore to elaborate on that grievance. That was neither here nor there, she admitted. The point was that those two horses must not be found anywhere near the smokehouse or her pa would be convinced she was up to her old tricks again. "That's the way he puts it," she said, breaking into a giggle, "*just let me catch you up to your old tricks again, young lady, and I'll cut you off without a penny.*" Money was a thought that turned the giddiest female sober, Ada noticed as Julia dropped the mimicry. "He just might at that. Or leave it tied up in my brother's hands so I can't get at it, which boils down to the same thing. You haven't met my brother—he's away just now taking the cure for what ails him—but believe me, he'll spend everything he gets on gambling and loose women, and Pa never questions *that* because he's a man!"

Ada sighed. Julia was too much in a rush to establish herself as more sinned against than sinning.

"All right, Julia, we'll remove Cullen's horse from the scene, but I hope you will not embroil me again in your deceptions. To be honest, I find them distasteful."

With an uncomfortable sense that Rose had been fully justified in discouraging her acquaintance with Miss Jessup, Ada went outside to offer the use of her horse to Patrolman Cullen. How awkward it would be, explaining to Mr. Vance! No need to worry, Cullen had taken on the task himself and Mr. Vance was already helping him rope together some fallen lengths of timber. A primitive affair when finished, like the travois she had seen the Indians use out West, but it served well enough. The two men rode off, dragging behind them the patrolman's dead mount. Julia looked disdainfully at Nicholas's straight back and wondered aloud that she had ever wanted to meet him. "Now that I see him close up, I think Paddy's twice as handsome. And a lot more *lively,* you can bet." Which led Ada to wonder which she disapproved of more strongly—Julia's conduct or her taste.

Mr. Vance returned alone, leading Ada's mount, to report that Cullen had proceeded to the station on foot. "A man devoted to his duty," was his dry comment. "He feels he must make a prompt accounting of his dead horse, now to be found alongside the public road." He gave a sardonic look at the remaining corpse. "I assume we may leave that poor beast, its reputation now untarnished, where it lays."

"That's true," Julia said and jumped up from the rock she and Ada had been sitting on. Now that there was nothing to worry about—and certainly the bright face she turned to Ada was free of any concern—their visit must be considered to have officially just begun. If they would follow the road up to the house, she would run ahead by a shortcut and vowed to beat them there.

Under the guise of a much-needed stretch, Ada searched for some way to politely refuse. This past half hour had surfeited her with Julia's conversation, which had centered on the judging points for fine horses and fine men. But the need to say anything was taken from her by the presumption of Mr. Vance.

"So sorry," he said firmly, "Miss Traherne must be getting back. She has a guest of her own at Kirkewode and is expected back at tea."

How dare he decide for her whether she would leave or stay! He made it sound as if she were a child on an outing with her governess! Furious though she was, Ada managed to keep back the explosive denial she had framed. It would be too unseemly to get into that kind of fracas in front of Julia. Forgetting that but a moment ago she had no desire to ever see Miss Jessup again, she suffered Julia's embrace, puppyish in its squirming ardor, and even gave back a convulsive squeeze all the while glaring at Mr. Vance over the girl's shoulder. *Of course* she would come again, and *soon,* she promised.

As soon as they had ridden out of earshot, she asked coldly what he meant by turning down Julia's invitation with no regard for her own wishes.

"Did I misread you then?" he asked mildly. "I thought I detected a certain lack of enthusiasm on your part for extending our visit."

"You're not so good at reading faces as you think you are. And may I point out that I am not a deaf-mute, I am accustomed to speaking for myself."

"Don't tell me you believe that story about the poachers."

Ada did not care for his sarcastic laugh. "There *are* poachers—even at Kirkewode," she retorted, glad to divert the argument along this path. "Caxton told me they had caught one just before I came."

"Be that as it may, surely you realize that any further intimacy with a young woman like that is undesirable."

"Oh!" Pure rage snorted from Ada. He and Rose made a very harmonious couple! "Spoken like a true Deventer!" she struck out at him. Her "oh!" this time was a sucking in of air, a futile attempt to recall that telltale sneer.

Excruciating silence. As if those words were stones dropped into an unplumbed abyss, and she was waiting for the impact of their landing. She stole a look at him—that sharp profile seemed exceptionally severe.

"How long have you known?" he asked at last.

There was no help for it. Ada knew the game she had been playing was at an end. "Since I saw your uncle at the opera."

It would seem from the direction of his gaze that he was more intent on the twitching of his horse's ears than on anything she had to say. "I must assume you have not yet shared this knowledge with Mrs. Deventer. May I ask why?"

Ada's answer was to bring her crop down smartly on her mare's flanks. "Race you back," she cried, determined to avoid any further interrogation. But she had something better in mind than the formal avenue of approach and departure they had just regained. She headed across the high meadowland that paralleled the river, in search of the fence she had first jumped to find herself on Jessup land. There it was, a girdle keeping Kirkewode's wilder growth within bounds. And there the opening in the treeline that marked the riding path on the other side. Ignoring Nicholas's alarmed halloo, she headed the mare straight for it and took the jump in fine style—or so she thought until she pulled up, once again on Deventer land, and allowed Nicholas to draw alongside her.

"You must loosen up on the reins, allow more neck extension," was his critical comment. Suddenly he stiffened in the saddle. "Did you hear that?"

They came to a halt, at strained attention, waiting for the mournful sound to be repeated. Somewhere close by a dog had howled. About to ride on, they barely heard the whimper.

Nicholas dismounted and strode into the brush. His "dammit"—more a signal of distress than an angry curse—brought Ada plunging to his side. She felt like cursing too when she saw Argos's bloody leg mangled in a steel trap. The tail flailed the ground feebly, the moist eyes were fixed with a pathetic eagerness on Nicholas Vance, and yet when the kneeling man reached out to unlock the trap, only quick reflex saved him from a vicious snap.

"It seems I owe Miss Jessup an apology," Nicholas said grimly, "there *are* poachers about. Look at that leg. And he'll not let me near it, he's in such pain. There's nothing for it but to shoot the poor beast, I'm afraid. I shall have to come back with a gun."

"Wait." Ada squatted behind the dog, impatiently assuring an anxious Mr. Vance that she would keep out of biting reach. "You can see the bone—how badly crushed I can't tell until we get him free—still I think he can be saved. It's just the kind of thing Dr. Stevens has a talent for, and since he's here he might as well be useful. At least, it's worth a try."

Nicholas agreed. The loss of Argos might prove more than Mrs. Haygood could bear. "In spite of all her talk about her son's need for company on the Other Side, she needs such company more."

Ada brusquely assumed command. Mr. Vance should stay with the dog, who at least recognized him as a friend. She would race back to Kirkewode, alert Dr. Stevens to prepare for surgery and return with an anesthetic. Once unconscious, the dog could be safely extricated from the trap. Without argument, Nicholas let her go, suggesting only that, while she was about it, she should also alert a couple of footmen to bring some kind of stretcher. "Argos is not exactly a lap dog, you know. I could put him across my saddle like a sack of grain, but that might prove a rougher ride than he could survive."

Ada lost no time beyond the moment or two it took to convince a stubborn mare that the proper turn to make was toward the castle, not the stables. She ignored Caxton's look of concern at her breathless state—a concern which was not diminished by her asking for Dr. Stevens. "In the Rose Room, miss, taking tea with Mrs. Deventer." Some dire catastrophe indeed, he must have thought, from the way she sprinted through the great hall.

Had she interrupted something, bursting in so unceremoniously? Or was it surprise, not guilt, that made those two figures on the sofa give such a startled jump?

"Really, Ada, one doesn't come to tea smelling of the stables," Rose said, quick to take the offensive. She was wiping her fingers on a frothy bit of lace. Francis was wiping chocolate off his chin.

"I did not come to tea—I came to get Dr. Stevens. We need his help."

Francis was on his feet, losing no time in what could only be a medical emergency. What had happened? Who was hurt? Where was the patient?

"A *dog?*" He stared at her incredulously, then his face took on the bruised color of anger. "Is this your idea of a joke?"

Ada's eye was still on a smudge his tongue had missed. She

could not trust herself to speak to him. Instead she addressed her plea to Mrs. Deventer, taking her case to a higher court. "It's Argos—he's been caught in a poacher's trap—badly hurt."

Francis wavered, he too looked to Mrs. Deventer for his cue. *Her* pet? he asked solicitously. An animal she was particularly fond of? If that was the case, then of course. . . . He left hanging what would follow next, but he resumed his seat, the better to display his reassuring bedside manner.

Rose's smile repaid him for his gallantry, but she let him know it was uncalled for. "A nasty-tempered beast that belongs to my chaplain's wife. Surely, Ada, there's someone at the stables who knows what to do with an injured animal—it's not suitable for Dr. Stevens to be bothered with something like that."

Ada swallowed her pride. "Please, Francis, it's a compound fracture of the nastiest sort. He won't survive unless he's operated on—and by someone who knows the latest surgical techniques—" she even attempted a flattering smile—"which is why I thought we were so lucky to have you here."

She ended with a helpless feminine flutter (am I really doing this? she asked herself) but it brought a softened look to Francis's face. It would have worked, he would have come, had not Rose put her hand on his knee—a "stay" command that Argos would have understood—and announced that she was glad to hear her own opinion of Dr. Stevens's talents so confirmed. "I have noticed before, Ada, what tender sensibilities you have where animals are concerned, but to me Dr. Stevens comes first. What would it do to his reputation to be seen doing kennel work?"

That had glued Francis firmly in place, she could not hope to dislodge him now. The ultimate humiliation—to play the helpless female and still lose the game.

Ada dropped all pretense to sweetness. "Since I have no reputation left to lose—" she sent Francis a scathing glance, "I will see what I can do myself. Do you still have the key to Papa's office?"

It was back in Caxton's hands, where it belonged, Rose told her reprovingly. She was not at all sure Ada's papa would care to have her tend a dirty animal in his surgery, nor would he care to have her—

Ada turned on her heel, not waiting to hear what else Papa would not care to have. She went in search of Caxton, snarling to herself: *And were you not a dirty animal once? Should you not show a little pity to those left in their original state?* But Papa's key in her hand had a calming effect, and once inside his office she had thought only for Argos's mangled leg and what procedure she must follow to repair it. Putting aside chloroform and a linen handtowel to take with her, she made up a solution of carbolic acid in a large porcelain bath and dumped in the contents of Papa's surgical kit, prepared another solution in the wash basin for her hands. She would need some wire . . . ah, in this drawer . . . and where did Papa keep his plaster of Paris. . . .

All in readiness, she closed the door behind her, only then remembering the need for a stretcher. Fortunately there was Thomas strolling down the hall. He gave a start when she called out his name, much surprised by her presence. Too surprised. Had she emerged a moment sooner, she suspected, she would have stumbled over him, eye to keyhole.

To one so curious, the sparseness of her information was a punishment that fit the crime. She told him only what was needed and where to take it, requiring first that he accompany her outside and help her remount. She galloped off, enjoying the thought of what wild imaginings she had implanted in his mind.

She found Nicholas on one knee, helplessly stroking Argos's head, making the clucking noises of a mother reassuring a feverish child. "It's going to be all right, old fellow, just you hold on a bit longer, it's going to be all right. . . ."

He looked embarrassed to be caught in so unmanly a pose. "I think he finds some comfort in hearing my voice. . . ."

"Don't apologize, Nicholas," Ada said, with a new warmth in

her voice, and passed him the towel soaked in chloroform. "Here, you're the one he trusts."

In the surgery, she was the one to be trusted, Nicholas made clear. He asked no questions beyond the whereabouts of Dr. Stevens, and even plunged his hands into the carbolic solution without demur, though the sting evoked a momentary grimace.

"You make a good operating room nurse," she said, as he stood by, handing over each instrument as requested, and supplying another whiff of chloroform when Argos gave signs of coming to.

"You make a good surgeon," he replied, watching with admiration as she cleared away the shreds of injured flesh and bone fragments, sponged up the blood, and fitted the parts of the bone together so precisely.

She wired the bone together, all the while chattering—a nervous rush of words she was unable to stop. "If you think I've done this before, you're mistaken. For the most part we are just herded into the amphitheater as spectators—like watching lions and Christians in an arena, you know—the women in a special section, of course, and you may be sure the view from there is not the best. This year I won the privilege of actually assisting, but that turned out to be—for me—mainly scrubbing up, but at least I got the chance to see. . . . Oh yes, they let me thread the catgut, as I am about to let you do. With Francis—Dr. Stevens—it was another story. They admired his work with cadavers so much, they even let him use the knife. Oh well, let's hope I paid attention in class—have you the needle threaded yet?"

The stitching finally done, she dressed the wound and made up the plaster of Paris, wondering how to make it clear to a dog that he must keep off the leg while the fracture healed. Nicholas suggested that two splints be arranged to protrude beneath the cast. "I see . . . to bear the weight . . . yes, that may work, and he'll hobble along like Pegleg Pete. . . . Mind you, I don't promise he'll be as good as new, but he'll survive, I'm pretty sure."

The job done, they faced each other over the still unconscious dog, exchanging a congratulatory smile. Ada suddenly remembered that she had never answered a certain question. "Don't worry, Nicholas—do you mind if I call you that, that's *one* of your names, isn't it?—"

"Please. It's the name I use, in fact." Looking at each other, they seemed unaware that the conversation had languished. Finally he said, "Don't worry about what?"

"Oh. That I will tell Mrs. Deventer who you are. Though of course I must tell Papa. But I'll make him promise to speak first to you before he takes any action. You'll have a chance to make your case, fair enough?"

More than fair, he granted. "But don't *you* want to hear my case?"

"No, no," she said quickly. She felt disloyal enough. He opened his mouth to speak and she clapped her hands over her ears. See no evil, speak no evil, hear no evil—like the little monkeys, a morally instructive threesome. "I will not talk about the Deventers behind their backs," she said loftily.

"Nobly put, Ada," he said, but with a grin that put her down a peg. "I've been thinking it's time I spoke to your papa anyway. I thank you for the opportunity."

He reached across the table and took her hand. Raw and red once more, she winced to see, but from the way he held it, it might have been as lily-pale as the Lady of Shalott's.

Never had Ada felt such ambivalence as in her anticipation of Papa's return. With each day that passed, Francis seemed more fixed in Rose's charmed circle. She wished Papa would hurry back and kick him out. Then hoped Papa would be delayed, remembering that once Nicholas's identity was exposed, the Deventers would kick *him* out.

By the end of the week, Papa had yet to show but Mr. Witten was sufficiently recovered to make a public appearance, though pale and subject to occasional tremors. Since he had no knowledge of her appearance at his bedside, she did not really expect his thanks, but she felt truly unappreciated when she and Nicholas called at the parsonage to inquire about Argos. No more than Mr. Witten did the dog recognize her as his benefactor, choosing instead to show his gratitude by licking Nicholas's hand. Mrs. Haygood would have liked to do the same, Ada was convinced. However, Nicholas had given her a full account of the operation and she was forced acknowledge that Ada had played a secondary role in saving her dear pet. "I shudder to think," she said, pressing Nicholas's hand, "what would have happened had you not heard him moaning when you rode by."

Ada's spirits sank to a new low after Sunday services in the chapel. Papa's continued absence was becoming a matter of concern. Nor were Dr. Haygood's sermons exactly spirit-lifting. This Sunday he had chosen as his text: *Behold, my brother Esau is a hairy man, and I am a smooth man.* An uninspiring verse, was Ada's first thought, but from those poor bricks what a grand edifice he managed to construct, providing yet another proof of how God knew his own. Those hairs of Esau betrayed the beast in man, the bristly evidence of his fallen state, whereas Jacob's skin, smooth as silk, showed the depilatory action of God's grace. You may delude yourself, announced that cold voice, sharp as the cutting edge of carbon steel, but always His hand is passing over his children, feeling for the hairy and the smooth, the sinner and the saved. Ada stole a glance at Francis to see how he was taking his first experience at a Kirkewode service, almost laughed aloud at his attitude of devout attention.

As soon as the service was concluded, she slipped away while Rose was presenting Francis to her chaplain as if he were another permanent member of the domestic congregation. She was having such bad thoughts about Francis and Rose Deventer—so inappropriate to a Sunday—she could not help but wonder if Papa was not right, she had been spiritually coarsened by her medical studies. She determined to spend the rest of the morning reading the Bible—a pious resolution that seemingly exhausted her virtue for she closed the door behind her with a discontented sigh.

However, she stretched out on the chaise longue with the Bible on her lap, toying with the idea of opening it at random. People did that sometimes, as a kind of soothsaying. Too much aware of the mirror across the room, she allowed one hand to fluff up her hair. Vanity, once awakened, seemed in constant need of reassurance, demanded now she take a look. The reflection that met her eyes so startled her, she gave a short shrill screech.

"Mr. Deventer!"

She scrambled to her feet and turned around. How long had he been there, standing beside the door, hands in pockets, staring at her with that penetrating, unblinking gaze? In those baggy knickers and low shoes, he must have come straight from an outing in the park.

"May I ask, sir, what you are doing in my room?"

He advanced, drawing out of one deep pocket a tangled glittery mass of jewelry. "There," he said, tossing what seemed a pirate's loot on the chaise, "that's for you. Is that enough?"

Ada gasped. The diamond star necklace, the rope of rubies and diamonds, the pearl choker—she had seen them all at one time or another around Rose's lovely neck. "Sir, those are your wife's jewels!"

His mouth opened, his cheeks spread, his eyes narrowed—the musculature of a laugh but no sound. "*She* won't care. She's got a new fancy man—two of 'em. I can count. I've seen 'em from my window, fine strapping lads, they'll keep her occupied."

There was something about his eyes—the sharp cut of the lids—that made her think of the cold predatory look of a lizard about to tongue a fly. Terror froze her to the spot. Movement—any movement—was imperative. She leaned over to pick up an emerald ring that had fallen at her feet. "You— you must handle these more carefully, sir. You'll damage the settings."

"Pooh," he said, "I'll get you more. Now I want to see those pretties I got a peek at—"

Ada backed away from the outstretched hand, instinctively guarding her breasts with crossed arms. "Please—*please*, Mr. Deventer, go away—leave me alone—I shall scream if you keep on like this—"

"Cunning, cunning!" He shook his head in open admiration. "I should have known a high-stepping filly like you wasn't to be taken in. I admit it—I've been holding out—but here's the lot!" With the triumphant air of a magician pulling a knotted string of colored handkerchiefs from his sleeve, he began to draw from his other pocket a rope of pearls—an unending length, it seemed. Ada had a fleeting vision of Rose in black and white descending the stairs of the Deventer town house on the way to the opera—

"Oh, do be careful, don't tug like that!" she cried impulsively as the string caught on a button of his sleeve. Pearls rained down on the rug. This was the moment for escape, Ada realized. Under the pretext of picking up the pearls, she had made her way almost to the door when she was seized from behind.

"You want to play horsey? I don't mind?" She felt his hand exploring underneath her bustle. With a hoarse cry of rage, she twisted around and raked his face with fingers turned to claws.

She had given him the warpaint of a savage—three bloody grooves down each cheek—but he seemed to feel no pain. She grasped his beard, pulled with all her might. It gave way with a rasping sound and she looked down in horror at the clump of red hair in her hand—pulled out by the roots!

"Don't *do* that," he said, suddenly deflated. He took the false beard out of her nerveless grasp. "Rosie wants me to always wear it, she doesn't like me hairless. . . ."

He was frowning at the mirror, nothing in his mind but the need to redress the damage she had done. She was forgotten, and yet she stood there, mouth agape, watching his pudgy hands slap the beard back in place. Then, as if awakening from a dream, she felt the power of movement restored to

228

her and she fled from the room. *Nicholas!* Only now could she scream, crying out not so much a name as a magic incantation against evil. Up the stairs, past Mr. Witten's door, she ran, faced with a nightmarish uncertainty as to which was Nicholas's room. *Nicholas!* she cried again and a door opened. She hurled herself at him with such force, he was rocked back against the wall.

Her response to his alarm came in dry gasps. He could not make out what she said. What jewels, he asked. His bear hug tightened as if to squeeze the answer out of her, but it served only to extract a wild arpeggio of laughter. He was asking the wrong question, she thought, he should be asking: And did you once see Deventer plain, and did he stop and speak to you?

"Mr. Deventer, plain enough, in my room—just now!" The giggles coming out of her were like bubbles of a dangerous chemical reaction. "He was trying—he attacked me, Nicholas— and I pulled out his beard! I had it in my hands!"

Kinder than a slap, but just as efficacious, was the firm press of lips on hers. "Stay in here," he said, closing the door of his room on her. Her rigid obedience lasted only as long as she could hear his running steps. In the ensuing silence, her mind played with new images of disaster: Nicholas squaring off against a sparring Mr. Deventer . . . or worse, Mr. Deventer creeping up the servants' stairs while Nicholas sought him on the floor below. Anything was better than being alone, shut in, passively awaiting the outcome. . . . She opened the door a crack to find the passageway was clear, and ran after her protector.

Standing in the middle of her empty room, Nicholas whirled around as she entered. "There's no one here," he said unnecessarily.

No jumble of diamonds and rubies and emeralds on the chaise. No scattering of pearls on the rug. The little table overturned in the struggle had been righted. The Bible which had fallen from her hands now rested in its rightful place by her bed. No sign at all of an intruder. She wondered that he seemed to still believe her.

"This time you stay put," Nicholas said grimly, "I'm going to beard him in his lair. He is certainly living up to all my father's reports of him—the governor was right, it seems, in refusing to believe a man like that could change."

And this time she obeyed, hovering in the doorway just long enough to see him disappear into the Deventer wing. Calmer now, she wished she had held Nicholas back. What could be gained by a row that would surely come to Rose Deventer's ears. It was her experience that wives preferred to believe in shameless hussies rather than in errant husbands, and she squirmed at the thought of the kind of interview with Rose that must ensue. All those Ann Arbor faces surfaced anew—Reverend Nichols and his wife, Dean Thwaite, the stationmaster ogling her even as she boarded the train, memory fudging on the features but recapturing intact all the condemnation and disdain. If only she had not lost her head but made a quiet escape, remembering that Papa was due back any moment now. When he heard what had occurred (even the expurgated version she was already preparing in her mind), he would take her away from Kirkewode under some polite pretext—she would insist on that—avoiding any unpleasant fuss.

So when Nicholas returned to report that Slade, still on guard before his master's door, swore that Mr. Deventer had just returned from a short constitutional and had not been out of his sight, Ada made no protest.

"He refused to let me see the man himself—fisticuffs, I decided, would be inadvisable," Nicholas said with a twitch of his lips. "Nevertheless, I'm afraid that Slade does not make a good liar."

Ada was almost perky at the thought that a scene might yet be avoided. "He *could* be telling the truth, Nicholas. I've been thinking . . . it's possible I fell asleep and had a nightmare of sorts—you know how real they can seem when you just wake up—" Ada faltered, reading in his eyes that she too made a poor liar.

He did not answer her directly but strolled over to the chaise and picked up a pearl that lay beneath it. He tossed it in the air and caught it with a quick snap of his hand, as if intent only on playing a boy's game.

"I'm afraid that won't wash, Ada. And I don't mean because of this little bauble. I'm sure that, given a moment, you could explain it away as well. The best evidence that Deventer was here is what you said about his beard."

"That it comes off?" The most nightmarish part, Ada would have thought.

"Exactly. It's supposed to be a family secret, but he has no hair—none at all. Even the eyebrows are false—"

"No eyelashes! That's what's so odd about his eyes!" Ada could not contain her chagrin at making so belated a discovery. She had noted the reptilian stare and yet had failed to notice an anomaly like that! "A congenital condition?"

She had succeeded in embarrassing the unflappable Mr. Vance. "Er—not precisely," he said, examining the pearl as if he had a jeweler's eye for its worth. "As a young man, he incurred—hmm—a certain disease. He was fortunate enough to be cured, but not before all his hair fell out."

"I see." Ada employed her most matter-of-fact manner. "*Alopecia syphilitica.*" Did he think she had gone through medical school without learning about that "private" disease? It was true there had been but one lecture on the subject (from which the ladies could be excused if they so desired). Granted that the odium attached to such patients was apt to stick to the physicians who treated them, it seemed to her the height of foolishness to ignore a disease that afflicted so many—one in every twenty if the latest figures were to be believed. And besides, as she had remarked to an unappreciative Francis, were physicians to restrict their services to the virtuous, they would soon wind up with no practice at all.

"I had forgotten your scientific training," Nicholas apologized. "Although in fact I have known even doctors to be offended by the mention of such complaints—agreeing with the ministry that it is a divine retribution for a misspent life and therefore beyond their province. In which case one would think my uncle's cure would equally imply divine forgiveness, but their thinking does not go so far." He ran his hand over his own thick fair hair and smiled. "Nor did my father's. I think he rather appreciated having so handy an object lesson to hold up to his son."

It was a brave show, this dispassionate discussion of venereal disease, but neither could meet the other's eye and Nicholas quickly returned to the problem of his uncle's present conduct. By contrast, that no longer seemed so embarrassing. With a convincing lightness, Ada shrugged it off. No doubt Mr. Deventer was accustomed to purchasing whatever he desired. It was true his overtures has been somewhat crude, but she was afraid (repugnant as it was, she forced herself to say it) she had been guilty of a typical female reaction. Hysteria had led to exaggeration.

"Do let it lie, Nicholas," she pleaded, uncomfortably aware that he did not believe her. In the end, she had to play her last card—Papa's imminent return. She was sure he would prefer to handle the matter himself.

"It is true, he has the right, not I." For a heart-stopping moment Ada thought he was going to ask, then and there, to remedy that situation. But instead he gave a short laugh and put the pearl in his pocket. "Perhaps I was guilty of a typical male reaction—the desire to be a Sir Galahad. But until your papa does return, I shall keep an eye on you. You must allow me that."

Secretly comforted by the thought, Ada graciously allowed him that. An unnecessary precaution, she was sure, but nevertheless she locked the door as soon as he was gone and felt the safer for it. Once again she took the Bible and settled on the chaise, but once again her thoughts were far too worldly. To keep an eye on her, Nicholas would surely suggest they spend the afternoon together. It was a little difficult to decide what gown to wear.

She sat up with a start—was there someone at the door? Her eyes widened with terror as she watched the doorknob turn.

"Ada! Are you in there?"

Papa! Ada sprang to her feet, rushed to unlock the door. Her welcoming hug was returned in full measure. Lifted off her feet, she was whirled around and around until breathlessly he released her, admitting she was a big girl now.

"Since when have you taken to locking your door?"

Not now, she decided silently. Never had she seen him look so happy, she would not spoil that with her own misadventure. And besides, he was not giving her a chance.

"Oh, Ada, a new day is aborning—for both you and me! I have so much to tell you, but later, later. Do you know where I've been this past week? Making a new future for us, away from Kirkewode, away from—Kirkewode. You were right of course—not an easy admission for a father to make to his own child. I have grown rusty, behind the times. That article of Fitz's—"

"You read it, Papa?" Ada's face lit up.

"Of course I read it, my little sawbones."

For once Ada did not object to that epithet. At best she had hoped he would read Fitz's paper on the sly. Not in her most sanguine moments, had she dreamed he would openly admit her opinions carried weight. Yet here he was, *seriously* discussing medicine with her!

"I do not fully agree with you," he warned, "I think you're jumping in too soon with surgery, but it is unforgivable that I did not even know what new ideas were in the market place. Well, I have just taken steps to remedy that. There is now a Postgraduate School in the city, where even an old codger like me can bring himself up-to-date without sitting in a pew with a bunch of young whippersnappers to make him feel a fool. That's something new, there was no such thing in my day." They laughed in unison at his use of that phrase which in her mouth had so enraged him. "Yes, I admit it, I had a day. And, by God, I'll have another, you'll see. In fact, that's how I feel—

as if a long night is over and the sun is just clearing the roof-tops and there are all these bird noises in my head and the smoke is just beginning to come out of chimneys and a fresh wonderful day lies ahead."

Could he be inebriated, Ada wondered—at this time of day and on a Sabbath? But she smelled nothing on his breath. Still it was hard to understand his euphoria until he announced he had been busy elsewhere too. He had rented a house in the city with two front parlors, one of which would make a fine office for his new practice. "And you'll be my assistant, in all but name—in front of the patients I'll call you nurse—how does that sound to you?"

She was so stunned he had to tweak a sidecurl of her loosened hair to evoke some response. "Oh Papa, you really mean it? You're truly leaving the Deventers? And we'll have our own house? And you'll let me help you in your practice?"

Amused at such a rush of questions, he responded to them all. "I do, I am, we will, and I count on you being my right-hand man. And Ada—" no longer laughing, he seemed struck dumb with shyness, about to speak, then thinking better of it, his red fringe of beard quivering as he struggled with his indecision.

Papa shy? Ada could not believe it. How endearing. For the first time in his presence, she felt grown-up, as if she had just noticed that her height was commensurate with his or that their eyes met at the same level. "Yes, Papa?" she urged him gently. "You wanted to tell me something?"

"Now is not the time," he said with his old briskness, and yet she saw he could not bring himself to leave without hinting at a future revelation. "You must not think I have been entirely rusticating these last years. Don't forget that I too have a predilection for research. For you it's Koch and Pasteur, for me it was Claude Bernard. I was in Paris when he died and you should have seen the funeral—you would have thought it was for a Napoleon, not a mere man of science. In this country, of course, no one cares if you have discovered some great truth, all that matters is can you turn a profit. Even so, my name may one day be on people's lips, you may yet be proud of your papa, Ada."

"You cannot let it go at that, Papa," she coaxed, holding him back by his lapels. "I want to know what you are working on—something important, I can tell."

Beard tilted upward, he squinted at the coffered ceiling. "Ha!" he grunted, satisfied that he had contrived a sufficiently enigmatic clue. "Let me tell you about the three chickens—"

"Oh, not a fable, Papa!" Ada groaned.

He laughed and pinched her cheek. Where was the grown up Ada now? She was his little girl again. "Not Aesop's chickens, you goose, M. Pasteur's. I have your interest now, eh? But since you put it in my mind, it makes a rather good fable at that."

Ada sat on the chaise, hugging her knees, transported to earlier happier days when she had listened thus to his stories of Greek gods, which Mama had frowned upon as unfit for a little girl's ears. "Once upon a time," he began, proving he shared the same memory. This too was to be a story of the gods—an argument between a lesser diety and the All-Knowing One. (Ada smiled; not a bad epithet for M. Pasteur, whom many a disgruntled colleague accused of all-knowingness.)

"The All-Knowing One had just proclaimed, in that annoying way of his, that anthrax, which could fell a mighty ox overnight, was helpless against a puny chicken. The lesser deity, determined to prove for once that the All-Knowing One was wrong, inoculated chicken after chicken with a virulent culture of the bacillus, but to no avail. He had to admit it, chickens could not be given the disease. Whereupon the All-Knowing One reversed himself—such high beings can be very provocative at times—and said that he would prove his superior powers by doing what the lesser god had publicly admitted was impossible. *He* would kill a chicken with anthrax.

"Now listen carefully. This is where the three chickens come in." Papa had dropped all playfulness. So serious was his tone that Ada swung her feet to the floor and sat up straight. "M. Pasteur inoculated a white chicken with anthrax, then put it into a cold bath. With the same culture, he inoculated a black chicken, but spared it the rigors of the bath. Two days later, he presented his chickens: The black chicken was completely healthy, but the white chicken was stone dead. Mind now, both had been inoculated with the same culture—there's a riddle for you."

Ada shook her head. A fable, she insisted. "The moral is, don't take a cold bath."

"No, no. I forgot the the third chicken—a speckled one. It was given the cold bath but no inoculation and survived as well."

Ada amended the moral. "Don't take a cold bath if you've just been shot full of anthrax."

"That certainly applies to chickens, my dear," he said. He looked inordinately pleased with himself but refused to entertain any further questions. "First you must tell me why the white chicken died and the black did not—I'll give you until luncheon to figure that one out, as I'm sure you will, a smart girl like you." Meanwhile he had too much to do to jabber away like this. He had yet to freshen up and then he must let Mrs. Deventer know of his return.

The thought of Rose had a sobering effect. He supposed the lady was displeased with his taking off like that? Reading the answer in Ada's face, he seemed to shrink a bit, drawing his shoulders together as if to conserve a dwindling warmth. A poor chicken doused in a cold bath could not have looked more dispirited. But Ada was not to worry, it would soon be all over, was his exit line.

Left alone, Ada felt the full force of Papa's news. Never again would she despair, or be tempted to abandon hope. In the twinkling of an eye, all could be changed, and happiness which had seemed forever destroyed, suddenly restored. *We are going to leave Kirkewode,* Papa had said it—just like that, all on his own. It was as if the hand of Providence had turned back the clock, erasing the last seven years, with all the strains that had developed between them. Only now was she disembarking from the ship which had brought her back to New

York, only now was she stepping onto shore, only now was Papa opening his arms to her. . . .

Yet even in her state of exaltation, M. Pasteur's chickens made themselves heard. It was disconcerting that she had never heard of that particular experiment—in a field she would have chosen for her own. Of course, anthrax no longer made the news, Papa must have cited work more than ten years old. Was probably in Paris at the very time, may well have heard M. Pasteur himself triumphantly report his results. Still, Papa had remembered it all these years. She had thought that he had abandoned, along with her and Mama, all interest in research as well. She was wrong, it seemed.

Yet the real riddle, she obscurely felt, lay not in those old facts but in what new use he had found for them. In the dressing room, she squatted on her haunches over her unpacked box of books. Texts were of little use in that field—even the revised editions could not keep pace with the current explosion of discoveries. Lecture notes held more promise, and she settled on the floor to moon over her dense, crabbed scribbling as over the love letters of an old beau. The pins-and-needles tingling of a leg asleep reminded her that the time for luncheon must be drawing near. Though she had found nothing to the point, on some other level her mind had been working all the while, so that in putting away her notes, she cried aloud, "How simple!" There was the answer, as if ready-made.

Carefully she checked the reasoning for a flaw. What did one do for a patient with a raging fever? Swab his body down with cold water. What was a bird's normal temperature? Close to 110° Fahrenheit if she remembered correctly—certainly a raging fever compared to that of man or cattle. If there was one thing she had learned in the pathology lab, it was the importance of maintaining the right temperature in culturing any organism. Simple indeed—it was normally too hot inside the chicken for the anthrax bacillus to survive, hence the fowl's natural immunity. In proof of which, M. Pasteur had lowered its temperature by means of a cold bath and *voila!* one dead white chicken. "How

237

clever!" she cried this time. She wished Francis were present so that she might brag to him how clever she was too.

Francis! She had forgotten to warn Papa he was here! If those two met at luncheon—and Papa unprepared—only a dreadful scene could result! Papa ranting about horsewhips and her disgrace, Francis nobly vowing to make amends—she would die of shame at such a public display of her private life. Ada closed her eyes and saw the public as Nicholas Vance. She opened them to check the mantel clock—thank heavens, there was still time to catch Papa in his room before he came down. Since French cooks had a regrettable tendency to be Papist—so Rose complained—they required the entire morning to attend the village mass and as a consequence Sunday's midday meal was a cold collation and never served before one.

For the second time that morning, Ada made a mad dash up the stairs. At first politely, then more vigorously, she knocked on Papa's door, refusing to accept silence as an answer. Tired from his exertions in the city, he might have fallen asleep. She walked in and called out hopefully, "Papa?" On tiptoe she approached the open bedroom. Why on tiptoe? she asked herself, I *want* to wake him. Resolutely put her foot down and marched forward, only to come to an abrupt halt. A glitter of gold on the floor beyond the threshhold caught her eye. There was no mistaking that little piece of foil.

A furious blush testified to her embarrassment—what if she had walked in on Papa and Rose Deventer in the very act of—? She would never have been able to look either in the eye again. She teetered for a moment in dread of making any further sound, nerving herself to tiptoe out.

It was the continued silence that held her—surely there should be *some* noise? Her blush deepened, that she should think such a thought. And yet how strangely quiet they were. She could hear a clock ticking in the bedroom. It had always seemed to her that clocks acquired an inflated sense of their own importance in an empty room, and this one made a sound like that.

Mrs. Deventer must have left, and Papa too. The desire to see was too strong, she stepped forward, stood in the doorway.

Her father was alone. He lay crosswise on the bed, still in his traveling clothes. As if he had sat for some time on the edge, trying to decide if it was worth the effort to get up. He must have decided it was not. On the rug at his feet, lay the gun. She forced herself to take another step. She could see now what was left of his face. She was back in the amphitheater watching her first operation. The young man across from her sank down in his seat, someone held his head between his legs. *I* won't faint, she heard herself saying.

But there was something wrong with her knees. She tried to move closer, but all color was fading. Even the blood was dirtying to a grey. Papa, she whispered, and crumpled to the floor.

Chapter 14

FRANCIS had taken over everything—Papa's office, Papa's practice, now Papa's place beside Rose Deventer in the chapel. Ada, arriving late, sat immediately behind the sober couple, made sure they heard the rustle of her mourning clothes, felt her breath upon their necks. Grief may have buried Mrs. Haygood on this estate as inconspicuously as her son, but Ada meant to make her presence known.

Only such unchristian feelings could have brought her to this Sunday service, knowing that Dr. Haygood would not fail to mention Papa. She would have liked to forbid him to utter Papa's name, but failing that, she had contrived to miss most of his opening remarks.

". . . the great loss this house has suffered. . . ."

Thank God, he was winding to a close. At least he had been allowed to play no part in the funeral. That had been arranged by Nicholas—a discreet, all but unattended service at a Universalist Church. There God was not so unforgiving, and Papa's grave would be distinguished from the others only by the newness of the stone. All souls would be saved, the minister had assured her, regardless of the nature of their sins. Or the nature of their demise.

". . . and in times like these, where may we turn for guidance and instruction if not to the Good Book. . . ."

All souls, Ada repeated to herself as Dr. Haygood fingered the black ribbon of his Bible and opened to his text. All souls save one. She was not ready to give up the satisfaction of seeing Rose Deventer burn in hell.

"My soul chooseth strangling rather than life. Job 7:15."

Strangling was the sound that came from Francis, while Rose Deventer inhaled through clenched teeth, as if sucking in her dismay through a straw. In the pause that followed, Ada could plainly hear the stirring in the rear, envisaged servants craning for a better view of her. The protracted silence tightened every nerve, but still Dr. Haygood's massive head remained bowed, as if in private communion with his God. Or as if he had come ill-prepared and had yet to conceive how best to refute Job's despondent cry.

As the bulging dome lifted, Ada braced herself, determined not to look away, however pointedly he referred to Papa's choice. Prepared though she was to be unmoved, she was shocked at the sight of his face. So a saint might look, writhing in torture, but nourished by a radiant vision of the heavenly host. She had feared to be singled out; instead she felt obliterated by the trance-like fixity of his eyes, so darkened by an inward concentration they seemed more black than blue.

"I have decided to discard the sermon I prepared last night." The raspy sound hardly carried to the front row. He spoke as if someone had him by the throat. "Poor words, I have just realized, compared to those delivered on this subject by a far greater preacher than I. These are sad times when such a man can be dismissed as a mere scrivener of entertaining allegory, when his most inspired creation can be called a *novel*." His voice, suddenly restored, filled the small chamber with its ringing scorn. "As if his *Pilgrim's Progress* had anything in common with that unclean literature you read today, these modern novels aswarm with libertines and desperadoes, with fine ladies given over to every vice, these foul imaginings that play their part in filling our insane asylums and penitentiaries and alms-houses and dens of shame!

"And yet how much more exciting than any penny dreadful trash is Bunyan's simple story so simply told—what adventure, perils and temptations are encountered when a Christian sets out to save his soul! It is the city of eternal life he is seeking, and Bunyan knew, knowing his own heart, how easy it would be to lose his way. Or worse, to give up, finding the route too arduous, the dangers too great. We are not all so fortunate to have with us a companion called Hopeful when we come to Doubting Castle, wherein lives the Giant Despair. Imprisoned there in a dark stinking dungeon, without food or water or sight of daylight or any chance of succor, even Christian's heart fails him. Doubly fails him, for he knows he is in such dire straits because of his own weakness: did he not turn aside into By-Pass Meadow, in spite of his companion's gentle warning, when the right road became too rough and stony for his taste?

"Moreover the Giant Despair has a wife, whose name is Diffidence, and it is she who counsels him how best to break Christian's spirit. She would, as is a woman's way, seduce him. Not with the usual visions of earthly delights, mind you, but with the far more seductive vision of death. Why choose to live, seeing life is attended with so much bitterness? So speaks a woman's tongue. We must not forget it was Job's wife who would curse God and die. Nor would Christian have been able to withstand the temptation without the manly presence of Hopeful by his side.

"Who among us has not spent time in Doubting Castle, in the hands of the Giant Despair? Who has not thought at some moment the grave would be easier than this dungeon of a life? Let me recall for you how Hopeful dissuaded Christian from committing that unpardonable sin. If to murder another man is anathema to the Lord, then how much more offensive is it to

His nostrils to murder thine own self? In the first case, you but commit murder upon a body, whereas in the second you kill both body and soul.

"Need I remind you of the everlasting torments of hell beside which all your present heartbreak and misery and pain will seem as mere pinpricks, the annoyance of a gnat? Is it, like Christian in Doubting Castle, mere bread and water that today's jobless lack? Let them remember that in hell the smell of burning flesh will take all appetite away. Does the tenement dweller in the city, like Christian in his dungeon, mourn the lack of light? There is no blackness deeper than the pitch-blende depths of hell! Those poor souls who could not await God's happy release but thought to be beforehand in finding ease of pain are even now turning on the spit, roasting in hell, the playthings of the Devil's minions, who feast upon the tortured screams—"

Ada could bear no more. She rose and left the chapel, softly closing the door on a voice that did not falter for a moment at her leaving, that still penetrated even so thick a slab of wood—a torture instrument itself, worthy of the Devil that he preached. Like a sleepwalker, she made her way through the corridors of the main wing to the morning room, where Francis found her some time later. Relieved to see her so composed, he expressed his own indignation at the sermon. "No one blames you, Ada, that was really laying it on too strong. Mrs. Deventer is mad as a hornet—she expressly urged him not to mention your pa's—er—passing on."

The black-garbed figure on the window seat did not turn. "She should spare herself," Ada finally said, without lifting her forehead from the glass. "He does not concern himself with Papa, it is his son for whom he has designed such comfortable quarters."

"Bully for you! That sounds more like my old girl. I tell you what, after lunch we'll take a little ride in the runabout—just you and me and Mrs. Deventer—it really is a bang-up day!" There was no response to his fake heartiness. He sat down beside her, took her hand. "Ada, you can't go on like this." He must have heard the edge of impatience in his voice, for he took a deep breath and spoke more gently. "You'll just make yourself sick, you know." Words failing him, he patted the inert hand he still clasped.

"Don't do that!" Ada cried sharply, pulling free, seeing too clearly Rose Deventer's hand being administered to in just that way.

Francis made an effort to swallow his chagrin. "I guess I spoke truer than I thought when I told Mrs. Deventer it's nothing personal, you don't want *anyone* to touch you just now."

"Oh, has she been complaining of me?" It was a listless question, requiring no answer.

"For heaven's sake, Ada, don't you think she's got reason to complain? First off, you all but call her a murderess—"

"I apologized for that."

"Yeah, just about as convincingly as a horse thief apologizes when the noose is around his neck. And now you hardly speak to her, you take the first chance to leave the room when she comes in, you snoot her when she tries to comfort you for your loss—her loss too, don't forget, your pa was more than her doctor, he was her dearest friend—"

"Oh-ho." Ada's smile was a fine piece of nastiness. "Did she confess as much?"

Francis was shocked. Was that why she shrank from the lady's touch? Then it was true, as Mrs. Deventer feared, she was in danger of becoming downright deranged from grief. A purer, nobler woman he had never encountered in his life, nor one more put upon by fate. "Her burdens are greater than any you will ever know, but she doesn't let them get her down. You don't see her going around with a long face, looking as if the world had come to an end—"

The smile was still there. "I forgot, Francis. You're her doctor now, on the way to becoming her dearest friend—"

He looked ready to strangle her. "I'll tell you what, my girl. It's not just my patience that's wearing thin, it's Mrs. Deventer's too. After that scene you pulled last Sunday night, any other woman would have demanded that you leave her house, but out of the kindness of her heart she insisted that you stay at Kirkewode until your pa's estate gets straightened out. And this is the thanks she gets. I wouldn't blame her a bit if she did kick you out."

Not even his slam of the door disturbed Ada's icy calm. Having brought him to the point of explosion, she had deliberately transferred her attention to the view outside that he might see how impotent he was, even at his most furious, to reach her. And yet he had. *Last Sunday night.* That was all he had needed to say to tear loose the scab of apathy, set the wound bleeding again. A full week ago—an anniversary of sorts—her whole world had crumbled, all happiness blackened out. It seemed to her in another lifetime that they had found her huddled on this window seat. In the morning room, though it was night.

The glass against her forehead then had been weeping from the cold. Her eyes were dry. When they turned up the gas, destroying the womb-like darkness of her solitude, they found her completely in control. Why a Commissioner? she had wondered, fixing on that trivial detail as if it were the most significant event of the night. Entering the room, he had trundled his abdomen before him, announcing in avoirdupois his importance before Rose Deventer could. Had he driven posthaste to this farthest reach of his domain to ensure that a great house like the Deventers would not be disrupted by clumsy locals? Or did he dream of achieving an audience with Mad Jack Deventer, in the recounting of which he could dine out for many a month? If so, he was doomed to disappointment. Mr. Deventer had taken to his bed in a state of shock—more distressed, it would seem, by his doctor's death than the man's own daughter.

Apologetically the Commissioner explained he must question her—if she was up to it? That she was so evidently up to it did not speak well for her in his eyes. Ada welcomed his disapproval—it was proof that she had risen above hysteria, that her fainting had been a momentary weakness. She answered each question briefly, to the point, marveling at the steadiness of the flat uninflected monotone that was now her voice. Even the critical question, when it came, aroused in her nothing but a desire to make known the truth. As the last person to have seen Dr. Traherne alive, could she recall anything he had said that would explain his taking his own life?

"Looking back, of course," the Commissioner had quickly added, assuring her that often things were said which at the time had no significance, from which no one could be expected to predict such an irrational act, but only later . . . "looking back" . . . he floundered, coming full circle.

So considerate an attempt to absolve her of guilt. Ada too determined to be kind. She would not lecture him on the danger of fabricating a theory from untested assumptions—the poor man simply did not have a scientific mind. *She* was not the last person to have seen Papa alive. The piece of gold foil in her pocket attested that. But even more serious was another erroneous assumption he had made.

"Not suicide," she corrected gently, "murder, I would call it."

Rose had gasped. "Oh, Ada, my poor dear!" And cast a meaning look at the Commissioner, who stroked his whiskers and cleared his throat and fixed his eyes longingly on the door as if he wished now he had left the local constabulary in charge.

"My dear Miss Traherne," he said in great distress, "I have seen the wound myself, there can be no doubt—"

"I saw it too, you know," Ada said. No one could question her reasonableness. "Legally you may be right, he pulled the trigger, but—" Ada bestowed on Rose Deventer a nod of polite recognition—"*she* drove him to it. I don't know what she said, but somehow she made him do it. Surely the law will take cognizance of such an act—"

Rose moved toward her, but stopped short as if encountering an invisible wall. There was no way for her pale face to grow paler, but her grey eyes were magnified by the watering of unshed tears. "Ada, my child. I know you cannot bear to hold yourself responsible, but that is no reason to thrust the blame on me."

246

"What's that, what's that? The girl's responsible, you say?"

"No, no, Commissioner, I did not say that. You must not think that. Nor you either, Ada. I am sure that he had fully recovered from the blow of your expulsion—there was some dreadful misunderstanding, Commissioner, at the medical school this young lady was attending—you would not believe it to look at her, such a pretty young thing, but she was just three months short of being a doctor! Such a learned young lady, yet too much learning can be dangerous thing for the female mind, don't you think, Commissioner? It is a risk I myself have preferred not to take. As I have often said to my dear husband: Mr. Deventer, you have brains enough for the two of us, so I leave it to you to tell me what to think. As, my dear friend, I leave it to you to tell me what to make of this terrible tragedy."

That was when the Commissioner took her extended hand to chafe between his own with a restorative vigor that would have better served for frostbite. Clever, clever Rose. Behold another fool eating out her hand. This was no time to question the bereaved, the Commissioner could see, the poor girl should be in bed under a doctor's care. . . .

Francis was right, of course. She could not go on like this or Rose would kick her out. And once Kirkewode's gates closed behind her, Rose would be safe. Ada fingered the gold foil in her pocket—she was glad now she had not mentioned it, for the police would surely have taken it away. Yet what would it prove except that Rose, too, had greeted Papa on his return, but as to why he had done this dreadful deed (she would say) she had no more idea than his poor deranged daughter. If not the hard evidence Ada had first thought, it served well enough as a talisman, giving her strength to carry on, hardening her decision to connive, to lie, to listen at keyholes, to play the most duplicitous role—there was nothing she would not do to find out how, and why, Rose had contrived to make a man like Papa put the muzzle of a gun in his mouth and blow the back of his head away. That she had done so, Ada did not for a moment doubt. Something had happened between the time he had left her, so eager for the new life he had planned, in which she at last was to fully share, and that blood-draining moment when she had seen his body on the bed, the coverlet splattered with his brains. That something was Rose Deventer.

Was it too late to mend her fences, to get back into Rose's good graces? *If we are to be honest with each other, it's all acting—* Rose herself had said. For the first time in her life, she would stoop to mummery and pretense. Hate must wear the face of love if she was to revive the intimacy they had once enjoyed.

Since it was Rose's custom to linger for a chat with her chaplain—not likely to be a pleasant one today if her wishes had been disobeyed—she might yet be caught before she disappeared into the Deventer wing. Ada lay in wait behind the armored guardians of the stairs and was soon rewarded by the sound of clicking heels. Slowly, with a despondent droop and dragging pace, she began to ascend, certain of being overtaken by that brisk step.

"Ada, my dear," Rose called out, more tentatively than was her wont. "May I speak to you—for just a moment, please?"

"Yes?" Ada stopped to ask, unwilling compliance in her pose. But that she had stopped at all—and spoken, if only a monosyllable that seemed forcibly squeezed from her chest—left Rose overjoyed. Not on the stairs, she pleaded and, eyeing Ada as if she were some recalcitrant and potentially dangerous pet, coaxed her into the Rose Room.

"Ada, you must listen to me," she said, as soon as she had closed the door, "I was as horrified as you by Dr. Haygood's sermon. I have just come from letting him know the full extent of my displeasure. I cannot speak for what Mr. Deventer may do when he hears of it." Ada, steeling herself to respond, was letting the moment slip by. "I know, my dear, that for some reason you blame me for your Papa's act—perhaps because of certain tragedies that have gone before—but, by all that's holy, I swear to you this was no disappointed lover evening up the score. There's been nothing like that between us for a long, long time."

Rose sighed, defeated by Ada's silence. The girl would not even look at her. "I had hoped that by being honest—" she shrugged and turned to go, had half opened the door before Ada's cry stopped her.

"Oh, Mrs. Deventer!"

Rose barely opened her arms in time to receive Ada's shaking body. "Oh my dear, my dear, my dear. . . ." For once the throaty voice held no sexual undertone, throbbed with a purely maternal ache.

Her face hidden, the words directed into the crook of Rose's neck, Ada found it easier than she had expected to make her speech. "Oh, do forgive me, Mrs. Deventer—"

"Rose. I am your—Rose now." Your mama, was the unspoken plea.

"Oh, Rose, such terrible thoughts I had—you have no idea—I must have been out of my mind this past week." Ada spoke in dry gasping sobs, the closest she could come to simulating tears. "When I saw Papa last, he spoke so strangely, in riddles he would not explain . . . all I could make out was that he planned to put an end to his life here at Kirkewode. He seemed so happy, Rose, how could I guess he meant *that* kind of end? I was sure you had discouraged him, convinced him it was too late for a man his age—I know he cared about your opinion, more than he ever cared for mine. If one can be *jealous* at a time like that, I must have been, to strike out at you so senselessly."

Was it the convincing force of her own words, or was it the comforting feel of Rose's embrace that caused the dam to break? Real tears were streaming down her cheeks, the first she had been able to shed for Papa. As if only now did it sink in that he was really gone, that she was truly an orphan, facing the world alone. She felt Rose's light kisses on her head, the low voice crooning forgiveness in her ear.

". . . To have lost your father was a heavy blow, but to have lost my daughter, too—for that is how I long to think of you— was even worse!"

It was like quicksand, this emotional terrain she had ventured upon. There was no longer a firm floor of hate to stand on, only this morass of long-buried needs—buried but still alive. How easy it would be to let go, to sink inextricably into that embrace, to be no longer on her own, but a child again, loved by Mama.

With her own bit of lacy lawn, Rose wiped the drenched cheeks, kissed the reddened lids and swore that if her skin did not have a regrettable tendency to blotch, she would be bawling too. "We're friends again?"

"Friends," Ada said and was told lovingly to run upstairs and wash her face, she looked a sight.

She washed more than tears away. Cold water slapped on her face revived her as from a swoon. Had she really been about to accept Rose's proffered love and protection? Not at all, she reassured herself, she had been carried away by the unexpected intensity of her performance. Should she need another career, perhaps she should consider the stage.

"Marie! What are you doing here—did you not go to mass with the others?"

The girl had entered so silently, Ada was startled to see the white fluted cap in the mirror. She did not wish to hurt Marie's sensibilities, but she could not bear the commiserating looks, the pitying sighs with which Marie paid homage to her loss. The truth was that, as a lady's maid, she now had little enough to do. What was there to choose between one mourning dress and another? Yet she was forever suggesting that Ada's hair be brushed or a new herbal tea be tried, or some strange-smelling poultice be left on overnight—no doubt a peasant remedy guaranteed to draw out grief.

She had not felt up to such a long carriage ride today, was Marie's excuse this time for being underfoot. And besides, Maxwell had passed on to her a secret of *les grandes dames* which she would be gratified if ma'mselle would try. This little bottle of golden salts dissolved in a warm bath not only invigorated the skin but lifted the spirits, evaporated *chagrin*—

"Oh do go away, Marie. If Sunday is not to be your day of

worship, at least let it be your day of rest. I know you mean it kindly, but you're getting on my nerves."

Ada was sorry to have hurt her feelings—Marie had departed with her mouth clenched so tightly, one would think she was suffering real pain—but hoped her outburst would have some lasting effect. She had no need of fancy salts to relieve her depression—that had been accomplished by her success with Rose Deventer. It was better to act, however foolishly, than to endure passively whatever blows the enemy saw fit to inflict. Her next move must be to join forces with Nicholas. Reading her frame of mind, he had not intruded on her solitude once the funeral was over and there was no other practical service he could do. So anxious was she to keep in motion, Ada refused to wait until luncheon and ran upstairs to his room.

"Oh never mind that." Ada dismissed his embarrassment as peremptorily as she had dismissed her maid. She had no time for a silly stricture against entering a man's room. Even sillier was his hustling into a coat, his frantic search for a piece of silk to conceal the open neck of his shirt—as if one did not see workingmen dressed like that every day. Without further ado, she demanded to know what he was doing here. At Kirkewode. In disguise. "I assume your Uncle Henry planted you here for his own purposes. Don't worry, I shall say nothing—in fact, I shall do all I can to help if, as I suspect, we have the same end in view."

Nicholas eyed her cautiously. "And what end is that?"

"Mrs. Deventer's end, of course. I do not intend to let her get away with it. She murdered Papa, you know."

Though there was no hint of hysteria in Ada's voice—very business-like was her tone—Nicholas quickly asked permission to close the door. "Ada, my dear, I'm afraid there is no doubt—"

Impatiently she stopped him. She was tired of people pointing out the obvious—that with such a wound, only Papa's hand could have pulled the trigger. But was it credible that a man afire with grand new plans would extinguish them like that? All week long she had been going over what Papa had told her—

over and over, searching for some clue, some indication of his fatal intent—over once again now to Nicholas. Could *he* see in those words a broken man? Could a man, intending suicide, be so happy, happier than she had ever seen him?

To her surprise, Nicholas was not immediately convinced. "I don't know, Ada, I remember my father telling me about Black Friday, the day Mr. Gould's corner on gold collapsed—on other people's heads, of course. A week later, father encountered a friend who had lost everything in that debacle and was amazed to see him in such high spirits, as if he did not have a care in the world. Remarkable recovery, my father thought, until he read the obituary in the morning paper. His friend had gone home that afternoon and put a bullet through his head."

For a moment Ada was shaken. Could Papa's euphoria have been like that—the result of a dreadful decision finally made? She shook her head. There was nothing vague about *his* high spirits—he had been very specific about his plans. Postgraduate study. Opening a new practice in the city. And why, in heaven's name, rent a new domicile if he looked forward to inhabiting a grave? "No, something must have happened after he left me, something that altered drastically his mood." She held out her hand, palm up, presenting the golden fan of foil. "She never admitted that she saw Papa that day, but I found this in his room."

At least Nicholas was paying attention now. Had she confronted Mrs. Deventer with her supposition, he asked, looking very serious. And was obviously relieved to hear that, aside from a sticky moment when the Commissioner was questioning her, Ada had said nothing. "I suppose I said some pretty wild things then, but I never mentioned I had any *evidence*." Her dry lips parted, baring her teeth in a feral grin. "Don't worry, I have just come from a very touching reconciliation. We're the best of friends again." Suddenly a wave of anger swept over her. "You're doing it again—making me tell you everything, while you tell me nothing!"

He would tell her everything, he swore, but not here, not in his room. Such scrupulous concern for her reputation. She almost laughed in his face—mirthlessly, to be sure—that he should care about the conventions at a time like this, but agreed to meet him for a walk directly after luncheon. The esplanade was to be their meeting place and Ada, arriving early, saw what a vantage point Nicholas had chosen.

"I see," she greeted him, with a gesture that encompassed the open space on all sides, "you wished to make sure we were not overheard."

An elementary precaution, he acknowledged. In a household as large as Kirkewode's, there was apt to be an eye at every keyhole. And besides, he would employ any trick to get her outdoors a bit and bring a little color to her cheeks.

"Trick?" She glared at him and he had to put out a restraining hand to keep her seated on the marble bench.

"No, no—a poor choice of words. I promise you the truth, but the truth, you will see, is hardly more than vague suspicions. And like yours, entirely unconfirmed."

To give credit where credit was due, Nicholas began, his Uncle Henry was the first to question the popular fable constructed by the press to account for the reclusiveness of the Deventers. True love triumphant and in residence at Kirkewode? Bosh, said Uncle Henry, something fishy was going on.

"I heard him once say to my father: Everyone knows *you're* a prig, Alsop, you're no fun, but why the devil won't he see me? To which my father replied: Can it be because you are a gambler and a scoundrel and a cheat? And Uncle Henry said: That's what I mean, Jack and I always got along."

Ada did not respond to his smile. She wanted to know immediately what conclusion his Uncle Henry had reached. None, she was told. But on the assumption that Rose Deventer was keeping Jack from his loving brother for reasons of her own, he had bribed a footman in the castle to serve as his spy.

"That fellow Thomas," Ada said, with immediate certainty.

Nicholas nodded. A man not worth his pay. All he could

report was that even within the confines of Kirkewode, Uncle Jack kept to himself. But then last summer the Deventers decided on a cruise, and at voyage's end Henry approached one of the stewards—a man well positioned to know a thing or two and quite willing to share the knowledge for a price. Henry examined him for more than an hour—an aimless barrage of questions that turned up nothing. And then—out of pure ill temper, if Nicholas knew his uncle, although Henry swore he had an inkling all along—the steward was asked if the two famous lovebirds still billed and cooed. His uncle, Nicholas apologized, was not one to forget the lady's background and had made the coarse suggestion that she might find entertainment more to her liking below deck with the crew.

"The answer to that was never had the steward seen a happier pair. Like honeymooners, he swore. In proof of which, he had a very funny story to tell. At Uncle Henry's urging, he told it." Nicholas's pause was so protracted that Ada asked sharply if she was supposed to laugh in advance. In a voice oddly remote, he continued. "Bringing tea one afternoon, the steward had failed to knock loudly enough and walked in to discover the two in an unclad state, somewhat entangled in a loving embrace. Nor could they disentangle—this was what struck the steward's risibility—since the lady's earring, the sole item of apparel she had neglected to remove, was caught in the matt of red hair on the gentleman's chest."

Hazel eyes, stony with disapproval, let him know she was not amused.

"My dear, you don't understand," he said gently, "the gentleman in bed with her—the gentleman who had accompanied her aboard the yacht—could not possibly be Jack Deventer. Uncle Henry realized that at once. You see, when Jack Deventer lost his hair, he lost it *all*—including that which distinguishes the masculine torso."

"But who—oh, of course—" Ada could not bring herself to say it.

"Yes, your papa," Nicholas said, eyeing her cautiously. "I was wondering if I should not spare you this—"

Ada's pride was up. She wanted no such delicate handling. The relationship came as no surprise to her, she quickly let him know. Nor caused her any concern. Her tension was evident only in the tight interweaving of her fingers as she stared down at her lap. All she had ever seen was the red hair on Papa's arms, but now she visualized the thick cushion on his chest, a pillow for Rose's head.

"What about Mr. Deventer?" she suddenly asked. "Surely he must have known."

"Exactly. That's what Uncle Henry finally could not swallow—the picture of Uncle Jack as the complaisant husband. Nor could I, when he looked me up in Europe and put all his evidence before me."

Not that there was much evidence of a positive kind, Nicholas admitted. A Pinkerton agent was hired to comb through Rose Deventer's past, but turned up little not already known beyond the fact that Slade was her brother.

Nicholas waited for Ada to show surprise. Disappointed, he continued, "For a short while, Uncle Henry thought the detective was onto something when he discovered that just before he died the lawyer, Mr. Kerne, had prepared a new will for Uncle Jack—"

At last his listener came to life. "Of course, that's it! It must have to do with money, that's all these people care about."

Yes, a promising lead, Nicholas said, but in a dampening way. "Thomas was prompted to make inquiries among the servants and turned up the fact that some document had been burned the day Mr. Kerne shot himself, and in that very room. The new will, Uncle Henry had no doubt."

Ada was afire with the prospect of justice about to be done. "Now that we know her motive, it should be easier to determine the means!"

"No, no, Ada, wait," Nicholas cautioned, "you go too fast.

Does it make any sense to dispose of the lawyer when the testator remains alive? Moreover, you do not yet know the terms of either will, and yet you are jumping to conclusions. Is this the scientific method I've heard so much about?"

Ada showed her contempt for such pussyfooting logic. Since the new will had been destroyed, they would never know its contents, but it was safe to bet—

"Don't. Don't bet on anything where Mrs. Deventer is concerned. As a matter of fact, we do know what the new will contained—the Pinkerton man got a look at the office copy. It's not likely that Mrs. Deventer would have put any obstacle in the way of its execution—quite the contrary. She was to get it all—the whole kit and caboodle—outright, no strings attached. From her point of view, quite an improvement over the will that still stands, the one drawn up at the time of her marriage. As it is, only half the estate comes to her, and that in the form of a trust to be managed by a reputable banker. It's clear that as a lawyer, Mr. Kerne had no high opinion of the new bride's ability to handle money. And, what must be even more galling to the prospective widow, the trustee is empowered to forbid inroads in the capital, which is for her use only during her lifetime, reverting upon her death to the other heir. This was always the concern of the Deventers, you know—to keep intact the estate, the reason they have held so firmly to primogeniture."

Ada could see Mrs. Deventer slipping from her grasp. "And I suppose," she said bitterly, in the tone of one betrayed, "the other heir is your Uncle Henry."

"No, my father. And upon *his* death, to me." He gave her an embarrassed look. "Under no circumstances, I'm afraid, would Mr. Kerne consider Uncle Henry a safe repository for the family fortune. Of course, a new will was to be drawn up immediately should there be issue to the marriage, and I was always warned not to set my expectations too high. But by now that seems rather unlikely, wouldn't you say? No, if it's a matter of *cui bono*, you must redirect your suspicions to me."

Never had Ada's mulishness been more in evidence. She glowered at him for muddying the waters instead of clearing things up. There *had* been a new will and it *had* been burned—how to account for it? Or the fact that Mr. Deventer had never sought to make another—was that not equally strange?

"I have a theory to explain it all," Nicholas said modestly. "If we assume that Mr. Kerne had long been pining for the fair Rose—though if you had met the man!" He burst out laughing.

"I did," Ada said, with no answering smile. "That seems the strangest fact of all—"

"Still, granted that beneath that desiccated exterior, there beat a young man's ardent heart, he might well have drawn up a new will on his own, to use as an inducement to the lady. Be mine, and I shall see to it that your husband signs this—that kind of fustian stuff would be of his generation. And when she said be off with you, you naughty man, he tore it to pieces, threw it in the fire, and then obligingly shot himself."

Ada wasted no time on a theory that made Rose out to be a heroine. Obviously something other than the Kerne affair had brought Nicholas here, and she demanded bluntly to be told exactly what.

All his Uncle Henry's invention, Nicholas was quick to disclaim. A wilder idea would be hard to find. "Uncle Henry is not known in the family for having an imaginative bent, but it is amazing how self-interest sharpens wit." Nicholas took a deep breath and made the plunge. "He put it to me that Jack Deventer was dead."

"But—that's not true!" A crazier idea she had never heard.

"I know that now—but at the time he made an almost plausible case. Judging Mrs. Deventer by himself, he figured she would do anything to keep her hands on the estate. Say that one of Uncle Jack's malaria attacks had done him in, might it not occur to her that his reclusiveness in life would serve her well in death? A quick secret burial and who was to know the difference? Your father, Slade and Mr. Witten—" he ticked them off—"all tied to her by blood or by affection. Maxwell? No greater love than hers, that's plain. Caxton too, no doubt, but if English dukes are so purchasable today, then certainly their servants have a price. She would have an impelling motive for such deceit. As long as the fiction could be maintained, she would have at her disposal all his wealth, instead of a measly allowance (so it must seem to her) doled out by a bank. Since her marriage, she had developed expensive tastes, you must admit."

"Unfortunately," Ada said bitterly, "Mr. Deventer is very much with us still."

"Yes. Well, I did not really believe in that tall tale. For one thing, I checked with some friends of mine on the Street and there had been no falling off in his activity there. Nor in his wizardry. Uncle Henry pooh-poohed that, it was all Mr. Witten's doing, he said. Neither of us knew then how sick Mr. Witten is. In any case, there seemed to be a mystery of sorts—sufficiently intriguing for me to come up with a plan of my own."

Ada nodded. "To bore from within. So you got a job in the Deventer office, incognito."

Frankly, he said, he had been bored from without—didn't know what to do with himself. For three years, ever since his father's death, he had lived in Europe, finding it easier there to endure the life of idleness that seemed a gentleman's fate (for a moment, Ada glimpsed a bitterness she had thought only women had cause to feel). Abhorrent as she might find the role of a spy, it promised him an occupation, at least. His disguise was simple—the removal of his whiskers—he had hardly recognized himself in the glass. But in fact such tonsorial measures had not really been required—had she noticed that people saw only what they expected to see? The fact that he was *known* to be in Europe was enough to render him invisible to any acquaintance he might meet.

A clerk's job in the downtown office was the most he had hoped for—a chance to see some papers, hear some gossip. With trumped-up references from a friend, easy enough to arrange. Certainly he had never expected to be offered this plum—a runner's job that transported him to Kirkewode. Why *he* should be chosen to serve as Mr. Witten's replacement, he found hard to understand, particularly since Uncle Jack had not set eyes on him. But Rose Deventer had. Ada decided not to feed his vanity, and kept the thought to herself. They would do as railroad magnates do and make a "pool," she announced. They would share all their information, however poor the gleanings, and plan jointly how best to uncover Rose Deventer's villainy—

"That is strong language, Ada," Nicholas said, looking at her with concern. "Are you aware how much you are beginning to sound like a certain lady whom, if I remember correctly, you once sharply criticized for allowing her reason to be swamped by grief?"

"You mean Mrs. Haygood. I was wrong. I am sorry." If he was thinking that his comparison had had the desired moderating effect, her next words disabused him. "I did that poor woman an injustice. Oh, don't look at me that way, Nicholas. I've just come to see there's method in her madness. But what she knows intuitively, I mean to prove by hard cold evidence."

He abandoned the effort to temper her fierce bias. They seemed to have already pooled their knowledge, he pointed out, and had reached the stage of joint planning. He hoped she would let him know what plan she had in mind.

Ada closed her eyes. She who had never believed in ghosts was learning they were everywhere. Papa, hand behind his back, marched to and fro along this esplanade, telling her the sad tale of the Haygood youth. *In the end, one loses all control.*

"I want Papa's notes." A cold factual voice. Not a quiver of emotion. "From what you say about the will, I can see why she is so concerned about her husband's health. The last thing in the world she would want is for him to pass away—which is something I once overheard Papa to say. The puzzling thing—so unlike Papa, I could not believe I heard him right—was that he spoke of another malaria attack as something greatly to be desired. But I think I know what he had in mind. He told me in the form of a riddle, just before he died. See if you can figure it out."

Now for Nicholas's benefit, she recounted the story of Pasteur's three chickens and waited expectantly for him to make the same connection.

"I think I understand why the white chicken died," he finally said, "but what has that to do with Uncle Jack?"

"Don't you see?" she asked in the exasperated tone of one belaboring the obvious. "What if Mr. Deventer is suffering from some disease *other* than the malaria which the quinine keeps more or less under control. A disease caused by a bacillus as yet unidentified, for which no cure is known. Now what if Papa had reason to believe that this bacillus is sensitive to temperature and cannot flourish in an environment that is too hot—like anthrax in a chicken, you see? And exactly what does a malaria attack provoke?"

"A fever!" Nicholas let out a low whistle.

"Is that not clever? Who would have thought of fever as a *therapy*? Had Papa not fallen under that woman's spell, what a great man of science he would have proved to be—I should hate her if only for that. His last words to me were that one day I would be proud of him—" Grief had her by the throat. She *was* proud of him, but it was too late to tell him now, too late. . . . In Rose's arms, her tears had had an acid aftertaste, but with Nicholas's arms about her, weeping seemed to heal.

Releasing her gently—as if to let her know he understood his role was to provide human comfort and nothing more—Nicholas wondered what such a disease could be. "It must be serious, if Dr. Traherne preferred to see him shaking with the ague. But *you* have seen him—did he look ill?"

Ada rewarded him with a smile at last, wan though it was. "No. I thought him to be in quite rude health." To know more, she would need to read through Papa's notes. But Francis had refused even their temporary loan, citing the inviolability of any patient's record.

"Then there remains only one thing we can do," Nicholas

said decisively. "Confront Uncle Jack directly. By hook or crook, I must get in to see him."

"Tell Mrs. Deventer who you are and *demand* to see your uncle," Ada urged. "How would she dare refuse?"

Nicholas shook his head. He had considered and rejected such a course. "She might simply take my demand to Uncle Jack and return with a note—ostensibly from him—refusing to see me, demanding that I leave his house. How could I counter that? And yet how could I be sure that he had been told of my presence, that the note was in his hand? I would have shot my bolt, you see, and no matter how strongly I might protest, Slade would toss me out on my ear."

To Ada, the prospect was discouraging. As Nicholas himself once said, it was easier for a rich man to enter heaven than the uninvited to intrude on Mr. Deventer. "I don't see how you will get in to see him."

"The same way your father used."

Ada was chagrined not to have thought of that herself. Then she remembered there was one door in Papa's bedroom she could not open. But Nicholas saw no reason to change his plan just because the door was locked. He had more talents than she dreamed of, he said with a grin. "My father's favorite charity was a home for wayward boys, and every summer he transported a handpicked few, more or less my age, to our country place upstate. We were to be a civilizing influence, I believe was what he had in mind. I don't know what they picked up, but I acquired some valuable pointers in how to survive in adverse circumstances. For instance, how to jimmy locks."

What other undiscovered talents did he have, she wondered? He was actually enjoying this, she suspected, whereas she was growing more and more uncomfortable. She would have put his burglar's skill to the test immediately, anxious to have it over with, but Nicholas was more cautious. Before venturing down those stairs, he wanted to be sure his uncle was alone and would remain so long enough to be fully questioned. There would be no second chance if they were prematurely discovered.

261

"We mustn't wait too long," Ada warned. "You know that Francis is slated to take over Papa's apartment, and that will make it all the harder." Mrs. Deventer was only waiting for her to sort out Papa's effects and have them removed, but—another spate of tears threatened—she had not been able to bring herself to face that dismal task.

Nicholas approved her weepiness strongly. "Good—the longer the room is left unoccupied, the better." Using that entrance, they would avoid all prying servants' eyes and need only concern themselves with the whereabouts of Mrs. Deventer, Mr. Witten and Slade. Afternoon was the best time—Nicholas's mind was busily working—Mr. Witten, exhausted, took then to his bed; Mrs. Deventer had her daily workout in the gym; Slade—leave Slade to him, Nicholas said with a confident grin.

"And Francis? He takes his new position as Papa's replacement very seriously—who knows when he'll decide to make his rounds?" Try as she would, she could not keep the bitterness out of her voice.

"Stupid of me to forget him," Nicholas said, looking as if he would like nothing better. "Perhaps I'd better leave him to you."

Leave him to Providence, he might have said. But neither he nor Ada could foresee the turn of events that would so conveniently remove Francis from the scene. Indeed, for the next few days, Ada all but abandoned hope for Nicholas's plan. A sudden turn for the worse in his new employer's health kept Francis almost constantly in the Deventer suite. Nothing to worry about, he answered Ada's inquiry, there was no real danger, Mr. Deventer's constitution was remarkably robust. Unfortunately, just as it seemed the ague had subsided, a more than usually severe attack was making itself felt. Diseases had a way, he informed her importantly, of gathering their strength for a last burst of virulence just before conceding defeat.

Rose too was fully occupied by her husband's relapse—so much the devoted spouse that it was not until the middle of the week that she appeared at dinner. Although she professed herself greatly relieved at Mr. Deventer's progress, there were lines around her mouth, a puffiness under the eyes that Ada had not seen before. How much she owed to "our dear Dr. Stevens" she made clear not only by her fulsome praise but in the misty softness of her grey eyes. Francis—Francis! whom Ada had thought was tough as dried jerky—blushed like a girl.

"You must take care of your own health," Ada said, surprised to find in herself such Machiavellian cunning. "If you go on like this, Dr. Stevens may find himself burdened with another patient. Do you not think, Francis, that Mrs. Deventer would do well to resume her daily exercise?"

Francis rewarded Ada with a pleased look at her concern for Kirkewode's mistress. She had obeyed his command to come to her senses. Exercise? By all means. He prescribed it with all his new authority.

"Ah, do I show it in my looks?" Rose asked in alarm. The point had been taken, Rose would no longer omit her daily sessions in the exercise room downstairs. Now if only Francis were as easy to handle. Ada wished she had Nicholas's confidence in the efficacy of her charms, but even at the height of their romance she had never produced in Francis his present spooniness. To use his own western brand of talk, he was roped and branded, the property of Rose Deventer. Ada, proudly confident that she would never be so owned, felt only contempt for a man turned into livestock. It was not Circe one despised, but the swine crawling on all fours.

Unable to shake off a new fit of melancholy, Ada excused herself early from the rather somber gathering in the drawing room. Rose, who had seemed hardly aware of her presence, looked up in dismay. "Oh, my dear, I have been so taken up with my own troubles, I've been no help to you at all. I mean to arrange matters differently, you will see. You will not be left so much alone. Which reminds me, Mrs. Haygood wishes to pay a condolence call—remarkable, is it not? Do you feel up to coping with the woman? If so, I shall have her to tea tomorrow afternoon."

Ada consented, though with such a glum look that Rose

laughed, not at all displeased to see that Ada shared her aversion to the chaplain's wife. But it was coping with Dr. Haygood—who surely would be present too, was he not the woman's keeper?—that Ada doubted she was up to.

Yet she marched downstairs at the appointed time determined to play her part in the dismal ceremonies society prescribed for the mourning state. And almost turned and fled on hearing Dr. Haygood's voice—his pulpit not his parlor voice—through the closed door of the Rose Room.

"—an unconscionable attack on the finest elements of society. I immediately canceled my subscription—" As Ada entered, Dr. Haygood brought his indignation to a premature close and advanced with his great head lowered like a battering ram. Ada stood her ground bravely, gave every impression of being gratified to hear that she was doing well to resign herself to the will of the Lord, whose judgment was infinitely merciful since our (Papa's) sins deserved a punishment infinitely worse. Mrs. Haygood, reputed to be the prime mover in this call, said nothing, but there was a strained look in her eyes, a silent pleading, that drew Ada to sit beside her.

Anxious to avoid any further reference to God's judgment, Ada begged them to continue the conversation she had interrupted. "I did not catch the subject, but it sounds quite dreadful."

Dreadful indeed. Some dratted fool, according to Francis, had written an article proclaiming the need for a People's Party and making the usual outrageous demands—free silver, eight-hour day, government ownership of railroads—

"And an income tax!" Rose interjected. "I wonder they're allowed to print things like that!"

"In my letter to the editor," Dr. Haygood said, "I ventured to question if the author had ever met in person one of those hard-hearted monopolists he was so occupied in denouncing. Having had that advantage myself, I wished to correct certain of his misconceptions. Millionaires, contrary to *his* impression, are the hardest workers of us all, I wrote, and have little time for those luxuries he rants about."

Rose applauded as at the finish of a concert, but Dr. Haygood meant to cite himself in full.

"And for what purpose do they tax themselves so strenuously and deny themselves so much all their lives? For what reason do they struggle like the titans they are to accumulate more wealth than they can ever use? Why, to relieve the hardship and minister to the comfort of the less fortunate, the idle, the dissipated, the poor and needy—in short, all those who misunderstand and abuse them!" He answered Rose's approving nod with a slight bow, then turned to Nicholas, demanding sternly, "Where would these so-called *people* be without our men of substance? Who has been more devoted than Mr. Cooper to the instruction and elevation of the working classes? And the great free library even now being built—whom have the *people* to thank for that if not a gentleman, the Honorable Samuel Tilden, who left the larger part of his fortune for that noble purpose?" Francis was next favored with his glare. "In many cases, they owe their very lives to those they so contemn. These fomenters of discord never mention such facts as the huge sums the Vanderbilts have provided for the Clinic of the College of Physicians that recently opened. Or—" he turned back to Rose, dangerously tipping his cup of tea—"the hospital our own Mr. Deventer has so charitably provided right here in Riverdale."

"Your dear papa," Rose said softly to Ada, "should be thanked for that—it was all his idea and planning, Mr. Deventer merely provided the money."

Ada looked into her drained cup as if to read her fortune in the leaves. Now that the dry spell had been broken, her eyes seemed never free of tears. Papa had never mentioned to her his civic concerns—how much more was there to him she did not know? She was glad that only Nicholas seemed aware of her struggle for composure, and grateful to him when he changed the subject.

"How is Argos?" he asked of Mrs. Haygood, who stared at him as if the name meant nothing. It was clear that for the moment neither Nicholas nor her dog held Mrs. Haygood's interest. Her attention was fixed on Ada. "I must speak to you—alone," she whispered with such desperation that Ada soothingly agreed.

Mrs. Haygood was feeling indisposed, Ada announced abruptly. "No, no, Francis." He of course must jump up to offer his professional assistance, but she knew how to take care of that. "This is a *woman's* matter, I will take her to my apartment."

Properly abashed, Francis gave way and Rose's murmur of polite concern barely concealed her eagerness to have the lady gone. Ada led Mrs. Haygood from the room, not upstairs but to the conservatory. The glass doors securely closed, the glacier melted, setting off an avalanche of words.

"Now you know, Miss Traherne, now you know! Here is proof indeed! You cannot doubt my Katie is truly attuned to the spirit world! You thought her foolish because she called you fatherless when you met, but her only error was in the timing of your loss. I am sure that Jonathan was there, though he could not make himself felt by *us*—that it was he who warned her in advance of your papa's death, she merely mistook the future for the past. The communication is not always *clear,* you understand. She comes to me again tomorrow evening, will you not join us then? It is sometimes easier to make contact with those who have freshly departed, whose earthly ties are just beginning to be dissolved. Come, Miss Traherne, and hear from your papa's own lips how that murderess killed him. As she killed my son, my only son!"

The beseeching hand was hot and dry, yet Ada shivered, chilled by this woman's touch. Did hate do that to one? Was she herself in danger of becoming such a ghoul, feeding on the souls of the dead in order to keep alive?

"I am not a believer, Mrs. Haygood," she said harshly, removing herself from the lady's grasp. Removing herself as well, she hoped, from the contagion of such madness. Upon their return to the drawing room, Ada did not resume her seat by Mrs. Haygood's side, but took an empty chair near

Rose. That realignment of forces did not go unnoticed. At the evening's end, for the first time since Papa's death, Rose kissed her good-night.

Gone was her obsessive hate, her preoccupation with revenge. In its stead, a strange emptiness, as if she had suffered another loss. Ada felt she should dissociate herself from Nicholas's plan—picking locks, creeping down back stairs, that kind of behavior seemed no longer justified—and yet she somehow failed to find the opportunity to tell him so. Using the mild weather as an excuse, she spent the next two days on horseback, exploring every corner of the Deventer estate. Retired immediately after dinner—"too exhausted," she truthfully complained. Fell asleep as soon as her head hit the pillow. She was grateful for oblivion.

On Friday, close to tea time, she and Rose met on the stairs, both flushed and damp with perspiration—she had just come in from the stables, Rose from the exercise room below. Ada was reminded that Nicholas must be impatiently ticking off the others, hoping she would see to Francis— No! Ada swore, kicking shut her door, she was no Mrs. Haygood, living only for revenge. And yet if she kept Francis safely occupied, it would be so easy for Nicholas to see his uncle—surely a nephew's right.

"No," she muttered, this time aloud, and Marie dropped the hairbrush. "Oh, for heaven's sake, Marie, don't be such a ninny." The girl looked as if she had been stabbed in a vital organ—was she unable to withstand the slightest scolding? Ada's temper flared. "Oh, go away—you're more bother than help, anyway." Marie's suffering compliance merely enraged her further. "And don't come back until you can show a better face," Ada shouted after her.

No day could be fairer than the Saturday that followed— spring had definitely arrived. Or so everyone announced, although Ada did not share in the general euphoria. All this smiling but underscored her own depression. Greeting her cheerfully at breakfast, Francis announced that on such a day he too would like to feel a horse between his legs and would join her on her morning ride.

Nicholas turned his head to mouth something at her. Ah yes, *afternoon,* not morning. When Rose too would be out of range, sparring with a phantom enemy while the real one upstairs made his way into her private quarters.

"I am not riding until after luncheon," Ada said. "Mrs. Deventer has been very patient with me but I mustn't put it off any longer—I plan to spend the morning in Papa's room, sorting out his things."

When Francis said too bad, he must look in on Mr. Deventer in the afternoon, Ada's shrug conveyed to Nicholas there was nothing more she could do. Whereupon the fates stepped in. There was no other way to look at it. When she came down to dinner, having spent the whole day in Papa's apartment more in weeping than in packing, the small gathering in the drawing room was smaller still.

"We'll not wait for Dr. Stevens," Rose informed her, "I'm afraid he'll miss his dinner, poor man. But that's often the fate of a doctor, your dear papa used to say."

So Papa had become a reverential source of wise quotations like Mr. Deventer. Even in death he had not escaped—thus would Rose continue to possess him. Ada felt revived by a familiar thrill of hate.

"Dear Ada," Rose said gently, catching the change in her expression, "am I not to even speak of your papa now that he has gone? There are certain wounds which heal only when exposed to air—I learned that from *him.*"

Ada accepted the reproach meekly and asked if Francis's absence meant that Mr. Deventer had been taken bad again.

"Thank heavens, no," Rose said, "it's only Marie."

"Marie?" Ada sprang to her feet as if an ambulance bell had clanged. "She has had another attack? She never even mentioned feeling ill—" Bad conscience cut her short. Nothing circumscribed one's world, shriveled one's heart, like unhappiness. She had been so absorbed in her own grief, no one else existed. When had she last looked at the girl? Or given her a chance to mention anything? Marie had not appeared all day and she had given it no thought beyond assuming the girl was in a sulk after last night's scolding.

"My dear child, there is no reason for you to be concerned," Rose comforted her, "Dr. Stevens will take good care of her."

Nicholas added his own reassuring note. "Mrs. Deventer is quite right, the girl is not being neglected. In fact, I heard Caxton send for a carriage and it is my impression that Dr. Stevens is taking her to the hospital. I am sure it will all work out for the best—"

Caxton stood in the open doorway, announcing dinner, but Ada had ears only for the noise she heard in the hall.

"That's Francis—they must be leaving now—I want a word with him before he goes." She caught up with him outside, just before he stepped into the waiting carriage. Inside the capacious brougham, Marie was half-reclining, enveloped in a carriage robe, nodding drowsily, already opiated.

"It is the appendix, isn't it? Has it perforated, Francis?"

"Do you think I'd be moving her in that case?" he said impatiently. There was a flush of excitement in his usually sallow face. "I just want her in the hospital until the fever breaks."

"Are you considering an operation?" she pressed him. She was shivering from the cold—March was no month to brave the night air without a shawl.

"Of course I am *considering* it," he snapped at her irritably. "If she is no better in the morning—we shall see."

He pulled down the jump seat to face his patient and instructed the coachman to drive on, leaving Ada with the impression that she had offended him with her questions. Or could it be, she wondered as she hurried to the dining room, that his rigid bearing, his tight voice meant only that he was afraid? Though he had been one of the chosen ones, allowed to assist in the operating room, this would be his first attempt at abdominal surgery unaided.

To Nicholas's inquiry of concern about Marie's condition, Ada answered with an irritability that rivaled Francis's. "You must ask Dr. Stevens that. Although I rather think he will operate tomorrow."

"If it is necessary," Rose said with an authoritative nod. "I gave my permission."

"Marie may have something to say about that. You should have heard her scream when I mentioned the knife to Papa."

"Marie will agree, I assure you, to anything Dr. Stevens orders. You know, Ada, there is something you did not consider when you chose the medical profession. A doctor must have a certain authority, and for that it takes a man. Do you not think so, Mr. Vance?"

Caught between the crossfire of grey eyes narrowed with humor and hazel ones bright with anger, Nicholas temporized by chewing slowly. "I am sure that if Dr. Stevens operates tomorrow, it will turn out to be exactly what is needed," he finally said.

Ada supposed that was what was known as diplomacy—that piece of blithering inanity. Was that all he could say of a life-imperiling infection that required such radical surgery—that all was for the best in the best of all possible worlds?

Suddenly Ada had a strangling fit—the turtle soup had gone down the wrong way. Over her napkin, she stared at him tearfully. He was not talking about Marie. Surgery was not what he had in mind.

"One must seize the moment," Nicholas said, carefully buttering a roll. "As I understand it, in such cases to wait is to court disaster."

Francis out of the way. The opportunity they had been waiting for all week. That was the meaning behind all that Panglossian idiocy.

Sleep did not come easily that night. Tired though she was, Ada lay in bed with muscles tensed as if she were still on horseback, about to take a jump. Up at dawn, she drew the heavy curtains to look out on a lowering sky that promised rain. A strong wind was coming up, to judge from the agitation of the trees. Hers was the stance of one determined to brave the elements, but she was paying little heed to the change in weather. She had dreamed of Papa—an exigent dream which faded even as she awoke but its import remained. She wanted Papa's notebooks. So would Papa reveal himself to her—not as a table-rapping ghost but in the workings of his mind. There was a chance, if she confronted Mr. Deventer directly, she might convince him to countermand Francis's decree and turn them over to her. Rose never tired of citing how fond he was of Papa. Aside from his gross behavior with women—she need fear no repetition of *that* with Nicholas by her side—he might be a generous sort of fellow.

So it was she nodded calmly at Nicholas when she joined him at breakfast. A glance at the front page of his newspaper reminded her what day it was. Oh, Nicholas, we cannot, not on a Sunday, she almost objected, restrained such foolishness in time. As if they planned some light entertainment, harmless enough in itself but inappropriate on the Sabbath.

The *Herald* was put aside. He had feared he was fated to breakfast alone, Nicholas apologized. "Dr. Stevens operated last night." Since Caxton was in the room, he was being very casual. "He has just sent word he will remain all day at his patient's side."

Their golden opportunity, so much she understood. Belatedly the real content of his news sank in. "The poor girl!" she cried. "Did Francis say anything about her condition?"

Caxton, with an apologetic cough for making himself visible, volunteered that Mrs. Deventer was much relieved. He understood the doctor had assured her the operation was a great success. Ada found some comfort in that report, although she knew a surgeon's definition of success was often questioned by relatives of the deceased.

"When does the carriage leave for St. John's?" she asked Caxton, pushing back her chair. "I shall have the coachman drop me off at the hospital—" So much for the golden opportunity, but she did not care. There was a chance she might be of use, if only as a nurse, in this critical postoperative period.

Caxton disabused her: there was to be no mass today for the Romans. Madam had just canceled the carriage, the coachman did not like the look of the storm that was brewing. Nor would chapel services be held. Dr. Haygood suffered from a weak chest and Mrs. Deventer had sent word that he was not to expose himself. Persuaded at last that she must wait until tomorrow, she asked Caxton for a fire in Papa's rooms so that she might finish packing, leaving Nicholas to his Sunday paper.

It did not take long for the coachman to be proved right, but within Kirkewode's thick walls, the storm's fury could be ignored. Even when a sudden shift of wind hurled bucketsful of rain against the windows, Ada thought little of the weather. Thought little of anything. It was best to keep the mind a blank, to move like an automaton, folding garments and emptying drawers as if the contents were mere things, no bits and pieces of a dead man that seemed to cry out, "You have no right to touch."

Knowing the bedroom would prove the most painful, she cleared it first, trying to keep out of her line of vision the cavernous bed in its bare-boned state, stripped of the mattress that had been as blood-soaked as the linen. Heedless of time, she failed to hear the bell for luncheon, nor did the tray sent up by a thoughtful Caxton interest her.

Now in the sitting room, she was confronted with less personal objects, for the most part Deventer property, belonging to the house. Even the desk, sumptuously fitted in gold and onyx, gave little evidence of use. A pristine blotter. A clear polish on the burled walnut top—not a speck of dust, it would take more than violent death to justify a slackening on the part of the Deventers' well-trained staff. In this elegant showroom piece, no intimacies would be revealed.

Because her guard was down, the contents of the shallow center drawer, mundane though they were, proved more than she could bear. The keys, the ticket stub, the watch—here Papa had emptied his pockets for the last time. A letter slit open hastily—witness that jagged edge—no doubt it had been awaiting his return. She picked it up and a pair of gold cufflinks rolled free, bringing Papa before her tear-filled eyes: train-weary, eager for a bath, skimming his correspondence even as he disrobed . . . and then some days later, the callous hand of an upstairs maid sweeping all this clutter of the dead out of sight, out of mind.

A chilling thought put a stop to tears. Had she done Rose Deventer a terrible injustice, did that letter contain such devastating news that Papa saw but one way out? If so, she did not wish to know. Had no right to know, she told herself, by such fastidiousness seeking to deny her dread. And might in fact have thrown it into the fire unread, had she not remembered the police had pawed through all the "effects of the deceased," as the fat commissioner had called them, and still were at a loss to explain such a shocking deed.

Fear dispelled, curiosity remained. She drew the letter out and sat down by the fire, was on a second reading when Nicholas appeared. So silent had been his entrance she suspected he was practicing a burglar's tread.

"It's going like clockwork," he announced complacently. "*She's* downstairs in the gymnasium. I checked on Witten, he's so full of laudanum he doesn't know where he is. Maxwell has retired to her room to rest her poor bunions. And Slade won't bother us—that I'm sure of."

Ada merely stared.

"Don't look so puzzled, my dear. He and I had a little bet on the Sullivan-Mitchell fight. We got the results in today's paper—39 rounds ending in a draw—much to Mrs. Sullivan's disappointment." He laughed. "She is quoted as wishing Mitchell had permanently done him in. I brought Slade some beer, spiked with a little stronger stuff, to celebrate our mutual victory. We could walk right in through the outer office and he wouldn't see a thing, but still it's more discreet this way. Now where is this locked door—I hope my childhood skills haven't grown too rusty."

Her only response was to furrow her brow. Had she forgotten why he was there, he asked sharply.

"Nicholas, listen to this." It was clear she had not heard a word he said. "It's a letter to Papa from a doctor in Boston—an old friend of his, I gather they met in Europe when they were both studying there—"

"Ada," he groaned impatiently, "can't that wait, we don't have all day!"

"Look, Nicholas." She rose from her chair to wave under his nose the sheets she clutched. "It is most curious. He starts out joshing Papa about his obsession with germs—and then he says, right here, Nicholas: 'your wild theory is not even new, old boy. Wild theories never are, I'm afraid. You are familiar with Astruc's *De Morbis Venereis,* I presume, but perhaps not with his journal. Let me quote a passage I ran across and made a note of, I think you will find it as startling as I did. *There are some who think that venereal poison is nothing else but a numerous school of little nimble, brisk, invisible living things of a prolific Nature which, when once admitted, increase and multiply in Abundance; which lead frequent Colonies to different Parts of the Body; and inflame, erode and exulcerate the Parts they fix on . . . in short, which without any Regard had to the particular Quality of any Humour, occasion all the Symptoms that occur in Venereal Disease.* Now what do you think of that as coming from Louis XIV's old doc? Still, old sport, before you abase yourself for being so behind the times, you should know that he goes on to dismiss the whole idea as absurd. To which I add a devout amen. Absurd, my dear fellow. Fashions come and fashions go, and just because your little animalcules are all the rage, it doesn't mean they should be used to explain everything—even the unfortunate condition of your anonymous patient.' "

She was reading to Nicholas's back, following hard on his heels as he strode past her into the bedroom. "Don't you see, Nicholas? Papa did have a theory—no, not that door, the one over there."

"Yes, something quite absurd, it seems." His mutter indicated that he was repaying in kind her lack of attention to the more important matter at hand.

"—And it has something to do with venereal disease." What was he doing, she suddenly asked. Picking a lock, he said shortly. Why not try Papa's keys, she suggested. At his exasperated look, she went to fetch them from the desk. None of which interrupted her train of thought. "What I want to know is, are you sure that Mr. Deventer was ever cured?"

"Of course he was. At a very private clinic, only the best kind of people admitted, the kind who can afford a hefty sum. Uncle Henry placed him there—they were thick as thieves then—and has since used him as a testimonial in recommending the same place to his many friends, no doubt on commission." He swore under his breath, having tried yet another wrong key.

Ada admitted reluctantly she must be wrong. Besides no doctor nowadays would call it wild to attribute so contagious a disease to a germ. Far more likely, she decided now, that Papa had something else in mind, for which that quotation served merely as a parallel.

With an "ah" of satisfaction, Nicholas felt the bolt draw back, pulled open the door on a dark flight of stairs. Ada's interest in the letter evaporated in the rush of cold air. Why conjecture about Mr. Deventer when they were about to confront the man himself? With a shiver of excitement, she crammed the letter in her pocket and caught up her skirt, ready to follow Nicholas down.

"Go *on,* Nicholas. We don't have all day, I remember being told."

She didn't like the way he was looking at her—with that sharp crease between his brows. "I never intended, Ada, that you should accompany me. These stairs lead to a gentleman's bedroom, which we shall be entering unannounced."

"I'm going too," she said flatly. "I have business of my own with your uncle."

But Nicholas refused to budge until she made some concession to the proprieties. He was to enter first and if necessary she would wait outside until his uncle made himself presentable. "All right, all right," she agreed and gave a little shove. Damn the proprieties, she muttered under her breath, taking a leaf from Julia Jessup's book.

The door at the bottom of the stairs opened noiselessly on well-oiled hinges. A momentary stiffening of Nicholas's back betrayed his surprise. Eager to see too, Ada pushed her way in and stood blinking, as if blinded by the light.

Rose. Everything was rose. The silk coverlet on the bed, the satin chairs, the fabric-covered walls, the marble of the fireplace, the enormous buttoned pouf of velvet (sized for two) drawn up close to the glowing coals. Even in her absence Rose Deventer occupied this room: her scent was everywhere. Stupid! Ada addressed herself angrily. To have believed, even for a moment, these private stairs were built to bring a doctor quickly to his patient's side.

"Are you surprised?" she taunted Nicholas for looking so uncomfortable. "We both knew that they were lovers." Though I prefer to forget it, she taunted herself. To show how unmoved she was, she walked briskly to the nearest door. "Mr. Deventer must have an adjoining room—"

Her wrist was caught in a tight grasp. "For once you will do as you are told. I go first, remember?" Besides, he had his bearings now. The door she had chosen could lead only to a long sitting room. "I get a glimpse of it occasionally when they enter through the office just beyond." He strode across the room to the door directly opposite, warned her with a stern look to obey his orders, and passed inside.

Waiting came hard. Restlessly she paced before the door, then moved to the window to check the progress of the storm. The rain had turned to sleet, the wind still made an incessant noise. A crack like a pistol shot made her jump—the limb of a tree has snapped off, was blown away before her eyes, so close the branches scratched the glass. Only then did she realize the peculiar blankness of her view. Where was the tree itself, which should be staring her in the face? The tree by which young Jonathan Haygood had climbed into Rose Deventer's room, to swear undying love, and then to die. She pressed her head against the cold glass and caught a sideways glimpse of its gnarled form, showing the raw wound of a freshly amputated limb. Poor boy, poor boy, was all she could think, understanding the true nature of his humiliation. How inept a Romeo to climb instead into the husband's room! It must have made a ludicrous scene—at which no one would ever laugh, the boy had seen to that.

Wrenching her thoughts away from that old tragedy, she stationed herself again by the door. How long did it take a man to make himself presentable? She put her ear to the raised center panel. I am no better than Thomas, intruded the discomforting thought which did not keep her from straining harder to hear what was being said. If only they were closer to the door, not at the far side of the other room.

She opened the door stealthily, a most discreet crack.

"Why do you ask such a silly question—can't you see?" The deep barrel-chested voice was unmistakably Mr. Deventer's. "I am showing you my money, you numbskull, that's what I'm doing. I keep it here—all in gold. No greenbacks, I won't have greenbacks, I've made that quite clear to Rosie."

"Sir!" Nicholas sounded unaccountably distressed. "You've had an—accident, I'm afraid. . . ." his voice drifted off.

An accident. That was all Ada needed to hear, she entered ready to offer her services. Her first thought was that Mr. Deventer had garbed himself to match his smoking room—a pagan Hindoo, needing only to wrap a turban around his wigless pate, smooth and shiny as a billiard ball. But he was in his bedclothes after all—apparently he preferred the new English fashion of pyjamas. Even more reminiscent of the golden Indies was the treasure he was squatting beside—an open chest into which he thrust his arms elbow-deep, withdrew a clutch of coins, dribbled them back like a child playing on the beach with sand.

What an odd skittering sound they made—where was the

clink of metal? There was something even odder about Mr. Deventer's backside. The silken trousers were plastered to his rear by a clotted mass. She saw the sepia stain, caught the foul smell. He half rose from his haunches and turned to show a ruddy face, beaming with a rather sweaty benevolence. Without the validation of a wig, how false the bristling brows now looked, how theatrical the beard.

Suddenly it was raining gold. Mr. Deventer was scooping up his treasure by the fistful, hurling it at Nicholas. "Crawl, my boy, get down on all fours, let's see you scramble for it! It's real gold and you can have it for the picking!" Ada threw up her hands to guard her face, for he had seen her now and was taking delighted aim. "And you, my pretty puss, can have it for the fucking!"

Nicholas turned on her a ferocious look. "Have you seen enough? It should be clear by now why no one is allowed to see him. Now get out and leave me to deal with him."

Ada picked up one of the golden coins that had so lightly stung her. HUYLER'S, she read around Miss Liberty's head. More chocolate in gold foil, but these minted like a double eagle.

"What are you going to do, Nicholas?"

"Get him back in bed, if I can—just *look* at that bed—and then make a quiet exit. I have no wish to encounter Slade, if you please—not with the head he'll have on him. But I want you to go this minute—"

"I'll go, I'll go," she said to calm him. Mr. Deventer was sitting peacefully on the floor. His pyjama trousers were open at the waist. He was pointing at her a purplish swollen—

"I'll go—" she gasped in a very different tone of voice, but from the sitting room came a noise that caused her to falter, turn back to Nicholas in alarm.

"Rosie," Mr. Deventer whimpered. "She'll make me *swallow* it this time—nasty stuff."

They could hear now the curses, the low voice bludgeoning her victim with contempt. " . . . you drunken scum, you rotten stinking piece of garbage, I should have left you in the gutter where you belong, how do you even know he's still in there, a herd of elephants could have come through and you none the wiser. . . ." The crash of breaking furniture drowned her out. Either she had thrown something or Slade was still wobbly on his feet.

Nicholas recovered first, motioned to Ada they must beat a quick retreat the way they had come, but Mr. Deventer raised his stentorian voice in an appeasing cry to angry gods: "I was taking my forty winks, just like you said, Rosie! It's the fellow in here—*he* made me get up out of bed!"

If she and Nicholas were paralyzed anew, so was the approaching whirlwind. Then Rose called out, "Ah, you have company, my dear? You hear that, Slade?" A good-humored voice again.

Nicholas made a quick adjustment in his plan. "Quick, up those stairs with you." He pushed Ada into the adjoining room and closed the door between them before she realized he had remained behind to draw the enemy's fire.

She hovered indecisively, fearing what Slade might do when he entered the room. But no sounds of carnage came through, only Rose's voice, at its most caressing. "Ah, it is Mr. Vance. You gave us a fright, young man. Slade, send someone to the call box to summon the police. Then clean up Mr. Deventer— he has fouled himself again. As for you, dear Nicholas, you surprise me—" at the ripple of amusement in her voice, Ada could almost see the fair head thrown back, the white throat extended—"you and I must have a little talk."

For herself, Ada would rather have faced Slade's charge than that soft chuckle. She turned and fled, leaving Nicholas to his fate.

Chapter 15

T HE rain had turned to snow, giving an ashen pallor to the night. Ada let the curtain fall, but even the heavy velvet could not muffle the insistent rackety roar of the wind. A nerve-wracking sound, like the bearing down of an enormous engine, always approaching, never arriving.

Even in her merino robe, she had been chilled by the bitter cold seeping through the window. She put more coal on the dying fire and huddled by its warmth. The clock on the mantel showed midnight and Nicholas had yet to come upstairs. *Must talk to you in strictest privacy. Your room tonight, after she retires. Remember, you know nothing.* So read the note he had slipped to her before they went in to dinner.

Ignorance, she thought bitterly, had been easy enough to portray. What had happened between those two that he should be seated in the absent Francis's place, treated to all the delicate attentions lately reserved for the Deventers' new doctor? There was no dearth of small talk—the Kaiser's death, a lurid murder out in Brooklyn, the chances of the New York Giants to win the pennant—in which both seemed equally at ease. Much more seemed to pass between them without being spoken, in the way of people with an understanding.

As for Kirkewode's mistress, never had she looked more seductive than in her new gown of black lace. Still in mourning, the color proclaimed, but beneath the filigree pattern of black roses shimmered a pale peach slip, the color of flesh itself. Here was a woman whose terrible secret had been discovered a few hours earlier, and the only concern she showed was for the weather, bemoaning the loss of a score of handsome trees, complaining the telegraph wires were down, mocking the papers' prediction of a light rain. Ada had fingered the crisp edges of the note buried under her napkin to convince herself it was not all a dream.

Not until Rose lit a cigarette, indicating the ladies would remain at table, did she mention the police. Granted there were bridges down, houses flooded, rescues to be made, when a Deventer summoned, they should come without delay.

"The police?" Knowing nothing, Ada decided, meant that she should show a certain maidenly alarm. "Has something happened?"

"Now would you expect a poacher to be out in such weather? Two of my men caught him when they went out to clear a road of fallen timber. He too must have believed the weather man. I suppose the police will pick him up tomorrow, but in the meantime we have to keep him tied up in the stables."

Mr. Witten had dismissed the subject with the suggestion that all poachers should be hanged. That gentleman's appearance at dinner had grown increasingly rare of late, but this night he had tottered in, proclaiming himself much improved. Ada did not believe it. Three times he had asked her when that young jackanapes was coming back. It had taken her a moment to realize he meant Francis. Three times she told him how serious an operation Dr. Stevens had just performed, that he would not leave his patient while the outcome was in doubt. The third time he was ready with his quip. "One thing I'll say for your pa, he wasn't such a cutup!"

Ada's failure to respond went unnoticed. All his attention was on his fair lady, it was her appreciative chuckle he had wanted to elicit. But, alas, Rose had not heard him. She was otherwise engaged. Later in the drawing room she had repaired this neglect by plying him with bonbons. For once Ada found a rationale for that childish game. At the table he had eaten very little, needed any nourishment he could be coaxed to swallow. And then Rose had given Nicholas a turn. The sight of him with closed eyes and open mouth, obediently awaiting delivery of the sweet, so sickened her that she had left the room.

The faintest scratching sound, but Ada was at the door in a rush, hardly waiting to close it before bombarding Nicholas with furious questions. What had kept him so long, did he know the hour, what had Rose said to him that afternoon, what had he said to her to make her turn so lovey-dovey?

"Keep your voice down." How uncomfortable he looked. "No one must know that I am here—"

"The proprieties again?" Still she lowered her voce. Found it difficult to give a scornful laugh sotto voce. "It seems to me that downstairs they were not much observed—"

"Stop it, Ada. All I want is to keep you out of this. For that, she must continue to believe you have no inkling of my uncle's condition. In fact, the reason that I am here is to ask you to leave. From now on your presence in this house will only be an added burden."

Ada stared at him. He was in deadly earnest. She had become a burden.

"Oh she can keep her blasted secret!" she exploded. "Who cares? Why should she, if it comes to that? It's not as if there were children—tainted blood, runs in the family, to protect them from the kind of talk. How noble of her to be so solicitous about the good name of the Deventers—the tribe which did not exactly welcome her with open arms."

She was sarcastic. He was bland. "How clever of you. Precisely the reason she gave for wanting no one to know—the need to protect the family's good name."

"Why did you not tell her you *are* the family? She still calls you Mr. Vance. What kind of game are you playing now, may I ask?"

"Frankly, I'm not quite sure I know." She noticed that he enacted puzzlement not by disturbing but by smoothing hair— running his palm down the back, as if the only problem he faced was its ineradicable tendency to curl. Too smooth already, she thought, eyeing him with an unwonted objectivity. Too smooth hair, too smooth face, too smooth voice—

"Then frankly, I shall be glad to leave. There is nothing to keep me here. I have packed Papa's things, my own will take little longer. You needn't worry, I shall be out before the week is over."

"Ada, you have not been listening." (Oh yes I have, she thought bitterly.) "When I said leave, I meant tomorrow. In the morning. I don't want you to spend another night in this place."

"Because of your uncle? I appreciate your concern—" A patent excuse. In that deteriorated state, Mr. Deventer was not likely to escape his guard.

"Uncle Jack is the least of my worries. *She* is the one I'm thinking of—"

"That's clear enough. And you think I'll be in your way. Let me put your mind at rest. I have no interest in whatever game you choose to play—"that was all she intended to say, the words that followed came of their own accord, "—though in some circles it may smack of the incestuous—"

She was taken by surprise or would surely have struggled harder. At first the kiss was hard as an argument, then softened, made insidious demands. She was still clinging to him when he straightened up. It was he who broke away. He had not intended—it was too soon—she was still in mourning—he hoped she would not think it was for such a purpose he had asked himself into her room.

"Stop looking at me like that, Ada!" he demanded, a man at the end of his tether. Though she enjoyed the sight, she meekly sat down by the fire and stared at her hands, feeling like the beggar-maid before the wealthy Cophetua. She would show him how well-behaved she could be, how obedient. A perfect ninny, she had always thought that beggar-maid, but she had never known there could be this kind of richness. "At least you cannot misunderstand me now when I say I want you out of here. She has something up her sleeve—an intriguing thought, I'd like to see it through. But not with you about— who knows *what* she's planning—"

"To seduce you, of course." There was a sudden tigerish gleam in the beggar-maid's eyes. "Ensure your silence by taking you as her lover—"

"So she would have me think." He was leaning against the mantel, the fire's glow lighting his face from below. The shadows threw his handsomeness into relief, added depth. Because his eyebrows were so blond, she had not noticed their ogive arch before, worthy of Mephistopheles. Sternly she suppressed the resonance of fresh desire as inappropriate to the seriousness of the moment. Besides, his thoughts were clearly elsewhere. "One thing you said, Ada, makes sense: such secrecy is uncalled for. Unless she has more to hide than my uncle's condition. The family would have taken care of Uncle Jack, there are plenty of sanitaria with proper alienists in attendance. And once he was legally declared incompetent, the estate would be professionally managed by our bankers. The whole mess would be taken out of her hands—you would think she would want that, wouldn't you. A woman with her attractions, though a bit long in the tooth, could have a brilliant social life with the income that would be made available to her. The kind of high living she must have married for, all expenses paid. And yet she chooses otherwise. Odd, wouldn't you say?"

Ada said nothing, being occupied with balancing "a woman with her attractions" against "a bit long in the tooth." Nor was any answer required. He had spoken as to himself, had now discovered that such a conversation could be continued in silence. His eyes, resting on her occasionally, took in only the surface of her, making her one with the furniture. She had thought the mystery was over when they discovered the nature of Mad Jack's disease. Not so, it seemed.

"Another lie," he said abruptly. "She would have me believe his madness has not been of long duration, that there are remissions, that she still hopes for a cure."

Ada reluctantly demurred. "There must be remissions of one degree or another. When I saw him last, he was not in *that* condition. I merely thought him—well, you know, the way men are—"

Nicholas took pity on her embarrassment. "Normally depraved?" His smile vanished, the line between his brows remained. "Yet I'll wager he has been mad—more or less mad, let's say—since they immured themselves in Kirkewode. She must have found him out on their honeymoon, poor lady, for it was right after that he came here, shut himself off from all society, changed his ways. Changed his ways, my God! The love story of the ages! You remember all that drivel in the press?"

Before Ada's eyes flashed a scene of summer splendor: a twirling parasol of lace . . . a white yacht languidly afloat on a deep blue sea . . . the wild splashing race of bronzed swimmers . . . real gold, not chocolate, they were diving for in those halcyon days. . . .

"Yes, I remember." She drew back the curtain again and stared at the bitter winter gale outside. As if her eyes needed to rest on something cold and white and arctic to extinguish the burning memory of that Mediterranean sun. "It began when they docked at Nice. When she first called Papa to attend her on their yacht. *He* was the one in need of a doctor, not she. Buckets of coins he was throwing overboard."

"Do you see what that means?" A stern question as Nicholas voiced it, bringing her back to the present. "Left to himself, my uncle would have thrown away the entire Deventer fortune. I am not privy to the exact amount it's worth today, but he is reputed on the Street to be in the Midas class. That, my dear, is the real mystery: who has been doing the speculating, manipulating, investing so successfully all these years?"

"Mr. Witten, surely."

He shook his head, stroked smooth again the wayward hair in back. "I don't believe it. Presumably I am being trained to replace him—a highly imminent event, judging by his appearance tonight. If so, then all he does is fetch and carry. A glorified runner, that's all my job will ever amount to. It's been clear to me for some time the real brain work is to fall on someone else. When Witten dies, I thought at first. But suppose that someone else is of the here and now, has existed all along. Consider this: Witten was *hors de combat* for a whole week—you recall his attack of dyspepsia?—and during that time a cool million was made on a transaction of amazing complexity. I confess I didn't understand myself the significance of what I was being told to do, my instructions coming step by step. Only after it was over, could I put it all together, see how this Weyderlander had been tricked to sell L & N short so that when he couldn't cover, because by then the stock he needed was in our hands, he had to beg us to bail him out. Which was done but at a blackmailer's price, rest assured." Again he smoothed his hair. "The timing, the execution all perfect, and Witten didn't know a thing about it, so much I discovered when he finally returned to the office. Obviously those orders—straight from Uncle Jack, I was to believe—came from this someone else. . . ."

Money. Always money. That was all any Deventer seemed to worry about. These mysteries he was propounding—she couldn't bring herself to care. Papa was dead—*there* was a mystery. And a young boy, just beginning his life. And an old man, whose lifetime of probity should have earned him a better end. These were mysteries to which he would never find an answer, no matter what intimacies he encouraged from Rose Deventer.

It was not jealousy but some deeper concern that suddenly caused her to say, "Take care, Nicholas, that she doesn't best you in this game you're playing. I'm afraid that she will feed you bonbons, not information."

He thought it jealousy, of course. "Your fears are unfounded, dear. It is true that before Dr. Stevens arrived on the scene, she made a few overtures in my direction which I rather enjoyed—purely as a game, you understand. But now—I don't know how to put this without sounding as irrational as Mrs. Haygood—my skin crawls at her touch, every muscle stiffens in revulsion. It makes me wonder how fortune seekers can endure to make love to the rich old women they make their prey. And yet my eyes tell me she has not changed, she is still as appetizingly lovely as before. Why then do I have this reflexive response as to something ugly, loathsome? What is more, she knows it. A woman of her experience can sense when her charms are not working. And yet she pretends to believe my pretense. Promises to satisfy me in *every* regard—tomorrow. Why not tonight, I asked her, making a fine show of heavy-breathing impatience. Her performance was even better—you know how she can narrow her eyes? Slits of smouldering passion, she would have me think—but regrettably, Mr. Witten was there. I wouldn't be surprised if his presence hadn't been commanded for just that purpose. Feeble as he is, he outstayed me at the end."

Ugly. Loathsome. If it were jealousy that pricked her, she would be relieved. But like the prodromal symptom of a festering illness, sensed in its early stage as nothing more than vague malaise, her anxiety remained.

"What do you expect to learn tomorrow? She will only tell more lies."

"A lie can be the obverse face of truth," he said, staring into the fire. "It is true I am meeting her on her own ground, the weapons of her choice, but I think it worth the risk."

Risk? What risk? If there were any risks—how her own fears picked on that random choice of phrase. The risk of being made a fool, he was quick to elaborate, seeing that she grew balky. The fate worse than death, in its masculine declension.

287

"Then you will go? Tomorrow? Just for my peace of mind, Ada."

With a struggle the beggar-maid reappeared. Whatever he wished. Yes, in the morning. No packing, no bags, no announcement of a final departure. But where was she to go, she meekly asked.

"To my house in the city. I will give you a note to my housekeeper. If you leave early enough to catch a commuter train, you will have only Caxton to deal with, she won't be out of bed. All you need say to him is that you have business in the city for the day—something to do with picking out your father's stone—he will not dare to question so pious a mission."

"Oh, Nicholas," she sighed when he kissed her good-night—a cautious peck—"when it comes to lies, Rose Deventer has met her match."

How much she hated Kirkewode she realized only now that she was quitting it. Like Christian released at last from Doubting Castle, she thought, anticipating tomorrow's freedom. She laid out the clothes she would wear—black serge walking suit, black cashmere ulster, black bonnet with its heavy veil. How efficiently Rose had moved in an emergency to see that she was properly attired to mourn. But even that funeral pile of blackness could not depress her tonight. Once in bed, she groped with her feet for the comforting warmth of the hot-water bottle, reached out to turn down the lamp. For the first time in weeks she noticed the fat naked cupids carved in the bed, examined them critically. Their expression was not so unpleasant as she had thought.

She awoke to an internal alarm in a room whose dimness made the time ambiguous. Seven o'clock, according to her bedside clock, but she had to draw the curtains to confirm that is was day, not night. What a day. It was hardly worth the effort to remove the crust of ice that had formed over the panes, for the sky had let down a curtain of its own, an opaque sheet of white, flapping wildly in the wind. Already drifts two feet high and the snow showed no sign of letting up. Impossible to believe this was almost the middle of March, that two days before the drifts her eye had treasured were of forsythia in bloom.

The ice-encrusted windows induced her to revise her selection of the night before: a second flannel petticoat, a fleece-lined pair of boots. Muffled to the chin, even thankful for the ugly bonnet, whose velvet ties were broad enough to cover her ears, she ran downstairs in search of Caxton.

"A carriage?" He looked down at her as at an uncomprehending child. "You have but to look outside, miss, to see how ill-advised it would be to venture out."

She had expected some such expostulation on his part, was ready to do battle. Her business in the city was most urgent, she insisted, she must be taken to the train.

"Ah, the train," he said, with evident relief. Not even Caxton cared to pit his will against a Miss Traherne with that determined look. "There *are* no trains, miss. They can't make it past Mount Vernon. And there has been a frightful collision at Dobbs Ferry. Many casualties, I'm afraid. We have just been informed of the situation by the policeman who has come to pick up our poacher. It's a veritable blizzard, miss, without a doubt."

Ada's heart sank. The idea of leaving Kirkewode had taken hold, she could not wait to get away. It seemed, however, she must resign herself to waiting out the storm. Removing her bonnet and coat, she consoled herself with the thought of breakfast and followed Caxton down the hall.

"Oh!" she gasped, for Nicholas had startled her, popping out of the morning room like a jack-in-the-box. Frowning her into silence, he drew her inside.

"I know," he forestalled her, "no trains. But I have spoken to Patrolman Cullen. He will take you in his van as far as Miss Jessup's. And as soon as the roads are clear, you can continue on into the city."

Stop and go, stop and go—she could not adjust so easily to this constant change of plans. An envelope was thrust on her— the note to his housekeeper, she supposed. "To Julia's?" She could not resist reminding him that he had practically forbade her to continue that acquaintance.

"A choice of evils," he said with a lightness that did not fool her. "Try to slip out unnoticed, will you? Under these circumstances, your departure will be difficult to explain. As for Miss Jessup—" his smile became more convincing—"tell her you are escaping my unwelcome attentions. She will go for the most outrageous story if it involves a man."

Ada wished she had never thought of breakfast. Hunger turned her protest into a whine. "I hate this underhanded way of doing things, I hate sneaking out as if I were a thief—"

"Don't worry, it will soon be all over." A light kiss, and he was gone.

She stood watch at the window, which gave her a view of the drive leading to the stables. How appropriate, she thought bitterly, when the police van came into sight. She had arrived at Kirkewode like a prisoner, was leaving much the same. A dash through the empty hall, a struggle with the door, and she was plowing through a drift toward the horses steaming through their nostrils like a train pulled to a stop. She had pictured herself riding as before on the box, but experiencing now a cold so intense it had paradoxically an almost scalding effect on her exposed face she was glad to see Cullen dismount and open the rear door of the van. He shouted something but she could not hear him over the noise made by the wind. To her surprise, after hoisting her up, he followed her into the van, sat on the long bench beside her and closed them in.

"It's a whistler the likes of which I've niver seen. I need to gather me strength for the long haul." Even in the van, his words emerged in little puffs of steam. She understood where his strength lay when he drew off his gloves and pulled a flask from his thick blue overcoat. "Sure and there's nothing like good likker and bad women to keep a man warm."

To Ada he sounded warm enough. But her immediate concern was the hulking form stretched out on the opposite bench. For a moment she thought it was a corpse, for even the head was covered by the grey horse blanket, only a pair of thick-soled boots exposed—the boondockers of a farmer. The slight rise and fall of the blanket relieved one concern, aroused another.

"Is he dangerous?" she whispered. She was not sure she cared to be shut in alone with a lawless poacher.

"Not in the blessed state he's in. Plumb likkered up, he is, he'll not be feeling the cold like you and me, miss. The boys took pity on him last night—Christian souls, every man jack of them—didn't want him to freeze in the tack room where they was keeping him for the law, in the person of yours truly. If it was up to me, he'd be there still, this ain't no weather to send man or beast out in. But seeing as how it's a big swell like Mr. Deventer what called in, the sergeant sez I'd better go while the going's good."

With a groan, he wrapped his long muffler over helmet, ears and chin until all she could see was the bridge of his nose, and forced himself out. The jerking of the van announced their start. Even Cullen's fine team found the going hard, took forever to reach the first turn in the drive, at which point the van was almost pushed over by the buffeting of the gale. The inert body of the poacher was thrown to the floor, rolled to her feet—gymnastics that evoked nothing more than a strangled snort. Righting herself, Ada tried to direct her thoughts to the warm welcome that lay ahead, the blazing fire, Julia's delighted surprise, but the farther from the castle the horses plowed their way, the more intense her anxiety. She wished there was more light—gloomy surroundings led to gloomy thoughts—but the only window was the small high opening in front allowing the driver to keep an eye on the prisoners inside.

Hers was an *unreasoning* fear, she scolded herself—if ever a man was competent to take care of himself, it was Nicholas. *Don't worry, it will soon all be over.* She repeated Nicholas's reassuring words to comfort herself. But it was Papa's voice she heard—the same last words he had uttered before he went upstairs to— Her fingers gripped themselves within her muff.

291

Nicholas would never—there was nothing Rose could do to make him—

A tapping on the glass drew her eyes upward. Cullen's face filled the small opening, fiery red, straining to tell her something. Mouth open like a fish, index finger moving in and out of the steaming aperture, and then before her jiggled the flask. She shook her head. No, she needed no such warming draught.

What was there about that pantomime that caused such an asthmatic stricture of her chest, made her skin crawl? Mouth open like a fish, index finger moving in and out. *Open your mouth and close your eyes! Open your mouth and close your eyes!* Rose's voice, that low coaxing murmur promising a chocolate surprise, promising other even sweeter delights—and in between the teeth and tongue, the cold black barrel of a gun! Had she gone mad—where did such a picture come from? She held her head, closed her eyes, still saw it plain: the pink lolling tongue, the dark abyss of throat, and slipping in with deadly care, the barrel of a gun! She knew—she *knew*—that was how it was done.

"Stop!" She was screaming now. Papa had not killed himself—Rose had murdered him! Oh, God—Nicholas too! He would be the next to be found with brains blown out, another victim of the Cloistered Rose! She was banging on the glass—Cullen had to hear her! Cullen twisted around, peered in, nodded—the van came to a stop, the door opened, Ada fell into his arms.

"We must go back! Back to Kirkewode!" She pushed aside the flask under her nose—"No, not that. Turn around, we must go back!" She had to yell into his ear to make herself understood.

"Can't do it!" he yelled back. "It's touch and go if we make it to Miss Julia's!"

Life and death—murder—Mr. Vance! It did not matter what catastrophe she threatened, he looked at her as if she was completely daft. He was pushing her up the step, back inside, ready to lock the door—Nicholas would never know! Twisting around, she caught him unaware with a hard jerk of her knee to his chin that sent him sprawling on his back in the snow.

Run! Run! The desperate command she gave herself was ignored by legs that found it arduous to move at all. A look behind told her she had no need to fear recapture. That bent figure was searching for what could only be his flask. Though the wind was mostly at her back, there was no way she could turn her face that it was not scoured by icy needles. The van had made but one turn, the way back could not be far, but it was like a nightmare, lifting one foot after another with such effort, inching forward at such a laborious pace. Even now Nicholas might be closeted with Rose Deventer, demanding explanations, receiving only death.

As if it too were impatient at her progress, the wind gave her a particularly vicious thrust, toppled her face down in the snow. She scrambled to her feet in frantic haste. The second time she rose a little slower, disoriented by the erratic gusts, the dervish dance of whirling snow so thick she could not see two feet beyond. Trying to hold her flapping veil in place, she could not see at all, ripped it off. Lashes, brows encrusted, the tip of her nose already numb, she kept her gaze strictly downward. The van's tracks, already half-covered, were parallel depressions of packed-down snow. Follow the tracks. With a maniacal concentration, she narrowed her vision to one thin smudged line, aware for a while of the furious pumping of her heart, a deeper ache of thighs with each lifting, the slow spread of a terrible fatigue strumming on her muscles, plucking them like strings, and then her mind grew blank. She no longer thought of where the track was leading, only that she must follow it. Now she was playing with a strange intensity that long-forgotten childhood game— step on the crack, break your mother's back. She missed, her foot had slipped in the icy rut, she fell. Poor Mama, her back was broken.

For a long moment, Ada lay where she had fallen. How luxurious the feeling. Beneath her, a cushion soft and yielding as a down comforter. Mama was tucking her in, pulling a warm white blanket over her, leaning over to croon a lullaby. . . . But he would not let her sleep. Nicholas was shaking her. Go away, Nicholas, she mumbled, but he kept shaking her. Open your eyes and close your mouth, he whispered to her. No, that's not right, she answered sleepily, it's the other way around. *Nicholas!* As if an electric jolt had passed through it, her body jerked, lifted itself to its knees. She stared in amazement at the great drift of snow directly ahead. Stared at the barrier that had formed it. The grey stone walls of Kirkewode. She had arrived without knowing it.

She never remembered how she covered those last few yards. Later, in a recurrent nightmare, she was to claw her way through a mountainous drift only to find her fingers too numb, her wrists too weak to open the massive door, to pound upon it helplessly, unheard, to pull the bell with her last ounce of strength, knowing as she sank into a final sleep that the bell had made no sound, it too was frozen. . . .

"She's coming to, Mr. Caxton."

"Good, Thomas, keep rubbing. We'll see if she can swallow now. . . ."

With the hot sweet liquid running down her throat, alcoholic fumes rising up her nose, Ada struggled to sit up. A kneeling Caxton held her in his arms before the fire, the footman had her hands. *Nicholas!* His name could not make it through her burning throat, she strangled instead.

"There, there, miss, easy does it. . . ."

Thomas would not let go her hands. The hot liquor was held threateningly to her lips, waiting to drown her next attempt at speech. The fire was drawing languid wisps of steam from her soaked skirt. To awake in hell could be no worse than this.

"Thank you, Thomas, that's enough," she croaked, pulling against his grip. She turned her head aside in time to deliver another proffered drink down her chin.

"It's Mr. Caxton you should thank, miss. If it was not for him sending me out to shovel off the snow—keep the doorway clear, he says, for what, I asks myself, who'll be coming in or

294

going out on a day like this? It gives me the creeps when I think another few minutes and you'd been frozen stiff!"

"Thank you, Caxton. I'm quite all right now."

She looked up into formal eyes, a symmetry of face showing for the woman in his arms an impersonal concern that kept intact the difference of status, the distance of sex. Tigers too have symmetry—Caxton could not be trusted. Nor Thomas, though he was supposed to be in Henry Deventer's employ. A man once bought could be bought again.

Once on her feet, she was judged fit to be asked what had driven her to expose herself to such a storm? A small relief—no one had seen her start out in Cullen's van. Easy enough to play the foolish female who did not know a blizzard when she saw one, had felt a childish urge to romp in the snow.

Disappointed he might be in her intelligence, but Caxton was satisfied with her recovery, instructed Thomas to see her to her room. Maxwell had taken to her bed, on madam's instructions, but he would find some young woman to send up shortly to assist her—an offer which Ada rejected with more vehemence than called for. However she was grateful enough for Thomas's arm as they mounted the stairs. As soon as they were out of hearing, she asked for Mr. Vance's whereabouts.

"At this time of day, he's always in with Mr. Deventer, miss."

"Could you take a message to him? I would like to see him without delay."

"Me barge in *there*?" Thomas gave an incredulous nod toward the Deventer wing. "Not likely. Slade would bounce me out on my ear. He'll be coming down soon enough for luncheon, miss, I'll tell him then."

It was not to be so easy then. In the cold hall, she had to clench her teeth to keep them from chattering. Yet somehow she must keep on her feet. In her room, leaning against the closed door, she waited out the receding footsteps. There was a blazing fire in the grate, evidence of Caxton's swift efficiency. From this distance it only made her aware of the sodden weight of her clothes. Her fingers, toes, the tip of her nose throbbed painfully, but all the rest of her was numb. So tired. Perhaps for just a minute—

Nicholas! That part of her mind which would not let go flailed her with his name. She cautiously opened the door—no one in sight—moved quickly down the hall oblivious to the flapping of clammy skirt, oblivious to the chattering she could no longer stop. Across the landing, through the door she had never entered before. Into an entirely different domain, another country. Desks, files, machines—in that corner a stolid safe, in the other a glass-domed ticker that she knew should be chattering too but was strangely silent. She stopped short, utterly confused. Amid these trappings of commerce, all proclaiming the sanity of business, that picture of Nicholas opening his mouth to death seemed so mad, so wild a fantasy, she might have turned and left had not Slade suddenly entered from the Deventers' private quarters.

At the sight of her, his head rocked back as if a fist had landed on his unprotected jaw. He was hamstrung by surprise. "What the devil are you doing here?" His scowl, registering confusion more than hostility, lifted momentarily. "You ain't got the ague, have you? The doc ain't here, he couldn't get through that stuff outside even if he tried."

"It's Mr. Vance I want. I must speak to him immediately."

"I just took him in to see Mrs. Deventer. I'll tell him when he comes out."

Ada swayed, hearing a cold clear voice in her head: he will never come out. She stared at the ticker's dome and saw as if reflected in its glass the long white fingers peeling back gold foil, holding delicately by the fingertips a chocolate bonbon.

"Could you not call him out?" Though the effort seemed to crack her face, she tried to smile up at him winningly. "It will only take a moment." Only a moment, the same cold voice mocked her helplessness, only a moment to blow his brains out.

The scowl was back. There was a mean look in his eyes as he

moved toward her. "You can have all the time with him you want when she gets through—she's giving him his walking papers."

Walking papers, repeated the same cold inner voice but with a different intonation. He was propelling her to the door. Ada dug in her heels. "Nicholas!" she screamed, more to drown out that voice in her head than in any hope of summoning him. The grin that slewed the thick features of Slade's face was nothing more than a rearrangement of old battle scars.

"Yell all you like—there ain't no noise that can come through them walls, they're double thick, stuffed full of wadding. Mr. Deventer likes his quiet."

The door slammed in her face. Slade had picked her up, deposited her in the hall with as little effort, as little emotion as he would a pair of dirty boots to be cleaned. All hope gone, it seemed pointless to keep struggling against exhaustion. Let go and it would embrace her like a friend. I tried, she whimpered, I really tried, Nicholas. Even you could not beat your way past Slade, we had to go down Papa's stairs—

Papa's stairs! Strangely dissociated from her body, her mind lashed her legs as with a whip. Up the stairs, into Papa's quarters, fresh flowers everywhere, virgin bedding, rooms holding their breath for their new tenant. *She* had not locked the door on her frightened scramble back, if only it were still— Oh God, she prayed and turned the knob. The door opened.

She must not run, must descend at a cautious pace. To fall, to lie helpless while just beyond Rose triumphed once again as impresario for death—Ada knew how that performance must run: poor lad, I had just discharged him, turned to my desk for his final pay, little did I know he would take it so hard. . . .

Another door to open, another prayer. The bedroom was empty. As if for first time, Ada took in its rose prettiness. Farce, not tragedy, was meant to be enacted here. All hallucination, then? One saw mirages in the desert. Perhaps in snowy wastes as well.

Nicholas laughed.

That sound of frank amusement came from the door she had first mistaken for Mr. Deventer's. The sitting room, Nicholas had corrected her. Rose was speaking now. The soft teasing murmur grew more distinct as Ada stalked it, moving soundlessly over double piles of rugs.

". . . of course you shall. Nicholas—I may call you Nicholas?"

His voice did not carry so well—too much the well-bred mumble. They were very cozy. And if she burst in, a wilder-eyed version of Mrs. Haygood, crying murder?

". . . don't underrate yourself, my dear boy," Rose was saying. "I may not be able to understand the ins and outs of it, but I am sure you played your part well. From the way you described him, this Mr. Weyderlander would have wrung my heart. Shall we put all that aside for the moment—too much business talk makes my head hurt. Instead. . . ."

All talk stopped. If she opened the door now she knew what she would see. And Nicholas would accuse her of ruining his fine plan. She must be suffering from an obsession, she could not get that terrible refrain out of her head: *close your eyes and open your mouth.* . . .

". . . surprise for you. Now close your eyes, there's a good boy. And open wide—"

Not in her head. Dear God, *not* in her head. "Nicholas—no! Don't!" As Ada hurled herself into the room, Nicholas whipped his head around, a stubby silvery barrel wavered, a finger gave its reflex jerk. Across the room, a pedestaled vase exploded into a shower of shards.

"My God!" With one hand Nicholas held Rose Deventer by the wrist, with the other he fingered a red nick on his chin. "A close shave, I call that," he said shakily.

The pressure of his fingers increased until, with a grimace of pain, Rose uncurled her fingers and the gun thudded softly at her feet. Ada rushed in to pick it up, held the snub-nosed barrel at arm's length as if it were a poisonous snake that might yet prove alive.

Nicholas eyed it with contempt. "A derringer. Fits in a vest-pocket, they advertise. Or in a lady's palm. Don't worry, it's a single-shot. Why not? She could hardly miss, could she."

In awe Ada watched Rose's eyes secrete two perfect tears, carefully calibrated drops in a chemical titration. The bruised wrist proved itself workable again in a distraught flutter. "What was I doing?" Rose asked in a faint voice.

Nicholas ignored her after a flicker of a glance that told her she was of no further account. He took the gun from Ada, tested the heft of its butt, cast a worried look at the office door, no doubt expecting the shot would bring Slade running. Soundproof, Ada told him.

The ruffled lace of Rose's sleeve gave miraculous birth to an infant square of lace. She dabbed at her eyes, reclined against the cushions, became the performer in the wings, awaiting her next cue.

"So simple!" Nicholas stood over her, muttering. "So fiendishly simple. Had you not arrived in time, who would ever have suspected I was not another suicide?"

Nicholas was in a state of shock, Ada could tell. He did not even ask what she was doing back at Kirkewode nor recognize her bedraggled appearance. In truth, she seemed to have passed beyond fatigue into another state—a lightness close to levitation. Extraordinary, her clear-headedness.

"*I* would have suspected," she consoled him. "Did I not say she murdered Papa?"

"Your father—you were right. The Haygood boy too? And we thought his poor mother deranged. Even Mr. Kerne's death one must question now. But why? For God's sake, why?" He seemed unable to bring himself to look at the perpetrator of so many crimes. It was of Ada he asked, "Look at her—is that a degenerate criminal type? Lombroso is wrong, physiognomy does *not* instruct us."

Rose Deventer did not intend to either, it would seem. She was absorbed in pleating a gold fan from the discarded foil of the last chocolate she had unwrapped.

"Perhaps she's as mad as Mr. Deventer," Ada said and

299

watched the fingers grow still. Nicholas was not alone in knowing that nasty little secret, Rose had grasped. "To *kill* you,
Nicholas, just to prevent her husband's madness from becoming known? Is not that a greater madness?"

"Yes, but I rather think—" a flush of excitement replaced his
pallor—"she was more concerned to prevent the questions we
would ask once his condition was exposed. Who is her real
paramour, the real financial wizard, the man into whose hands
she has placed the entire Deventer fortune?" His face hardened. For the first time, he addressed Rose directly. "His name,
madam. I mean to have it before we leave this room."

The carefully pleated fan was crushed into a wad. Rose flung
it into Nicholas's face. "The man! The man! Always the man!"
she cried. "Do you think I need a man to tell me how to bring the
Street to its knees? Do you think it takes a man to judge a market's weakness, know its strength, gain a fortune on someone
else's loss, ride the coattails of someone else's coup? Is it in that
silly thing between your legs you keep your brains? *Mine* are in
my head, not where I keep my sex!"

Sex. She spat the word at him with such venom that he recoiled. Seeing which, she threw back her head and laughed. A
free open laugh, as if that one moment of rage had cleared
away the clotted phlegm of a lifetime's disgust. "Not that I
haven't used that too, when needs must. In my salad days that
was all I had. My capital, my stock. It got me hauled aboard
many a rich man's yacht—part of the provisioning, you might
say—where I completed my education. My Groton, my Harvard. A rum lot, my professors—but millionaires. Millionaires!
How richly that word rang in my ears—the clink of gold in
every syllable. I learned by listening at table, quiet as a mouse,
playing with the baubles they gave me—so they thought—while
they talked of business, business being all they knew to talk
about. I caught on quick enough—after all, it was not so very
different from the shell games and the loaded dice they used in
the back room at MacReady's stables—"

Abruptly she whirled, confronted Ada with a contemptuous

demand. Did Ada know the difference between stocks and bonds, and the uses that could be made thereof? An astonished Ada shook her head—no, she could not bind the cluster of the Pleiades, or loose the bands of Orion. The proud rigid figure mocked her ignorance. That was primer stuff.

She was striding up and down before them now, there was no stopping her. The low voice grew raspy, dewy beads of sweat rimmed the sharp twin peaks of her lip, her pale skin took on a lubricious sheen. Nicholas and Ada exchanged an unbelieving glance—this was a lecture they were being forced to attend! Hers was the power, she would have them know, to turn bulls into bears, bears into bulls, an alchemy to transmute bits of worthless paper into good hard gold. When buying a railroad, Ada heard herself advised, both creditor and debtor be. Did she want the stock to rise? Pay dividends. Did she want the stock to fall? Call in the bonds. "That's what they call playing both hands against the middle—a child's game. But the time came when I was matching wits with the likes of Keene and Woerishoffer and Villard and Morgan and the Little Man himself—oh, oh, then the fun began!"

To an invisible public she delivered her harangue, but all the while, out of the corner of those long grey eyes, she searched Ada's face. It is from *me* she wants applause, Ada realized with dismay. It is for me she is preening like a peacock, displaying not voluptuous curves but convoluted mind. Ada looked away. A deeper embarrassment she had never known.

"Enough—" Nicholas managed to interpose—"I am willing to accept the fact that you alone have managed your husband's money. Managed well—I accept that too. A grim necessity drove you to it. But had you only let the family know—"

"The family!" Rose's stare implied she could not have heard aright. "That loose screw of a brother—Henry? Or that bookish fop Alsop, the nose-in-the-air kind of swell who thought making money was a vulgar trade? No, it was up to me—I could do it, I knew. And I did! But always with a sword hanging over my head."

301

That damn will, she groaned and cursed the man who drew it up. Kerne did not even let her know the contents until too late, Jack being incompetent by then to make another. That little pettifogger, she raged, that upright member of the bar! "There was nothing upright about his other member," she sneered, "I can vouch for that. He should thank me for providing him so romantic an end. A regular Romeo, you would have thought, reading the papers."

Nicholas drew in his breath aghast. Was she openly admitting then that none of these deaths was suicide, even Mr. Kerne had been killed by her hand? She answered willingly enough—so willingly that Ada wondered if she did not find something like relief in speaking of what had been unspeakable for so long. Kerne had deserved it, was her delivered judgment. She held that man responsible for his own death and all that followed. Had he drawn up a reasonable will—but instead to take all the money out of her control when Jack died, to pension her off like a domestic servant!

"You killed the poor man just for that?" Ada cried in horror. "For revenge?"

Rose looked at her nonplussed. "What has revenge to do with it? I have no taste for melodrama. Perhaps I should not have trusted your papa's judgment, but he assured me the latest siege of malaria had left Jack all but cured. Your papa was quite excited, dear, with his new theory—something about Jack's madness being caused by germs, which the fever had killed off—quite mad it sounded to me but there was no denying Jack showed improvement. It didn't last—it never does—but of course I did not know that then, I was quite hopeful. Now was the time, I thought, to get a new will made while the lawyer would find him of sound mind.

"Mr. Kerne was sent instructions to draw up a proper one, leaving everything to me outright. The day he brought it over for execution, Jack was so quiet, so well behaved, I was sure he could pass inspection. After all, it would take him only a few minutes to sign—Slade and your papa were the witnesses, they would see to that. Oh, everything was going fine—I was my most charming with that dried-up dustball of a man, I gave him tea, flirted enough to addle him a bit, and warned him Jack still held to his seclusion, would just affix his name and leave. Then Slade brought Jack in. I could tell something was wrong, there's a look he gets, but if it went quickly enough. . . . Then what does that fool of a lawyer do but demand that Jack read it through. Jack tried, but he couldn't keep his mind on all that legal gobbledegook. And when Jack doesn't understand, he gets upset. I held my breath when Mr. Kerne passed him the pen. And what does my lord and master do?" A loud peal of laughter startled her two tense listeners.

"He *pissed* on it. I mean, he *pissed* on it, just that. Took out his dick and sprayed it good, then turned his water on Mr. Kerne. He was playing fireman, I believe. I was ignored—I didn't have the equipment—but all the menfolk were asked to join in. When your papa and Slade finally got him out, Mr. Kerne dried himself off, tossed the will in the fire, and turned on me his pitying eye. The man's mad, completely mad, he sighed, the world's misunderstood you, my dear Mrs. Deventer, and so have I. Ah yes they had, I thought. And so did he, to imagine I would allow him to spread the news, have Jack declared non compos mentis, and take the management of the estate out of my hands! Men are so stupid, Ada. In time I'm sure you will come to agree with me. I had often thought how easy it would be, when they sat panting, with drooling mouths—it proved easier than I dreamed."

"For God's sake, madam—you would have been well provided for, there was no reason for you to fear—"

"Provided for?" Rose screeched, and looked as if she would have liked to rake Nicholas's face with her nails. "With *my* money? The money I had made? To have a piddling allowance doled out? It takes large sums of money, you fool, to operate successfully on the Street. Oh, Mr. Kerne explained it all to me—clothes, jewels, French cooks, any frippery my heart desired, send in the bill, it would be paid. All very fine, but for

303

me the real pleasure has always been in the fight—the besting of an opponent who outweighs you by ten million, a feint to the chin, the knockout blow delivered, and he falls at your feet! Did you not see how Weyderlander had to truckle, get down on his knees, plead for mercy, when he over-shorted and I had the stock he needed? Was he not spurting blood? He came out of it with the skin of his teeth, and I the richer by a cool million! You don't play that sort of game with a lady's pocket money."

Never had Rose Deventer looked more beautiful. Ada could not take her eyes off her. And yet had she not seen the luminous glow before? Her first evening in the castle . . . the ladies withdrawing after dinner . . . Slade intercepting his mistress with the important business telegram from Kansas City. Only Rose could take it in to the great tycoon. A little trouble getting her husband back to bed, she had explained on her return. Ada had thought she understood. What other kind of trouble would leave behind so high a color in a lady's cheeks, so exhilarated an air, such a sparkle in the eye, add that thrilling note to the low voice. In her innocence, it was the smell of rampant sex her nostrils had detected. Ada knew now it had been a darker passion. Something had happened in Kansas City and Rose Deventer would turn another million, bring another Weyderlander to his knees. That musky smell was of money—the power of it in her hands.

"And the Haygood boy?" Nicholas asked harshly. "I suppose he too stumbled on the truth?"

The glow abruptly faded. Rose looked ten years older. Poor boy, he had climbed into the wrong room, encountered Jack at one of his worst times. It had hurt her, but she had no choice.

"But why Papa?" Ada had trouble finding her voice. "Papa had kept your secret all these years—"

"Ada, dear Ada—" So lovingly was her name pronounced, accompanied by such a yearning look, Ada moved back. "It was the most painful thing I've ever had to do. I loved your papa. Owed him much. However wild his theories, he did keep Jack alive. Even sufficiently improved at times to put in a personal

304

appearance for that great admirer of his, Dr. Haygood. And it proved convenient that he shared with Jack the same complexion and build. Once he had grown a matching beard, we could even take a holiday—God knows we needed one occasionally—and it did no harm to have a Jack for occasional public show. Believe me, Ada, I feel more a widow than were it Jack who had passed away. Dr. Stevens will do his best, but frankly he does not inspire the same confidence. Still I suppose I must make do with him."

Ada was always to believe that for a brief moment Rose herself had teetered on the edge of madness, refusing to admit that anything had happened to destroy her tenure as Kirkewode's mistress. As if indeed a widow, she had progressed before their eyes through all the stages of mourning, from inconsolable grief through quiet resignation to the hopeful conviction that she would make do, life must go on. On and on and on, something inside her brain must have been shrieking even while in their eyes she read the judgment that would send her to the hangman's noose.

As if in answer to that cold judgment, she asked abruptly, "Do you remember, Ada, when you accused me before the Commissioner and I said that if anyone was to blame, it was you? That's true. Would he have wanted to leave me had you not come? I could even have permitted that—he had earned a place of special trust—but there was the paper he was writing which he counted on to make his name. A scientific paper on his fever treatment for the insane. Did you know he believed Jack's madness came from an old case of the pox? I told him that was nothing new—Dr. Haygood would have said much the same. But right or wrong, he could not be allowed to publish anything that might call attention to Jack. Anonymous case history indeed! What other patient did he have all those years—how long do you think it would take people to think of that? He agreed to wait until Jack died. But then you came. And I saw how much he wanted to raise himself in your opinion, make you proud of him. And I knew, once he left Kirkewode, he would be too impatient for that fame he believed awaited him. . . ."

"Stop. I don't want to hear any more." Ada looked as if no fire would ever warm her. "What happens now, Nicholas? What do we do with her?"

He shrugged. At the moment, nothing. The blizzard that was raging outside would keep her prisoner well enough. It was Slade who worried him. He would feel better with a bullet in the gun.

Gone was the haggard murderess. Rose moved to the escritoire. Even now her bustle made exquisite play of her undulating walk. To Nicholas she handed a little box of ammunition. "There, do you feel better?" Even now there was a cajoling lilt to her voice. "But Slade need not worry you, my dear fellow. He knows nothing of all this. No one knows—I want to make that clear. Sam, Caxton, Maxwell—they've served me well in keeping Jack's condition from public knowledge, that was my right—but for the rest, they must be held blameless. Do you promise?"

"If it's as you say, of course," Nicholas said carelessly. Nevertheless he slipped a cartridge in the gun.

"Good." It was as if she had struck a deal. With the lightest touch, as if enclosing a billet-doux, she folded Nicholas's fingers around the gun. "See how easily it can be concealed? Now come with me. I'll show you how to handle Slade."

Before they could stop her, she had passed through into the office. Still mistress of Kirkewode, still in charge, leading where they must follow.

"Ah, Slade, I've had second thoughts about discharging Mr. Vance—he has persuaded me to give him another chance. The telegraph still out? Oh well, it must be even worse in the city— no business will be done today. I hereby declare a holiday! You may go downstairs, ask Caxton for some beer."

No order could be more to his liking. He jumped to his feet with a grin. The creases suddenly reversed into scowl as he took in Ada's presence. "How did *she* get in? Not by me, I swear!" Reassured by Rose that his vigilance was not in question, he was on his way, stopped to deliver a message which the promised refreshment had almost driven from his mind. "Witten's taken bad, wants to see you. Reckoned it could wait, since you said you was not to be disturbed on no account?"

It was strange to see the trepidation of this hulking brute whom even Nicholas did not care to face unarmed. Had he done right? The small eyes sunk in their puckered beds strained to read his fate in Rose Deventer's face.

"Good boy, Slade," she said gently. The mound of pulpy flesh rejoiced, turned back when she called again, "Slade."

Had he ever heard such tenderness in his name? Confusion was plainly writ in his slow-witted gaze. Rose seemed to have forgotten what she meant to say.

"All the beer you can drink."

Once he had left, she asked permission, meekly as a child in class, to answer Mr. Witten's call. Comfort to a dying man was hardly to be denied. Alone with Nicholas, Ada found the silence in the office preternatural. Perhaps it was the lack of chatter from telegraph or ticker. It was as if this were a battlefield which had seen an unexpected armistice declared, the troops dispersed, nothing left behind but the war's debris.

Seeing Nicholas struggling with his doubts, she said, "It's true enough about the blizzard, Nicholas, it'll keep her safe inside. It's a miracle I survived even the short distance I had to make."

All thought of Rose evaporated, concern for her was the order of the day. He had sought to send her out of harm's way, never had he envisaged she would be so foolhardy as to—on the verge of scolding, he suddenly braked. Whatever had brought her back, he was grateful. She had saved his life, so it was hers—was not that how it went?

"And at needless expense, my dear. It was yours already." His smile vanished as he took in her sad state. "Off to bed with you, not another word, I'll hear the details later. I'll stay here awhile, see if the telegraph service gets restored. The sooner we get through to the outside, the sooner the police will come. Now don't argue, straight to bed, or I'll carry you there myself."

Ada was in no mood to argue. She would not have minded if he had exercised that threat. And when she reached her room, she would not have minded if Caxton had disobeyed her and sent up a maid. To undress required too much effort. Standing by the fire, she stepped out of soggy skirt and petticoats, pulled off wet stockings, wrapped herself in the merino robe and decided that would do.

The howling of the wind, far from abating, had increased to banshee shrillness. Banshees, Cullen would have told her, heralded a death. Poor Mr. Witten. Little black book or little black bag, all the same to him. Just as well, for he was dying with neither priest nor doctor at his side. Should she not see what could be done to make his passing easier? The fire had warmed her, she had been as tired as this before. Many times during those long tours of duty at the clinic. The call of a dying man—she was still doctor enough to answer that. She pushed aside the thought that the call had been for Rose, not her. She could not admit that what she was answering was a banshee call, a superstitious dread.

She was halfway up the hall when a movement on the landing caught her eye. In such gloomy light that armored contingent always seemed to come to life. But she had no such rational answer for the ghostlike flutter of white. Her heart jumped.

"Rosie! Rosie!"

The terror was no longer hers, but Mr. Witten's, embodied in that frantic cry. A ghost almost in fact, there was so little corporeal substance left to fill the nightgown which wavered in and out among the armored knights, then flung itself in a heap on the railing, calling down again, "Rosie! Rosie!"

Ada ran to rescue him from what threatened to be a headlong fall. Not shoulder, but scapula and clavicle was all she felt beneath the linen in her grasp. "Mr. Witten, please! You must get back to bed." She could carry him in one hand, she thought. How had he found the strength to get down the stairs? And yet he struggled to escape her hold with the galvanic force of a creature already dead but responding with reflex muscle twitch to some powerful current's flow.

"Rosie, don't leave me! You promised never to leave me, don't leave me now!"

Ada let go. Rose Deventer stood in the great hall below. A sable-cloaked figure drawing on her gloves, ready to display her elegance abroad. Ada descended slowly, steadying her voice to a reasonable tone, as if to coax a dangerous beast back into its cage. "You don't know what it's like out there, Rose, you won't survive ten minutes in that blizzard."

As if she were alone, unobserved, had not heard, Rose gathered her cloak around her, but loosely—the lady of fashion disdainful of the protective value of her furs, flaunting them purely as evidence of wealth. The mirror in the entry hall held her for a moment. Only when at the door, hand on the heavy pull, did she acknowledge Ada's presence. The look cast over her shoulder stopped Ada in her tracks. So Argos, bloody and mangled, had looked up at Nicholas, begging for release from the steel-toothed trap.

A torrent of bitter cold air whirled through the hall. With a final shudder, the door was closed. Still Ada could not move. She must tell Nicholas, of course. And yet, as if she sought some reason to delay, she remembered Mr. Witten, abandoned to his grief. First she would get him back to bed.

Before she reached the white nightgown on the floor, she knew she would not find Mr. Witten in that heap of linen, that discarded cloth. Not abandoned. Not left behind. His Rosie had taken him with her, after all.

Epilogue

ITH much whistle blowing and horn tooting, the *City of Paris* slowly moved out into New York Bay. Most of the passengers were still on deck watching the tall buildings of Manhattan recede, but honeymooners have a way of avoiding crowds.

"Alone at last!" Nicholas cried in a mock heroic way, having just closed the door on the purser, who had presented the compliments of the captain and would the Deventers join him at his table. Ada looked at her husband with a fondness she feared was growing excessive. She hoped that in Paris she would not find him too distracting, for she meant to work hard. Dr. Jacobi would never regret giving her this chance.

What a wonderful woman, Ada thought, as she did at least once a day. A woman not afraid to admit she made mistakes, who had checked with Ada's professors at Michigan and confessed herself impressed with their glowing praise. At that second, far more pleasant interview, Ada was struck speechless by the suggestion that she matriculate at the École de Médecine. "I myself had to enter by the side door to emerge through the front, but I have some influence now, I think I can do better for you. It is fortunate you have a command of the language—you will have no trouble with the examination, I'm sure." And the French, Dr. Jacobi concluded with a broad smile, would find her *character* just what a woman's should be.

The greatest medical school in the world, where Dr. Jacobi herself had obtained her degree! Ada was still a bit awestruck at the future thus arranged for her. When she put it to Nicholas, he had sighed romantically "Ah, Paris!", hoping to get her dander up, but on the whole he had been most understanding. Even when she pointed out that she would have little time for him, he did not protest. "Then I shall have to find something else to do. I've been thinking I might go into government. I don't have Theo Roosevelt's taste for politics exactly, but there are other ways to perform a public service. I'll look up old Brasewell at the State Department." For a Deventer, of course, old Brasewell had come through, and Nicholas was to busy himself as an undersecretary in the Embassy at Paris.

He would be the perfect diplomat, he lied so well. Ada wondered she had not thought of it herself, after observing him in action protecting the Deventer name. She had agreed with him that nothing would be gained by public disclosure of Rose Deventer's crimes, God's justice having preempted man's. To this day, that love story of the ages remained intact. Poor Mrs. Deventer, another eminent victim of the great blizzard, to be mourned along with Senator Conkling. Her husband too, in a way—had he not been driven mad with grief when they brought in her frozen body, had to be put away in an asylum? A story like that, once started, maintained itself. Even his death three months later was reputed to be of a broken heart. Rose would have liked that, Ada thought.

Had she ever questioned Nicholas's goodness, his disposal of his uncle's estate would have been answer enough. "It's not Deventer money, it's really *hers*," he had said when asking her consent to donate the greater part to the Society for the Prevention of Cruelty to Children. A particularly appropriate charity, he thought, having heard the ugly account of Rose's childhood. But his goodness was something she was not allowed to praise. "What need have I of such a sum?" he had retorted with a grin. "Once you get your medical degree, I count on you to support me in the manner to which I am accustomed."

Somewhere in her trunk lay Papa's notebooks. There they must stay, less case report than personal diary, dreadful cries from his heart. For slowly as his theory had developed—that his patient's syphilis had only seemingly been cured, was raging now in his brain, the cause a germ, the cure a fever—equally slowly grew his conviction that his patient's wife, the woman he loved, was evil to the core. Even before the suicides, he had sensed it: *Not my daughter, no. Ada she shall not touch.* Later he had written: *These suicides, how convenient!* but never doubted the deaths were self-inflicted. His conclusion was that Rose Deventer was a witch. Literally a witch, Ada realized, reading on, dumbfounded that he could entertain such superstitious rubbish. Hardly a journal to establish his scientific fame.

"I do think," Nicholas interrupted her sad thoughts of Papa, "we should check out our quarters in this so-called floating palace. If the bedroom is not comfortable, I shall demand another suite."

"I think we should," Ada agreed, with just the same housewifely concern. But on the threshold she suddenly stiffened. "Oh, Nicholas. Do forgive me, but I just remembered—I must get up on deck!"

Ignoring his look of dismay, she ran out of the suite, down the corridor, up a short flight of steps into the open air. Nicholas found her in the crowd at the railing and ruthlessly shouldered his way to her side.

"My dear, not seasick already?"

She shook her head and pointed. "I wanted to see *her*—I was afraid it was already too late. Oh Nicholas, is she not beautiful?"

"Is that all?" he said with great relief. "Do you mean to tell me you've never seen the Statue of Liberty?"

"No. At least, not like that."

For Ada it was the final healing of all wounds, at last to see the Lady as she was meant to be—whole and entire.